GRANTA BOOKS

BUDDING PROSPECTS

T. Coraghessan Boyle was born in New York's Hudson Valley and now lives near Santa Barbara, California. He is the author of four other novels: *Water Music, East is East, World's End* (which won the 1988 PEN/Faulkner Award for fiction) and *The Road to Wellville*, and four books of short stories, most recently *Without a Hero*. His fiction has appeared in the *New Yorker, The Atlantic, Granta, Harper's, Playboy* and many other magazines.

Also by T. Coraghessan Boyle

NOVELS

Water Music

East is East

World's End

The Road to Wellville

SHORT STORIES

If the River Was Whiskey

Greasy Lake

Descent of Man

(Published in one volume, *The Collected Stories of T. Coraghessan Boyle*)

Without a Hero

T. CORAGHESSAN BOYLE

Budding Prospects

GRANTA BOOKS
LONDON
in association with
PENGUIN BOOKS

GRANTA BOOKS
2/3 Hanover Yard, Noel Road, London N1 8BE

Published in association with the Penguin Group
Penguin Books Ltd, 27 Wrights Lane, London W8 5TZ, England
Viking Penguin, a division of Penguin Books USA Inc., 375 Hudson Street, New York, NY 10014, USA; Penguin Books Australia Ltd, Ringwood, Victoria, Australia; Penguin Books Canada Ltd, 10 Alcorn Avenue, Toronto, Ontario, Canada M4V 3B2; Penguin Books (NZ) Ltd, 182–190 Wairau Road, Auckland 10, New Zealand

Penguin Books Ltd, Registered Offices: Harmondsworth, Middlesex, England

First published in the USA by Viking Penguin Inc, 1984
This edition published in Great Britain by Granta Books, 1995

1 3 5 7 9 10 8 6 4 2

Copyright © T. Coraghessan Boyle 1984
All rights reserved

Grateful acknowledgement is made to the following for permission to reprint copyrighted material:
Bug Music Group: Lyrics from 'Semi-Truck' by Bill Kirchen and Billy C. Farlow. Copyright © 1980 by Ozone Music (BMI). Administered by Bug Music. *Ice Nine Publishing Co, Inc*: Lyrics from 'Truckin'', music by Jerry Garcia, Bob Weir and Phil Lesh, words by Robert Hunter. Copyright © 1971 by Ice Nine Publishing Co, Inc. *Jobete Music Company, Inc*: Lyrics from 'Money (That's What I Want)', words and music by Berry Gordy and Janie Bradford. Copyright © 1959 by Jobete Music Company, Inc. Used by permission. International copyright secured. All rights reserved. *MCA Music:* Lyrics from 'Satin Sheets', words and music by John E. Volinkaty. Copyright © 1972, 1973 by Champion Music Corporation, New York. Used by permission. All rights reserved. *Screen Gems–EMI Music Inc*: Lyrics from 'So Much Trouble', words and music by B. McGhee. Copyright © 1952, 1978 by Screen Gems–EMI Music Inc, 6920 Sunset Boulevard, Hollywood, CA 90028. Used by permission. All rights reserved. *Taco Music, Inc*: Lyrics from 'Beat on the Brat', words and music by The Ramones. Used with permission of the publisher, Taco Music, Inc. *Viking Penguin, Inc*: Excerpt from *Death of a Salesman* by Arthur Miller. Copyright © 1949 by Arthur Miller. Copyright renewed © 1977 by Arthur Miller. *Zora Delta Music*: Lyrics from 'Farm Blues', words and music by Robert Williams. Copyright © Zora Delta Music. All rights reserved. Used by permission.

According to the Copyright Designs and Patents Act 1988, the proprietor hereby asserts his moral right to be identified as the author of this work

Except in the United States of America, this book is sold subject to the condition that it shall not, by way of trade or otherwise, be lent, re-sold, hired out, or otherwise circulated without the publisher's prior consent in any form of binding or cover other than that in which it is published and without a similar condition including this condition being imposed on the subsequent purchaser

Printed in England by Clays Ltd, St Ives plc

This book is for my horticultural friends.

Plough deep, while Sluggards sleep; and you shall have Corn to sell and to keep.

Benjamin Franklin, *The Way to Wealth*

"Why, boys, when I was seventeen I walked into the jungle, and when I was twenty-one I walked out. And by God I was rich."

Arthur Miller, *Death of a Salesman*

PART 1
Preparing the Soil

Chapter 1

I've always been a quitter. I quit the Boy Scouts, the glee club, the marching band. Gave up my paper route, turned my back on the church, stuffed the basketball team. I dropped out of college, sidestepped the army with a 4-F on the grounds of mental instability, went back to school, made a go of it, entered a Ph.D. program in nineteenth-century British literature, sat in the front row, took notes assiduously, bought a pair of horn-rims, and quit on the eve of my comprehensive exams. I got married, separated, divorced. Quit smoking, quit jogging, quit eating red meat. I quit jobs: digging graves, pumping gas, selling insurance, showing pornographic films in an art theater in Boston. When I was nineteen I made frantic love to a pinch-faced, sack-bosomed girl I'd known from high school. She got pregnant. I quit town. About the only thing I didn't give up on was the summer camp.

Let me tell you about it.

Two years ago I was living alone. I woke alone, flossed my teeth alone, worked at odd jobs, ate take-out burritos, read the newspaper and undressed for bed alone. The universe had temporarily pulled in its boundaries, and I was learning to adjust to them. I was thirty-one. I sat at the lunch counter with men of fifty-one, sixty-one, eighty-one, slurped tomato-rice soup and watched the waitress. Sometimes I had dinner with friends, shot pool, went to the aquarium, danced to a pulsing Latino beat in close, atramental clubs; sometimes I felt like a bearded ascetic contemplating the stones of the desert.

On this particular night—it was in late February—I stayed in. I was reading, absorbed in an assault on K2 by a team of Japanese mountaineers, my lungs constricting in the thin burning air, the deadly sting of wind-lashed ice in my face, when the record—*Le Sacre du Printemps*—caught in the groove with a gnashing squeal as if a stageful of naiads, dryads and spandex satyrs had simultaneously gone lame. I looked up from my book. Rain knocked at the windows like a smirking voyeur, small sounds reverberated through the house—the clank of the refrigerator closing down, the sigh of the heat starting up—the fire crackled ominously round a nail in a charred two-by-four. At that instant, as if on cue, the front buzzer sounded. It was after twelve. I gave the tube a rueful glance—zombies in white-face drifted across the screen, masticating bratwurstlike strings of human intestine—put down my book, cinched the terrycloth robe round my waist, and ambled to the head of the stairs. Insistent, the buzzer blatted again.

My apartment was a walkup on Fair Oaks, three blocks west of the Mission. The house was a Victorian, painted in six colors. I had four rooms, a deck, a hallway and a view. Before the intercom went dead, the signal had become so weak and static-jammed I wouldn't have recognized my mother's voice—or Screamin' Jay Hawkins doing "I Put a Spell on You," for that matter. I stood at the head of the stairway and pressed the door release, more curious than apprehensive, and watched three shadows dodge in out of the wet.

There was a flash of lightning, horns and violins shrieked and reshrieked the same tortured Slavic measure like a tocsin, they were coming up the stairs, *thump-thump-thump*. For one nasty moment I stepped back, cursing myself for so blindly buzzing them in—gray forms, strangers, junkies, Mexican confidence men—when I saw, with relief, that it was Vogelsang. "Felix," he said.

"Hey," I responded.

He had a girl in tow, her hair clipped short as an East German swimmer's and bleached white. Behind her, three steps down, a guy in his late twenties, wearing rubbers and a yellow rain slicker that gave off a weird phosphorescent glow in the dull light of the hallway. All three of them looked as if they'd jumped off the Bay Bridge four or five times: noses dripping, hair plastered, water dribbling from collars and shoes. Vogelsang was grinning his deranged grin. "It's been a while," he said, clapping my shoulder.

It had been two months. Vogelsang lived in splendid isolation in the hills above Bolinas, making money nefariously, practicing various perversions, collecting power tools, wood carvings, barbers' poles and cases of dry red wine from esoteric little vineyards like Goat's Crouch and Sangre de Cristo. He also collected antique motorcycles, copper saucepans, espresso machines the size of church organs, sexless mannequins from the fifties (which he painted, lacquered and arranged round the house in lewd, arresting poses), bone-handled knives, Tahitian gill nets and a series of cramped somber oil paintings devoted to religious themes like the decapitation of John the Baptist or the algolagnic ecstasies of the flagellants. Every few weeks he would descend on San Francisco to prowl junk shops, cruise North Beach and attend sumptuous mate-swapping parties in Berkeley. Norman Mailer would have loved him.

At this juncture, he maneuvered the girl forward. I noticed that she was wearing a delicate silver ring through the flange of her right nostril, and that her toenails were painted black. "This is Aorta," Vogelsang said. I labeled her instantly: sorority girl cum punk. She was probably from Pacific Heights and her real name was something like Jennifer Harris or Heather Mashberg. She gave me a hard look and held out her hand. Her hand was as wet and cold as something fished out of a pond. I ducked my head at her and sucked back the corners of my mouth.

"And this," Vogelsang was saying, gesturing toward the slickered figure three steps down, "is Boyd Dowst, a friend of mine from Santa Rosa."

The rain slicker seemed to erupt in response, and a big bony hand lunged over the top of the rail to grasp mine. I was staring into the face of a Yankee farmer, angular, big-eared, eyes the color of power-line insulators. "Now living in Sausalito," he said, clawing at his dripping hair with his free hand. The other hand, the friendly one, was still pumping at mine as if he expected my fingertips to squirt milk or something.

I was barefoot, my bathrobe was dirty, the skipping record ripped at my nerves like a two-man saw. I invited them in.

Vogelsang strode into the living room, unzipped his sodden jacket and draped it across the back of a wooden chair, characteristically brisk and nervous in the way of a feral cat attuned to the faintest movements, the tiniest scratchings. He smelled of rain and something else too, something musky and primal. It was a minute before I realized what it was: he reeked of sex. When he'd arranged the jacket to his satisfaction, he turned to enlighten me on this and other matters, pausing only to produce a plastic vial of breath neutralizer and squeeze off two quick shots before launching into a monologue describing his recent acquisitions, touching on improvements to his property in Bolinas and the progress of his investments in the commodities market, and giving a lubricious play-by-play account of the urbane orgy he and the girl had attended earlier in the evening. He spoke, as he always did, with a peculiar mechanical diction, each word distinct and unslurred, as if he were a linguistics professor moderating a panel discussion on the future of the language.

I puttered round the apartment, half-listening, changing the record, lowering the volume on the TV, digging out an ashtray, four bottles of beer and a plastic envelope of pot. Vogelsang followed me, step for step, lecturing. Dowst and the girl sat on the couch. As soon as the pot hit the coffee table, Dowst snatched it up, opened the Baggie and sniffed it—breathed it rather, like a snorkeler coming up for air—made a disdainful face and tossed the bag back down as if it contained some unspeakable refuse on the order of dog turds or decomposing sparrow eggs. I caught this out of the corner of my eye as I was slipping Stravinsky back into his jacket.

"Boyd's just finished up his Master's degree at Yale," Vogelsang said, easing down on the arm of the couch and taking a swig of beer for dramatic emphasis, "in botanical science."

I pulled up a chair. "Congratulations," I murmured, glancing at Dowst, and abruptly changed the subject—who wanted to hear about some overgrown preppie and his academic laurels? I'd been that route myself. I said something about the rain, then made a bad joke about the quality of the entertainment at Vogelsang's party.

"You don't understand," Vogelsang persisted. "*Botanical science:* he can grow anything, anywhere."

I nodded. The girl was looking at me as if I were a sandwich in the window of a delicatessen, and Dowst was squinting at a copy of *Scientific American* he'd dug out of the pile of newspapers on the floor. Muffled shrieks came from the TV. I glanced up to see the heroine trapped in a hallway made of flimsy plasterboard while the hairy arms of zombies—I marveled at their insatiability—punched through the walls to grab at her.

Vogelsang set the beer down, fished the mouth spray from his pocket and treated himself to a single squeeze, the puff of soapy atomized liquid like a cloud of frozen breath on a cold morning. "I closed a deal on three hundred and ninety acres in Mendocino County today," he said. "Remote as the moon, with a cabin on it."

Dowst looked up from his reading. "And with year-round water." I noticed that he hadn't bothered to remove the rain slicker. It billowed round him like an aniline tent, a glistening yellow barber's gown tucked in at the neck. He pawed ineffectually at a strand of wet hair that dangled alongside his nose, then went back to the magazine.

"That's right," Vogelsang added, "a creek and two separate springs."

It was twelve-thirty. I'd heard *The Rite of Spring*, it was raining, I was tired. I wondered what Vogelsang was driving at. "Sounds nice," I said.

"We're going to start a summer camp." He was smirking, as if this were the punch line of a subtly developed joke. Dowst chuckled appreciatively. The girl sat hunched over her untouched bottle of Moosehead lager and stared through the wall. I got up and switched on the radio.

There was the sudden hollow thumping of a distant bass drum, some machine-shop noises, and then a strange detached female voice pushing ice through the speakers:

The best things in life are free
But you can save them for the birds and bees,
Give me money, that's what I want.©

"Listen, Felix," Vogelsang was saying, "how would you like to make half a million dollars, tax-free?"

I sat down again. All three of them were watching me now. "You're joking," I said.

"Dead serious." Vogelsang was giving me his Charlie Manson stare. He used it when he wanted you to know he was dead serious.

"What," I laughed, bending for my beer, "running a summer camp?"

"*Cannabis sativa*," Dowst said, as softly as if he were revealing one of the secret names of God.

"We're going to grow two thousand plants." Vogelsang was studying the vial of breath neutralizer as if it were inscribed with the hieroglyphs of economic calculation, with cost-ratio tables and sliding scales for depreciation and uninsured loss. He looked up. "Figure half a pound per plant. One thousand pounds at sixteen hundred dollars a pound." He raised the vial to his mouth, dropped his jaw in anticipation, then thought better of it. I said nothing. The plastic tube tapped at his pursed lips, mesmeric, lifting and falling to the pulse of the music. "I put up the capital and provide the land, Boyd comes in every few days to oversee the operation and you provide the labor. We split three ways."

Suddenly I was wide awake, brain cells flashing like free-game lights in a pinball machine. Vogelsang didn't make mistakes—I knew that. I knew, too, that he had a genius for making money, a genius of which I'd been beneficiary on two serendipitous occasions in the past. (The first time we went partners on a battered Victorian in the Haight, put out three thousand dollars on a twenty-thousand-dollar purchase price, refurbished the place for fifteen and sold it for a hundred. The second time he merely phoned, gave me the name of a broker, and told me to buy as much zirconium as I could. I had eight thousand dollars in the bank and I was out of work. I made more in a week than I'd made all year.) No: if Vogelsang was behind it, it would go. As certainly as Segovia had been born to finger a fretboard or Willie

Mays to swing a bat, Vogelsang had been born to sow pennies and reap dollars. Thirty-three, and already independent of any visible means of support—he hadn't held a job since I'd known him—he nosed out investments, traded in commodities both licit and illicit, bought and sold buildings and property and God knew what else—and all with the unshakable confidence and killing instinct of an apprentice Gould or Carnegie.

And his timing was exquisite, I had to admit that. He'd come to me at just the right moment, a year and a half after my divorce, a time when I was depressed and restless, a time when I was beginning to feel like a prisoner in solitary. Half a million dollars. It was as if the head of NASA had just asked me if I'd like to be the first man to walk on Mars. There were risks involved, sure, but that was what made the project so enticing—the frisson, the audacity, the monumental pissing in the face of society. Vogelsang wasn't going to grow a hundred plants or a hundred and fifty, he wasn't going to be content with fifteen or twenty thousand—no, he was going to grow marijuana like Reynolds grew tobacco. My blood was racing. When I looked up into the three faces intent on my own, I was already halfway there.

"I don't know a thing about growing marijuana," I said finally.

Vogelsang was ready for this. "You don't have to," he said, lifting himself from the chair arm, "—that's Boyd's department."

"But two thousand plants . . . can one person handle that sort of thing?"

"No way," Dowst said, rustling his rain slicker.

"We figure you'll need two full-time people to help out. Who they are and how you pay them is up to you. You could hire them on a straight salary, or split your five hundred into shares. But whatever, they've got to be willing to give up the next nine months of their lives, and above all they've got to be"—here he paused to come up with the right word—"discreet."

Rain hit the roof like pennies from heaven, the icy voice on the radio was chanting *Money, give me money,/Money, give me money.*© We were all standing, for some reason. Dowst and Vogelsang were grinning, the girl's face had softened with what I took to be a sort of truculent amicability.

"How about your friend up in Tahoe," Vogelsang said, as if he'd had a sudden inspiration (I realized at that instant he'd been playing me all along, like a street-corner salesman, a carnival barker making his pitch). "What's his name . . ." (he knew it as well as I) "Cherniske?"

"Phil," I said, half to myself. "Yeah, Phil," as if I'd stumbled across the solution to a baffling puzzle.

Vogelsang took hold of my hand and pumped it in a congratulatory way, Dowst showing all his long gleaming teeth now, the girl fighting to keep the corners of her mouth from curling into a smile. I felt as if I'd just come back from sailing around the world or whipping the defending Wimbledon champ. I didn't say yes, I didn't say no, but already Vogelsang was lifting his half-empty Moosehead bottle and calling for a toast.

He had an arm round my shoulder, zombies disintegrated on the TV screen as heroes lobbed grenades at them, the cold voice chanted *money* in my ear, the smell of musk, of conception, of semen and the dark essence of the earth fired my nostrils, and then he flung up his hand, bottle clenched tight, like an evangelist called to witness: "To the summer camp!"

Chapter 2

There was nothing in my early upbringing to indicate a life of crime. I wasn't beaten, orphaned or abandoned, I didn't hang out on street corners with a cigarette in my mouth and a stiletto in my pocket, I wasn't mentally disfigured from years in a reformatory or morally and physically sapped as a result of shooting smack on pigeon-shit-encrusted stoops in the ghetto. No: I was a child of the middle class, nurtured on Tiger's Milk and TV dinners and Aureomycin until I towered over my parents like some big-footed freak of another species, like a cuckoo raised by sparrows. I knew algebra, appreciated Verdi, ate veal marsala, sushi and escargots, and selected a good bottle of wine. My record, if not spotless, was tainted only by the most venial infractions. There had been the usual traffic violations, an unfortunate incident on the steps of the Justice Department during one of the Washington marches, and a fine for carrying an open container on the streets of Lake George. But that was about it. Certainly, like any other solid citizen with inalienable rights, I broke laws regularly—purchasing and consuming controlled substances, driving at a steady sixty-five on freeways, fornicating in water beds and hot tubs, micturating in public, knowingly and willingly being in the presence of persons who, etc., etc. On the other hand, I didn't litter, extort, burgle, batter, assault, rape or murder. At thirty-one, endowed with the cautiousness and conservatism of maturity, I could arguably consider myself, if not a pillar, then at least a flying buttress of bourgeois society.

Still, two hours after Vogelsang had left, and despite a weariness that verged on narcolepsy and a steady blinding Niagara of a rainstorm, I was on my way to Lake Tahoe to take my first irretrievable steps into the lower depths.

At four a.m. I pulled into a truckstop and sat hunched over the counter on a cracked vinyl stool, spooned up grease and eggs, listened to moronic country-inflected yodeling from the jukebox, and drank eight cups of coffee that tasted of death and metal. The rain had stopped, and I watched myself in the dark, water-flecked window for a moment, my face lit by neon and the flashing lights of semis, and saw that my eyes glared and cheeks bristled with the look of criminality. Or tiredness. Then I left some money on the counter, stumbled out to my rust-spotted Toyota, and drove on up the hill to where dawn was flaring over South Tahoe.

I missed the turnoff for Cherniske's place, everything uniform at this altitude, snow on the ground like a fungus, trees as alike as a forest of Dixon pencils. Without thinking, I swerved to cut a U-turn and was nearly annihilated by a California highway patrolman doing about ninety on urgent business. The thing that saved my life—and the patrolman's—was the supersiren with which the CHP car was equipped, the sort of deadly, heart-seizing klaxon fire trucks use when approaching intersections. I was halfway through my illegal U-turn, horizontal to the flow of traffic and already obstructing an entire lane, oblivious to sirens, lights, the possibility of runaway logging trucks, when the klaxon slapped me like an angry hand. My foot went to the floor, tires squealed, brake drums clapped like cymbals, and the Toyota lurched to a halt as the CHP cruiser careened past the front bumper, inches to spare. As he passed, the patrolman gave me a quick sharp look of murderous intensity—a look that said, I would shoot you here, now, no questions asked, as automatically as I would shoot a rattlesnake or a junkyard rat, but for this appalling emergency that requires my dedication, bravery and expertise—and then he was gone, a pair of taillights skidding round a corner in the distance.

Mortified, I pulled the car round just in time to avoid the

shrieking ambulance for which the cruiser had been running interference, humbly shifted gears, signaled, and swung onto the wet glistening blacktop road that snaked through the trees to Cherniske's place. Almost instantly there was a thump, the wheel was jerked from my hand, and the car veered wildly for the shoulder and a clutch of nasty russet-barked pines. I'd been driving since I was sixteen and, groggy though I was, rose to the occasion, snatching the wheel back and regaining control without missing a beat. Calmly, almost clinically, I noted the cause of my minor emergency: there was a groove in the road. A deep insistent gash that seamed the right-hand lane like a furrow, as if some absentminded sodbuster had neglected to lift the plow blade while rumbling home on his tractor. I would have thought nothing more of it but for the fact that the groove seemed to be going in the same direction I was, turn for turn. I followed it down Alpine Way to the end, left on Lederhosen Lane, left again on Chalet Drive, and then, amazingly, into Phil's driveway and right on up to the bumper of his sagging '62 Cadillac.

Phil's house—a two-story chalet/cabin/condo/duplex—was silent, the windows dark. It was seven a.m., and the early light had been absorbed in a low ceiling of ropy cloud the color of charcoal. I swung out of the car and examined Phil's Cadillac: it was pitched forward like a crippled stegosaur, tail fins in the air, and the right front fender and a portion of the hood had been crumpled like tinfoil. Looking closer, I saw that not only was the tire gone on that side, but the brake drum and wheel as well. The car was resting on a sheared splinter of axle, from the apex of which the groove raveled out up the driveway, down the blacktop road, and out to the highway. The engine was still warm.

No one responded to my knock. This was no surprise: I hadn't really expected a formal reception. At this hour, Phil and his assorted roommates would be entering the first leaden phase of deep sleep, having closed the bars in California and roamed the casinos of Stateline, Nevada, until dawn. The door was unlatched. I stepped in, sleeping bag under my arm, thinking to curl up on the couch, wake when they did, and put my proposition to Phil over breakfast. It was colder inside than out, and the place had a familiar subterranean smell to it—a smell of underwear and socks worn too long, of stale beer, primitive cooking and a species of mold that thrives under adverse conditions. The shades were drawn, but there was light enough to distinguish generic shapes: TV, armchair, couch, bicycle, lamp, log. I groped my way to the couch, unfurled the sleeping bag and sat down.

This was a mistake. As my buttocks made contact with flesh and bone rather than Herculon and Styrofoam and I began to intuit that the couch was already occupied, a quick lithe form jerked up to shove at my chest, rake my face and gasp a few emphatic obscenities. "Noooooooo," the voice—it was feminine—half rasped, half shrieked, "I've had enough. Now get off!" I found myself on the floor, muttering apologies. Then the light exploded in the room as if it had come on with a blast of noise, and I was staring up at a tableau vivant: the girl's white naked arm poised at the lamp switch, her furious squinting eyes, high breasts, the lavender comforter slipped to her waist. "Who the hell are you?" she hissed.

"Felix," I whispered, somehow feeling as if I were covering up the truth, "Phil's friend."

She glared at me as if she hadn't heard. Her hair was a cracked fluff of peroxide blond, her eyes were green as glass marbles, she had no eyebrows. I watched her nipples harden in the cold. "I'm looking for Phil," I said.

"Who?" The tone was barely under control, the upward swing of the interrogative a scarcely suppressed snarl. "Listen, mister"—drawing the comforter up under her armpits—"you better get your ass out of here or, or I'll—" She never finished the phrase, gesturing vaguely and then fumbling for a cigarette on the coffee table.

This is what an inept rapist must feel like, I thought. Or a cat burglar who catches the Mother Superior with her habit down. Despite myself, I found I had an erection. "Phil," I repeated. "Phil Cherniske? The guy that rents this place?"

Suddenly the rage went out of her face. She looked up at me over her cigarette as she lit it, shook out the match and took a deep drag. Eyebrowless, she looked like Humpty-Dumpty or the Man in the Moon, too much pale unbroken space between eyes and hair. I watched her exhale a blue cloud of smoke. "Oh, Phil," she said finally, wearily, as if she'd just experienced a revelation that hadn't seemed worth the effort. "He's in jail."

Phil and I had been close all our lives. Our parents had been friends before we were born, we'd attended the same elementary and secondary schools, had quit separate colleges in the same year. Phil went west, I stayed in New York. I got married, went back to school, dropped out, found a job selling life insurance to pensioners with trembling hands and hated myself for it. Phil made a brief splash in L.A. (Pasadena, actually) as Phil Yonkers, *sculpteur primitif*. He roamed junkyards with the avidity and determination of a housewife at a Macy's white sale, collecting fascinating slabs of rusted iron, discarded airplane wings, scalloped fenders, anvils, stoves, washing machines, useless but intrinsically edifying cogs, springs and engine parts from obsolete heavy machinery. These he would weld together in random configurations, hose down to encourage oxidation, and offer for sale.

I remember a brochure he once sent me in advertisement of his first (and last) show. The cover featured a poorly reproduced photo of the artist (the sagging pompadour, pointed nose, emaciated frame and wandering eye) grinning in the lee of a gargantuan iron monster that dripped oil like saliva and seemed to be composed around the gap-toothed shovel of an earthmover and a set of pistons frozen at descending intervals. The text indicated that the piece was titled *Madonna and Child*, and compared the artist to Herms, Smith and Keinholtz. Unfortunately, the show had to be canceled the afternoon it opened, owing to irremediable structural damage to the building that housed the gallery. The immense, crushing weight of Phil's pieces, combined with the exuberance of his friends and acquaintances—who turned the sedate, champagne-sipping gathering into a foot-stomping celebration of rock and roll and the sculptor's muse—fractured several floor joists and collapsed a section of the foundation. Phil did manage to sell one piece—three table saws welded together beneath a corona of conjoined lug wrenches molded in the shape of a butterfly's wings—to a retired tool-and-die-maker from Boyle Heights. Then he went into the restaurant business.

The restaurant business, as far as I can see, harbors a greater assortment of misfits, bon vivants, congenital crazies and food, drug, and alcohol abusers than any other métier, with the possible exception of the medical. Phil, disappointed in his effort to combine artistic expression and pecuniary reward, was only too willing to give himself up to the pharmaceutical oblivion of the world of waiters and *plongeurs*. He stood before a blazing grill at a steak house in Boulder, washed dishes at a Himalayan restaurant in Montpelier, tended bar in Maui, Park City and Aspen, bisected oysters on Bourbon Street. For a time, like most restaurant people, he attained restaurant nirvana, opening his own place. He borrowed money from his parents, his friends, relatives whose existence he'd forgotten, went partners with a savvy Greek in his mid-fifties, opened an impeccable haute-cuisine eatery in the suburbs of Sacramento, and went broke in nine months. Bad location, he said, but he later confided to me that the savvy Greek had been skimming money off the top. When I came to town that early morning with the proposition Vogelsang had made me, Phil was employed as a dishwasher at the Tahoe Teriyaki and, as I learned from the girl on the couch, temporarily incarcerated.

I blinked at her two or three times. My eyes felt as if they were bleeding. I staggered to my feet, dragging the sleeping bag like the corpse of a dead enemy, fumbled my way out the door, across the blackened and pissed-over snow, and back into the Toyota. Ten minutes later I pulled into the courthouse lot where the Eldorado County Sheriff's Department maintained its drunk tank and holding facility.

If the stereotypical desk sergeant is loose of jowl, corpulent, balding and noncommunicative, the man I encountered at the Sheriff's Department didn't break any new ground. A cardboard container of coffee steamed on the counter before him, his eyes were as puffed as a prizefighter's, and his loose jowls were reddened with a thousand tiny nicks and abrasions that gave evidence of a recent and clumsy shave with one of the new, ultramodern, reclining-head skin-whittlers reinvented by Gillette, Bic and the rest each month. I wear a beard myself.

"Excuse me, officer," I said. "I'd like to put up bail for someone you might be holding here." I felt like Raskolnikov in Myshkin's office, born guilty, guilty in perpetuity, guilty of everything from not honoring and obeying my parents to adolescent masturbation and stealing cigars to the larger and more heinous crimes of adulthood. I wanted to blurt it all out, confess in spate, be shriven and forgiven. Uniforms did that to me.

The desk sergeant said nothing.

I repeated myself, with a slight variation, and began to think wildly of all the possible permutations of this simple communication I might have to sift through until I hit the right one—the combination that would set clicking the tumblers of the policeman's speech centers—when I hit on revealing the name of the incarceree after whom I was inquiring. "Cherniske," I said. "Philip T."

Still nothing. The man was immovable, emotionless, a jade Buddha serenely contemplating some quintessential episode of a TV police show, perhaps one in which a mild-mannered desk sergeant is moved to heroics by the sick and sad state of society, leaping out from behind his deceptive mask of lethargy to pound drunks, pleaders, crooks and loophole-manipulating lawyers back into the dirt where they belonged. I tried again, this time making it a question: "Phil Cherniske? Brought in this morning? Public intoxication?"

The thick neck swiveled like a lazy susan, the blue beads of the eyes hesitated on me with a look of hatred or impassivity—I couldn't tell which—and continued past me to focus on an object over my left shoulder. The officer's next motion was almost magical, so abrupt and yet so conservative of energy: his chins compressed briefly and then relaxed. I looked over my shoulder to a wooden bench flanked by a battered water cooler and a forlorn flag. "You want me to wait over there?" I said, my voice unnaturally loud, as if in compensation for his rigorous silence.

I watched his eyes for the answer, in the way one watches the eyes of a stroke victim for life. They squeezed shut, slowly, tenderly, then flashed open again—he could have been a dragon disturbed in its sleep—before drifting down to contemplate the steam rising from the cup. I turned, obsequiously dodging leather-booted, black-jacketed, hip-slung patrolmen, who stomped and jangled across the scuffed linoleum floor, and started for the bench. Halfway there, pausing to maneuver around a fleshy colossus who stood yawning and scratching before the water cooler, I was suddenly arrested by a summons at my back, a croak really, like some barely breathed disclosure of the oracle. "Sixty-five dollars," the voice whispered.

I gave him three twenties and a five. As the crisp folded bills passed between us, I felt we'd attained some sort of brotherhood, a moment of truth and accord, and I took advantage of it to ask the sergeant if he could possibly tell me when the prisoner might be released. His eyes were glass. Five fat fingers lay on the bills like dead things. When I saw that no answer was forthcoming, I wheeled round, irritated, and blundered into an officer dressed in the uniform of the California Highway Patrol, replete with mirror shades, Wehrmacht boots and outsized gunbelt.

"Oh—excuse me," I gasped, regaining my balance and letting the final vowel trail off in a little bleat of urbane laughter meant not only to implicate him in a shared responsibility for our collision and the foibles of the human condition in general, but to assure him that it had been purely accidental and that, just as he would think no more of it, neither would I. I was grinning like an idiot. He was not grinning. The shades in fact seemed to draw his eyes together into a single horrific cyclopean mask that rendered the rest of his face expressionless. He stood there a second, rocking back and forth on his heels, then tore off the sunglasses. "You," he snarled.

"Me?" The smile had gone sick on my face. I recognized him in that instant, the guilt I'd felt on entering the station house infesting me like a cancer, my mind racing through the minuscule store of legal knowledge I'd accumulated under duress in the past, thinking moving violation, his word against mine, *judicium parium aut leges terrae*.

All for naught. He threw me against the wall in an explosion of shoulders and arms and began to shout in my face. "What in *Christ's* name do you want here?" he spat, his voice breaking on the expletive. The room had gone silent. All the others—big, beefy local cops—looked up from their coffee and clipboards and took an involuntary step or two toward us, like a defensive backfield converging on the ball carrier.

I began to offer an explanation when my antagonist bellowed for me to shut up. His hands pressed my elbows to the wall. He was breathing hard, his upper lip was wet and his eyes shone with the fierce fanatical glow of righteousness one recognized in the eyes of Muslim zealots. A black plastic plate over his shirt pocket identified him as Officer Jerpbak.

There in the police station, up against the wall, physical harm and worse shouting me in the face, I found a moment to indulge myself in the luxury of philosophy, to acknowledge my debt to empiricism, causality and John Locke. A mere eight hours ago I'd been padding round the apartment in my bathrobe, listening to the rain and Stravinsky preparatory to turning in. All was right with the world. And then the Grail, in the form of half a million dollars, sashayed through the room and I ducked out into the rain, inserted the key in the ignition of my Toyota, welcomed the answering shriek of the enervated engine, and drove here, to Tahoe, where I had managed to make an enemy of the most desperate and lawless sort—a cop—simply because I'd been in the wrong place at the wrong time. Suddenly I felt indescribably weary. "Get your fucking hands off me," I said.

Officer Jerpbak responded by spinning me around like an Indian club and slamming me back into the wall in the classic shakedown position. "Spread 'em," he snarled, patting me down with all the finesse of a middleweight working out with the body bag. He gave elaborate consideration to the genital area, all the while breathing obscenities over my shoulder. "You fuck," he whispered, his voice trembling at the breaking point. "You stupid-ass dildo motherfucker: you nearly killed me out there, you know that? Huh? Huh?" His breathing was furious, incendiary: I could hear the hardened snot rattling in his nostrils. All I wanted at that moment was to swell to Laestrygonian proportions and murder him, pound the other beefeaters to hamburger, set fire to the station house and go home to bed. Instead, I listened to the harsh jangle of handcuffs and relaxed under his grip.

"You know who was in that ambulance?" he demanded, leaning into me with one broad hand while he fumbled with the other for the cuffs. "Huh? Huh?" It was a quiz, that's what it was. Twenty questions. Hit the jackpot and win two free tickets to the Martial Arts Exposition. "Merv Griffin, that's who, shithead. Merv Griffin." There was reverence in his voice—he could have been naming the Pope's mother or the winner of the Miss America Pageant—reverence, and outrage. "The man took twenty-two stitches in his thumb—he could of bled to death." Suddenly he was shouting again. "You hear me? Huh? Huh?"

My hands were torn from the wall and forced behind me, there was the cold bite of the cuffs, the furious breathing, and then, just when things had begun to look grim, the soft restrained tones of a second voice, deus ex machina: "John, John, take it easy." I looked over my shoulder. Officer Raab had joined us. He had a head the size of a beachball, crimson face, white hair. His voice was as soothing and softly modulated as a shrink's. "John," he repeated, "the man hasn't done anything. He's here to bail somebody out is all."

Jerpbak wheeled round on him. "I don't give a shit." There was a whining edge to his voice, the young hothead reluctantly deferring to a higher authority, and I realized in that instant that Jerpbak was no older than I. It was a jolt. I could have submitted to a middle-aged cop—an Officer Raab or the mute desk sergeant—could have rationalized the father figure's need to assert himself and all that, but with a coeval like Jerpbak the experience was humiliating, deeply shameful. A whole series of childhood episodes suddenly flooded my mind. I saw every physical confrontation in a flash, tallied up the wins and losses, counted the times I'd backed down, conjured the faces of the class bullies and extortionists as if they were snapshots in a riffled deck. *No older than I*. I jerked my neck at Officer Raab. "You don't get these cuffs off in two seconds, I'll sue everybody in this place for false arrest, and, and"—I was so wrought up I nearly sobbed the word—"brutality."

Officer Raab had a soft puffy hand on Officer Jerpbak's upper arm. They'd moved off a pace, and the older man was whispering in the younger's ear like a lover. I watched Jerpbak: he looked like a cobra having his hood stroked. When I opened my mouth, Raab glanced at me as if I were a bit of offal—talking offal, something of a curiosity perhaps, but for all that worth no more than a cursory glance—and then moved off across the room and down a pitted corridor, Jerpbak in tow.

I was left standing in the middle of the room, hands manacled behind my back. Every cop in the place was staring at me. After a moment's hesitation, a wizened little deputy crossed the room, released the cuffs and told me in a quiet voice to wait on the bench. I was exhausted, confused, furious. I eased down on the bench, breathing in gasps, adrenaline bubbling in my veins like grease in a deep fryer. Two minutes later I was snoring.

I was awakened by a pressure on my arm and a voice repeating my name. It was Phil. He looked as if he'd just emerged from the third tier of an opium den, his eyes drooping, shirt torn, hair wedged to one side of his head, and he was smiling the fragile smile of a man with a terminal headache. "Shit!" he said, breaking into a grin, and then he repeated himself six or seven times, alternating the exclamation and my name like a cheerleader trying to rouse a stand of lethargic fans. I blinked twice. There were pins and needles in my feet. All the fearsome G-forces of the spinning planet tugged at me as I rose wearily to exchange the backslapping hug we'd used in greeting ever since we saw *Beau Geste* together at the age of fourteen. "Kid," I said. Then we stood there looking at each other for a moment, both of us grinning now, until Phil said he didn't know what I was doing in Tahoe but that I couldn't have come at a better time and did I happen to have another sixty-five dollars on me.

I did. I'd stuffed some bills in my wallet as I left San Francisco—a hundred and sixty dollars or so. Sixty-five and sixty-five was one-thirty, I was thinking as I reached for my wallet. That left me nothing to eat on and an expired Shell card for gas. I asked him what he needed it for.

Phil was rubbing his temples. He looked up at me out of bloodshot eyes and let the air whistle through his teeth. "For Gesh."

"Who?"

"Gesh. He's the new roommate. They've still got him back there," indicating the rear of the building, "and I'd have to wait till the bank opens before I could bail him out. Crazy Eddie we're going to have to take up a collection for."

Crazy Eddie was the third roommate. He'd been behind the wheel when the road had insidiously narrowed and the triangular sign with the insistent arrow had sprung up in front of the bumper. Crazy Eddie flattened the sign and then took out three or four of the steel posts behind it before the right front wheel of Phil's Cadillac sheared off and the car spun to a halt. All three of them had been drinking and eating Quaaludes, and their judgment was gone. They pulled themselves out of the car to assess the damage and saw that they had annihilated the guardrail of a narrow bridge somewhere off the main road. Black trees stared down at them. Water hummed under the bridge. Crazy Eddie expressed his regrets to Phil and offered his condolences with regard to the condition of the car. Phil asked him if he knew how to get home. Eddie applied in the affirmative, and they stumbled back into the car. Then he revved the engine and lurched out into the far lane, trailing sparks. The police followed the furrow to Phil's house, arrested Phil in the act of urinating against a tree, dragged the comatose Gesh from the back seat, and proceeded into the house, where they peeled Crazy Eddie from the girl on the couch and booked him for DWI and leaving the scene of an accident. Bail was fifteen hundred dollars.

"I see what you mean," I said, referring to Eddie's dilemma, counted out the sixty-five dollars and watched Phil re-count it for the mute desk sergeant. Ten minutes later Gesh staggered down the pitted hallway, an officer at his side. He was wearing a watch cap, a reindeer sweater and a drooping khaki overcoat the Salvation Army might have rejected.

A roomful of cops, stenographers, fingerprint filers, minor functionaries and shackled suspects watched Phil introduce us. I saw cheekbones cut like slashes, unfocused eyes, a stubble of beard. The overcoat concealed a big man, two hundred pounds or more. There were nicotine stains on his teeth and one of his eyebrows was divided by a white scar. I nodded, made a stab at a smile. Gesh was unsteady. He fell back on one heel, covered himself by grabbing my hand in a bleary soul shake, and murmured, "Aces, man."

Outside, it was snowing. Dry white pellets sifting down with a hiss. We tramped silently across the white expanse of the parking lot, the wind in our faces, a line of smeared footprints snaking out behind us and climbing the steps of the stationhouse in mute incrimination. Gesh jerked open the door of the Toyota and pitched headlong into the back seat. He was asleep by the time I cleared the snow from the windshield and thumped in beside Phil. My stomach was sour, my head ached. I wondered what in God's name I was doing in a snowstorm in Lake Tahoe at eight-thirty in the morning.

I glanced at Phil. He was grinning at me, his wandering eye so far out of alignment it could have been orbiting the socket. Then he began to laugh, a braying gasping high-pitched shriek that choked on each breath only to come back all the stronger on the next. I couldn't help myself. Delirium, hunger, sleep-deprivation: whatever triggered it, suddenly I was laughing along with him. Roaring. Beating the steering wheel, throwing my head back, struggling for control and then looking at Phil and collapsing all over again. This was hilarious—the snow, the parked car, the police—all of it. "Phil," I gasped, my voice cracking with the absurdity of what I was about to say, "Phil, listen, how would you like"—I broke off, laughter nagging like a cough, the sheer silliness of it—"how would you like to make a quarter of a million dollars?"

Chapter 3

She stood at the door, looking through us, incongruous in an apron that featured a pair of chipmunks brandishing oversized carving knives and the slogan *Why dontcha come up and see us sometime?* Woodwork gleamed behind her, dried flowers threw shadows like teeth against the wall. I smiled. No response. We'd heard the music from the road the instant we stepped out of the car. Now, in the open doorway, it was an assault, loud enough to ionize gases, impair hearing, score the lining of the brain. There was an aggressive smell of cookery, too—garlic sizzling in olive oil—that constricted my throat and poked like a finger at my gut. It was drizzling. Cold. Aorta looked down at her feet, then up at my face and away again. "Hello," she said.

Phil and Gesh shuffled behind me like a pair of thugs. Somehow, somewhere, Phil had dug up a khaki overcoat identical to Gesh's—double-breasted, pleated, belted, and encrusted with stainless-steel loops and couplings that flashed like badges—and they were both wearing fishing hats with the brims pulled low. Aorta stepped back, Gesh paused to grind out his cigarette in the upturned palm of a headless mannequin outside the door, and then we were in.

The door closed with a heavy, airtight thump, like the door of a bank vault, and we found ourselves in a narrow hallway crowded with hunting trophies. Teeth, horns, nostrils. More dead flowers. Dumb-staring eyes. Javelinas drew back their lips to expose tusks the color of tobacco, mule deer thrust out their antlers, a wizened black creature I didn't recognize seemed to be devouring itself in a frozen tumult of tooth and claw. "Well," I said pointlessly. The music raged, the smell of food tore at our stomachs. I shouted out introductions, my companions ducked their heads distractedly, Aorta stifled a smile—was she naturally fractious or merely shy?—and then turned to lead us down a series of hallways and a flight of stairs to the lower level of the lodge she shared with Vogelsang.

She left us in what had once been the ballroom—big floor-to-ceiling windows and a view of treetops and ocean—and disappeared through a swinging door at the far end of the room. I caught a glimpse of Vogelsang, in chef's hat and apron, standing over a stove as the door swung back on itself. Phil dropped into the sofa as if he'd been shot, and Gesh strode directly to the amplifier and cut the volume. The silence was thunderous. One minute a desperate ragged voice had been raging in my ears over the amplifed thump of tribal drums, and in the next I could detect the smallest sounds: a spoon rotated in a pot, the hiss of a gas burner. As if in compensation, the cooking smells seemed to intensify, tempering the atmosphere like a mother's touch.

The room was huge, vaulted like a cathedral, and literally encrusted with the objects of Vogelsang's collecting mania, as cluttered and baroque as a hall in the Museum of Natural History. Which is not to say that each article didn't have its precise place or that a single piece was displayed to disadvantage. The Tahitian gill nets were suspended from the ceiling, softening the effect of the open beams, a gleaming espresso machine climbed the wall like an instrument of torture, knives and guns were arranged symmetrically on hooks over the fireplace, the oil paintings—richly framed and fastidiously hung—occupied a nook over a party of mannequins and stuffed badgers in coats and T-shirts grouped round a table in the corner. There was a long dining table in one section of the room, a TV and stereo cubicle in another, a museum display case containing pottery shards and fossilized human bones just to the left of the kitchen door. You could spend a week poking through it all and still have another eight rooms to tour.

"Hey," Gesh was saying, "did you see this?" Phil got up to join him and whistle in appreciation; I laughed. He was standing over one of Vogelsang's taxidermic triumphs, a pair of bobcats doing the lindy, claws entwined, knees bent, heads thrown back in Dionysian ecstasy. Beside them, a cakewalking salmon leaped into a lampshade, the soft-white bulb protruding from its mouth like an egg in a comedy routine.

Gesh was trying his index finger against the incisor of one of the bobcats when the kitchen door heaved open and Vogelsang burst into the room, grinning wide. "Welcome, welcome," he said, pumping my hand, clapping Phil on the back, and hesitating ever so slightly before reaching for Gesh's hand. Vogelsang had discarded the white hat and apron, and was wearing a T-shirt that announced: I'M OK, YOU'RE OK. There was a moment of confusion over the handshake—Vogelsang coming straight on for the businessman's handclasp, Gesh cocking his wrist for the soul shake—and then Vogelsang was asking us what we'd like, cocktail, beer, pot, sherry, mulled cider, a nice dry not-too-tart zinfandel he'd come across at a little vineyard in Sonoma County?

Gesh asked him what kind of beer he had and Vogelsang listed six or seven imported brands. "Yeah, that sounds good," Gesh said, sinking into the sofa and raising a work boot to the coffee table, "beer."

Vogelsang was a little edgy—I could tell by his diction, which got ever more precise, sprinkled with "I shall"s and "pardon me"s, as if he were trying out for the role of Prince Charles in a made-for-TV movie of the future monarch's lovelife. He was out of the room and back in an instant with our drinks—Phil and I had asked for scotch—and a tray of antipasto. "We're having Italian tonight," he said. "I hope you fellows don't mind. I make my own pasta, and I've been simmering the sauce since I turned out this morning."

I couldn't help grinning: he was amazing. Entrepreneur, culturato, expert mechanic, carpenter and electrician, collector nonpareil—and gourmet chef to boot. We murmured our assent, the congenial guests. "Sounds great," Phil said.

There was a silence. Vogelsang was twisting a wineglass in his hands. Perched on the arm of the sofa, he looked like a bird of prey, his nose hooked like an accipiter's, the blond hair cropped close as feathers. Phil and Gesh were sunk into the couch like cephalopods washed up on the beach. Vogelsang's tone was different now, terser, more businesslike. "So you fellows know all the details, correct?" He looked at me. I nodded.

Gesh stirred and pushed himself up with a grunt, as if it required a herculean effort, took a long swallow of beer, and then looked Vogelsang in the eye. "No," he said, something obstinate and combative creeping into his voice, "why don't you tell us about it?"

For the past week and a half Phil had been occupying the spare bedroom at Fair Oaks, and Gesh had been sleeping on the couch in the living room. It had taken them a single day to wrap up their affairs in Tahoe (Phil phoned the Tahoe Teriyaki, shouted "I quit" at the bewildered busboy who picked up the phone and then hung up, having forgotten to identify himself; Gesh simply failed to show up for his bartending job). The Cadillac was chalked up as a loss, the girl on the couch—her name was Nelda—was given responsibility for the chalet/cabin/condo/duplex, the landlord was berated and abused via telephone, and close friends were lied to (the official story was that Phil and Gesh were moving to San Francisco to work with me in the remodeling trade). It was rumored that Crazy Eddie's mother was wiring bail money, so Phil felt he could rest easy on that score, and he closed out his bank account with a check for $32.14. "Well," he said with a grin after he'd hung up on the landlord, "the only thing now is to pack up all of this shit," gesturing at the mounds of arcane artifacts that littered the floor like the leavings of an aboriginal tribe, "and hit the road."

We strapped Phil's skis to the top of the Toyota, along with three or four cardboard boxes of key belongings and priceless mementoes, like the lacquered conch shell he'd brought back from Miami Beach and the history reports he'd been saving since the ninth grade. He lashed his mattress to the boxes, which were in turn lashed to the skis, which were fixed to the Toyota's roof by means of a frayed bit of clothesline snaked through the windows and granny-knotted at the level of the driver's forehead. His record collection, acetylene torch, and guitar took up the entire back seat. Gesh was easier. His worldly possessions amounted to two Safeway bags stuffed with odd bits of clothing—chiefly dirty underwear, judging from the top layer—and a box of paperback books.

When we had it all together it was nearly dark. The mattress—it was a new king-sized sleep-eze deluxe special model and Phil couldn't bring himself to part with it—sagged over the rear window and mushroomed out from the top of the car like a pulpy carapace. I asked Phil if he was sure the rope would hold. "This?" he said, cinching a limp strand of clothesline to the radio antenna. "Are you kidding? You could take this thing through a hurricane and then drive coast to coast and back again." He patted the mattress. "No: this baby isn't going anywhere."

As we were crossing the Bay Bridge four and a half hours later, a sudden gust lifted the mattress off the roof and deposited it beneath the wheels of a semi loaded with ball bearings. When it broke loose it took a box of mementoes with it, slamming at the roof of the car like an angry fist and then tearing back with a heart-seizing rumble and a rush of wind. "What was that?" Phil gasped, jerking awake.

"I don't know," I said, trying to account for the sudden visibility through the rear window. "I think we lost something."

Gesh's voice was flat and emotionless. He could have been a radio commentator noting a minuscule change in hog futures. "Your mattress," he said.

We stopped in the inside lane. Trucks shrieked by with a suck of wind, tires hissed like death, the hair beat crazily at our heads. I could barely catch my breath, each truck tearing the oxygen from my lungs like an explosion. The mattress had already been flattened along three-quarters of its length. Phil made several feints to rush out and nab it, but the traffic was mindless. Sixty miles an hour: *whoosh*, *whoosh*, *whoosh*. The bridge swayed with the thunder of the big semis. There was a stink of diesel fuel, gull shit, the dead man's tide. We shrugged our shoulders and eased back into the car.

For the next nine days we divided our time equally between making preparations for our move to the country (Phil purchased an imitation Swiss Army knife with a corkscrew the size of an auger, Gesh washed his underwear, and I bought six snakebite kits) and deliberating over how we would spend our respective shares of the profits accruing from the summer camp. Gesh was going to reserve the first ten thousand of his $166,666.66 for a blowout at the carnival in Rio, then invest the balance in a thirty-five-foot sloop and cruise the Caribbean with dusky-skinned women, eating lobster and pompano. Phil was going to pay off his debts and maybe open another restaurant—a New Orleans–style fish house with a tile floor, teak booths and big lazy overhead fans. I was worried about taxes. I figured I could buy another neglected Victorian and clandestinely pump cash into it while simultaneously writing off the cost of labor and materials. At any rate, we all agreed that we were sick to death of scrambling for a living and that here was our chance to set ourselves up for life.

"I'm tired of busting my ass for somebody else," Phil said, as if he'd been accused of liking it, "and then being so depressed I've got to spend every nickel I make on cocktails and tranquilizers."

Gesh grunted his assent. My eyes burned with indignation over the wrongs and inequities Phil had suffered—not to mention the wrongs and inequities I'd suffered myself. "I know what you mean," I said. We were sitting around the living room, idle and impatient, and we were profoundly drunk.

Society was rotten to the core, I said. It was dog eat dog and every man for himself. I was fed up with academics, real-estate agents and carpenters alike. You gave them everything—heart and soul and sweat—and they gave you nothing in return, not even the satisfaction of a job well done.

Phil said he knew exactly how I felt.

Gesh was perched on the windowsill, staring into his glass. After a moment he raised his head. "Society sucks," he said with real vehemence, and then waved his hand in disgust. "That happy hippie crap." I knew what he was driving at. The whole hippie ethic—beads, beards, brotherhood, the community of man—it had all been bullshit, a subterfuge to keep us from realizing that there were no jobs, the economy was in trouble and the resources of the world going up in smoke. And we'd bought it, lived it, invented it. For all those years.

His laugh was bitter. We were older now, he said, and wiser. We knew what counted: money. Money, and nothing else.

It was late afternoon, the day before we were to dine at Vogelsang's, work out the last-minute details and then head up to the summer camp. I felt good. I felt ready. As ready as I had ever been for anything in my life. For six months I'd been idle, living off what I'd made from my last remodeling job (the housing market had closed up like a fist) and the pittance they gave me at the community college for teaching a summer course in freshman English, sinking lower into the pit of inactivity, self-denigration and loneliness. Now, sitting there in the glow of anticipation, the moment rich and immediate, Phil and his friend at my side like supporters at a pep rally, I felt purged of all that. Sunlight suffused the room like a dream of kings, Bruce Springsteen was singing about the Promised Land, we were drinking gimlets from a pitcher. I looked out over the rooftops of the city and pictured a fleet of ships lying at anchor, masts stepped and washed in golden light, and I felt like Coronado, like Cortés, gazing on the vessels that would take them across the flashing seas and into the vestibule of the treasury of the gods.

"Saltimbocca alla romana," Vogelsang announced, backing through the door with a platter in each hand. "With steamed asparagus, and homemade pasta on the side."

The table was littered with the remains of the first four courses, with beer bottles and fiascos of wine. After the antipasto, Vogelsang had served a dish of agnolotti, a brodo di pesce and caponata. About halfway through the soupcourse, Dowst joined us, bobbing into the room in blazer and button-down shirt, apologizing for his lateness and showing us a mouthful of gleaming equine teeth. We were eating so hard we barely noticed him.

When the meat had gone round, I tore a hunk of bread from the fresh-baked loaf and made a joke—in dialect, with Chico Marx flourishes—about the "unafortunate congregation of our-a late associates at-a the Appalachian lodge-a." Phil laughed. "This is more like the last supper," he said. No one else cracked a smile. There was a silence, broken only by the moist rhetoric of mastication and the ring of silverware. Finally Phil looked up and said: "Good stuff, Vogelsang. It jumps in your mouth."

Vogelsang said he knew the chefs at Vanessi's and Little Joe's personally, and that he'd been invited into the kitchen on several occasions. He was eating a minuscule portion himself—no more than a single bite of each dish—and supplementing it with what looked like soggy cornflakes. "You're not eating?" I said.

"Oh, God." Vogelsang looked offended. "This stuff is much too rich for me." He was eating a mixture of dried flaked fish and pine nuts. The saltimbocca stuck in my throat.

"Listen, Herb," Gesh broke in, "why don't you fill us in on the house and all—you know, what sort of thing we can expect up there." The silence that fell over the table was absolute: no fork clattered, no lip smacked or tooth champed. Vogelsang's Christian name was Herbert, but no one called him by his Christian name, not even his mother. He was known as Vogelsang, pure and simple. One of his girlfriends—I can't recall her name—began calling him "Vogie" after the three of us had sat through a double bill of *The Big Sleep* and *To Have and Have Not*. The next time I saw him he was alone.

Gesh's words sank into the silence, absorbed like the butter that oozed into the hot bread before him. Gesh knew perfectly well that our benefactor hated to be addressed as Herb or Herbert or any other variant of his given name—I'd specifically warned him against it—and Vogelsang knew that Gesh was trying to provoke him. But if Vogelsang was anything, he was imperturbable. I'd never seen him angry, had never seen him display any emotion whatever, for that matter. To be angry, frightened, happy, moved, was a weakness, a loss of control—and Vogelsang never lost control. "Certainly," he said, flashing Gesh a smile, "what do you want to know?"

Gesh was tearing at his veal with knife and fork, talking through the wedge of it stuffed inside his cheek. "Well, shit," he said, "I mean we're going to be living out there in the asshole of nowhere for the next nine months while you're chewing the fat down at Vanessi's—I want to know what kind of shape the place is in, does it have running water and electricity and all that?"

"Oh, yes," Vogelsang said, reaching for his fish flakes, "yes, it has all the essentials."

"You've got a generator for electricity," Dowst said. "Runs off an old Briggs and Stratton engine. The water comes from a big redwood holding tank just up the hill from the cabin."

"The place is perfectly adequate," Vogelsang said. "With a

little work it could be really cozy." Aorta was sitting beside him. Her eyes caught mine and she smiled—she actually smiled—before looking down into her wineglass. I watched a piece of veal disappear between her black lips, then turned my attention back to Vogelsang. "It used to be a hunting lodge back in the twenties," he was saying. "Great view, you've got a hilltop overgrown with fir and oak and madrone. There's even a couple of redwoods."

I could see the place. Or rather I could see the cabin we'd rented each summer when I was a kid. It was in Vermont, by the side of a lake. There was the smell of pinesap and wet leaves, the close comforting feel of tree trunks grown so thick your eyes couldn't penetrate a hundred feet. In the morning, loons cried like lost souls and tanagers whistled outside the window. I remembered sitting around the stone fireplace at night, sunburned and happy, playing hearts with my father. This was going to be all right, I thought. Soothing. Rustic. An adventure. When I tuned back into the conversation, Dowst was talking about worm castings and the need for soil preparation. "The drainage stinks up there," he was saying, "too heavy a clay content. So what you've got to do is create your own environment for each plant—a sand-mulch mixture for drainage and root expression, and the worm castings for nitrogen . . ."

Later, over espresso and millefoglie, the lights turned low and Vogelsang's museum fading into the shadows, we got down to business. The cabin, the supplies, the equipment, the seeds, the eight-dollar per diem Vogelsang would front Gesh, Phil and me each week above and beyond our share of the final profits, the disposal of the mature plants (Vogelsang had a connection who would buy all we could produce, cash up front, no questions asked)—all this was easy. It was Gesh who asked for clarification of the one point that had crouched in all our minds like a stalking beast: "What if we get busted?"

Vogelsang handled it with perfect sangfroid. "I know nothing about you. I'd bought the land as an investment, and was surprised to hear that anyone was on it, shocked and stunned that illicit activities were taking place there. Under the table, of course, I pay all legal fees."

Dowst had come alive at the mention of the verboten word. "First offense," he said, sipping at his coffee. "No one's going to jail—a fine and probation, that's all." I couldn't be sure, but I thought I saw his hand quaver as he set the cup down.

Gesh looked angry—he opened his mouth as if to say something, then thought better of it. Aorta was expressionless. Across the table from me Phil eased back in his chair, the effects of the scotch and wine evident in the skew of his bad eye. He was already in his new restaurant, eating oysters at a marble-topped bar. I didn't know what to think.

"Don't worry," Vogelsang said, "I'll take care of you."

Chapter 4

Perhaps it was the strange bed, the smell of the sheets or my excited imagination, but my dreams that night were exclusively erotic. Faces leered and tongues lapped, a thicket of pubic hair sprang from the ground, breasts and buttocks sprouted beneath me like vegetables, like fruit, ripe and wet and stippled with dew. Then I was downstairs, in the ballroom. Aorta was pinned to me, naked, her tongue was in my mouth, pasta bubbled on the stove, a legion of stuffed otters, beavers and bobcats stiffened their hackles, she was massaging my abdomen with the strange stiff bristle of her bleached hair. Then she broke away. Cruel and silent as the sphinx, she shifted round the room, playing with herself, taunting me until I lunged for her.

In one of those odd conjunctions of dream and reality, I was awakened by her voice. "Felix," she was saying, her voice throaty and raw, as if cracked with sexual exhaustion, "everybody's up." I forced my eyes open. She was standing in the doorway, wrapped in a white robe, and she looked smaller than I'd remembered her, shrunken somehow, vulnerable. It was a moment before I realized what it was: she wasn't wearing any makeup. No black lipstick, no punctured eyes, no skin-prickling claws. "Vogelsang's making breakfast," she whispered, hoarse, hoarse, and then turned and shuffled off down the hallway.

She was right. He was making breakfast: I could smell it. Coffee, Canadian bacon, flapjacks, eggs: the aura of the logging camp suffused the room, penetrated to the core of my being, and in that instant the genitive urge gave way to the alimentary. I jerked myself up and fumbled through my duffel bag for one of the new flannel shirts I'd bought for the summer camp. It was cold. As I buttoned the shirt, bacon in my nostrils, the chill air slapping at my thighs like a cold hand, I looked round the room with satisfaction. A moosehead hovered over the bed, the split-pine walls glistened with varnish, my jacket hung—simplicity itself—from a coat tree in the corner. I slipped into my jeans and workboots, feeling like a candidate for a cigarette ad.

Downstairs, in the big room we'd vacated in the dark, full of dark fears, there was a flood of sunlight. Everything was gleaming, pricked with light, from the glass of the display cases and the burnished copper of the espresso machine to the wild grinning eye Phil cast at me as I stepped through the doorway and held my hands out to the hissing fire. Phil was already at the table, hunched over a mound of flapjacks and a glass of fresh-squeezed orange juice; Gesh sàt beside him, his plate empty, a Bloody Mary clutched in his hand as if it were the ejection lever of a flaming jet. I listened to the distant whine of a tea kettle, and to Vivaldi, who was measuring out the irretrievable moments as if to be sure we all had enough.

Vogelsang startled me. He slammed through the kitchen door, arms laden—coffee pot, pitcher of cream, a platter of eggs in poaching cups flanked by flat red slabs of bacon. He was wound up, so brisk he seemed awkward, each movement an effort to contain the flashes of energy that jerked at his fingers and set his limbs atremble. I thought he was going to lift off the floor and flap round the room like a cockatiel sprung from its cage, but he managed instead to set the platter down and boom a greeting at me. "Felix!" he shouted. "It's about time." He was wearing a running suit, chevrons at the shoulders, stripes down the seams of the legs. Too loudly, and far too cheerfully, he informed me that he'd already run seven miles and loaded the back of the pickup with our equipment.

I sat down and began to consume eggs. Vogelsang crouched at the head of the table, lecturing in spasms, alternately gulping fistfuls of garlic pills and ginseng and dosing himself with breath neutralizer. "Picks, shovels, a wheelbarrow," he said, interrupting himself to swallow a desiccated-liver tablet. "A couple rolls of barbed wire and a come-along, and two little Kawasakis I've just finished overhauling. It's all in the truck. Plus some odds and ends: an axe, a set of socket wrenches, claw hammer, that sort of thing. Oh: and the two-by-fours and whatnot for the greenhouse. Boyd will be up there at the end of the week, and he's going to bring up the worm castings and seeds and all the rest in his van."

Gesh was wearing a torn flannel shirt that featured cowboys with lariats, his hair was in aboriginal disarray and his eyes looked as if they'd been freshly transplanted. He mixed himself another Bloody Mary, threw back two Quaaludes and gave us a sick grin.

"You'll need the bikes for patrolling the place once you get the crop in—three hundred ninety acres is no putting green, you know—and for handling the irrigation system during the dry months. But the first thing you've got to do—and this is vitally important—is to get that fencing up." Vogelsang paused to shake the vial of breath spray irritably, set it down on the table and fumble in his pocket for another. Phil was reading the sports page. Gesh looked as if he were about to fall into his drink.

Half an hour later we were milling around Vogelsang's driveway, preparatory to setting off on the four-hour drive to Mendocino County and the wild venue we would tame like the pioneers and prospectors we were. Gravel crunched under our feet. Birds piped and throbbled. Sunlight fell through the trees with a cheering insistence and the air was like milk. Vogelsang was fussing around the vehicles, cinching ropes and rearranging cartons of supplies, but I wasn't paying him any attention. I was feeling the pulse of things, suddenly aware of that richness of color and texture you take for granted until you see it represented in oils or illuminating the big screen in a darkened theater. The smell of eucalyptus was as sharp as recollection.

Then Vogelsang was pumping my hand. Aorta stood beside him, restored to impermeability behind her layers of makeup and a black vinyl jacket. "Good luck," Vogelsang said, reasserting his promise to look in on us in a week or so. Phil fired up the vehicle our benefactor had provided for us—an ancient, fender-punched Datsun pickup—and I climbed into the Toyota beside Gesh. "Where's the ticker tape?" I called, grinning, as I turned over the engine and wheeled up the drive, feeling heroic, poised on the verge of greatness, ready for anything. The gears clattered, I waved my arm off, Phil fell in behind me and Gesh began to snore.

By the time we reached Santa Rosa the sky was the color of dishwater and sunk so low I had to turn the lights on. At Cloverdale, just below the Mendocino County line and fifty miles or so from Willits, our point of reference, it began to rain. Not with a burst of lightning or a roll of thunder, but with the sudden crashing fall characteristic of coastal precipitation.

The hammering on the roof woke Gesh. He said he felt like shit. "Raw and unadulterated," he added, slitting a cellophane Mandrax packet with his teeth. "How about we stop for a cup of coffee and wait till it clears?"

We watched the water heave down the windows of the Hopland Coffee Shoppe in big scalloped sheets. It was so dark it could have been dusk shading into night. Phil was soaked through—apparently the truck's window wouldn't roll up. "Just my luck," he said gloomily, and asked Gesh for some pharmaceutical help. Gesh, who seemed to have an unlimited supply, slipped him three Quaaludes. I took two. For equilibrium. It was ten-thirty in the morning. We waited until the waitress stopped refilling our coffee cups, shrugged our shoulders and hunched out into the rain.

Willits, the rain-blurred sign announced some fifty minutes later, had a population of 4,120 and stood at an elevation of 1,377 feet. We passed a series of diners, motels and gas stations, Al's Redwood Room, and a Safeway market. The town seemed contained in a single strip, stretched out along Highway 101 for the convenience of tourists intent on the redwood forests to the north. It was as bleak and barren and uninspiring as an iceberg bobbing in the Bering Sea. Gesh and I caught glimpses of it through the beating windshield wipers. "For the next nine months," I said, a trace of retardation in my voice as a result of the drug, which shifts your system down a couple of gears into a sort of prehibernatory torpor, "this is our closest urban center."

"Urban center," Gesh repeated, his voice as lugubrious as a noseblow. "Shee-it."

Fifteen miles north of Willits we were to turn off on a blacktop road, follow it past a place called Shirelle's Bum Steer and six or seven tumbledown farms, and then up a gravel drive to a gate that opened on "five point three miles of unimproved dirt road," to quote Vogelsang's directions. Fine. But it was raining so hard we missed the turnoff and Phil nearly slammed into my tail end when I braked to cut a U-turn. I rattled up on the shoulder, hit the emergency flasher and ran back to confer with him.

The intensity of the rain was staggering: I felt I was carrying a sack of potatoes on my back as I jogged the twenty steps to the pickup and poked my head through the open window. Rain tore at the back of my neck and sent exploratory tributaries down the collar of my jacket. A lone logging truck hissed up the highway, spewing water, and vanished in the haze. "What's the story?" Phil mumbled, each word played out on a string like a yo-yo winding down. The sagging pompadour was flattened across his forehead and a drop of water depended from his nose.

"Vogelsang said fifteen miles from Willits. I read fifteen and a half on my odometer. The road we just passed must be it."

Phil was shivering. The iris of his wild eye looked like an ice crystal in a cocktail glass. "Christ," he moaned, "I hope so. All's I want to do now is sit in front of the fire and crash for a couple hours."

Shirelle's Bum Steer greeted us like a shout of affirmation as we lurched across the highway and onto the presumptive road. I could hear Phil honking his joy behind me as we sped past the place—a ramshackle country bar attached to a house in need of paint. A pair of mud-streaked pickups huddled beneath the drooling oak out front, the hand-lettered sign was pitched at a drunken angle, and a single sad Coors neon glowed in the window like a candle at the shrine of a martyr. I took it in at a glance, noting bleakly that this was our nearest outpost of civilization. "The Land of the Rednecks," Gesh muttered, and added that he felt like Lewis of Lewis and Clark, or maybe it was Clark, and then we were rattling over a raging tributary of the Eel River (in summer it would subside to a series of fetid, mosquito-breeding pools) and threading our way up a valley between cropped, long-faced hills that bristled with pine like so many unshaven cheeks. We were counting off tumbledown farms and scouring the left-hand side of the road for a block of stone that protruded from the ground like an admonitory finger—our indication to swing into the next road to our right—when Gesh shouted "Eureka!" and I cut hard into a dirt road that was coincidentally the brown rippling bed of a stream.

Suddenly we were going uphill—climbing a precipice—the tires groping for purchase, water slashing at the fenders, the engine cranking with a propulsive whine and carrying us fifty or sixty feet in a headlong rush before the wheels sank to the hubcaps in a sea of reddish mud. Phil, loaded down with the barbed wire and Kawasakis, was able to develop better traction, and careened wildly up the hill and into the back of the stalled Toyota. I don't recall the sound effects, whether there was a crunch, a shriek or a thud. But my head flew forward as if on an urgent journey of its own, the windshield groaned and then flowered in silver filigree, and the trunk latch popped open, forever. I looked at Gesh. He was cursing, and there was blood on his forearm.

Then we were all out in the downpour, ankle-deep in mud and roiling water. Trees loomed over us like cupped black hands, the rain lashed our faces with a thousand stings, I rubbed my forehead and discovered that an object the size and consistency of a golf ball had been inserted beneath the skin in the vicinity of my left eyebrow. For a moment we just stood there, hunched like lost souls awaiting the ferry across the river of lamentation, cursing softly. Then Gesh plunged into the undergrowth like an enraged bull, tearing at ferns and briars and poison oak, knocking down saplings, uprooting stumps. I thought he'd gone mad.

Meanwhile, Phil had begun to dance around the road, wringing his hands and rotating his head as if he were trying out an esoteric new routine for Alvin Ailey. "Hey, I didn't know—" he began, but I waved him off. "I'm okay," I said, noting at the same time and with the dispassion of a man in a movie theater watching the *Lusitania* go down, that my duffel bag had been thrown from the trunk and into the center of the streambed. The heavy khaki cloth had gone dark with wet, and debris had already begun to collect against it. Inside were my shirts, my socks, my underwear, my sweaters. I took hold of the dripping strap and jerked the bag up out of the mud, nearly dislocating my shoulder in the process. Phil helped me heave the sodden thing back into the trunk, and together we managed to secure the ruptured latch with a piece of wire.

Suddenly Gesh emerged from the woods, his face cross-hatched with welts and contusions, the trench coat flapping about his knees. He was dragging a downed tree the size of a battering ram. For a moment we just stood there gaping at him, our hands at our sides, rain crashing through the trees, mud swirling at our feet. It was as if we'd just been wakened from a dream of sleeping. "Christ ass," Gesh shouted, "give me a hand, will you?"

I could feel the drug loosen its grip—think of a crouton drawn from a pot of fondue—and then I was at Gesh's side, jerking furiously at the wet, moss-covered log. Phil fell in beside me, and we maneuvered the thing alongside the car, then staggered into the undergrowth for another. We worked silently, grunting at one another, each locked in his own thoughts (I was thinking of hot showers, hot soup, electric blankets and thermal underwear). Everything dripped, thorns raked at our wrists and faces, sowbugs crept up our arms, rain hissed in the branches like a stadium packed with disgruntled fans. As Phil and I wrestled with a half-petrified log, Gesh jacked the Toyota out of the mud. "All right, push!" he exhorted, the jack at its apogee, and the three of us leaned into the fender and then jumped back as the car slammed down on the makeshift platform with a percussive splintering crack. Then we jacked up the other side.

There was a smell of slow rot on the air, of mold and compost. Birds mocked us from the trees. Our hands and faces were black with loam, as if we'd been buried and unearthed and buried again. Gesh tried to light a cigarette. His pants were torn at the knee and the trench coat hung from him like a wet beach towel. Phil was clowning. He bent to scoop up a handful of mud and slap it down across the crown of his head, like Stan Laurel at the conclusion of a pie-throwing skirmish. It wasn't funny. "Okay," Gesh growled, flinging down the wet cigarette and spreading his big hands across the indented bumper of the Toyota, "why don't you see what you can do?"

I wiped my hands on the seat of my pants and slid into the driver's seat. The car was musty and cold, the windows opaque with wet. I turned the key, took note of the answering roar (we'd lost the muffler apparently), and watched the wipers flail at the rain. Then I revved the engine, peeled the bark from the logs and hydroplaned up the road as far as I could go, my co-workers slogging madly behind me like refugees chasing after the Red Cross wagon. When I bogged down, the whole process started over again: heave, haul, crank, shove. Sometimes I'd manage to make a couple hundred feet; other times I'd come wheeling off the log grid and sink instantaneously in the mud. The rain was no help: it fell steadily all afternoon. And we were, as I was later to discover, climbing a vertical drop of something like six hundred feet from the blacktop road to the cabin.

Finally, after four and a half back-breaking hours, we reached a point at which the road began to level out, and when I came off the launching pad for what must have been the twentieth time, I kept going. The car fishtailed right and left, low-hanging branches swooped at the windshield, the cheers of my partners faded in the background, and I kept going. There was a short straightaway, a series of *S* curves and then a wide sweeping loop that brought me up into a rain-screened clearing about the size and shape of a Little League field. I didn't know where I was going, slashing through swaths of waist-high weed and thumping over frame-rattling boulders and mounds of rusted machine parts, hooked on the idea of momentum . . .

Until I saw the cabin.

No, I thought, no, this can't be it, as I slammed on the brakes and skidded into a heap of scrap metal that featured a rusted boxspring and the exoskeleton of the first washing machine ever made. I'd experienced hiatuses between expectation and actuality before—who hasn't? But this was staggering. Hunting lodge? The place was an extended shack, the yard strewn with refuse, the doorway gaping like an open mouth, like the hungry maw of the demon-god of abandoned houses demanding propitiation. Someone—Vogelsang, no doubt—had nailed tarpaper up on the outer walls in place of shingles, and there was a ridiculous white cloud of sheet Styrofoam lashed across the roof (in the hope of forestalling leaks, as I was later to learn). One thing I was sure of, even then, sitting stunned behind the fractured windshield of the stalled Toyota: no one had lived in the place for twenty years. Or more.

Inside, it was worse. The roof leaked in eight places, the front door had blown in and torn back from its hinges, a furious collision of sumac and vetch darkened the windows. I dropped my duffel bag on the cracked linoleum floor (a floral pattern popular in the forties), and walked round the main room as if I were touring a museum. The room was L-shaped, roughly divided into kitchen and parlor. I paused over the .22 holes in the kitchen wall, the gas-powered refrigerator that had been nonfunctional for thirty years, the sink stained with the refuse of forgotten meals. There were two small bedrooms off the parlor, and a crude staircase that led to a third in the attic. The kitchen door gave onto a partially enclosed porch that connected with a dilapidated storage shed. Beyond the storage shed, a rust-pitted propane tank (Pro-Flame) and a grim, tree-choked ravine. I took all this in, shivering, and then turned to the stove.

There were two stoves, actually. One was a range—combination gas and wood, circa 1935—and the other was a squat wood stove made of cast iron. There was no wood. All the clothes I owned were soaked through, my shoulders had begun to quake involuntarily, I was exhaling clouds. Something had to be done. Beyond the brown windows lay 390 acres of pine, hardwood and scrub, every stick of it wet as a sponge. I pictured myself back out in that dripping tangle, snapping off branches and peeling back strips of sodden bark, and dissolved the image as abruptly as I might have switched channels on the TV. Then I thought of the storage room, and slammed through the kitchen door in a rush, inadvertently flushing a bird that had been roosting in the porch beams. It flew up in my face like a bad dream, and then it was gone.

The storage room was penumbral, cluttered with refuse. There were bundles of yellowed newspaper (TRUMAN CALLS FOR FAIR DEAL; DIMAGGIO UNRAVELS SOX), staved-in gasoline cans and remnants of what might once have been a hand loom. I stepped into the low-ceilinged room as I might have stepped into Pharaoh's tomb, treading carefully, keeping an eye out for lucre—or rather, in this case, the merest splinter of anything combustible—among the heaps of rags, cans and bottles that flowed across the floor and slapped at the walls like the spillage of some diluvian tide. Dust lay over everything, white as pulverized bone. When I snapped a chair leg across my knee, a pair of sleek dark forms shot through the jagged window on the near side of the room. Rats, I thought absently—or maybe ground squirrels. Five minutes later I had a respectable pile of furniture fragments and odd pieces of lumber. I set it atop a bundle of mildewed newspaper, hauled the whole mess back into the main room, checked the flue on the stovepipe, and realized I didn't have any matches.

This was too much. I cursed. Kicked something. And then threw myself down on the stinking sun-faded sofa opposite the cold stove. Dust rose in a mighty swirling mushroom cloud and settled on my wet jacket. For a while I just sat there shivering, listening to the rain percolate through the ceiling and spatter the ancient linoleum, the storm laying down a screen of static outside. Then I heard the laboring engine of Phil's pickup, churning its way up the mountain. They were in for a surprise, I thought, lifting myself from the sofa and gazing out through the open door at the raked and rugged hills, the trees like claws, the gray distance that couldn't begin to suggest the gaps between ridges.

Impatient, jittery, wet to the bone, I paced the room half a dozen times and then thought of looking over the bedrooms again, with an eye to staking a claim on one of them. The nearest was unremarkable: four walls, crudely done (some misguided soul had attempted to put up slabs of sheetrock and had given up halfway through the job), a torn mattress set atop a boxspring, a broom handle nailed diagonally across the far corner to serve as a clothing rack. I moved past it, down the narrow hallway that led to the bathroom, and then into the back bedroom. It was as spare and Essene as the first. The walls were pine slats, there was a boxspring propped up on wooden packing crates, an unfinished window looked out on the trees. At first I almost missed the calendar nailed to the inside of the door. But the door swung to on uneven hinges, and when I turned, it was staring me in the face.

A calendar. I could hear the pickup rattling into the yard, the engine wheezing like a miler's lungs. The picture over the month-and-date portion of the calendar featured a woman in a cloche hat, her face averted, skirt pinched to reveal her legs—a dull, brownish, Norman Rockwell sort of thing. But it wasn't the picture that caught my eye. It was the year—1949, the year I was born. Odd, I thought, and then I noticed the month. November. My month. I could feel the blood rushing to my stomach, as if I'd been hit in the midsection, the impossible, nagging cosmic joke of it, the heavy black pencil strokes an act of the will, irrefutable, closing in on the very day. My day. My birthday. Circled in black.

I stepped back involuntarily. "Hey, Felix!" Gesh was shouting from the front room. "You in there?" It was one of those moments that annihilate a lifetime of empirical assumptions with a sudden mocking laugh. "Felix!" Gesh shouted. I stepped back another pace, as bewildered and disoriented as if I'd just been slapped.

Something was wrong here, and I didn't like it. From childhood I'd been taught that there were answers for everything, that the square root of four was two, that the sky was blue because of the diffraction of light through dust particles in the atmosphere, that life originated from the action of an electrical charge on simple proteins. I was not superstitious. Like anyone else, I knew that in an infinite and multifarious universe, the most bizarre coincidences were commonplace, were calculable probabilities. Nonetheless, I wanted to quit. Right then, right there, my face smarting and heart hammering, I wanted to quit.

PART 2
Germination

Chapter 1

Let me tell you about dirt.

Brown dirt, red dirt, black dirt, yellow dirt. Dirt that sucks at your shoes, blackens your fingernails and seams the creases of your hands, dirt that dries to dust on the faded linoleum and settles in your lungs at night. Friable dirt, liquid dirt, dirt clods, bombs and bricks, sandy dirt, loamy dirt, dirt that reeks of corruption and slow rot. Dirt. The foundation of all things, the beginning and the end. We are made of dirt, not water, and in dirt we shall lie. At the summer camp we ate dirt, washed with dirt, slept in dirt in dirty sleeping bags; at the summer camp, no doubt about it, we lived close to the soil.

You don't encounter true dirt in the city, with its shoulder-to-shoulder buildings, its cement and its blacktop. But it is there—down in the sub-basement like a nasty primordial secret, clenched in the strangled roots of the trees, crushed beneath the heaving floor of the Bay itself. Dirt is problematic in the city, an element you perceive theoretically, intellectually. You don't become aware of it on the experiential level until you dive for a Frisbee on the tame suburban grass of Golden Gate Park, and there it is—dirt—on the calf of your white pegged jeans. Or you come down in the morning to find minuscule grains of black dust on the windshield of your car, or take a stroll past a building site and see some actual raw hard-core dirt exposed like a cavity in a rotten tooth. Dirt, you say to yourself, how about that? Still, it's an anomaly, an exception to the rule. You think about air in the city. You think about water, gasoline, broken glass and dog shit. But not dirt. Dirt just isn't relevant.

It was relevant that first night at the summer camp.

We found ourselves in the purlieus of nowhere, cold, hungry, exhausted and wet, our hair, skin and clothing layered with mud, which is of course simply protean dirt. Disappointment choked us. Weltschmerz glinted in our eyes. Our hands were black as potatoes dug from the ground, black as the hands of the mechanic I'd known in New York when I was selling insurance. He'd held up his hands to me one afternoon as I came in to reclaim my car. "See these hands?" he said. I looked. The skin was uniformly black, as if it had been dyed or tattooed, the nails were gone, black callus gave way to gray. "You think you got it bad," he said. "At least you don't have to get your hands dirty." It was a revelation: ineradicable dirt, stigmatic dirt, dirt as an unbridgeable social barrier. I'd tried to picture him at the Waldorf or Gracie Mansion, making polite conversation and passing the croissants with hands that looked as if they'd been exhuming corpses. Now, and for the next nine months, we'd know how he felt.

A gust of wind rattled the windows. I shivered. We needed heat, we needed hot water, we needed soap. Phil pried some rusted two-penny nails from a sagging outbuilding and nailed the door shut, while Gesh kindled the fire with his lighter and then hunted up a Coleman lantern. I didn't know what to do. Voodoo drums were pounding in my ears, a fist beat at my stomach, the witchery of the calendar as unsettling as an effigy transfixed with pins. I couldn't help it: I was shaken.

"Come on, man," Gesh said, wadding up newspapers and feeding them into the stove, "snap out of it. You know as well as I do the whole thing is just that shithead Vogelsang's idea of a joke—big laugh, you know?"

It was true that Vogelsang had been up to the property at least twice already, and true, too, that his sense of humor was skewed, to say the least. I remembered the newspaper file he'd once produced for me. A manila folder crammed with the responses to ads he'd placed in *The Berkeley Barb* and *The Bay Guardian*. One of the ads read "Man or Beast? Love Animals . . . But Love Them the *Right* Way," and gave a P.O. box number. He received twelve responses, one of which came from a male zookeeper who expressed a fondness for big cats and whips, and another of which invited him to spend the weekend on a sheep ranch in Marshall. Still another gave the vital statistics on a wire-haired pointer named Rex, suggested a liaison, and was cosigned with a woman's name and the print of the dog's right forepaw. Vogelsang never told me if he accepted.

And then of course there were the stuffed animals and the mannequins and all the rest. Yes, I thought, he's capable of it—and I even pictured him digging the old calendar out of the storage shed, his face lighting with perverse inspiration as he circled the date and nailed the thing to the wall. But in the same instant I felt the tug of superstition, and I saw an unknown hand, three decades back, painstakingly marking the date of some future event in a pathetic expression of longing—or worse, apprehension.

While I was agonizing over a pencil smudge, Phil was scorching his eyebrows in an attempt to ignite and adjust the pilot on the water heater. He finally succeeded, with a *whoosh* that agitated the windows and singed his pompadour as neatly as if he'd paid twenty-five bucks for a flame cut. Abashed, I took charge of dinner. While we waited for the pièce de résistance—hot water—I opened three cans of beer, an institutional-sized bucket of Malloy's Red Hot Texas Chili, and a loaf of white bread. Exhausted, we sprawled in front of the stove, baking like pots in a kiln, the mud crusting and peeling from us in stringy lumps while we sipped warm beer and mopped up cold chili.

Then we turned to the bathroom. There was a sink, a bathtub, a toilet (which, like the facilities on railway coaches, simply opened on the ground below; but whereas the railroad apparatus worked on the principle of fecal dissemination, ours relied on gravity and the slope of the ravine). The tub looked as if it had last been used to disinfect lepers, the porcelain pus-yellow and ringed with the strata of ancient immersions. It was a color that reminded me of the urinals at the old Penn Station, filth beyond redemption. I brought the Coleman lantern closer, and we examined the calcium-flecked fixtures, the husks of desiccated insects, the network of cracks that veined the inner surface of the tub like the map of a river delta. We stood there, as hushed as if we were gazing on the ruins of Lepcis Magna, until Gesh broke the silence. "Me first," he said.

"Hey, wait a minute," I protested. "Let's at least draw lots or something."

"I did most of the pushing out there," Gesh said, but without much conviction. He looked like one of those New Guinea shamans who make masks of dried mud, his head big as a pumpkin, each strand of hair braided with dirt.

"Doesn't matter." Phil's tone was crisp, businesslike. He produced a box of wooden matches, shook out two with sober-faced gravity, halved one and turned his back. Then he swung round, the three matchsticks protruding from the plane of his clenched fist like pins in a pincushion, and presented his hand first to Gesh, then to me.

Phil got the long one. "Flip you for seconds," Gesh said, the coin already gleaming feebly in the dull glow of the lantern. "Tails," I said, and lost.

Phil ran the water till it went cold. Then he shrugged out of his clothes, flung them in a silty heap beneath the sink—where they would undergo a gradual petrifaction as the weeks dragged by—and eased into the tub, moaning like a man in the throes of the consummate orgasm.

We watched from the doorway. "Five minutes," I shouted, checking my Benrus.

By the time my turn came round, the water was tepid, and the color and texture of the Mississippi in flood. No matter. This was real dirt I was covered with—stinking, fermenting, wildwoods dirt—and there would be no peace, no sweet surcease from care, until I got it off me. Besides, I reflected as I lowered myself into the soup, as last man to bathe I could linger as long as I liked.

I didn't. The water went cold almost immediately and the tap water was colder still. I lathered up, rinsed off, patted myself with a wet towel and made for the back bedroom, the ominous calendar and my damp sleeping bag. I was beat, every joint rubbed raw. Rain lashed at the roof, tiny feet scratched in the corners. I slept like a zombie.

We were awakened by a thunderous pounding at the door—Anne Frank's moment of truth, the men in the black boots come to drag us away. The sound reverberated through the house, deafening, insupportable, terrifying. We'd done nothing illegal—yet. We had no pot, no seeds even. There was no reason to be alarmed, but we were alarmed. No, not simply alarmed—panicked. I rushed out into the main room in my underwear, heart slamming at my ribs, to see Phil's stricken face peering from the shadows of the front bedroom. It couldn't have been later than six-thirty or seven. "Hallo?" a voice boomed. "Is anybody in there?"

"Just a minute," I called, dancing round the cold floorboards, my nervous system simultaneously flashing two conflicting messages: *Be calm* and *Sauve qui peut*. Phil had vanished. I could hear him thumping into his pants, coins spilling like chimes. Something crashed to the floor. "You'll—you'll have to go around to the other door," I shouted, hugging my shoulders against the cold, "this one's been . . ." I hesitated. "This one's been nailed shut."

Gesh's head appeared at the top of the stairwell, between the rails of the crude banister one of our troglodyte predecessors had erected. "Get rid of them," he hissed. "We can't have fucking people—" but he cut himself off in mid-sentence: the kitchen door had begun to rattle.

I reached the door at the same instant it was thrust open, and found myself standing toe-to-toe with the very archetype of the rural American, the living, breathing, foot-shuffling image of the characters who populate the truck stops of America, vote for neo-Nazis and mail off half their income to the 500 Club or the Church of the Flayed Jesus. Rangy, fiftyish, he was dressed in overalls, plaid hunting jacket and a Willits Feed cap. His face was seamed like a soccer ball, a wad of tobacco distended his cheek, he reeked of cowshit and untamed perspiration. "Hallo," he roared—he could have been greeting someone six miles away—and extended his hand. "Lloyd Sapers," he said, still too loudly. "I ranch the place next door?"

I shook his hand gravely, the elastic band of my Jockey shorts tearing at my flesh like masticating teeth. I was wondering both how to get rid of him and how to indicate, without arousing suspicion, that we were antisocial types who neither sought nor welcomed unannounced visits and least of all friendly relations with our neighbors, when he brushed past me and strode into the room as if he'd just assumed the mortgage on the place.

"Seen the light last night," he said, drawing himself up and spinning round like a flamboyant prosecutor exposing the sordid and incontrovertible truth to a scandalized world, "heard you, too. Comin' up the road. All afternoon, it seems like." And then he laughed, way up in the back of his throat.

Somehow, things had gotten out of hand. Here I was, shivering like a wet dog and dressed only in my underwear, standing in the middle of the dirty, disused kitchen of a shack unfit for human occupation, engaged in a bantering conversation with an utter stranger, a man who by his very presence had to be considered an enemy. The discolored lump over my left eye began to throb. "Look," I said, "I don't mean to be rude or anything, Mr. Sapers, but—"

"Call me Lloyd."

"—but it's early, and I—"

He burst out with a laugh so sudden and sharp it startled me. "Early, oh yeah, I'll bet," he shouted, and flashed me a knowing grin.

At this point, Phil appeared behind him, shuffling his feet and bobbing his head. His bad eye, I noticed, had gone crazy. Normally it was just slightly out of plumb, but under duress it began to rove as if it had a life of its own. Standing there in the gray light in his rumpled clothes, he could have been an elongated Jean-Paul Sartre contemplating a street full of *merde*.

Sapers swung round on him and seized his hand. "Glad to meet you. It's a pleasure, it really is. Haven't had nobody out here for thirty years now," he said, "except for that bonehead that was up here last summer in his house trailer—Smith or Jones or whatever the hell his name was. He was up to no good, I'll tell you that." The rancher delivered this information with a sad shake of his head, then pushed his cap back with a sigh that was actually a sort of yodel, and asked if we had any coffee.

I don't know what I was feeling at that moment—curiosity,

shock, fear, annoyance. That someone else had been up here before us, and that he'd been up to no good—this was news. Who was he? Why hadn't Vogelsang told us? And what about this nosy old loudmouth who was perched on the edge of the stove now, as comfortable as if he were counting sacks of hog manure in his own living room? We couldn't afford to have him snooping around—or anybody else, for that matter. But how to get rid of him? Abstractedly, I watched Phil bend to the stove, stoke the embers and lay some scrapwood on top. Then I ducked out of the room to get dressed, as jittery as if I'd swallowed a handful of amphetamines.

When I slapped back into the kitchen, hoisting my pants with one hand and clutching boots and socks in the other, Phil was heating water for coffee and Sapers was rattling on about the property, the weather, his wife, hoof-and-mouth disease, Ronald Reagan, taxes, deer hunting and just about anything else that came to his fevered mind. He was like a man who'd just emerged from six months in solitary, like the sole survivor of a shipwreck, Crusoe with a captive audience: he could not shut up.

As if he'd read my thoughts, our neighbor looked up at that instant and fixed me with a gaze as steady and intense as a stalking predator's. For an instant I saw something else in him, something raw and calculating, but then his eyes went soft, and he was the grinning bumpkin again. "Sure hope you don't mind me going on like this, but unless I go into town I don't have nobody much to talk to, outside of Trudy, that's my wife, and my son Marlon. And Marlon, he's a good boy, but he ain't got much sense, if you know what I mean." (I didn't know what he meant, but in time I was to be enlightened on this score, as on a host of others. Marlon was nineteen, he weighed three hundred and twenty pounds, stood six feet tall, wore glasses that distorted his eyes until they looked like tropical fish in a hazy tank, and was so severely disturbed he'd spent the better part of his adolescence in the violent ward of the state mental hospital in Napa.)

Phil fished a can of Medaglia d'Oro from one of the bags of groceries we'd hauled up with us, found a cracked cup in another, and poured the intruder a cup of coffee strained through a paper towel. "This used to be the old Gayeff place, you know," Sapers said, blowing at his coffee. I wondered how he was going to manage to drink it and chew tobacco at the same time. "Ivan, now there was a character. Had hair like a nigger on him, kinky and black. A real tippler he was, too. He'd get himself liquored up on a Friday night, whale the piss out of his kids, blacken the old lady's eyes for her and then run into the woods mother-ass naked and howl like a dog. Ivan the Terrible, we used to call him."

Suddenly Sapers looked as if he'd been stricken—he turned his head away and nearly dropped his cup. Then he leaned over and spat feebly in the sink. "Oh, but listen," he stammered, avoiding my eyes, "I didn't mean to . . . oh, what the hell: I may as well level with you. Mr. Vogelsang told me what you fellas are doing up here."

It was as if he'd announced that the place was surrounded. The words drilled into me like slugs, Phil scalded his hand and cursed sharply, I could feel the hairs rising on the back of my neck. "He *what*?"

"Well, naturally. Since we live so close and all, he had to tell me." The rancher paused to send a mauve stream of tobacco juice into the sink. Then he gulped at his coffee and glanced up tentatively: he'd put his foot in his mouth, and he knew it.

By this time Gesh had appeared, looking terrible. He was scowling, as irascible and dyspeptic as a member of the Politburo, the scar that divided his eyebrow gleaming like the mark of Cain. I thought of the moment in *The Treasure of the Sierra Madre* when the interloper arrives at the prospectors' camp and they decide to murder him rather than give up their secret.

If there was blood in the air, Sapers didn't seem to notice. He shook hands with Gesh, made a jocular reference to Phil's haircut, spat in his coffee, and proceeded to enlighten us as to the nature and extent of the information he'd received from Vogelsang. The story came out gradually, but as soon as we began to get the drift of it, we played right along. It seemed that Vogelsang, thinking of everything, had told Sapers that he had some friends who were writers—really first-rate, mind you—but that they had a severe and debilitating problem with alcohol. He was going to let them live up at the camp for six or nine months so they could dry out, get some writing done and batten on sunshine and good clean country living. It was about as lame a story as I'd ever heard.

"Hey," Phil said, as soon as Sapers paused for breath, "I'm not ashamed of it. I've had my problems with the sauce, and I'll be the first to admit it. I'm here to straighten out or lay down and die."

"Amen," I said.

"Yes, sure," Sapers boomed, looking relieved. "I had an uncle that used to hit the bottle—Four Roses, quart and a half a day. It's a disease is what it is. Just like cancer. And I'm shit-for-hell glad to see you boys determined to lick it."

Without warning, Gesh stepped forward, snatched the cup from the rancher's hand and flung it against the wall. "Frankly," he said, his voice curling round a snarl, "I don't give a shit about your uncle, or you, or your half-assed opinions either. If you think you can come around here, brother, and lord it over us because we might've had a problem in the past, well you're dead wrong, I'll tell you that right now."

Sapers seemed to shrink in that instant, his neck as red and thin and sinewy as a turkey gobbler's, his open shirt big around as a life jacket. Gesh loomed over him like the statue of the Commendatore come to life. "I . . . I . . . listen, I never—"

Gesh shouted him down. "We have feelings, too, can you dig that? What do you think we are, some kind of human garbage or something? Huh?" Raging, Gesh jerked the leathery little rancher off the stove, both fists bunched under his collar. "We're shit, right? Just because we take a drink once in a while? Right? Right?"

Sapers was a man of straw, a bundle of clothes. He seemed to have shrunk away entirely, his essence concentrated in a reddened oval of face, stained teeth and hissing nostrils. "Don't," he panted, his hands tugging at Gesh's wrists. "I drink! I drink myself! Me and Trudy, why—"

But Gesh wasn't listening. His features were contorted, his shoulders heaving with rage: he pulled Sapers to him like a lover, and then flung out his arms and sent the rancher reeling across the room. "Son of a bitch," Gesh roared, advancing on him. "Son of a self-righteous, teetotaling, holier-than-thou bitch. I'll kill you!"

Our partner's words hung in the air, ringing with the faint reverberations of saucepans and empty bottles, thrumming in our ears, but Sapers wasn't there to appreciate the sonic aftereffects: he'd slammed through the kitchen door and bolted round the corner of the storage shed like a missionary in the land of the cannibals. We watched him out the kitchen window, jogging across the field, stumbling and then pitching down the slope of the ravine that divided our property from his. When he broke stride to glance over his shoulder and catch his breath, Gesh flung open the window and heaved a Coke bottle at him. "I'll kick your ass," Gesh bellowed, shaking his fist, and Sapers was off like a world-class sprinter, knees pumping, head bobbing, cutting a wide wet swath through the weeds until he disappeared in the cleft of the ravine.

As soon as the rancher was out of sight, Gesh slammed the window down and collapsed as if he'd been hamstrung. He looked up at us, a big, shit-eating, Cheshire-cat grin on his face, and then he hooted and beat the floor like a drunken chimp. Phil had to grab hold of a chair for support, I was wiping hilarious tears from my eyes. "Hoo-hoo," I said, the long double vowels trembling with appreciative vibrato. The kitchen was dingier than ever, last night's chili-crusted plates in the sink, coffee stains on the wall, the shelves rife with dust and the tiny splayed tracks of rodents, and none of it mattered: we were laughing.

"Critics' Circle Award," Phil gasped. "Best impression of a crazed degenerate—"

"—by a crazed degenerate," I added.

"Ham of the year," Phil said, applauding.

Gesh folded his arms across his chest, stretched out his legs and leaned back against a thirty-year-old midden of blackened pans, nonreturnable bottles and eviscerated cans. "Shee-it," he said.

Chapter 2

That night we sat around the wood stove and listened to the rain pick at the Styrofoam on the roof. We were too tired to worry about baths. After routing Sapers and breakfasting on leftover chili, we'd spent the better part of the morning (in a drizzle that softened the landscape till it looked like a Monet, and coincidentally kept us wet as manatees) tinkering with the five-H.P. lawnmower engine that would theoretically furnish us with electricity. We'd approached it with caution. Separated from the mechanism that provided its ens, and bolted to a slab of iron, which in turn rested on a platform of cinder blocks, it was like a monument to a forgotten civilization, no more functional than one of Phil's junk sculptures. It was cold, it was rusted, it was grease-clogged. There were belts, pulleys, wires, pipes, what I took to be a dynamo, and a thick black cord that looped over the roof of the storage shed and disappeared into the house. A crude metal bonnet protected the apparatus from the elements.

"Gently," I warned, as Gesh stepped up and gripped the plastic pull handle that was pinned to the top of the engine casing like a bow tie. He hesitated an instant, threw me a glance over his shoulder, and then leaned into the thing as if he were Indian-wrestling a mortal enemy. His arm jerked back three times in quick succession. From deep inside the inert block of metal there was a faint answering clank of gears. Nothing more. Gesh tried the pull half a dozen times before Phil suggested that the engine might be out of fuel. "Or maybe it's old gas," I reasoned. "You know, maybe it's gone stale or something."

We siphoned gas from the Toyota and added a pint to the inch or two of pale liquid we discovered in the engine's reservoir. I took my turn at the pull. Nothing. We removed the spark plug and cleaned it. We checked the belts and wires and laid our hands against the cold metal casing like faith healers. Still nothing. Gesh fiddled with the carburetor in a way that indicated he didn't know what he was doing. Phil looked over his shoulder. I've never been mechanically inclined myself.

We knocked off at noon, gulped reheated coffee and swallowed Velveeta sandwiches like pills, and then went out to put up the three-strand barbed-wire fence that would keep cattle and deer out of the growing areas. As soon as we left the house, the drizzle gave way to a deluge—plastic rain-colored sheets hammered into the ground, no sky above, buckling rivulets below. My nose was running. I felt as if I hadn't been warm—or dry—in a month. "Okay," Phil said, bending over a roll of wire, "you grab one end, I'll get the other."

Stringing barbed wire involves the use of a come-along, an insidious forged-steel device that operates on the leverage principle. You bind the thing to a sturdy tree trunk, crank the wire till it's tight enough to strum, and then affix said wire to a post or tree by means of a U-clip. It is nasty, back-breaking work. And what made it even nastier was the terrain we found ourselves confronting.

When you're growing a contraband crop you can't just step out the front door, plow up a field and sow seeds as if you were raising corn, pumpkins and squash. No, you've got to be discreet. And with discretion in mind, Dowst had suggested we plant in widely separated patches—in the midst of existing stands of vegetation—as a means of subverting aerial detection. During the dry months, he'd explained, our plants would be the only viridescent vegetation for miles, and if concentrated, they would stand out like oases in a desert. Unfortunately, the only planting area he'd selected and laid out at this point happened to be located on a hillside with a slope comparable to that of Mauna Loa. We negotiated this hillside throughout the afternoon, shredding our hands, stumbling, lurching, falling, haphazardly stapling the wire to saplings and clumps of poison oak, cursing Vogelsang, cursing Dowst, cursing ourselves. It was dark when we quit.

Gesh did the cooking. He tended his two frying pans and the big pot of steaming water on the back burner with the scrupulosity of the *cuisinier* at La Bourgogne. In one pan, he fried eggs; in the other, pork chops. The pot of water was eventually converted, through the miracle of modern science and the chemical wizardry of General Foods, to a steaming, plethoric mass of mashed potatoes. At the moment of truth, when all three dishes had simultaneously reached the apex of culinary perfection, Gesh inverted both frying pans over the pot of instant mashed potatoes and beat the resulting mélange to a froth with a spoon the size of a Ping-Pong paddle. "Soup's on," he said, jabbing a serving spoon into the midst of the glutinous mess—it stood erect—and setting the pot down on the table.

After dinner, we sipped cocktails (eight-ounce vodka gimlets, very dry) and stared at the wood stove. Phil hauled out his guitar and gave us a nasal rendition of "So Much Trouble" (*My baby left me, my mule got lame,/Lost all my money in a poker game,/A windstorm came up just the other day,/Blew the house I lived in away)*, and then suggested we tell jokes to while away the time. We had to do something. It got dark at six and we had no television, no stereo, no radio, no lights even. I refilled the glasses while Phil told a hoary joke about a tractor, a bloodhound and a farmer's daughter. The response was less than enthusiastic: neither Gesh nor I could even muster a grin. "Give me a break," Phil said. He was seated cross-legged in front of the stove. His face, neck and hands were pocked with welts, as if he were suffering from chicken pox or scarlet fever. "It's your turn, Felix," he said, as I handed him his drink. "Tell us a joke."

I said I didn't know any.

"Gesh?" Phil said.

Gesh looked first at me, then at Phil. The Coleman lantern squatted on the table behind him, and it threw his shadow over the room, enormous, jagged, looming and receding as he leaned forward to light a cigarette or set his glass down. "What's the closest you ever came to dying?" he said.

"Me?" Phil sipped at his drink, looking like a whiz kid who's just been handed an intriguing equation. He produced a wad of toilet paper and blew his nose thoughtfully. "I don't know—I guess it was the time I was working construction and nearly had a dump truck fall over on me. It was weird. I was too worried about looking stupid to be scared." He pulled back the door of the stove and chucked in the wad of toilet paper: the room flared for an instant, then the iron door fell to and the shadows sprang back to reclaim the corners.

"I was nineteen, working for minimum wage and doing construction on this golf course in Westchester—they were adding a back nine to go with the nine they already had, and we were doing everything from digging trenches for the irrigation pipe to raking up stones and seeding the fairways. Anyway, the foreman, he's this character right out of *The Untouchables* or something—Italian, heavy accent, square as a wooden block—and he wants volunteers to drive these three broken-down dump trucks he's got, hauling dirt. There's about thirty of us there—a couple of black guys in their late twenties, early thirties, and the rest a bunch of long-haired college kids. I'd never driven a truck in my life, but when the foreman says 'Who can drive this thing?' I raise my hand. I thought it was funny that the older guys—the black guys—never looked up from their shovels, but shit, the way I saw it, it was a hell of a lot easier to cruise around in a truck than break your ass digging ditches."

"I can relate to that," I said, holding up my blistered hands.

"So I get in the truck. The pedals are the size of frying pans, two feet from the floor, the steering wheel's like an extra-large pizza or something, there's this dumping gear I've never seen before." Phil looked up at me. "You remember that summer I worked at Loch Ledge." I nodded.

"Anyway, six guys are coming with me. Two in the cab, the rest hanging on to the outside. We're going to pick up a load of dirt and then bring it across the property and spread it. So I get down there at the base of this big hill and there's another truck in front of me, idling, while this guy in a caterpillar—union worker, middle-aged, making two hundred bucks a day—fills up the truck. This is great, I'm thinking. Getting paid for just sitting here.

"Then it's my turn. He fills me up so the dirt is mounded up over the roof of the truck, stones clanking off as I grind it into gear and head up this narrow dirt road, real steep, up the side of a cliff that overlooks this little stream they dammed up for a water hazard. Halfway up, in first gear, the bands start slipping. I'm going full out, foot to the floor, and the truck is standing still—overloaded, I guess. So I hit the brake. Nothing. The engine's screaming, the truck is sliding backwards and I'm totally powerless.

"That's when the other guys abandon ship. College kids, like me. Stupid, crater-faced, do-or-die types. They leap off the sides, open the door and jump. I don't know what to do, don't even think about it. All I know is the foreman'll eat me for breakfast if I wreck the truck, so I just hang on, foot to the floor, bands slipping, the truck inching backwards. I was dead, from stupidity, from not knowing that I could die, from not even considering flinging open the door and jumping."

Phil was grinning. "But I'm not dead—though I think I will be if we have to go through much more of the sort of bullshit we went through today."

"So what happened?" Gesh asked.

"Oh. It was simple. The guy on the bulldozer saw what was happening, steamed up the hill like he was coming off the starting flag at Le Mans, caught me with the bucket and pushed the whole business right up the road and onto level ground. I was within about three feet and ten seconds of being crushed under Christ knows how many tons of dirt and I didn't even really know it."

Ice cubes rattled in our glasses (we'd been provident enough to bring up six bags of ice in a pair of plastic coolers). Wood hissed in the stove. We mulled over Phil's story in silence for a moment before Gesh turned to me. "How about you, Felix?"

I laughed. "The closest I ever came?" I laughed again, remembering. "It's short and sweet," I said, "nothing like Phil's. But it's weird and mystical almost. Did I ever tell you about this, Phil?"

"I don't think so."

"It was when I was living in New York with Ronnie and we rented that summer place for two weeks—I think it was about a year after we got married. You remember the place, Phil."

Phil took a long pull at his drink and made a face. "In Lake Peekskill, right?"

In Lake Peekskill. A bungalow that belonged to my Uncle Irv and that stank of cat shit and mold. We'd been living in the city and we had no money. Irv let us have the place cheap. It seemed like a good idea at the time.

"That's the place," I said. "You remember how it smelled?"

Phil nodded, Gesh leaned forward. I told the story.

There was sun the first couple of days. I set up a volleyball net, swam across the lake, charred meat on the outdoor grill. I was Mr. Country all of a sudden. Ronnie did crossword puzzles. Then the rain started. A low-pressure system that hovered over New Jersey like a judgment and gave us four solid days of thunderstorms. When the sun finally poked through again I was burning to get out—we were wasting our vacation. I asked Ronnie if she wanted to take a hike in the woods.

"The woods? Isn't there enough woods right here to satisfy you?" We were hemmed in by maple, willow, white birch. Hummocks of unmowed grass fled from the wall of the house, ducked under a barbed-wire fence and flowed out into a field where cows were lowing. I shrugged my shoulders. What I wanted was deep woods, solitude, the pale clerestory light that filters through the trees and settles over you like an ancestral memory. Ronnie eased into a lawn chair with a tube of tanning butter, her prescription shades, a magazine and a radio. I told her I'd be back in a couple of hours.

It was August. Humid, the trees drowning in green. I drove to the state park and followed a rutted dirt road through a close dark tunnel of hardwood and pine. It was a one-lane road. There were no other cars. Eventually I reached a primitive bridge that might or might not have supported the weight of the car. Afraid to chance it, I backed off the road as far as I could and stepped out to have a look at the stream rushing under the bridge.

The stream was high and roiled, swollen with runoff from the previous days' storms, hurling debris over its banks, slamming at the base of the bridge as if it would annihilate it. I don't know what I was thinking of—I was a city dweller, and I'd never been out in the woods alone in my life. Perhaps it was some recollection of Boy Scout camp or the cabin my parents had rented when I was younger, or perhaps it was simply an instinctual need to experience nature in some primary, unsanitized way—at any rate, I decided to follow the stream into the green tangle that swallowed it up.

If I had vague stirrings of the excitement that must have infected a Hilary or a Cabeza de Vaca, they were quelled almost instantly—others had been here before me. With a vengeance. They'd guzzled beer, blasted shotguns, changed babies, gobbled tortilla chips and carved their names in tree trunks. As I went on, though, following a rough path that dodged in and out of the tumble of rocks bordering the streambed, the signs of civilization began to disappear. There was still the occasional Schlitz can or shell casing, but I began to get the impression that I'd penetrated more deeply into the forest than the average day-tripper, and I felt a swelling of pride. When I came across a natural pool fed by a steady plunging waterfall, I settled down on a rock and ate the Hershey bar I'd brought along, careful to fold up the wrapper and tuck it in my pocket.

The water gulped and hissed like a dozen Jacuzzis, birds whistled in the branches, sunlight broke through the treetops to fracture the surface of the pool. I felt at peace, in tune with things, I felt like Huck Finn, Nick Adams. There were no serpents in the forest, there was no poison ivy, nothing to bite or sting or discourage. Why hadn't I done this more often? I thought, munching candy. This was great, this was exhilarating, this was nature.

It was at that moment that a thunderous, splintering crack sounded behind me and I was suddenly raked along the right side of my body and swept aside as if I were nothing, a dustball, a speck of dander; then there was a booming crash and an explosion of water that soaked me through. A tree had fallen. My arm was scraped raw, my clothes were wet, there was bark and sawdust in my hair, ants scrambling down the back of my neck. The base of the tree lay beside me, as big around as the Washington Monument; the far end of it was sunk into the pool at my feet.

I'd told the story before. It was at this point in the recitation that I looked up and held my audience's eyes, the old loon with his hand on the wedding guest's arm: "If I'd been sitting twelve inches to the right, I would have been crushed."

Gesh whistled. "That's some story."

"CITY MAN HEARS TREE FALLING IN FOREST," Phil said, quoting an imaginary headline and hooting into his gimlet.

My hand trembled as I lifted my drink from the box of canned beets that doubled as an end table. I always felt odd telling that story, no matter how I tried to make light of it. I hadn't been crushed, I hadn't contracted leukemia at fourteen or run my motorcycle into a fence. To remember it, to describe it, was to admit not only that I could have been crushed in any one of a thousand ways, but that inevitably I would be, as all of us would. It was a thing you didn't think about. Maybe that's why Gesh suggested it.

I stood abruptly and began to rifle through the bags of groceries that lined the crude kitchen counter and competed with garbage for space on the floor. Shaken, light-headed, filled with the soul-barer's exhilarating sense of communion and absolution, I let my fingers do the thinking. Cold tin, cold aluminum. Shapes. The muffled clatter of air-tight cans. Finally I came up with a can of black olives. I borrowed Phil's Swiss Army knife, serrated the lid and sucked back the oily dark essence of Greece—or rather the San Fernando Valley—and settled back down beside the stove.

Then it was Gesh's turn.

He fingered the scar that split his eyebrow. "I got this in a car crash," he said. "I was driving, shit-faced drunk. A red Triumph I borrowed from a girl I was going out with. Went through a stone wall at sixty and the thing burst into flame. Some stranger pulled me out. I was unconscious."

He rolled up his shirt to expose a triad of short angry welts. "And this I got down in Mexico. Some shithead in a bus station said something to me in Spanish I didn't like the sound of, so I hit him. He stabbed me three times."

I said something weighty like "Holy shit."

Gesh looked pleased. He liked to think of himself in heroic terms—biggest, toughest, smartest, strongest, able to leap tall buildings at a single bound, eat the most Quaaludes and still stand up and wash the dishes. Raised in Echo Park and educated in abandoned clapboard houses and the alleys out back of Sunset Boulevard, he'd been through it all—gang fights, juvenile hall, doping, moping, expulsion from his high school honor society, and two years of the worst the UCLA classics department could dish out—and he never let you forget it. After a pause of suitable dramatic duration, he said, "But I've been closer than that, a lot closer."

We leaned forward.

"It was the Sirens," he said, "they lured me onto the rocks. One siren, anyway. Her name was Denise. Short, tight ass, skin like ice cream—like toasted-almond ice cream. I met her on the beach in Venice, summer before last. We were having a party and she was somebody's cousin or sister or something, in a white two-piece that offered up her nipples like hors d'oeuvres. She walked up to me and traced the scars on my stomach with the tip of her finger. 'Where'd you get that?' she says. 'Gall bladder?' When I told her, her eyes went funny for a second, narrowing like little periods and then opening wide, green light, let's go.

"We went. She took me home with her—she had money, a ground-floor apartment in Manhattan Beach with a little patio and cactuses that must have cost five hundred bucks apiece. Next day we went out to lunch. We went to the zoo, saw a band at the Whisky. Then two days later she called and asked me did I want to go out on her father's sailboat. Sure, I said, why not?"

Phil said he'd been sailing exactly three times in his life, twice on lakes and once on Long Island Sound. All three times he'd ended up in the water.

Gesh lit a cigarette and exhaled a cloud of blue smoke. "That's about as much experience as I'd had, too, fooling around in lakes and coves in those little fourteen-foot jobs, Sunfish or whatever you call them. But this boat was big, thirty-five feet or so, bobbing in the water at Marina del Rey like a big white coffin. . . . I mean it had bunks and a galley with this little stove and refrigerator, Stolichnaya in the freezer, teakwood decks, the works. It was called *The Christina Rossetti*—after some poet her mother'd studied in college, Denise said.

"She said she knew what she was doing, but we had a lot of trouble just getting the sails up and making it out of the marina without hitting anything. But after that, with the whole wide blue sea out there, it was easy. The boat ran itself. Every once in a while the sail would come round and Denise'd tell me to haul on this line or that, but it was no big deal—it wasn't like we were going anywhere or anything. Shit, I began to enjoy myself. The sun was flaring away, there was a nice breeze blowing, Denise looked edible in this black bikini. I mixed us some cocktails and slipped my hand in her pants. We did it right there, standing up, her holding onto the wheel, the boat rocking, seagulls flapping by. It was fantastic, like being on an island or something—nobody around for miles. There was no reason to put our suits back on."

Gesh looked up at me. "Sounds great, huh Felix? Paradise on earth, right?"

"Yeah," I said, "but I've got a feeling this is where it turns nasty."

"Nasty? That doesn't even come close, man—this was fucking horrifying. One minute I'm getting laid and sipping a martini, the next I'm in the water. What happens is the wind comes up all of a sudden while we're lying there on the deck, stroking each other and getting hot to do it again. I've got a hard-on like a steel rod and I lift myself up to stick it in her when the boomline breaks and this fucking pole comes slamming around and catches me under the chin. Next thing I know I'm in the water—the ocean. Miles from shore. I can't even fucking swim that good, and I'll tell you"—he was holding my eyes—"snakes may be your thing, but mine is sharks. I'm scared shitless of them. I don't even go in over my head at the beach because I'm afraid some saw-toothed monster is going to rip my legs off. Really, I don't care how I go, just so long as I don't wind up as shark shit."

I watched as Gesh extracted rolling papers and an envelope of pot from the pocket of his dungaree jacket. He rolled a joint thin as a Tootsie Pop stick and passed it to me. I lit it, took a drag, and passed it back.

"So anyway, Denise jumps up and starts wringing her hands and screaming and whatnot, and then runs back to the wheel and tries to swing the boat around. Meanwhile, I'm churning up the waves like Mark Spitz—it's amazing what you can do when you have to—and the boat is drifting away. Drifting? I mean it was flying, really moving out, sails humming and everything. I wasn't in the water ten seconds and it was already fifty yards away. Then it was a hundred yards, two hundred, and then it was gone.

"Christ. I was in an absolute panic. For about the next ten minutes I swam for all I was worth, the chop of the waves crowding me in, gulping water, stopping every few seconds to kick myself up as high as I could and try and see something. Water, that's all I saw. No land, no boat. Nothing. It was cold. There was salt in my eyes. It was then, completely by accident, that I blundered into a life preserver—*The Christina Rossetti*, it said in big red letters. I felt like I'd been saved, right then and there. I hooted for joy, heaved myself up on the thing and waved my arms. She'll be back any minute, I thought, soon as she gets the goddamned boat under control. She'll be back, she's got to be.

"I was in the water for six hours. Shivering, praying, scared full of adrenaline. I kept making deals with the Fates, with God, Neptune, whoever, thinking I'd trade places with anybody, anywhere—lepers, untouchables, political prisoners, Idi Amin's wives—anything, so long as I'd be alive. I remember I kept looking down to where my feet disappeared in the murk, feeling like they were separated from my body or something, sure that at any moment they'd be jerked out from under me. I thought about *Jaws* and *Blue Water, White Death*. Thought about the guy who got hit by a white shark off the Farallons and was dragged down about a hundred feet by the impact and said the happiest moment of his life was when he felt his leg give at the knee."

The joint had gone dead in Gesh's fingers. He was staring down at the floor and seeing waves, his face sober with the memory of it, nobody laughing now. I wondered why he was telling us this, what the point of the exercise was. At first I thought he'd been boasting, letting us know how tough he was, how hip and cynical and experienced with the ladies. But now, looking at the way his face had gone cold, I realized that wasn't it at all.

Phil got up with a snap of his knees and fed a bundle of pine branches into the stove. There was a fierce crackling and an explosion of sparks as he slammed the door and eased back down on the blistered linoleum. "So come on," he prodded, "don't keep us in suspense—finish the story."

I made some noises of encouragement and Gesh relit the joint.

"I spotted seven boats that day," he said, shaking out the match, "and I shouted my lungs out, tried to throw the fucking life preserver up in the air—anything. But nobody saw me. That was the worst. You'd get your hopes up, thinking, I'm going to make it, I'm going to live, and you'd start paddling for the boat, screaming like a wounded rabbit, and they'd just coast right by as if you didn't exist, as if you were dead already. Then the sun went down. If they couldn't see me in the light of day, what chance was there they'd spot me in the dark? None, zip, zero. I began to cry—the first time I'd cried since I was a kid. There was a hole inside of me. I was shivering nonstop, like a machine about to break down. I was dead.

"Then, just after the moon rose, this gigantic cabin cruiser—fifty feet long at least—comes cutting across the waves straight for me. It was lit up like Rockefeller Center at Christmastime, they were having a party. I could see them, gray heads, cocktail glasses, two women in low-cut dresses. 'Help!' I scream. 'Help!' The engine was chugging away, waves slapping the bow: they couldn't hear me. I fought my way toward the point where I thought the boat would pass and tried once more, screaming till my throat gave out. Then, like a miracle, like statues bleeding and the dead coming to life, one of the gray heads turned. 'Here!' I shouted. One woman touched the other's arm and pointed."

Gesh's voice had quavered. He sat in silence for a moment, running the tip of his tongue over his upper lip and then wiping his mouth with the back of his hand. "They didn't even have the radio on," he said, waving his palm in frustration, "they didn't even know I was out there. Luck is all it was. Blind luck. I came on board naked, racked with shivers, two miles off Palos Verdes in the most shark-infested waters on the southern coast. One of the men aboard is a doctor. He tells me I'm suffering from hypothermia and makes me get into this down jacket, wraps me in blankets and gives me hot pea soup. Which I hate.

"When we get back, Denise is waiting on the pier along with a bunch of news reporters and guys in Coast Guard uniform. She's barefoot, still in her bathing suit, with a shawl wrapped around her shoulders. I don't know what came over me—I should have been filled with joy, right, glad to be alive and all that—but when I saw her there looking like the distraught heroine I just thought, You stupid bitch. You worthless piece of shit. Somebody was snapping pictures, flashbulbs bursting, she was running down the planks with her arms outstretched like it was the end of a movie or something, and I just couldn't take it. I gave her a stiff arm like Earl Campbell—caught her right in the breastbone—and sent her sprawling over the edge of the dock, ten feet down, into the blackness. There was a scream and a splash, and suddenly everybody cleared a path for me."

That was it. Finis. Gesh sat there, big and rumpled, something like a smile of satisfaction tugging at the corner of his mouth. "I don't believe it," Phil said. "You really pushed her in?"

Gesh looked as self-righteous as a fundamentalist at a book burning. He drained his glass and flashed us a grin. "Bet your ass I did."

Phil started it, with a snicker that gave way to a bray. Then I joined in, counterpoint, and finally Gesh, three-part harmony. We were drunk. We were alive. And for the second time that day, we were laughing. We laughed impetuously, immoderately, irreverently, wiping tears from our eyes. Late into the night.

Chapter 3

"All right. You won't actually need to know about this for another two weeks or so, but you may as well get an idea right now." Dowst leaned on the haft of his shovel, patting at his face with a red bandanna. Behind him, banks of mist obscured a sick pale sun, light spread across the horizon like putty. At his feet, a hole. Raw yellow earth, gouged out like a boil or canker sore. "You want to go down about two, two and a half feet, and make it wide around as a garbage can lid." Suddenly he was grunting or wheezing in the oddest way, like a horse with a progressive lung disease. It took me a minute before I realized what it was: he was laughing. "Or a"—he wheezed again—"or a big cut-glass punchbowl."

It was a joke. Phil, Gesh and I glanced at one another. Ha-ha.

We were standing over the hole, our breath steaming in the cold damp air, watching Dowst like Botany 101 students on a field trip. It was seven a.m. Gesh was wearing a black turtleneck maculated with grease stains (the result of a breakfast mishap), Phil was hunched in the carapace of a paint-spattered K-Mart sweatshirt, and I was sporting one of the flannel shirts I'd bought for the country, now torn and dirtied beyond recognition. Dowst was wearing eighty-dollar hiking boots, pressed jeans and the yellow rain slicker he'd had on the night I met him. "This," he said finally, "is the model hole. Once you get the fences up you're going to have to dig two thousand of them."

Gesh had a cold. He dredged the mucus from his throat and spat noisily. "While you're sitting on your ass in Sausalito, right?"

"No, no, no, no, no—I'll be right here the next three or four days at least, working side by side with you. We've got to get those fences up and start the seedlings before we get too far behind schedule."

"And Vogelsang?"

Dowst tucked the bandanna in his pocket and pushed the hair out of his eyes. "He said he'd be up tomorrow."

"Shit." Gesh focused on a fist-sized stone and hammered it against the side of the house with a vicious swipe of his boot. "That's what he said a week and a half ago."

Dowst had showed up at dusk the previous evening—eight days after the appointed time. For a week and a half we'd been on our own, isolated, bewildered, putting in twelve-hour days with the come-along and then collapsing on our soiled mattresses at night. Once the initial hillside had been fenced (we called it the Khyber Pass in tribute to its vertiginous goat-walks and sheer declivities), we erected a greenhouse to specifications Dowst had given us in Bolinas. It was a joy compared to fencing. I took charge, relieved to be doing something I was familiar with, and we threw up the framework in an afternoon. Then we nailed Visquine—clear sheets of plastic—over the waterlogged studs and painted the whole thing green, khaki and dirt brown: army camouflage. "I feel like we're going to war," Phil said over the hiss of his spray can. His right hand and the sleeve of the jacket from which it protruded were a slick uniform jungle green, owing to a sudden wind shift. Gesh stood beside him, his arm rotating in a great whirling arc, spewing paint like smoke. His jaw was set, he was squinting against the fading light. "Damn straight," he grunted.

Then we began to get itchy. Neither Dowst nor Vogelsang had showed up and we had no further instructions. And yet Dowst had repeatedly impressed upon us the vital necessity of keeping on schedule. The plants had to attain their optimum growth by September 22, when the photoperiod began to decrease. Once the daily quotient of sunlight was superseded by a greater period of darkness, the plants automatically began to bud—it was built into their genes—and that was that. The later you got your seedlings into the ground, the smaller your plants would be when the autumnal equinox rolled around—and the smaller the plants, the smaller the harvest. You didn't have to be a botanist to appreciate how all this smallness would relate to net profit.

"So what do we do?" I asked. We were inside now, sipping at the evening's first cocktail. We'd just driven the final nail into the greenhouse, the moon was up and the birds were crouched in the trees, grumbling like revolutionaries. "Just sit around?"

Gesh was in the kitchen, rattling pans and slamming drawers. "Mr. Yale is fucking up on us already," he said, swinging round and slapping a blackened pot of ravioli on the table. "How could we ever be so stupid as to trust somebody with a name like Boyd Dowst?"

We'd put in a tough day in damp, forty-degree weather. The fire was warm, the smell of food distracted us, canned ravioli, boiled potatoes and pale yellow wax beans had appeared on our plates. There was coffee, orange juice and something that resembled a foot-square brownie. Outside, the hiss of wind and a spatter of rain. We ate in silence, our eyes gone soft with the first chemical rush of hunger gratified, facial muscles swelling and contracting, saliva flowing, throats clenching and stomachs revolving in mindless subjection to the alimentary imperative: chew, swallow, digest. I listened to the scrape of utensils on the tin plates, glanced at our beards, our tattered clothes, the ramshackle roof that sagged over us, and thought how apt Phil's military metaphor had been—we *were* like irregulars, some cadre of the People's Army holding the line in a remote outpost, guerrillas taking refuge in the mountains. Of course the metaphor had its limits—we were capitalist guerrillas, after all.

"We could use a day off," Phil said after a while. "We can't do anything without Dowst and Vogelsang. I mean, what do we know about plants anyway? Christ, I never even had a wandering Jew."

"That doesn't matter," I said.

"No? What are we supposed to do then—fence in the whole three hundred and ninety acres? I say we take tomorrow off and just lay up and rest—or maybe go into town, see what kind of nightlife Willits has to offer."

Gesh was shaking his head. "Uh-uh, Felix is right. Look, I'm not up here for my health—I'm going to bust my ass, tear my hair out, do everything I fucking can to make sure I see that hundred and sixty-six thousand come November—and I say we pick out another growing area on our own."

Next morning we took the come-along and went looking.

It was a good move psychologically. We were riding the crest of accomplishment, the dreariness and hardship of the first week behind us, one area already fenced and the greenhouse erected, and now, when we had every excuse to sit back and wait for instructions, we were seizing the initiative. Here we were, men of action, hard, tough, ready for anything, off to wrest a million and a half dollars from the earth. But where to begin? There was an awful lot of territory out there: trees uncountable, rocks, slopes, sheer deadly drops, gaping gulleys, hardpan flats that mocked pick or shovel, thickets of thorn and manzanita as close and sharp as teeth. "What we need," I said, lacing my sneakers, "is something hidden, level and not too far from the house." We were milling around the front yard, belching softly over breakfast. "Good luck," Phil said.

The property sloped sharply toward the dirt road that linked us (however tenuously) with the outside world, and then dropped off beyond it to the south and east. To the north was Sapers's house, inconveniently located at the extremity of his property, no more than two hundred yards across the ravine from ours. (We couldn't believe it—the two places combined must have been close to a thousand acres, and yet the houses were within shouting distance. Wagon-train mentality, Phil called it, his voice saturated with disgust.) To the west, the mountain we were situated on rose another two hundred vertical feet before petering out in a smooth bald crown of rock. Since we wanted southern exposure—that much we knew at least—we started down a crude ancillary road that looped away from our driveway and wound round the southern slope like a waistband.

You didn't have to be Natty Bumppo to see that the road had been in disuse for some time. Branches had begun to close over it, saplings sprouted in the hollows dug by ancient wheels, clumps of poison oak made forays into the shoulders. There was evidence of animal life, too, most notably mounds of excrement flecked with seeds and bits of nutshell. I stopped at one point to tie my shoelace, and when I caught up with my co-workers they were bent over a glistening coil of feces that had been deposited smack in the center of the road. "Dog shit," Gesh announced.

"There aren't any dogs up here," Phil said. "I bet it's raccoon shit."

"What about coyotes?"

"Whatever it is, it looks pretty big," I said.

Gesh was racking his brain, mentally thumbing through the pages of some old battered *Fieldbook and Guide to the Mammals of the Pacific Northwest*. "Bear shit?"

We glanced around us as if an entire zoo were crouched in the bushes, eyes blazing, ears cocked, great pink tongues lapping at paws and hind ends. Then Phil straightened up, shrugged, and looked off down the road: the wonders of nature had an intense but short-lived appeal. We moved on.

Surprisingly, the road began to level out farther on down the mountain, until finally we came upon a strip that showed evidence of recent use. The faint impress of tire tracks was visible beneath a grid of weed, and here and there a bush had been lopped or a tree limb severed. Moments later we came across a garbage-strewn path that intersected the road at a forty-five-degree angle and then plunged into a thicket as dense as something you'd expect to find in the Great Dismal Swamp. "What do you make of this?" I said, hesitating.

Gesh grunted. The path was well worn, the bushes clipped back. "Jones," he said.

Jones. Enlightenment came like a blow to the back of the head. My pulse rate accelerated. Undifferentiated fears assailed me like bats exploding from a cave.

Phil looked perplexed, as if we'd been talking in code. "Who?"

"That dipshit farmer, remember? Somebody was up here last year, he said, somebody that was up to no good. Somebody named Jones."

"Or Smith," I added, but Gesh was already lumbering through the undergrowth, striding along like a Bunyan, and I hurried to keep up. I don't know what I expected to find—half-eaten human carcasses dangling from the trees, a cache of automatic weapons or an angel-dust factory—but I should have guessed. "Wait up,"

Phil called. Weeds slapped at my face, a branch snagged the sleeve of my shirt. I focused on Gesh's back, birds hissed in the trees, something darted off through the bushes, and suddenly we were standing at the edge of a sunlit clearing between walls of oak and laurel. I took it all in at a glance: the gray splintered tree stumps, the chicken-wire fencing, the sunken rims of the holes. Strips of corrugated aluminum had been driven into the ground at the base of the fence, as if at the border of some suburban zucchini patch, and hundreds of twelve-ounce Styrofoam cups littered the area, crushed underfoot, caught up in the roots of bushes, while deflated plastic bags advertised a Polk Street party supply house. There was garden hose, too, great sun-bleached coils of it, and crumpled half-empty sacks of fertilizer from which jagged clumps of weed had begun to sprout.

Gesh stood in the midst of this desolation, hands on hips. Phil and I were spouting expletives and taking the name of God in vain. We were like children exposed to the ugly underbelly of Fantasyland, the dirt and grease and grinding gears beneath the pristine forest floor. "Pot!" I shouted, surprised at my own emotion. "The son of a bitch was growing pot up here and Vogelsang never said a word about it."

It was true, it was incontrovertible. If the Leakeys had problems interpreting the archaeological record at Olduvai, this was a snap—it couldn't have been clearer had Jones left a diary with photographs. He'd used the Styrofoam cups to sprout his seedlings, and he'd dug the holes—as we would—to create a controlled environment for his maturing plants. But what went wrong? Or had it gone wrong? Maybe Jones was in Rio at that very moment, parading around in a Nixon mask and doing cocaine till his septum dissolved. I had a fleeting vision of palm trees, the girl from Ipanema, the mask, the cocaine and a water glass of dark Jamaican rum, but it was almost immediately supplanted by a vivid recollection of the Eldorado County Jail and the look of unreasoning hatred on Officer Jerpbak's face.

"Hey, what's this?" Phil said, fishing a flat wooden object from the weeds. I saw rust, a spring and a coil of steel wire. It looked like a rat trap.

"Looks like a rat trap," Gesh said. I studied the ground. There must have been fifty of them in plain sight. I remembered the rats or squirrels I'd seen the first day—big brown things the size of footballs. There was a connection here, a nasty connection. But I wasn't ready to make it.

For the next ten minutes or so we poked around Jones's growing area (Smith, Jones: was anybody really named Smith or Jones?), uncovering rat traps, checking the chicken wire fences, gazing up at the sky in an effort to gauge the area's vulnerability to aerial detection. Then we continued along the road and discovered that it gradually wound back on itself and joined our driveway just below Sapers's house. On the way back I said I didn't like the fact that someone had tried to farm the place before us. Phil didn't like it either. "I wish I knew whether Jones was lying on a beach in the Bahamas or out on bail," he said. Gesh spat in the dirt. He was climbing the hill with his long loping strides, breathing hard. "At least we know where to put the fence up," he said.

Three nights later, after we'd refenced and cleared Jones's plot (we dubbed it "Jonestown" by way of honoring our unknown predecessor and out of a perverse sense of humor that laughs in the face of its own defeat), we heard the sound of a well-tuned engine straining up the hill. All three of us were outside in the gathering dusk as Dowst's sky-blue van lurched into the front yard and skidded to a halt. The first thing Dowst said was "Sorry I'm late," as if he were overdue at a cocktail party. We said nothing. "I had to finish up this article on the walking-stick cholla for *The Cactus and Succulent Journal*, and I just got buried in my notes." He shrugged. "Well, listen: I hope you can appreciate my position—I had to deliver on time and there were no two ways about it. I'm sorry."

He looked like a page out of an L. L. Bean catalogue: fisherman's sweater, duck hunter's vest, skeet shooter's cap. We regarded him with unremitting hatred. He'd been writing articles and we'd been stringing wire.

"So," he said, clapping his hands and rubbing the palms together as if they were wet, "I see you've got the greenhouse up."

Our heads turned like beads on a string. The greenhouse sat in the corner of the yard like the centerpiece in an exhibition of avant-garde sculpture, its camouflage colors disguising it about as effectively as the brick-oven red of my Toyota. "Yeah," Gesh said finally, turning to Dowst, "no thanks to you."

That night we sat around the stove, smoking the pot Dowst had brought us, examining the Skippy jars full of seeds that would make us our fortune, and listening to Dowst's assurances that everything was all right and that the few days we'd lost really wouldn't matter in the long run. The resentment we'd felt when he first stepped from the van had begun to wane, and Phil broke the ice socially by offering him some of the corn chowder he'd been boiling for the past three days. Dowst feigned a grateful smile and said he'd already eaten. I told him he could sleep on the couch, but he said he'd just as soon sleep in the van—which he'd equipped, incidentally, like a pimpmobile, with cherrywood paneling and shag carpet. "Okay," I said, "have it your way."

In the morning we found ourselves in the front yard, lined up like refugees and licking egg yolk from the corners of our mouths, while Dowst plied his shovel in an exemplary and instructive way. The air was dank. A crow jeered from the rooftop. We listened to the hiss and scrape of the shovel, the sudden sharp clamor of metal and stone. We watched Dowst's flailing elbows, his sure foot, we counted the seams in his designer jeans. And then, when he stood back, wiping the sweat from his brow with a red bandanna, we edged forward, silent, curious, awed and disgruntled, to contemplate the model hole.

Chapter 4

I was against it. Gesh was for it. Phil wavered. But when we came within sight of Shirelle's Bum Steer, the bed of the pickup loaded to the gunwales with groceries, twelve-ounce Styrofoam cups, half-gallon bottles of vodka, seam-split sacks of worm castings and steer manure, three rolls of chicken wire and a battery-powered Japanese tape player Gesh had picked up at a yard sale, Phil braked, downshifted and spun the wheel, and we rumbled into the parking lot like Okies on parade, lurching to a halt beneath the sorry bumper-blasted oak that presided over the place in long-suffering martyrdom.

There were three other cars in the lot: two mud-caked Chevy pickups and a Plymouth Duster with bad springs. A dog that looked like a cross between a malamute and a hyena regarded us steadily from the bed of the nearer pickup. "Just one," Phil said, holding up a finger and draining a can of Coors in a single motion.

"Or two," Gesh grinned.

"Okay," I said, gulping down my beer. "But remember what Dowst said."

"Fuck Dowst."

"No, really—we can't be too careful."

"Loose lips sink ships," Phil said, swinging out the driver's door.

"Right on," Gesh shouted, drumming at my shoulder blades as I heaved open the door and flung myself from the cab.

For a moment we just stood there in the glutinous muck of the parking lot, the hyena-dog's yellow eyes locked on us, the tavern door as forbidding as the gates of Gehenna. We were feeling guilty. Dowst had laid down the law, ex cathedra—we were to pick up the groceries and supplies and head directly home. No stopping. Not at diners, bars, burger stands—not even at the post office. It was absolutely essential that we keep a low profile, talk to no one, remain anonymous and invisible. You strike up a friendly conversation—with the checkout girl, the man at the Exxon station, the old lady peddling stamps at the post office—and you're dead. Dowst assured us, with Puritan solemnity, that the locals could spot a dope farmer a mile off.

"Maybe we shouldn't," Phil said.

I studied the dog, the scarred tree, the massive weathered windowless slab of redwood that barred the entrance to Shirelle's inner sanctum. The Duster, listing to the right, sported a bumper sticker that proclaimed: I'M MORAL. It looked like rain. "Yeah, I guess we shouldn't," I said.

"Shit," Gesh said. Nobody moved.

In that instant the decision was taken out of our hands. The door suddenly burst open and a woman emerged, an aluminum beer keg cradled in her arms like the decapitated head of a lover. She was in her early forties, dressed in black spandex pants, a lacy Victorian blouse and a pair of aniline-orange spike heels, with ankle straps. I registered bosom, flank, false eyelashes and a shade of mascara that was meant to coordinate with the shoes. There was a moment of hesitation as she locked eyes with us; then she flashed us a smile, tossed the empty keg down outside the door and invited us in. "Goddamn," she said, and it was almost a bark, "you guys going to stand out here all afternoon or come on in and join us?"

Inside it was dark as a closet, the windows grimed over, a few feeble yellow bulbs glowing here and there. Two men sat at the bar, hunched over beers; three others slouched at a table in the back, their faces ghoulish in the blue light of the jukebox. All five were wearing straw hats worked into nasty, rapierlike peaks, work shirts, Levi's and boots. They shared a look compounded of shock, indignation and irascibility in equal portions, as if we were the last thing they expected to encounter in the shadowy depths of Shirelle's, and the first thing they'd like to stamp the life out of, followed by rattlesnakes, rats and weasels, in that order.

Shirelle ducked behind the bar, wiped her hands on a dirty towel and gave us a pert, expectant look. We were milling around, searching our pockets, shuffling our feet. The jukebox thundered with the strains of hillbilly-trucker music: *Don't let your cowboys grow up to be babies* and *Tears in my beers, can't keep a head up over you.* Gesh ordered shots of rye and beer chasers. We sat. Gallon jars of pickled eggs confronted us, a faded souvenir pennant from the Seattle World's Fair, dusty bottles of Bols crème de menthe, Rock & Rye and persimmon liqueur. The bar was smooth as a salt lick with generations of abrasion, the soft sure polish of sleeves and elbows. We threw down our shots like mean hombres and then took economical little sips of beer.

Shirelle leaned back against the cash register and lit a cigarette. "Haven't seen you guys before," she said. "Just passing through?"

"No," I said.

"Yeah," Gesh said.

"We're heading over to Covelo," Phil said, working a country twang into his voice.

"Covelo?" Covelo was the end of the road, a hamlet that gave on to Indian reservation, national forest, mountain. No one but game wardens and liquor salesmen went there.

Phil leaned across the bar, confidential. "We've got a load of smallpox-infested blankets for the Indians."

Shirelle stared at him for a minute, blank as an oil drum, and then she let out a whoop of laughter so sharp and sudden it made me spill my beer. No one else cracked a smile. The faces by the jukebox drew together, beaked, craggy, a glimmer of blue-black Indian hair. Shirelle laughed like a woman who's not responsible for her actions, breaking off to hack into a fist glittering with painted nails. She laughed till tears dissolved her makeup. Moles appeared out of nowhere, lines tore at her eyes. "Hey," she gasped finally, "let me buy you another one, you funny guy," and she reached out to pinch Phil's cheek.

An hour later I reached for my wallet and spilled a pocketful of change on the floor. I waved at it vaguely, and then slapped a ten-dollar bill on the bar. "Another round," I said. Shirelle and Phil were dancing, their groins locked like machine parts. Gesh was shooting pool with the Indians in back, and I was engaged in conversation with George Pete Turner at the bar. I was also leering shamelessly at Shirelle's daughter, who'd been summoned from the house to help the other customers while her mother helped Phil.

The daughter's name was Savoy—surname Skaggs, as George Pete informed me. Delbert Skaggs had left Shirelle ten years back to run off to Eureka with the Cudahy twins, Natalie and Norma. Turner was squinting at me through a haze of Tareyton smoke, his voice low and confidential. There was more to the saga, but I wasn't listening. No. I was down from the hills, back from exile, and I was ogling Savoy's butt with all the mendicant passion of a Charlie Chaplin, out at the elbows, pressing his nose to a plate-glass window rife with cream puffs and napoleons. The girl couldn't have been eighteen, let alone twenty-one. But she looked good. Very good. Golden arms, a low-cut sweater top, violet eyes—one just slightly but noticeably smaller than the other. She caught me staring, and I asked her where she'd got her locket from.

"This?" She fished the gold heart from her cleavage and stared down at it as if she'd never seen it before. Then she giggled, showing small even teeth and an expanse of healthy pink gum. "Eugene gave it to me before he went into the army." George Pete Turner's whiskery face hung at my shoulder like a salami in a delicatessen. He was nodding in confirmation. "He's stationed in Germany," she said. "Wiesbaden." She pronounced it *wheeze.*

I didn't know what to say. I watched her as she carefully set the three sizzling beers down on coasters and lined up the shot glasses, cocked her wrist and expertly topped them off. "Nice," I said.

"Did I tell you that Ted Turner in Georgia—the tee-vee magnet—he's my second cousin?" George Pete's voice had a nagging edge to it, each word a desperate raking claw fighting for a toehold. He was talking to the side of my face. I ignored him.

Savoy leaned over the bar and arranged the shot glasses in a neat little circle before me, the locket dangling enticingly from her throat. I could smell her perfume. Behind me I heard the click of the pool balls and a voice I recognized in a moment of epiphany as Phil's, singing along with the jukebox. "Satin sheets to lie on," he crooned, every bit as passionate and downhome as George Jones or Merle Haggard, "Satin pillows to cry on." I don't know what came over me, but I reached for the locket.

"Hey," Savoy said, pulling back in slow motion, chin lifting to expose the unbroken white line of her throat.

My hand traveled with her, the button of gold pinched between my thumb and forefinger, the palm of my hand coming into inevitable contact with her breast as she straightened up. I was leaning over the bar. My hand was on her breast and I had her by the locket. "Nice," I said again, stupidly. "Very nice." She was grinning. George Pete's eyes were like raging bulls, and I felt suddenly, with all the clarity of Cassandra, that something unpleasant was about to happen.

I was right.

The door swung back with a shriek and Lloyd Sapers lurched into the barroom, so drunk his feet failed him and he slammed off the doorjamb like an errant cueball. Our eyes met. I dropped locket and breast, looked away, looked back again. In that instant of looking away, a shape had obliterated the doorway, hulking shoulders, belly, head, hands like catcher's mitts, feet of iron: Marlon.

Gesh and the Indians had paused over their pool game—elimination—Gesh arrested in the act of lining up a shot, cuestick bisecting the bridge of his fingers, angles mentally cut. He looked up at the door with a quizzical expression, as if he'd just turned a corner and found himself in the middle of a parade. Phil, entirely oblivious, had worked Shirelle up against the jukebox and was grinding away at her like an escaped sex offender.

"Well, Jesus H. Christ and all the saints and martyrs," Sapers roared. "If it ain't the teetotalers."

At that moment, George Pete Turner—he was, I later learned, the prospective father-in-law, sire to the absent doughboy and guardian of the family jewels—hit me in the left ear and knocked me from the bar stool. I made a four-point landing, on hands and knees, in a puddle of beer. Lloyd Sapers laughed. I'd been blind-sided, sucker-punched, humiliated. Crouched there, poised between mercy and grief, I could hear the fearful grinding of the earth as it slipped round its axis. And then the shadow of Sapers's son fell over me and I knew I was doomed.

When I came out of my cringe I saw that George Pete Turner was being restrained by his drinking companion, a toothless beardy old sot who couldn't have weighed more than a hundred and ten pounds, and that Marlon, who was merely blinking curiously at me, had the face of a fleshy Boy Scout. Savoy had emitted a short truncated gasp and then faded to the far corner of the bar, Phil was glancing over his shoulder in surprise, Shirelle's eyes were abandoning the smokiness of passion and hardening for action, and Gesh was advancing on the bar, gripping his cuestick like a Louisville Slugger. The Indians were ice statues, drinks locked in their hands like glacial excrescences, and Johnny Cash, his basso rattling the glasses on the shelves, was letting me know that he, too, walked the line. And then, as quickly as it had erupted, it was over.

Marlon, it turned out, was no threat at all. He had a mental age of nine, and was inclined toward violence only in private, isolated circumstances—if someone inadvertently got between him and a plate of food, for instance. He was massive. A barely contained spillage of viscid flesh, titanic, crushing, monumental. But puerile. Dangerous only *in potentio*. He stepped over me, feet like showshoes, bellied up to the bar and asked, in the pinched, whining tones of the preadolescent, for a Coke.

"Hey-hey," Sapers said, clucking away in some orphic backwoods code, as he staggered forward to help me to my feet. Shirelle was standing beside George Pete, who looked abashed. He apologized, and shook hands with me, but wouldn't look me in the eye. "Guess I've had one too many," he mumbled, zipping his lumberjacket, shoving through the door and vanishing into the night.

Gesh eased his cuestick into the wall rack, buttoned his torn trench coat and said, "Let's hit it, Felix. Come on." He had a hand on my elbow. Sapers had cringed and backed off a step when Gesh advanced on us, then turned his head and shouted something about the weather to George Pete's toothless comrade, who was no more than two feet away from him. My ear throbbed.

I felt vague and disoriented, as if my blood had somehow evaporated. Phil, his face solemn, gathered my money from the bar and held out my coat.

"Bye, honey," Shirelle said as we made for the door.

I looked back over my shoulder at the figures stationed round the room, Shirelle lushly replicated in her daughter, the slouching, twitching Sapers, George Pete's wizened cohort, the Indians gliding in brilliant liquid motion over the pool table, and Marlon, mountainous, his big pale glowing visage hanging over the scene like a planetary orb. No one looked particularly sympathetic.

"Could I please have another Coke?" Marlon piped.

The door was swinging to. I heard Sapers's shout, indistinct, competing with the jukebox and the clatter of glasses—I couldn't be sure but I thought he was hollering about crops, now's the time to get them crops into the ground, or something like that. Boom, the door slammed. Faintly, from within, I could still hear him: "Drunks!" he shouted. "Hypocrites!"

Then it was quiet. But for the hiss of the rain.

"Oh, Christ," Phil said.

It was dark. The rain fell in cataracts. We ran for the pickup, sloshing through ankle-deep puddles, everything a blur. We should have walked. There was something in our urgency, in the frantic quickening pace of our legs, that triggered a corresponding impulse in the all-but-forgotten hyena-dog that had stared so implacably at us as we entered the bar, and had waited patiently through the decline of day and the onset of the steady chilling rain for just such an opportunity as this. I was halfway to the truck when a silent lunging form streaked from the shadows and fastened itself to my pant leg with a predatory snarl. Tripped up, I pitched forward into the darkness with a splash, aware of mud, water, the exploratory grip of jaws. And then I was face down in the rank wet dirt, rolling and tumbling like a man afire, flinging up first one arm and then the other as the dog raged over me in an allegro furioso of snapping teeth and stuttering growls. "Rimmer!" a voice shouted close by. George Pete's voice. "You get out of that now!" And the dog was gone.

A mere twenty seconds had been extracted from my life. The violent conjunction of bodies, the interrupted flight, the accelerated heartbeat, the mud, the torn clothing, the raising of welts and breaking of skin—the assault was over before it began. I pushed myself up and limped to the truck, my sleeves shredded and pants flapping. Phil and Gesh were huddled inside. The engine roared, wipers clapped. "What the hell happened to you?" Phil said as I pulled myself into the cab like a flood victim flinging himself over the gunwales of the rescue boat. What could I say? Talk was cheap. I shrugged my shoulders.

Back at the summer camp, I took one look at Dowst's censorious face and told him to go fuck himself. Then I dabbed my wounds with alcohol and slogged out to help my co-workers evacuate ruptured sacks of groceries in the grass and haul dissolving bags of manure to the storage shed. It was no fun. At one point Phil turned to me, rain in our faces, cans of beets, niblet corn and garden-fresh peas at our feet, the sorry scraps of superstrength, double-bottomed bags in our hands. "Okay, so we screwed up," he said. "I'll be the first to admit it." The flashlight picked out a soggy loaf of French bread at my feet. Rain sifted through the trees. "We screwed up," Phil repeated, "but at least we had a good time."

Chapter 5

Oiled, glistening, wicked, they lay on the table in grim tableau, in the sort of menacing still life you see in the newspapers under the headline ARSENAL SEIZED. Guns. Three of them. A .22, a twelve-gauge shotgun, and the most lethal-looking thing I'd seen outside of the reptile house at the San Francisco Zoo, a .357 magnum pistol.

"You can't be too careful," Vogelsang said, grinning his diseased grin. He was wearing a one-piece khaki jumpsuit, boot to throat, the kind of thing favored by astronauts or kiddies toddling off to bed. The gloves, hood and gauze face mask were neatly arranged on the crate beside him. Aorta, in a sheeny metallic jacket, was watching me as I fingered the weapons.

It was lunchtime. Soup was boiling over on the stove, the windows were steamed up. Our guests had just stepped through the door, weapons bristling, commandos on a raid. Vogelsang greeted me by name, nodded at Phil and Gesh, then spread the firearms out on the table. Phil hovered over the blistered wooden counter, masticating a bologna sandwich with the intensity of a beaver felling trees, and Gesh, sweat-stained and filthy, was propped up on the couch with a beer. Dowst was in the greenhouse, where he'd been all morning, planting seeds in twelve-ounce Styrofoam cups.

"So how's the moon launch going?" I said.

Vogelsang gave me a blank look, then grinned and tugged at the front of his jumpsuit. "You mean this?" he said. "Poison oak. I get it like the bubonic plague and leprosy wrapped in one."

I hefted the shotgun judiciously, sighted down the barrel like a sharpshooter. Actually, I'd only fired a gun once in my life. Eleven years old, a Boy Scout for two months (after which I quit: too much marching and knot-tying), I lay on my belly in the dirt and clicked off round after round at a bull's-eye target. I remembered the firecracker smell, the snap of the report, the quick thin puff of smoke. The scoutmaster leaned over me, his face stubbled with whiskers, and breathed terse commands in my ear. "Sight," he whispered. "A hair to the left. Squeeze."

The gun was surprisingly heavy, the trigger light: death instantaneous and irrevocable. "Do we really need this sort of thing?" I said, trying to sound casual. "I mean, a pistol that could blind an elephant—isn't that a bit excessive?"

Gesh grunted. I couldn't tell whether it was a grunt of disparagement or agreement. I glanced at him. He was sipping beer, eyes squinted over the tight high cheekbones. I knew the look: he was sorting things out, ordering the priority of his grievances before opening up on Vogelsang.

Vogelsang laughed. He'd led patrols in Vietnam, shot people from cover, garroted underfed Asians in secrecy and silence. "Look, Felix, you're going to have a million and a half dollars' worth of pot out there. Not only do you have to worry about the law, but you've always got the possibility that some hunter or one of these dirtbaggers will blunder across it. What would you do in their place? You know, out in the woods, poking around—maybe even looking for an illegal operation? I know what I'd do. I'd take it, no questions asked."

If at some point I'd glamorized the outlaw life, the romance of the scam and all the rest, if at some point I'd pictured myself a latter-day Capone or Dillinger or Bugsy Malone, I suddenly saw the stark and nasty underside of the whole operation. Guns. I'd never imagined I would have to defend myself with a gun. *Quit*, a voice whispered in my ear. *Get out now*.

Vogelsang was studying my face, grinning still. He was enjoying this. "Come on, Felix," he said. "Really, it's no big deal." He paused to produce the ever-present vial of breath neutralizer, working it rapidly between his palms as if he were starting a friction fire. "Chances are maybe one in a hundred that anybody'll come around. But don't you want some insurance if they do?"

What could I say? Vogelsang was pooh-poohing me, Aorta regarded me appraisingly, Phil and Gesh seemed to accept the presence of firearms as casually as they accepted the pork cheeks in bologna or the nitrites in beer. I was a man, a dope farmer, an outlaw and a flimflammer. The gun was as much a tool of my trade as the come-along or spade, and I would just have to get used to it. I shrugged.

Meanwhile, splayed out on the couch, his eyes like coiled snakes, Gesh had apparently sorted out his various complaints and decided to make his presence known. Suddenly he crushed the empty beer can in one callused fist and sent it rocketing across the room like a three-and-two fastball; it hit the kitchen wall with a cowbell clank, and rebounded neatly into an overflowing bag of garbage. Four heads turned toward him. "Listen, Herb," he said, a peremptory edge to his voice, "I think we got a few things to discuss, brother, and guns is the least of them."

Here we go, I thought. I could feel the dollars slipping from my pocket, the seedlings wilting, the clash of personality like an early frost, an ill wind, like blight and scale and rot. Vogelsang cocked his head and leaned forward, his lips tight with a thin bemused smile. He could have been a headmaster bending an ear to an ingenuous and sadly misinformed pupil.

"First of all," Gesh said, his voice strangled with the effort to control it, "I don't like this business of you sniffing wine corks down at Vanessi's and la-de-dahing around Bolinas while we're busting our asses up here with no electricity and broken-down equipment, in the fucking rain, freezing our balls off, and then the quote *expert* shows up a week and a half late, and you, you come waltzing in the door like this was a costume ball at the Lions' Club or something. . . ."

Phil was licking mustard from his fingers, both irises locked in alert alignment, while Aorta, unconcerned, a creature of another species, insentient, slow-blooded, ducked through the doorway with sacks of groceries and laid them on the counter like the offerings they were. Gesh's voice nagged on, expressing deep and insupportable disaffection with everything, from lack of direction and equipment to the leaky roof and the holes in his boots and underwear. I could see the lines being drawn, the sides forming up: slaves and overseers, coolies and satraps, workers and bosses.

> *Yes, you know when I begin to farm,*
> *My old boss he didn't want to furnish me,*
> *He had one mule name' Jack, an' one name' Trigger,*
> *All the money for him an' none for the nigger.*

So could Vogelsang. He was nervous, hyperkinetic, scratching round the room like a dog looking for a place to squat. Pursing his lips, he did his best to look thoughtful and conciliatory—contrite, even. When Gesh finally wound down, Vogelsang parried with sympathy, promises, a waved fistful of cash—he actually extracted a roll of bills from his pocket and waved it like a flag of truce—and a pep talk worthy of Winston Churchill in his finest hour. He planned to stay for the next six days—*at least*, he said. He'd brought groceries, supplies, equipment, booze, cash, pot, a Monopoly board, cheap paperbacks, a four-wheel-drive vehicle. "And Boyd," he said, summing up, delivering the clincher, "Boyd's planning to stay on without a break until all the seedlings are in the ground and the growing areas enclosed."

"Seedlings, shit," Gesh growled, but I could see that he was mollified. In the space of three minutes Vogelsang had managed to reassure us that we hadn't been neglected, that he'd foreseen everything and was prepared to lay out the capital to meet all our needs, and that, most important, our project was not doomed to failure, not at all—no, this was just the beginning. Everything was all right. We were going to make it. We were going to beat the system. We were going to be rich.

And then, seeing his opening, Vogelsang took the offensive. "I might remind you, friend," he said, his words diced as if by a dozen quick knife-strokes, "that I'm the one who's putting up the capital for this little venture, and that I'm under no obligation to be up here at all. In fact, once things get rolling, you're going to see less and less of me."

"Less?" Gesh lurched out of the chair. He stopped three feet short of Vogelsang, jabbing his index finger at him. "You tell me: what's less than nothing?"

The smile was frozen to Vogelsang's face. For an instant something flickered in his eyes, something like emotion, but he killed it.

And then Phil was stepping between them like a rodeo clown, shuffling his feet and ducking his shoulders. His mouth was full and we couldn't catch what he was saying at first, but he was bowing and sweeping his arm in a grand comic gesture. Then he swallowed, hefted the blackened pot from the stove and set it down on the table. "Soup's on," he said.

There were two and a half gallons of soup. Unidentifiable chunks of meat or vegetable matter bobbed in a greasy slick that reeked of black pepper and garlic. It was food, that's all that mattered. We crowded round the caldron like the half-starved bricklayers of *Ivan Denisovich*, ravenous after a long morning of physical labor. Hands grabbed for bread, spoons, bowls. Vogelsang, I assumed, would decline to join us.

I was wrong. He dipped his bowl into the pot like a true son of the proletariat, squatted down before the stove, and broke bread with us. Perhaps he didn't have the faintest idea of how people related to one another, perhaps the quotidian range of human emotion was an enigma to him, but there was no denying this: he knew how to take charge of the situation.

After lunch, Vogelsang tinkered with the generator for ten minutes or so and then fired it up with a sudden blatting roar that obliterated the solitude of the hills and froze my heart like a block of ice. "Shut it off," I screamed, bursting from the house, where the lightbulbs had begun to glow dimly. He glanced up at me, then leaned over and shorted the spark plug with a plastic-grip screwdriver. "Works fine," he said.

"But the noise—they'll hear it for miles. It's like Pearl Harbor or something." (I could picture the town sheriff spilling his coffee every time we started the thing up. "What the sufferin' Jesus is *that*?" he asks the basset-faced deputy. "It's them city boys," the deputy says, "up on the old Gayeff place. Lloyd Sapers says they're growin' corn or somethin' out the side of a mountain. What you make of that, Ormand?")

Vogelsang stood. "Yes, well—you've got a problem there. Maybe you could use it sparingly, huh?"

Then he was off with Dowst for a tour of the plantation—an antebellum cotton farmer overseeing the darkies' efforts—while we labored with come-along and fence-pounder at growing area number three, a grassy slope we'd dubbed "Julie Andrews's Meadow" because its blues and greens looked like something done in CinemaScope. That night there were six of us for dinner, and as we sat beneath the brownly glowing lightbulbs and suffered the ratchetting shriek of the generator, we found we had some rethinking to do and some hard questions to lay bare.

"I can appreciate how hard you fellows have been working," Vogelsang said, "and I think that second growing area you've picked is ideal, but some of the fencing you've done is . . . well, I don't think you've got the idea."

We were seated on the floor, gathered in a semicircle round the wood stove. Dowst, Vogelsang, Aorta, me, Phil, Gesh. Dowst and Vogelsang were eating reconstituted black mushroom soup and freeze-dried paella out of plastic bowls from Dowst's backpacking kit. The rest of us—Aorta included—were eating blood-raw steaks, canned beans and French bread, courtesy of Vogelsang. A jug of Cribari red occupied the place of honor in the center of the floor.

"What do you mean?" Phil said.

"Well, listen. I don't think we have to string barbed wire around the growing areas." I began to protest—we'd nearly killed ourselves over that wire—but Vogelsang anticipated me. "Now hear me out—this'll save you a lot of work. The way I see it, and Boyd agrees with me, the only place we need barbed wire is along the border of Lloyd Sapers's property."

"Now he tells us," Phil said.

Gesh filled a twelve-ounce Styrofoam cup with wine and glared at Dowst and Vogelsang as if they'd just nailed his mother to a tree. Phil wiped his plate mournfully, while I toyed with a crust of bread, overcome with the sort of plummeting despair you feel when you're driving coast to coast and suddenly realize, in the dead of night, that you've been going in the wrong direction for the past three hours, the oil light is flashing, you're nearly out of gas, and your dog is not curled comfortably asleep in the back seat as you'd supposed, but was abandoned along the strip of crapped-over grass at the last truck stop. I watched as Dowst sucked beige droplets of soup from his mustache. His shirt was pressed and his hands were as white and unblemished as bars of soap. Aorta chewed steak.

"It's the cows the barbed wire will keep out. And the cows are ranging all over Sapers's place, and ours, too. Right, Boyd?"

Dowst nodded, dabbing at his mustache with a paper towel. "We saw three of them on the property today. And you know what that means—the cows get lost and then the cowboys come looking for them."

"Right," Vogelsang said, the paella going cold in his lap, "that's what I mean. We fence the property line—just on Sapers's side—and then we avoid that sort of, ah, confrontation."

"And the growing areas?" I said.

"Deer fencing." I watched Vogelsang raise a forkful of rice to his lips, then put it down again. "Clear the area, fence for deer, dig the holes, lay the irrigation pipe and watch the plants grow."

"One deer," Dowst said, holding up a single finger for emphasis, "could eat twenty plants in a night. And the barbed wire does nothing for them—they just jump right over it."

Gesh suddenly got to his feet, stalked across the room and out the door. Left ajar, the door swung lazily back on its hinges, and the room filled with the clatter of the generator. "What's with him?" Dowst said. I shrugged. The noise was excruciating. I was about to get up and slam the door when the lights failed and the roar abruptly died—with a choking, throttled cough and an explosion of backfire. One thousand, two thousand, three—I counted off the seconds as we sat in absolute, intergalactic darkness, the silence drawn over us like a cloak. Then a light appeared, wavering, and Gesh stepped back into the room with a Coleman lantern.

"Too much racket," he murmured. "Makes me nervous."

Vogelsang was nodding in affirmation. He'd repaired the generator as a concession to our needs, but I knew he was against it. Perhaps—and the thought was like the first trickle of gravel that precipitates a landslide—perhaps he'd perforated the muffler or something to make it louder still, his way of subtly demonstrating that comfort wasn't worth the price of exposure. Certainly the thing could be heard from the main road, and who knew what sort of visitors it might attract—people like Sapers, or worse. (Sapers's place glowed with cheap, silent, efficient wattage, incidentally. The PG&E line climbed the mountain as far as his house, and as I would one day discover, he'd paid a tidy sum for the privilege. But that's another story.) "I think you're right," Vogelsang said, and I suddenly realized it was the first time he and Gesh had agreed on anything.

Gesh set the lantern on the table, stepped between Vogelsang and Dowst, eased himself down beside Phil and reached for his plate. Dowst murmured something to Vogelsang about the temperature in the greenhouse, Gesh addressed himself to a mound of pinto beans, and Aorta turned to me and asked, as if she'd been considering the question all evening, "You into music?"

"Music?" I echoed, as if I'd never heard the term before. "Yeah. Sure. Of course. Who isn't?"

"Ever hear of the Nostrils?"

I'd already failed. I shook my head sadly.

"I sing with them."

"Oh, yeah? Really?" This was the first time she'd initiated a conversation, the first time she'd said anything in my hearing other than yes, no, hello, goodbye. I was interested. I was also, after three celibate weeks on the mountain, consumed with lust. I studied the slope of her breast, the swell of her calf, the neat red laces of her suede hiking boots, and tried to picture her engaged in deviant acts. Outside, in the greenhouse, seeds were sprouting.

She shifted her buttocks, bent to her plate and took a forkful of meat. "Yeah," she said, white teeth, black lips, chewing. "I think you'd like us." She was about to say more when Gesh cleared his throat and said, "So, Herb, why don't you tell us about Jones."

Silence.

Vogelsang looked uncomfortable. He looked besieged, hunted, weary, looked like a man who could think of better ways to spend his time—pressing pasta and stuffing weasels, for instance. I wondered how long he could keep his equanimity. "Who?" he said.

"You know: Jones. Dude that was up here last year, growing pot?" Gesh never stopped pushing, but he was right. If Vogelsang was hiding something, we were entitled to know about it.

"I don't know why you didn't tell us," I said. "It seems pretty significant, doesn't it, to know that somebody tried to farm the place before us?"

"No big deal," Dowst said, cutting in. "We knew he'd been busted—"

"Busted?" There was a chorus of cries.

"—and we figured he'd probably been doing some farming up here, but we never found any evidence of it."

"Yeah, and I'll bet you looked real hard, too," Gesh said.

"Busted?" I repeated, incredulous.

"On the highway, Felix," Vogelsang said, in control again, "miles from here. The way I heard it, he was sitting in a line of cars—they were doing roadwork and only one lane was open—and he tossed a joint to this long-haired ditchdigger. Five miles up the road the CHP nailed him for possession. Stupid, that's all."

"But he had a trailer up here," I said. "You must have known he wasn't up here for his health."

"Yes, well. As Boyd said, we assumed he'd been doing a little cultivating, but that really didn't affect us. He had an address someplace in North Beach. I figure he got a little paranoid after the bust, harvested early and cleared out—if he harvested at all."

Dowst smoothed the collar of his shirt and then set the plastic bowl down beside the plastic utensils. He could have been on a camping trip to commemorate his tenth-year Andover reunion. "So there's nothing to connect Jones with the place—it's irrelevant. Jones is irrelevant."

"Not if El Ranchero Grande next door knows about him," Phil countered. " 'Up to no good' is what he said."

"Yeah." I was getting incensed, strung-out, suspicious. "And if Sapers thinks Jones was up to no good, what do you suppose he thinks we're doing? Writing? With a come-along?"

Vogelsang shrugged. He looked tired.

Jail cells, I thought, dawn raid, yellow toilet, hardened criminals, buggery. I was picturing the three of us, shackled together, jackets pulled up over our heads, half a dozen Jerpbaks prodding us with nightsticks, when Gesh suddenly hammered the floor with his fist. He was shouting. "Come on, Vogelsang, you son of a bitch—you put Jones up to it, didn't you? Huh? Just like us."

Aorta's eyes glowed like neon. Dowst swiped at his hair. I could hear crickets or locusts or something going at it outside as if they were laying down the backing track for a horror film. With exaggerated calm, Vogelsang leaned forward to pour himself a glass of wine. He took a long sip, and then held Gesh's eyes. "I'll show you the deed to the property," he said. "I bought the place in February. From a fellow named Strozier—Frederick C. W. Strozier." Vogelsang shifted his gaze now, expanding his field of vision to include Phil and me. "Go ask him. Maybe Jones was working for *him*"—giving us the Charlie Manson stare—"just as you, my friends, are working for me."

Gesh muttered an obscenity, his voice so thick it could have been dubbed. I wondered if he'd been rat-holing Quaaludes.

"You're in or you're out," Vogelsang said, hard now, no patience left, the bargain-driver and market-manipulator. "Either trust me or pack it in."

I knew at that moment I should take him up on it—pack it in, get out, get clear. But I didn't. I couldn't. We'd just got there, the seeds were burgeoning in the dark moist earth of the greenhouse, Rio awaited. "Okay," I said, answering for all of us. "Okay. But no more secrets." And then, almost as an afterthought: "What about the calendar?"

No reaction.

"You know what I mean, Vogelsang, come on. The calendar, the one you dug up in the shed and hung in the bedroom." I felt something rising in my throat—gas, maybe. My heart had begun to hammer. "The calendar," I repeated. "The joke."

He looked up at me as if he hadn't heard, looked up as if he were deaf and dumb. His face was blank, no glimmer of comprehension in his eyes. He could have been aphasic, could have been a tourist who had no grasp of English. Worse: he could have been innocent.

Like the Savior at Golgotha, Vogelsang stayed three days. On the morning of the third day he arose and assembled us for instruction in the use and maintenance of firearms. We stood out front of the house confronting a series of makeshift targets—bottles, cans, Mason jars, a grid of two-by-fours faced with plywood and clumsily inscribed with sagging concentric circles. This last, mounted on stilts and angling backward like an artist's easel, explained the persistent hammering that had jolted me awake at the hour of the wolf. I breathed on my hands and then thrust them into my pockets. It was foggy and cold, dew beading our vehicles and the mounds of rusted machine parts that lay scattered in the high grass like the remnants of a forgotten civilization. Clumps of mist clung to the trees like balls of hair in the bristles of a brush. The model hole, a few yards to our left, was water-filled and rimmed with fingers of ice.

I was contemplating our new vehicle—an open Jeep of ancient vintage with big heavy-grid tires that had unfortunately gone bald—when Dowst emerged from his van, clean-shaven and alert. There was a notebook clenched under his arm and a row of pens clipped to his pocket—he could have been back at Yale, loping off to attend an early lecture on bryophytes. He slogged his way through the weeds, sidestepped the hole and joined us on the improvised firing line. "Going to take notes?" I said. Phil giggled. Dowst gave me an odd look, held out the notebook and flipped through the pages for me. I saw maps of the property, pages of calculations and formulas, notes on fertilizers, soils, mean temperatures and annual rainfall. Humbled, I ducked my head and spat in the grass.

Then the door slammed behind me and I turned to watch as Aorta picked her way toward us. "Good morning," she croaked, her voice ragged and raw. The cropped hair lay flat against the crown of her head; she was makeup-less and huddled in her silver jacket like a runaway. I rubbed my palms together and gave her a weak smile.

"Anything happens," Vogelsang was saying, "and your obvious choice is the shotgun." His eyes were hard, glacial, veins stood out in his neck. I was thinking of drill instructors, Fort Hood, recruits dying in basic training—eighteen years old and their hearts give out—when Vogelsang handed me the gun.

I didn't know what to do. I was prepared to fire the thing—in fact, in a childish sort of way I was looking forward to it. But not first. No. First I wanted to watch Vogelsang bring it to his shoulder, sight down the barrel, squeeze off a round or two; I wanted to hear the roar, see the target totter, gauge the force of the recoil. Life was full of surprises, most of them unpleasant. Why rush into things?

Vogelsang was lecturing, his words coming at me as if from a great distance: "Ithaca. Twelve-gauge. Pump. Double-ought shot." I held the gun stiffly, like an artificial limb. Flesh soup, I thought. Ground round. Then Vogelsang took my arm and indicated a target set apart from the rest—a pillow perched atop a peeling three-legged end table, no more than thirty feet away. He had painted a Kilroy face on it, eyes, nose, slashes for eyebrows, and a big grinning circus mouth. "Go ahead, Felix," he said. "Let it rip."

I felt silly. "That?"

"Go ahead."

I put the gun to my shoulder and squinted down the barrel. The sight was a flap of metal, an *M*, and I peered through the cleft of it with one eye shut, lining up first the table, and then the big sloppy mouth of my bitterest enemy, the crop-stealer, the desperado, the rip-off artist. It was like taking a photograph. Dying color. I concentrated on an image of Robin Hood splitting arrows, held my breath, and pinned the trigger.

There was a roar. The table splintered, the pillow exploded in a puff of feathers: now you see it, now you don't. I was startled—not only by the volume of the blast but by the violence of the recoil, which slammed at my collarbone like a karate chop—so startled I nearly dropped the gun. Through the ringing in my ears I could hear Vogelsang's laughter. I suppose it was funny, my juggling the thing as if it were hot, my confusion, my fear. The ineluctable modality of the risible. "Well shot, Felix," he said between gasps. "You see my point?"

I saw his point. Where table and pillow had formerly stood,

there were only feathers, sifting down like a meteorological aberration. There was no reason even to aim the thing. Just blast away. Destruction. Devastation. Annihilation. I saw his point. But I didn't like the way in which he'd made it. Not especially. So I turned round, hands trembling, and pumped another shell into the chamber—Vogelsang's face went cold; beyond him I could see Gesh, Phil, Aorta, Dowst, smiles freezing as if the wind had suddenly shifted and brought with it a whiff of something foul—and then swung leisurely on the other targets.

"Hey!" Vogelsang waved his arms. "No!"

I wasn't listening: I was aiming. Fifty feet. What was that—a cider jug? Yes. I could read the label. Apple Time. Unsweetened. "Felix!"

Cold steel, hot blast: the gun answered for me. And then again, and again.

Chapter 6

In all, including Phil and me, there were seven customers in the café when the CHP cruiser swung off 101 and nosed into the parking lot. We were sitting at a window booth. Relaxing. Eating. Enjoying a supply run and a two-hour break from the routine of the summer camp. In the booth across from us, a brittle-haired woman in her mid-fifties carped at her daughter, while the daughter's daughter, a two-year-old, kicked at the tabletop. The other denizens of the place—aside from the withered old crone in the checked mini-skirt who performed the multiple functions of chef, waitress and cashier—were two old men, in identical overalls and sun-bleached shirts, who sat at opposite ends of the counter, stolidly blowing into cups of coffee.

Nearly four weeks had passed since we'd last seen Vogelsang, and during that time we'd made determined progress, managing to enclose eight of twelve growing areas, fence the property line between our place and Sapers's, dig twelve hundred holes, and reverentially transplant every last one of the healthy seedlings Dowst had sprouted. Unfortunately, less than twenty percent of the seeds had proven viable, and we wound up with only about fifteen hundred seedlings, a third of which fell prey to some mysterious enervating force in the greenhouse—fungus, leafhoppers, gamma rays, locusts, who could say? Dowst had assured us that he would come up with additional seeds to replace those that had failed. Of course, we would have to scale down our original estimate a bit, but still, even though the second crop would get into the ground a bit late, we should nevertheless come close to the full thousand pounds we'd projected. He was an optimist, Dowst. We looked at it philosophically. So we harvested nine hundred pounds instead of a thousand. Big deal. We'd be rich anyway.

I watched as the cruiser slunk across the lot, weaving in and out of potholes with a muscular grace that suggested a carnivore at ease—a panther, belly full, gliding along the path to its lair. Behind the windshield, which alternately reflected the clouds and darkened to transparency, I could make out the rigid forms of the officers themselves, twin pairs of mirror shades, a riot gun framed menacingly in the rear window. I looked away. And found that I was clutching a laminated menu: Two Eggs Any Style, Super Chili Beef Burger, Corn Dog—Try It! The waitress hovered over us with pencil and pad, and Phil, his voice saturated with ennui, was ordering. "The special," he said. "That's the stuffed cabbage with chili, right? And it comes with a side of coleslaw?"

The waitress nodded her ravaged head. "That's right, honey." She must have been seventy, thin, with a sunken chest and flat feet. Her hair was dyed moonlit brown, and it played girlishly across her cheek as she bent forward.

"I'll take the Super Chili Beef Burger, too," Phil said. "On the side. And another glass of milk, please."

I ordered tuna on rye and a bowl of soup. Violins, converging on the maudlin strains of yet another country hit, whined from hidden speakers. Clouds expanded and contracted along the backbone of the sky. A fly batted at the window.

Then the door swung open behind me, footsteps scuffed across the floor, and the grid of seats heaved as a pair of oversized hominids settled into the booth at my back. I stole a glance out the window and saw that the cruiser was empty. "I'm telling you, you just can't operate that fast," a voice snapped in my ear before descending to an urgent rasping whisper. A second voice, also whispering, interrupted to hiss a reply. The back of my neck began to itch.

I reached for my coffee cup, found that it was empty, and signaled for the waitress. She looked up alertly, slid the Pyrex pot from the stove and started down the aisle—only to continue past as if she hadn't seen me. She halted opposite the newly occupied booth at my back. "Can I get you boys some coffee?" she said. There was a pause in the disputation as both voices broke off to breathe "Please," and then the rasping continued, covered momentarily by the splash and trickle of hot liquid. Phil reached across the table to nudge me, then indicated a point over my right shoulder and broke into a grin. "You see who just joined us?" he whispered.

I scanned the front page of the local paper, trying to ignore him. FUNDS CUT FOR RODENT CONTROL, I read. HARRIET SEARS HONORED BY FATIMAS OF THE FEZ. DROUGHT IN NAMIBIA. And then, with a shock that built in my chest like the thump of a boxer's speed bag, I came across the following:

ALL IN A (FIRST) DAY'S WORK

> Officers of the CHP detained two Bay Area men early this morning when a routine traffic stop turned up nearly 3 kilograms of marijuana seeds and a small quantity of cocaine. Esig "Bud" Jones, 29, of San Francisco, and Aurelio Ayala, 26, of Daly City, were apprehended near Pt. Cabrillo on the Coast Highway. A spokesman for the Highway Patrol speculated that the seeds may have been intended for local cultivation in the highly lucrative "sinsemilla" marijuana trade that many feel has become one of the county's biggest cash crops. Both men are awaiting arraignment in the county jail. Bail has not yet been set.
>
> This is where the story ends. But it had its beginnings in the Ukiah substation yesterday evening when patrolman John Jerpbak reported for his first day of duty with the Ukiah division. Officer Jerpbak, a native of Willits who many will remember as a star halfback for the Willits Wolverines, had requested the transfer from his post in Lake Tahoe because, in his words, "I wanted to do my part in fighting this thing right here where my friends and family (*Cont. Page 2*)

My fingers were trembling. We were thirty-five miles from the ocean, and yet the surf was roaring in my ears. Phil leaned across the table and gestured toward the young mother: "You know, she's not half bad." I didn't answer, couldn't answer. I scanned the room like an impala checking the high grass for movement, the presence at my back swelling to nightmare proportions, and then turned the page.

There he was. Jerpbak. Clipped hair, cleft chin, eyes like arrows in flight. The story went on for two columns. I read about Jerpbak's intrepidity in identifying and apprehending the suspects, I read about Jerpbak's father, who'd sold insurance in Willits for thirty years, about his sister, his mother, his wife (the former Jeannie Jordan). And finally, the conclusion of the piece, familiar, congratulatory, an editorial backslap: "Welcome home, John."

I ate tuna fish, but I didn't taste it—I could have been chewing cardboard smeared with mayonnaise. My stomach contracted, acid rose in my throat. I looked up to see the waitress flirting with one of the old men at the counter—leaning into him like a dance instructor—while his counterpart stared dolefully into his coffee cup. Phil waved a monstrous, chili-dribbling burger in one hand, and a fork in the other. He was relating the plot of the science-fiction trilogy he'd begun two nights ago. I wanted to leave. Split, vanish, dissolve. Toss my money on the table, hunch down in my jacket and slink out the door.

"So Bors Borka, he's the hero, finds himself on this planet where instead of only two sexes, they have five, all of which are necessary—all together—for an orgasm." Phil took a bite of his burger, delicately lapping the extruded chili from between his fingers in the process. "There's this penislike thing, the *omphallus*, that sticks out of this lake made of protoplasm, and it branches into three stalks. Then there's this viridian creature sort of like a female, only instead of a vagina—"

"Phil," I said, pressing both hands to my temples. "Let's get out of here."

"What's the matter?"

I tucked the newspaper under my arm. Strings and oboes tugged at the chords of "Jailhouse Rock," rain began to natter at the window, the old man at the counter slipped his hand up the waitress's dress. "I've got a headache."

Phil gave me a look of shock and dismay, as if I'd just suggested he share his food with everyone in the restaurant and then mail the leftovers to the Underfed Orphans Society. He took a quick bite of his Super Chili Beef Burger and a forkful of stuffed cabbage. "Christ," he muttered, digging for another hurried mouthful. "You sure?"

The booth trembled as one of the patrolmen shifted in his seat. I nodded at Phil, then glanced up nervously and found myself staring into the young mother's eyes. They were black, those eyes, soft and ripe as pitted olives. But I didn't want olives, I wanted escape, seclusion, anonymity. I looked away in confusion, focusing on the Campbell's Soup display and making a show of moving my lips as I read the labels: Chunky Mediterranean Vegetable, Turkey with Avocado, Plantain Broth. "All right," Phil said, frowning. "All right—just let me finish what's on my plate. I can take the burger with me."

I pushed away my half-eaten sandwich and motioned for the waitress. She was poised over the second old man now, refilling his cup while he stared morosely into the knot of his hands. "The check," I pantomimed. She ignored me. Jerpbak, I thought, the name howling in my ears. This was bad karma, malicious fate, the beginning and the end. I waved my arm. "Check, please," I mouthed, fighting for restraint. Behind me, the rasping continued unabated, officers of the law engaged in private business, their flesh and mine wedded by a thin slab of plywood and Naugahyde. Someone coughed. And then, as if a hot wire had been applied to my temple, a nasty certainty leapt through my brain: Jerpbak was sitting behind me. Jerpbak himself. Of course. Who else?

Suddenly I was on my feet. Jerpbak, Jerpbak, Jerpbak: the name beat with my pulse. It all became clear in that instant—he'd tracked me down, spider and fly. He was a Heat, a Holmes, a Javert. He'd seen the guilt on me like a dye, like the thief's tattoo, and he'd known in that moment what I was doing in Tahoe. Yes, and now he was waiting, that's all, waiting till the plants were grown and the buds mature, biding his time till he could swoop down on us when it would hurt most. Phil looked up at me, a smear of chili at the corner of his mouth. "I'm, I'm . . ." I stammered, digging a five from my pocket and flinging it down on the table. Then I took a deep breath, steeling myself. At the count of three I was going to swing round, lower my head and stride out the door.

One Jerpbak, two Jerpbak, three: I pivoted and found myself locking eyes with a scowling cop in his late forties who looked as if he'd devoted his life to the invention of instruments of torture. There was no trace of sympathy or decency in his face, but I felt like embracing him, buying him a cigar, stuffing twenties in his pocket—he might have been an inveterate suspect-beater and civil-rights abuser for all I knew, but he wasn't Jerpbak. The realization so elated me that I lurched forward and tripped over his slick black-booted foot. As I tumbled past him, fighting for balance and yelping an apology over my shoulder, I caught a glimpse of the second cop, the one whose back had for the last ten minutes been so alarmingly contiguous to mine. A glimpse of reflecting shades, cleft chin, clipped and parted hair. That was enough. I slammed into the cigarette machine, tore open the door and flung myself at the cleansing, quickening rain.

A moment later the door eased open and Phil joined me on the front steps. He asked if I was all right. I told him I just needed a little air, that's all. We started for the pickup in silence, raindrops slanting down like so many straight pins. I hardly noticed. All that mattered was that they were watching us (I knew they were, as certainly as I knew that forests are immovable and men born of women), observing the way we lifted our feet and hunched our shoulders, noting the make of the truck and the license plate number, idly fingering their handcuffs. Police surveillance, I thought. Undercover operations. Tapes, photographs, body hairs. Suddenly I saw myself at the window of the cabin, opening up on them with the shotgun, stopping bullets with my teeth, vanishing in a puff of smoke. I slipped the keys into Phil's hand. "What's this?" he said. "You don't want to drive?"

"No, I don't feel up to it," I said, climbing into the passenger's seat. The pickup was loaded with plastic pipe in twenty-foot lengths, with four fifty-five-gallon drums and a gasoline-powered water pump. I was trying my best to look like a tourist or hitchhiker, but I knew it was hopeless. We might as well have painted the truck Day-Glo orange with vermilion pinstriping and the legend DR. FEELGOOD'S FARMS. We were dope farmers—that was as readily apparent to any fool on the street as our species identification—dope farmers stockpiling equipment for their irrigation system. I hunched down in the seat.

"So," Phil said, grinding the ignition, "I didn't tell you the best part yet." I was mute, cataleptic. He went on anyway. "Well, Borka ducks into this cave to escape a column of Termagants from the planet Terma, when he miraculously comes upon four of the sexes trying to get it on—but of course they're missing the fifth link, which just happens to be this armless man-sized thing with a little penis and a prehensile tail. So here comes the space hero, fascinated, watching these four weird creatures go at it, heaving and rocking in frustration . . ."

The truck jerked back, drawing away from the café like a missile from the launching pad. I fought the impulse to look up. Fought it, and lost. As Phil swung around and shifted gears, I snatched a glance out of the corner of my eye. I saw the cruiser with its gold badge of justice, the cracked cinder blocks of the front porch, the little box of the café with its picture windows and advertisements for corn dogs and thick shakes. Light fell from the windows in slabs. I could see nothing. And then, just a flash: dark forms, bereft of animation, as shadowy and insubstantial as the figures in a dream.

Chapter 7

That night, after we'd unloaded the truck and put dinner on, I spread the Jerpbak article out on the kitchen table and motioned for Gesh to have a look. Gesh had spent the afternoon digging holes, and he was stretched out on the couch like a corpse, a hot toddy in one hand and Book One of *The Ravishers of Pentagord*—Phil's trilogy—in the other. From the front bedroom I could hear Phil strumming his guitar and moaning softly. "What is it?" Gesh said. "What have you got—drugs?"

My throat thickened. I didn't think I could get the words out. "It's an article. In the paper. Come take a look."

Gesh sighed, pushed himself up and started across the room. I was poised over the gray newsprint, scanning the article for the twentieth time, each insidious phrase poking at me like a hot scalpel. Gesh was in no hurry. He paused to refresh his toddy and slip a tape into his cracked-plastic battery-powered tape player (he'd unearthed two cassettes in the glove compartment of the Jeep Vogelsang had left us—something unidentifiable that sounded like a diva gargling in the shower, and an ancient Grateful Dead tape that repeatedly stuck on "Truckin'." He opted for the latter).

Busted, down on Bourbon Street,
Set up, like a bowlin' pin . . .

I watched Gesh's face as he read the article. When he'd finished he took a sip of his toddy, looked up at me and said "So?"

"So?" I could feel the floodgates opening wide. "What's with you? Don't you know who this joker is?" I was shouting, rapping Jerpbak's photograph with the back of my hand as if I could tear him in the flesh.

Gesh looked less certain of himself. He shrugged.

"This is the maniac that threw me up against the wall in the Eldorado County Jail when I bailed you guys out. Now he's here, dedicating his life to busting dope farmers—I mean, doesn't that strike you as a little strange?"

Gesh just stared at the paper, his jaw locked. The tape player slammed away at "Truckin' " over and over again: *Truckin'* . . . *Truckin'* . . . *Truckin'* . . . I stalked over and hit the eject button. "Doesn't it?"

"Yeah," he murmured. And then more forcefully: "It's a pisser. A real weird coincidence and a bad break. But nothing to go crazy over."

Phil appeared in the doorway of his room, the guitar strung round his neck like an umpire's chest protector. "What's all the commotion?"

I showed him the article. He held the paper close to his face, licking his lips and sucking in his breath in quick little puffs as he read.

"We just have to be extra careful, that's all," Gesh said.

Phil folded the newspaper neatly and set it down on the counter. Then he looked me in the eye, poker-faced, and hit the refrain of "I Fought the Law and the Law Won."

"Very funny," I said.

If Phil could clown about it, I couldn't. I was tense, shaken, wired to the breaking point. Things were conspiring against us, all our sweat and toil come to naught: we weren't going to wind up rich, we were going to wind up in jail.

"We'll stick to the back roads," Gesh said. Back roads? What was he talking about—there were nothing *but* back roads. "And instead of buying supplies in Willits, we'll go all the way down to Santa Rosa, where nobody'll notice."

I didn't want to end up in jail. But even worse than the thought of jail was the thought of the bust itself. A dozen troopers, in riot helmets and flak jackets, bursting through the door at first light, roughing us up, rifling our possessions, hauling us off in sorrow and subjection—it had become the standard nightmare. Still worse was its corollary, its sad and inevitable conclusion: detection would mean the end of the project, the failure of the farm.

Something had happened to me over the course of the past few weeks, something that transformed me with each crank of the come-along and thrust of the shovel: I'd become a believer. Perhaps it was the evangelical fervor with which Phil, Gesh and even Dowst regarded the project, perhaps it was the callus I'd developed on my hands and feet or the strips of muscle that corrugated my back and swelled the veins of my arms—but whatever it was, I'd been bitten more deeply than I realized. If I'd entered into the thing as a lark, an adventure, attracted as much by the action as the money, I was now fully, absolutely and zealously committed to making it work.

How else could I have gone on, day after day, pitching dirt and hammering fenceposts like a flunky? How else if I wasn't certain in the very root of my being, in the last looping curve of my innermost gut, that we would succeed? *No gains without pains*, Poor Richard said. *Plough deep . . . and you shall have corn to sell and to keep*. Yes, indeed. We would subdue the land, make it produce, squeeze the dollars from it through sacrifice, sheer force of will and Yankee gumption. It was the dream of the pioneers themselves.

But I was no pioneer. I was edgy, nervous, a chronic quitter. If I understand now how deeply involved I was in the summer camp—it *had* to succeed, not so much for the money itself or what it could buy, but as the tangible and final result of our labor, the fruit of our enterprise, the proof of the dream—I did not understand it then. Not that night. Not there in the kitchen, my face hot with the glow of the lantern and the shock of Jerpbak. Maybe I was being irrational, loosing my fears like hobgoblins and bogies—but then the calendar and Jerpbak's reemergence were irrational, too. I was spooked. I was angry.

"Okay," Phil said, "we're all a little paranoid. But just because of one newspaper article and a couple of cops that just happen to sit behind us in a diner, for Christ's sake . . ." He waved his hand as if he were swatting gnats.

Gesh ran his fingers through his hair, then settled himself on the edge of the table and folded his arms. "Yeah," he said after a moment, "I think you're blowing things way out of proportion, man. Sure it's bad news that this fucking jerk is launching a one-man crusade to bust dope farmers, but you got to remember there's a lot of dope farmers out there. To think he's out to get you is insane, it's preposterous."

"Dr. Freud, I presume?" Phil said. He tried to shake my hand but I pulled away.

"I mean, do you really think he bugged the ashtray in your Toyota or something—just because you made an illegal U-turn?"

I had to get out. The pressure was building in me like beer on a full bladder. I snatched my jacket from the chair and slammed out the door.

The night was torn with ragged clouds. Stars whitened the gaps, crickets pulsed like a heartbeat. Somewhere a tree groaned. There was a breeze—damp, fragrant—a southerly breeze that smelled as if it had rattled coconut palms and lifted the scent from hibiscus and frangipani. It wafted up now, a touch of warmth, out of the darkness that engulfed our lower growing areas. I gazed at the sky, clear in the interstices all the way back to the molars of the galaxy, and did not think the least thought about man's fate, the unfathomable universe or group sex on Pentagord. I thought of things worldly and quotidian. Jerpbak. The greenhouse. Mysteriously blighted seedlings.

I breathed deeply—spring breeze, late April already—urinated in the model hole and fumbled my way to the greenhouse. The feather-light door swung back on the hinges I'd installed, and I stepped in and surrendered to the rank wild odor of working soil, of fertility and the dark germ of life. Dowst's flashlight hung from a bent nail just inside the door. I found it and let the tube of light play over the ranks of Styrofoam cups, the stunted and late-emerging plants we'd yet to put in the ground and the flashing strips of aluminum foil Dowst had tacked up as reflectors. He'd arranged the planters on racks in ascending tiers—like grandstands—with a narrow footpath in between. Still agitated, I threaded my way up the path, thinking to find solace in the still, burgeoning atmosphere. It was a mistake. With the healthy plants already in the ground, the place looked barren. I surveyed it slowly, dismally, the husks of dead plantlings brushing at my pants, new growth spotting the remaining cups like a sprinkle in the desert.

Dowst had left for Marin three days earlier, in quest of the seeds we so desperately needed to make up our deficit (with just over a thousand seedlings planted, we needed at least nine hundred more to approach our original estimate). There were, he insisted, entrepreneurs who let their fall crops go to seed to provide for the germinatory needs of people like us—for a price, of course. A price that would come out of our net profit. And though it was a pity that the germination rate of his own seeds hadn't been higher—that's nature's choice, he said, clucking his tongue—he was confident he could obtain more than enough new seeds to suit our purposes. As I stood there counting cups in the tenebrous cave of the greenhouse, I hoped he was right.

Nearly three-quarters of the cups were empty. In some there was no evidence whatever that anything had been planted; in others, wilted brown stalks gave testimony to some inscrutable depredation. Phil maintained that the locusts were responsible—couldn't we hear them screeching in the trees? Gesh thought it might be aphids. Or beetles or something. Dowst, standing firm on the quality of his seeds, theorized that a fungus may have been attacking the roots of the young plants. I was puzzled, distressed. I'd watched the infinitesimal green filaments emerge from the earth, crooked as sweetly as dollar signs, and then come back the following morning to see that they'd been grazed to the root as I slept. Night after night I stalked the greenhouse, sitting in darkness, breath suspended, ears perked, waiting for the telltale crunch of mandibles or the scurry of soleless feet, and always I'd been skunked. There was nothing there—neither beetles nor aphids. Nor snails, leafhoppers, fruit flies or flying sheep for that matter. Just a silence, a silence so absolute I imagined I could hear the seeds rupturing their shells. Now, as I probed the cluttered corners with the flashlight, a sinking defeated feeling took hold of me—as if I'd been crushed under and sucked dry like a bad seed—and suddenly I understood that I was looking at the greenhouse for the last time.

It was an old feeling, compounded of fury and despair, a

choking impotent rage that could only be salved by turning away, by running. I'd felt it when I reread the same page of Carlyle for the fiftieth time, stuffed my books in a trashcan and took the bus for San Francisco while Ronnie waited tables and old Dr. Pengrave sat checking his watch and fussing over the exam questions he'd never get to ask me. I'd felt it in Boston, looking out from the projectionist's booth at the nodding heads and listening to the furtive clatter of white port bottles on the stained cement floor. I'd felt it when I was out of work and out of luck and Ronnie came home and told me she'd been accepted in the MBA program at Wharton and I looked up from my magazine and told her I wasn't moving. Yes: then especially. I remembered the look on her face, the way she held out the acceptance letter as if it were the deed to an oil well or a certificate of beatification. I put you through four years of grad school, she said. Four years. Now it's my turn.

Death, defeat, futility, that's what the greenhouse said to me. I turned my back on it. Like a magic lantern—magnetic, irresistible—the flashlight pulled me across the junk-strewn morass of the lot and on up to the door of the Toyota. I dropped the flashlight in the high grass, dug for my keys and fired up the car with a roar. A moment later I was yawing through the undergrowth and heaving down the gutted road to the highway. The headlights grabbed at the darkness like pincers, trees rocked over me, a deer sprang up and vanished like an illusion. I thought of my apartment. Of movie theaters and Thai food and color TV. Of my stereo, my drip coffee maker, of daily newspapers, books, magazines, of the society of men—and women. Branches swiped at the windshield, a rock exploded against the undersurface of the car, ruts and gullies grabbed the wheel from me and flung it back again. Carefully, carefully, I told myself. I was on my way home.

By the time I reached the blacktop, I was thinking of baseball. I don't know how or why—free association, I suppose. It began with a vision of the players emerging from the dugout against a green that ached, and the feel of the cold salt air of Candlestick Park. I could smell the sour scent of beer in wax cups, flat before it's been tapped, and then I panned across the crowd: men in T-shirts, women in print dresses, the legions of kids in the bleachers waving their outsized gloves. I thought of balls wrapped in black electrician's tape and bats that shudder in your hands, and then finally of Little League and my own eleven-year-old self. The memory was like a splinter under the nail.

Small for my age and late to develop, I'd devoted my life to baseball with the passion of an apostle: baseball was the be-all and end-all, the highest expression and fundamental *raison* for life in the cosmos. Regrettably, my skills were incommensurate with my enthusiasm, and I'd been shunted to right field the previous season—right field, the least dynamic, least significant position on the team, the venue of hacks and losers—and through the winter I burned to prove myself capable of playing closer to the action. That summer I tried out for third base. The hot corner. Where Brooks Robinson and the Boyer brothers routinely dove for scorching liners, leapt to rob batters of extra base hits, scooped up bunts as if they were gathering flowers, and in general demonstrated more skill, guts and panache than anyone on the field. All winter I'd shoveled snow and scrubbed dishes, hoarding nickels, dimes, quarters, the big flat shining half dollars I got for clearing the neighbors' sidewalks, saving for the ne plus ultra—a new Wilson's pro-style Big League infielder's mitt endorsed by and stamped with the signature of Brooks Robinson himself. Eventually, a twenty-five-pound sack of change in hand, I trundled into the sporting-goods store and bought the glove. I worked it and oiled it, and when the snow was gone I was out till dark every day, fielding grounders. I practiced continually, obsessively, practiced till I could handle anything—bad hops, skimmers, liners, dribblers and worm-burners. I was ready.

We tried out on a sweet sunny day in June. The field was new, freshly bulldozed and totally barren. There were stones and pebbles everywhere. Five of us competed for third base while the coach, a laconic veteran of the Korean War whose son was the star pitcher, hammered grounders at us. The first kid handled every ball with fluid ease; the next two flubbed them miserably. Then it was my turn. Thirty-thousand ground balls had been hit to me over the course of the past three months; I was practiced and assured, ready for anything. The first ball came slamming at me over the rocky hardpan of the infield, I bent for it and it took a bad bounce, careening over my shoulder and into the outfield. All right, I thought, the field is like a gravel pit, don't let it get to you. The same thing happened with the two succeeding chances. Humiliated, raging, I charged the next ball as soon as it came off the bat, pounced on it as if I were killing something for the pot, and heaved it six feet over the first baseman's head. The coach looked disgusted. He spat in the dirt. Two more, he said. And then, before I'd even set up, the next ball came rocketing at me. I moved back, adjusting as it skipped over the stones in its path, and at the last instant I lifted my glove for the inevitable hop. No hop. The ball went right through my legs and on out to the left-field fence, where a bored-looking kid with an underslung jaw shagged it back.

Object, movement, the elusive patterns of fate: I had never in my life been so stung with despair and self-hatred. Even before the coach could bring the bat to his shoulder for my final chance, I came out of my crouch and flung my new Wilson's pro-style Big League infielder's glove into the parking lot. Then I ran. Ran through a gale of shouts and laughter, mounted my bike and pedaled up the street as if the Furies were shrieking in my ears. My breath came in sobs. At home, I found my mother sitting at the kitchen table with a crossword puzzle. It wasn't fair, I told her, choking on the bitterness of it. I tried, I did. She pushed back her chair, got up from the table and looked down at me from her five feet and eight inches, sleeves rolled up, earrings dangling. Quitter, she said.

The memory arrested me. A moment before I'd been doing seventy, outracing the headlights, intent on San Francisco, and now I found myself slowing. Degree by degree, almost unconsciously, my foot eased up on the gas pedal. Signs, trees, fenceposts drifted up and trickled by, forty, thirty, twenty-five: I nearly pulled over. I was thinking of Phil and Gesh back in the cabin, sitting down to their fatty, starchy, tasteless meal, cracking jokes and dreaming the dream. Then the car rounded a bend and two dim spots of neon emerged from the darkness, soft and alluring, beacons in the night. I swung the wheel, and for the second time in my life pulled into the pitted parking lot of Shirelle's Bum Steer.

Chapter 8

I sat in the car debating with myself. The threat of Jerpbak and the desolation of the greenhouse tugged me in one direction, undifferentiated needs and personal loyalty in the other. Was I walking out, or was I going to see this thing through? A pithy question. I sat there chewing on it as the night settled in around me and the jukebox thumped seductively from behind the yellowed windows of the tavern. At first, I had no intention whatever of going in—I'd stopped in the parking lot solely to think things out—but then I began to feel that what I needed was a drink. Just a single drink, something comforting and calming—a warm cognac, for instance. But no, it was too risky. I'd been burned once—the thought of the previous debacle at Shirelle's made me wince—and it would be foolish to tempt the Fates yet again. No: a drink was out. Absolutely and positively.

After a while, though, I found myself casually examining the other cars in the lot, as if they could somehow give me a clue to their owners' personalities, mores and penchants for unprovoked violence. There were three of them, all American-made, all beat. I recognized the sagging Duster with the I'M MORAL bumper sticker, but the others made no impression on me. The Duster, I realized, must have belonged either to Shirelle herself, one of the Indians or the wasted old character who'd restrained George Pete Turner on the unfortunate and only occasion I'd encountered him. But George Pete, as I vividly recalled (and here I unconsciously reached down to rub my calf in the vicinity of his dog's initial assault), drove a pickup, as did Sapers. The chances, then, were that neither was present. Of course, all this was purely speculative in any case, as I had no intention whatever of passing through that redwood door.

It was then that I had an inspiration. I'd been sitting there for nearly half an hour, getting nowhere, when it suddenly occurred to me to call Vogelsang. He was, after all, the manager of this operation, wasn't he? Its guiding light and chief executive? I pictured him cozily ensconced with Aorta in his Bolinas museum, calmly chewing fish flakes while he rearranged his femur collection or sorted through his box of glass dog eyes. Yes. I'd call the son of a bitch and lay the whole thing in his lap, force him to make the decision for me. Hello? he'd say. Vogelsang, I'd say, this is Felix. I'm quitting. Yes, of course—why hadn't I thought of it before?

The hinges of the big redwood door grated like marrowless bones, cigarette smoke and rockabilly yelping enveloped me, one foot followed the other, and once again I found myself standing before the bar in Shirelle's Bum Steer. The place was precisely as I'd remembered it, no detail altered: the gallon jars of pickled eggs and bloated sausage, the souvenir pennant, the dusty bottles of liqueur. Shirelle, in mauve eyeshadow and a pink see-through blouse that looked like the top part of a nightie, was hunched over the telephone at the far end of the bar. In back, the customary Indians leaned over the pool table as if they were part of the décor, while at the bar, two old men were engaged in a raucous debate. "I say it was the best thing I ever tasted in my life," hooted the first, who seemed to be the randy old coffee drinker from the diner—or his morose counterpart. "Aaah, you're a iggorant shitsack," said the other, whom I recognized as George Pete Turner's emaciated crony. "Any fool knows you can't cook a decent piece of salmon without a slab of fatback pork to season the pan."

I took a seat at the end of the bar and glanced significantly at Shirelle, who ignored me. She was exchanging passionate tidbits over the line with some up-country Lothario—Delbert Skaggs's most recent successor, no doubt—and had neither time nor inclination to see to the needs of her customers. I was annoyed. But even more so when I saw that she was using the public telephone—obviously the only one in the place—which hung from the wall in a disused nook at the nether end of the bar. I dug out a ten-dollar bill, creased it, and laid it on the counter. "Shit," snorted the old boy from the diner, "and I suppose them beans you fed me and Gerard last Saint Pat's day was supposed to be something fancy, huh? Chili con carney, Texas style, is what you called it, didn't you?" Pool balls clicked behind me, one maudlin jukebox tune dissolved in a jangle of trebly guitars and another started up without pause. I slapped the bar and jerked my finger at Shirelle.

I watched as she poured a final dollop of lewdness into the receiver, set it on the bar and came toward me, bosoms heaving beneath the flimsy blouse. She gave me a toothy smile that didn't show the least hint of recognition—just as well, I thought—and said, "What'll it be, honey?"

I ordered a Remy with a soda back. She poured herself three fingers of vodka and served me the cognac in a smudged water glass.

"You call them beans? I'd as soon have eat my own socks as that hog swill."

"Godammit now, McCarey," George Pete's crony snarled, "you're going to get me steamed you keep up like that. Thirty-seven years I put in in that kitchen at Tootses' in San Jose and I'll be a bare-assed monkey if I can't out-chop, out-fry and out-charbroil a sorry scumbag like you any day of the week."

"Thanks," I said, as Shirelle set my drink down. "Are you going to be using the phone much longer?"

"Oh, no, no, no," she said, already leaning back toward the recumbent receiver like a dancer doing a stretching exercise, "just a minute or two more, that's all."

I lingered over my drink. Not simply because cognac is meant to be lingered over, but because I had neither the money nor the intent to overindulge: I was there to make a phone call. Period. I thought about nothing, the music droned on without pause, George Pete Turner's crony waxed passionate on the subject of batter-dipped okra. When my glass had been empty for some minutes, I motioned once again for Shirelle, but she didn't seem to notice. She was bent over the phone, both hands cradling the mouthpiece, her rear projecting at an angle and twitching idly. I began to develop an intense dislike for her.

I slapped the bar again, more violently than before. This time not only did Shirelle look up, but the two epicures as well. They'd been arguing a fine point of ham-hock preparation—whether to add flat or fresh beer to the stock—and both now desisted to turn and give me a wondering, distracted look. Shirelle again set the receiver down and joggled toward me. "Another?"

I pushed the glass forward. My voice was strung tight. "The phone?" I said.

Her laugh was like a bird of prey, shooting from its perch to swoop down and stun its object with a single explosive thrust. "My God!" she shrieked, "I'm so embarrassed! You know, I just forgot all about you, honey." She puckered her lips and blew me a sympathetic kiss. "I'll just be a sec," and then the phone was stuck to the side of her face again, for all the world like some kind of malignant growth.

I was on my third drink before I finally got to the telephone. I couldn't seem to find Vogelsang's number in my wallet, so I had to go through information, losing a fistful of dimes in the process and systematically alienating three or four operators. He wasn't listed, of course—except under one of his many aliases. The aliases were a joke, like the ads he ran in *The Berkeley Barb*. Dr. Bang was one of them. I tried it. No listing. With the aid of a fourth cognac, I began to recall others: O. O. Ehrenfurt, Malachi Mortis, Teet Creamburg. Nothing. I was frustrated, angry, nervous—each failure seemed to intensify the crisis, drum at my stomach, raise the ugly specter of Jerpbak from the grave of distilled spirits in which Shirelle had helped bury it. Just as I was about to give up, I remembered a company name he'd used two or three years back—Plumtree's Potted Meats—and I had the exasperated operator try it. To my surprise and everlasting relief, she did show a listing for Plumtree.

My fingers trembled as I dialed, the words etched in acid on my tongue: *I'm quitting, getting out, flying the coop, throwing in the towel*. There was a click, the line engaged, and I was suddenly assaulted by a mechanical hiss immediately followed by an ineptly recorded version of "Sweet Georgia Brown" done entirely on Moog Synthesizer and what sounded like an off-key triangle. After a full two minutes of this, Vogelsang's recorded voice came over the wire:

> What is home without
> Plumtree's Potted Meat?
> Incomplete.
> With it an abode of bliss.

This was succeeded by a rasping evil snicker that suggested nothing so much as a Bluebeard or a Dr. Mengele in the midst of one of his experiments, and then the click that disengaged the line.

None of this had given me much satisfaction. Whereas a moment before I'd been anticipating the release of unburdening myself—of arguing, cursing, demanding explanations for the inexplicable and allowing myself to be soothed by Vogelsang's crisp, confident tones and professorial diction—I was once again adrift, already two sheets to the wind and utterly paralyzed with indecision. What to do? Buzz into San Francisco and stuff loyalty, camaraderie, responsibility and trust, or creep back to the summer camp like a condemned man waiting for the blade to fall? I didn't have a clue.

Huddled there in the corner and clutching the receiver as if it were a resuscitory device, I sipped at my drink and glanced forlornly round the room. A blue haze of cigarette smoke blurred the atmosphere and dimmed the feeble flicker of the wall fixtures (which were molded, I noticed, in the shape of steer horns). I could just make out the form of the three Indians, all lined up in a row now, gravely chalking their cues and contemplating the configuration of balls on the table before them as if it held the key to the secrets of the universe. Shirelle had joined the two epicures at the bar and was engaged in a hot debate over the length of time a three-minute egg should be cooked.

I finished my cognac. In combination, and on an empty stomach, the drinks were beginning to have a twofold effect—first, of intensifying my feelings of guilt and disloyalty, and second, of exacerbating the panic I felt over the nasty coincidences that had begun to infest my life. I sat there, half-drunk, warring with myself. I probed an ear for wax, toyed with a coaster that showed a red-nosed man crashing a car through his own bedroom wall, tapped my feet on the brass bar-rail. And then, as I couldn't decide what to do—I found I was unable either to let go of the receiver or to get up from the barstool—I thought I might as well take things a step at a time and put something on my stomach. When Shirelle turned to pour herself another double vodka, I ordered a beer and two pickled eggs.

I don't know what it was—the taste of the eggs, the odor of the vinegar or the odd amalgam of egg, vinegar, soda cracker, and beer—but I was suddenly skewered with nostalgia. These eggs, this beer, this depressing disreputable rundown backwater dive—together they recalled other eggs, other beer, other dives. I thought of a college friend who'd spent every waking moment cloistered in a saloon killing piss-yellow pitchers of draft beer and whose only sustenance derived from beer nuts, beef jerky and pickled eggs. Brain food, he called it. He drank up his book money, his date money, his food, rent, gas and clothes money, he grew pale, his flesh turned to butter. I worried about him—until I quit school. The graduation announcement came the following year, his name prominent at the top of the page, summa cum laude. I thought of a girl named Cynthia, who climbed mountains, wore lederhosen over her rippling calves and once let me creep under a table in a dark bar and stick my head between her thighs. I thought of fights, forged ID's, vomit-streaked Fords. The eggs tasted as if they'd been unearthed in an Etruscan tomb, the beer was flat. I ate mechanically. Faces drifted into my consciousness, epoch by epoch, counters on an abacus. Then I thought of Dwight Dunn.

Like Phil, Dwight was a touchstone. We'd gone to school together, double-dated, squeezed pimples side by side, we'd struck out, scored, experimented with tobacco, alcohol and drugs together, we'd postured, pronounced, chased the same women, earnestly discussed Nietzsche and Howlin' Wolf late into the night. Dwight had been best man at my wedding; when his father died I flew in from the West Coast and sat up with him. We were children, adolescents, bewildered adults. Dwight had stayed in New York—he was living on East 59th Street now and working for a public relations firm—but we'd kept in touch. Unlike Phil, he was a straight arrow, steady—I could picture the baggy chinos, madras shirts and Hush Puppies he favored, and the look of pained concentration (as if he'd been forced to decipher *Finnegans Wake* while undergoing electroshock treatment) the contact lenses gave him. Dwight, I thought, alcohol tugging at my flesh, good old Dwight. At that moment I was visited with my second inspiration of the evening: I would call him, call him and listen to his soft stuttering laugh and the comforting rhythms of his speech.

I dialed like a man in a burning building. Come on, I thought, counting the clicks, and then the information operator was on the wire, quick and efficient, and I scribbled the number on my bar napkin and called collect.

"Hello?" Dwight's voice sounded distant, weary. For an instant I thought I'd wakened him—but no, it was just after ten in New York.

The long-distance operator interceded with a deadpan impression of Desi Arnaz: "Colleck call for anywan from Fee-lix: will you 'cept the charge?"

"What?" A tapping came over the line, and I envisioned a repairman in Kansas hammering a downed wire back in place. "Yes, yes—put him on."

"Dwight?"

"Felix?"

"How you doing?"

"Fine," he said. "What's up?"

I couldn't tell him, couldn't give him specifics anyway. "Oh, I don't know. I'm a little depressed." Just then Shirelle threw back her head and laughed like an abandoned old whore with a meter on every orifice. "Did I tell you I'm rooming with Phil?"

We talked for half an hour before I understood the reason I'd called. "Listen, Dwight," I said finally, "you think you could read me something from one of your notebooks?"

Dwight was a compulsive record-keeper—no, he was pathological, half a step removed from the crazy who keeps his own feces in labeled fruit jars. Not only did he list every experience he'd ever had—everything from breaking up with his girlfriend, rupturing his spleen or being victimized by pickpockets in Madrid to buying a pair of shoelaces—he kept track of every meal he'd eaten, the clothes he wore, states, counties and municipalities visited and distances traveled, gifts given and received, feelings felt, gas, electricity and water consumed, the number of points he'd scored in an intramural basketball game in junior high, cab fares, tips, the books he'd read, movies he'd seen (including where and with whom), records, shoes and nose drops purchased, every bowel movement, hiccough, belch and whimper of his life. He could tell you how many streetlamps line FDR Drive and how many times he'd passed under them, give you a blow-by-blow account of a trip he'd made to visit his grandparents when he was thirteen, describe Radio City Music Hall in terms of the number and texture of the seats.

I could appreciate what he was trying to do—each of us to a greater or lesser degree has the same impulse, after all, the same need to impose order on our sloppy irrational lives in the face of an indifferent universe. I could appreciate it, and benefit from it as well. My past and Dwight's intersected at any number of points: he'd recorded my history, too.

Within moments I could hear the rustle of turning pages, and then Dwight's familiar nasal tones: "Know how many points you scored against Fox Lane on January 18, 1967?"

Nineteen sixty-seven. Amazing. I had a vision of myself—alive, free, untrammeled and untroubled, dribbling an inflated sphere up and down a polished wooden floor as if nothing else in the world mattered. "How many?" I breathed.

"Twelve." A page turned. "You remember who else was on the team?"

I listed them, all of them, right down to the benchwarmers—the thyroid freaks with the pinheads and the muscular little guys who weren't quite quick enough to make first-string guard.

Then he was reading: "June 10, 1969. Picked up Felix at eight p.m. in my father's Charger, took fifteen point two gallons of gas at thirty-one cents a gallon for a total of four seventy-one, and then drove to Port Chester to pick up Sherrie Ryan and Ginger Beardsley. I was wearing my new maroon bellbottoms and . . ."

The voice went on, precise and evenly modulated, the voice of order and reason, the voice that proved my past and promised the future. I just listened, nodding, memory blooming like a field of clover. We must have talked for an hour and a half. I was working on my third beer and sixth egg when we finished, and feeling that God was in His heaven and all was right with the world. "Dwight," I said, my voice a pant of gratitude, "thanks." The receiver fell into its cradle with a click gentle as a kiss.

When I finally looked up, I saw that the Indians had gone—the light over the pool table had been extinguished and the rear of the bar faded into shadow. The two epicures at the bar were still there, though, and I saw that they'd been joined by a hefty young couple who brooded over a pair of highballs like inspectors from the Bureau of Alcohol and Firearms. Shirelle was nowhere to be seen.

Suddenly George Pete's crony lifted his head and roared, "Soak them beans, for Christsake!" as if he were announcing a cavalry charge. The other old fellow seemed pretty far gone—he just waved his hand vaguely.

I was feeling better than I had for weeks. I'd made my decision (of course I was staying; I'd go to jail forever—welcome it—lock myself in at Attica with savage perverts or swim out to Devil's Island, before I'd let down my friends and buddies), and it was as if I'd been set free, the fetters loosened, no more vulture come to feed on my liver. How could I even have thought of quitting? There was nothing more vital than the kind of friendship I had with Dwight, with Phil, with Gesh, and it was worth any sacrifice to sustain it. The alcohol spoke to me, my abraded nerves sank into their sheaths like sleeping tortoises. I felt light, holy, ecstatic: I could have gotten up and kissed everybody in the place.

What I would do, I decided, was have one more cognac to celebrate the rite of passage I'd endured, and then head on up the hill to the summer camp, get a good night's sleep and go out in the morning to cultivate my garden, as resigned and sensible as Candide on the shores of Marmora. As if on cue, Shirelle reappeared, emerging from the door behind the bar with a case of no-name scotch, gin, vodka and rum. I smirked at her like some dapper character out of a forties movie and knocked over my empty beer glass. "Shirelle," I said, my tongue somehow glued to the roof of my mouth, "one more Remy, please. With a soda back." And then, as if this simple request needed amplification: "I'm celebrating."

Shirelle's eyes were veined with red, as if she'd just finished a hundred laps in an over-chlorinated pool. The bottle floated in her hand like a helium balloon, and on the first pass she missed the glass entirely, splashing bar, coaster, her left hand and my right with expensive imported booze. Then she connected, filled the water glass halfway, wordlessly snatched up my money and lurched over to join the fat-faced pair at the other end of the bar.

"Half a quart of vinegar, a box of peppercorns and a whole shaker of salt—the whole damn thing—to a gallon of water," George Pete's crony said.

"What's that for?" asked the broader of the two new arrivals, who seemed to be female. "Footsoak?"

"Oh, gawd." George Pete's crony rolled his bulging eyes. "Ever'body's a iggoramus tonight—that's my genuine Chesapeake Bay crab boil."

The other old boy, the one in coveralls, was asleep, hands in his lap and forehead pressed to the bar as if he were a devotee of some obscure Far Eastern religion.

I felt warm. A voice mewled over the jukebox: *Well, here I stand,/All alone with a broken heart,/I took three bennies/And now my semi-truck won't start*. Time escaped me. I had another cognac.

It was then, just after I'd ordered the second post-phone-call drink—or was it the third?—that I felt a pressure on my arm and turned to see that someone had taken possession of the stool next to mine. I was too far gone to be startled: it was Savoy. Her hand was on my arm, a tall frosted glass of Coke sizzled on the bar before her. She was wearing a low-cut blouse and one of those complicated uplift bras that separate the bosoms and present them like ripe mangoes. "Hi," she said. "Haven't seen you in a while."

"Oh," I said, shrugging, waving my hand and licking the tips of my fingers like a third-base coach in the throes of a seizure, "it's no big thing. Been keeping busy, that's all." Eugene's locket clung to her throat like a magnet. I wanted to lick it.

"Yeah?" she said, grinning wide. "You living around here now or what?"

Boom, went the jukebox. *Boom*, *boom*, *boom*.

"Wanna dance?" I said.

She shook her head no and took a sip of her Coke. Pink lipstick, white straw. "Your name's Felix, right?"

I nodded. "And you're Savoy." I grinned like a deviate, like a billy goat.

She ignored me. Sucked thoughtfully at her straw a moment. "So you guys living up here now or what?" she said, repeating her question with a slight but significant variation.

"Blood raw!" roared George Pete's crony.

His interlocutor, who'd partially revived and propped his head on a bent elbow, squinted one eye and hissed, "Your ass!"

"Not really," I lied.

She laughed, a rich musical sound that inflamed every fiber of my reproductive tract. "No," she said, leaning into me, "I really want to know. I like you guys, I do."

"Well, if you put it that way," I said, making a stab at wit and raising my eyebrows to acknowledge the sexual innuendo, "we live in Berkeley, but we've been coming up here a lot—oh, it must be three or four times now—to go fishing, you know, trout and all."

"Come off it. You're living up by Lloyd Sapers's place, aren't you?"

"Sapers? Never heard of him."

She looked offended, her mouth puckered in a little moue. "What do you take me for—stupid or something?"

"Hah!" shouted George Pete's toothless compatriot, apropos of some culinary conviction forcefully expressed. "Hah! Hah! Hah! Don't make me laugh."

Savoy was staring into my eyes, cold and intent. A moment ago I'd felt warm, lit up, ready to lick the world: now I felt cold, cold, cold. "Come off it," she repeated, as if she'd forgotten her lines. "Come off it, will you? Everybody in town knows what you guys are doing up there."

PART 3
Efflorescence

Chapter 1

In June, the weather altered abruptly. Whereas before we'd shivered through a perpetual riveting downpour that made every moment of hole-digging or fence-stringing a curse and a trial, now suddenly we blistered under an unmoving sadistic sun. It was as if we'd been magically transported—house, weeds, garbage and all—from the windward coast of Scotland to the desert outside Tucson. One night the wind rattled up out of the south with the choking roar of an invading army—trucks in low gear, feet tramping across the roof—and in the morning it was clear. And dry. So dry that Phil's pompadour went permanently limp and our bathtowels stiffened to the consistency of redwood bark. You could feel the change in your nostrils, in your throat; you could hear it in the dry, tortured groans of the house, see it in the shimmering air and wilting weeds and in the slow-wheeling helices of vultures riding the thermal currents. Ninety-five degrees, ninety-six, one-oh-two. Lizards appeared from nowhere, as if they'd been conjured from the air, hummingbirds hung like mobiles over the bells of flowers, streams fell back and left their banks exposed like toothless gums. Mud caked, dried, fragmented to dust. The arid season was upon us.

We were ready for it. As ready as the reddest-necked cracker in the Imperial Valley, as ready as the Israelis on the Negev. Or so we thought. By May 31, when workers elsewhere were grilling hot dogs and singing "God Bless America," we were putting the finishing touches to an elaborate irrigation system engineered by Vogelsang, approved by Dowst and realized (i.e., hauled, hammered, cut, glued, joined and bled over) by Phil, Gesh and me. The mainstay of this system was a used gasoline-powered water pump for which Vogelsang had paid $100 at a foreclosure sale. Theoretically, the pump would suck water from the year-round stream at the base of the mountain, force it through the camouflaged lengths of one-inch plastic pipe we'd laid and connected, and then push it all the way up the mountain's five hundred fifty vertical feet and into the big horse-troughs situated above the Khyber Pass, our highest growing area. From there, the water would gravity-feed to smaller reservoirs consisting of clusters of fifty-five-gallon drums, and thence to the hand-held hoses from which we would provide each plant with the two to three gallons of water it needed daily.

The first problem we encountered was a familiar one: noise. When all the pipe had been painted, laid and linked, and all the connections made to the reservoirs, we gathered at the base of the hill to fire up the pump and inaugurate the system. It was a ceremonial occasion, and we stood around clutching slippery cans of beer while Vogelsang bent to make minute adjustments to the gasoline feed, the filter, the carburetor. Mosquitoes whined, the stream slid over obstructions with a languid splash and trickle. I thought of railroad men come together for the driving of the final spike, or boutonniered politicians toasting the first explosive rush of water that flooded the Erie Canal.

The day was hot, one of the first true scorchers we'd had, the sun raging through the trees like a forest fire. We were swallowed up in the clot of vegetation that lined the streambed, and it seemed as if the leaves caught and held the air until it reared up and slapped us in the face. Gesh was running sweat, his eyes slits, cheekbones glistening as if they'd been oiled; Phil's clothes were soaked through; I could taste the salt on my lips. Only Vogelsang seemed oblivious to the heat. Dressed in goggles, gloves, surgeon's mask and jumpsuit, and with a .44 magnum strapped incongruously round his waist, he had spent the better part of the morning creeping through the scrub to inspect each joint and coupling along the pipeline. Now, as he hunched over the pump with wrench and screwdriver, I was surprised to discover that not a single damp spot darkened the khaki jumpsuit. I was marveling over this revelation—*he doesn't even sweat*, I thought in amazement—when he stood, brushed the knees of his pants and jerked the starter cord.

Our cheers were drowned in the roar of the engine, which was at least six decibels louder than the one we'd abandoned outside the cabin. The beers popped soundlessly, blue-black coils of exhaust clutched at us before twisting off to darken the sky, the engine screamed its animate agony. Phil looked unhappy, Gesh gritted his teeth. If Vogelsang was disturbed, he gave no sign of it—he merely stood there, arms akimbo, staring down at the thing as if he were contemplating a painting in a gallery. Aorta never even turned her head. In shorts and halter top, she perched on a rock in midstream and serenely tapped her foot to a private rhythm, her ability to register auditory shock evidently impaired through her association with the Nostrils. *Rat-a-rap-rap*, screamed the engine, *rap-rap-rap*. Gesh bellowed something in my ear, but it was lost in the machine-gun rattle of the engine; I concentrated on swallowing without choking on my tongue. After five minutes or so, Vogelsang shut the thing down, then lifted his surgeon's mask and turned to us. "You'll have to dig a pit."

We dug. Four feet down in yellowish clay. Sweat flowing, mosquitoes harassing, beer gone sour in our throats. Then we set the pump in the trench, threw a slab of plywood over it and buried the muffler in sand. "That should do it," Vogelsang said.

As Gesh, Phil and I started up the hill, he turned the engine over again and I thought at first we were under attack, the fulminating blast of machinery so unexpected, so obscene and startling in the quiet of the woods. Phil shouted something to the effect that laboratory rats chewed off their own feet when subjected to loud and unremitting noise, but already the trees had begun to muffle the blare of the pump, taking the edge off it in the way a mute softens a trumpet. We would barely hear it from the house, I realized, but Gesh, who had long since identified Vogelsang as the enemy, wasn't mollified. "Terrific," he said, loping up the hill. "That's about as subtle as the London blitz."

The second problem was more complicated, human rather than mechanical. The problem was Lloyd Sapers. According to legal agreement, Sapers had access to the central road bisecting our property and plunging down into the valley to the southeast. This was his fire road—his escape route in the event that the primary road was blocked by fire, no mean consideration in an area that grew progressively drier until at the end of the season the hills were as volatile as balls of newsprint soaked in gasoline.

On the morning after we'd broken in the irrigation system, Vogelsang, Aorta and I were gathered around the breakfast table while Phil and Gesh watered the Khyber Pass and Dowst huddled in the greenhouse, trying to perform horticultural miracles with a handful of withered seeds and a bucket of Nutri-Grow. Since his arrival two nights earlier—he'd come, reluctantly, to oversee the completion of the irrigation system—Vogelsang had been jumpy as an air-raid warden. Nervous about everything from poison oak to pot poachers to detection and arrest by the DEA, FBI, IRS and the Willits Sheriff's Department, he was practically clonic, every facial muscle twitching, fingers drumming the tabletop, legs beating like pistons. In a word, he was wired.

This was understandable. With a forest of eighteen-inch plants in the ground, we were all edgy—they had the goods on us now—but Phil, Gesh and I had come to grips with our fears. Or at least we tried to obliterate them through the abuse of drugs and alcohol and an unwavering commitment to the sustaining visions of Rio, Cajun seafood houses and fat bank accounts. We had no other choice: unlike Vogelsang, we had to live with the threat of exposure day in and day out. For well over a month, for that matter, I'd been living with the knowledge of what Savoy had said to me that night—*everybody knows what you guys are doing up there*—a festering little secret, hidden close. Before the words had passed her lips I was on my feet, pretending I hadn't heard her, making apologies. I glanced at my watch, slapped my forehead, shrugged into my jacket and staggered out the door like a hamstrung deer. When I got back to the cabin, the lights were out. Just as well, I thought, inching my way through the darkness to my room, spun round with alcohol, panic and the finality of my decision. I was in this thing to the end: Give me pot, or give me death, I thought, giggling to myself. No teenager with an uplift bra and unsized eyes was going to scare me off it, nor Jerpbak, voodoo calendars or shotguns, either. I could take it, liberated by the pledge I'd made myself, burst from under the pall of the sickness unto death and into the light of faith. But why worry Phil and Gesh?

Now, with Vogelsang twitching across the table and rattling on about Krugerrands, gypsum and Oriental rugs, I couldn't resist sticking it to him just a bit, as he'd stuck it to me over the issue of the guns. "Oh, by the way," I said, cutting him off in the middle of a panegyric to Bokharan weavers, "did I tell you a plane came over the other day?"

Vogelsang set down his spoon, shot a glance out the window and then fumbled in his pocket for the vial of breath neutralizer. "Really?" he said, a barely perceptible sob cracking his voice.

"Cessna, I think. One of those little jobs with the sculpted cockpit and the propeller out front?"

He nodded. His features were drawn together, a string bag tightening at the neck, and the veins in his temple began to pulse.

The plane had come roaring over the hill, big as a truck, no more than three hundred feet up. It buzzed the house twice, then circled the property and vanished over the far ridge. When it appeared Phil and I were out in the yard, fully exposed, unloading lengths of PVC pipe from the back of the pickup. First there was the explosion of noise, then the dust and the big swooping shadow, and then Phil was bolting for the house shouting, "Load up the car!" He'd actually tossed two boxes of his priceless mementoes into the back of the Jeep before I could calm him down.

"Probably from that airstrip in Willits," Vogelsang said. "One of those weekend daredevils."

I shrugged. "Whatever. But it wasn't pleasant, that's for sure. With two thousand holes in the ground this place must look like Swiss cheese from up there."

Vogelsang rapped the tabletop with the vial of breath sanitizer, then raised it to his mouth for a quick fix, as if vigilance against halitosis were the first step in his plan to subvert detection and subdue the world to his fiduciary advantage. Aorta slouched over an uneaten bowl of Familia, absorbed in a copy of *Soldier of Fortune* magazine, her nose ring flaring in a ray of early-morning sunlight. I was about to amplify the story of the Cessna—*the eye in the sky*, Gesh had called it—when suddenly the cabin began to tremble on its frame and a rumbling burst of sound threw me from my chair.

Earthquake? Lightning bolt? The Russian invasion? The three of us lurched back from the table and rushed to the window, where we watched in stupefaction as an odd little parade passed in review. Sapers, on a huge thundering bulldozer, was steaming along the road adjacent to the house, followed by his son, Marlon, on a flatulent Moped. Intent on the controls and hunched in his filthy coveralls, Sapers never even turned his head; Marlon, his glasses glinting in the sun and big fleshy thighs and rear engulfing the bike as an amoeba might engulf a food particle, looked up, flashed us the peace sign, and then vanished into the trees along with his father.

For an instant we were immobilized, struck dumb with panic and outrage. Then all three of us were out the door in blistering pursuit. "What the hell does he think he's doing?" I choked as we leapt obstacles in the field and sprinted into the narrow roadway like hurdlers coming on for the tape. I was incensed, mortified, shot through with homicidal rage. What if he blundered off the road and into one of the growing areas? What if he caught sight of Gesh and Phil with the hoses or heard the pump? Vogelsang cursed, a series of truncated, doglike grunts, as he pumped his legs and flailed his goggles like a weapon; Aorta, gritting her teeth, ran neck-and-neck with us for a hundred yards or so before she stumbled and pitched forward into the dirt. We hardly noticed.

Vogelsang and I were nearly at the bottom of the hill, a few hundred yards east of the water pump, when we ran out of breath and slowed to an agitated, stiff-legged walk. Hearts hammering, we hurried along the roadway until we emerged from a stand of laurel to see Sapers up ahead of us, maneuvering the bulldozer as if he were taking evasive action. As we drew closer, we could see Marlon standing in the shade of a tree and drinking something from a thermos, while his father dropped the blade of the bulldozer and began slamming away at the surface of the road. "Oh, Christ," Vogelsang said, quickening his gait, "he's grading the road."

He was indeed. We watched helplessly as he reversed gears, swung right and left, rumbled forward behind a ridge of detritus, cleared culverts, crushed vegetation, leveled and de-rutted the nearly impassable roadway. Gears wheezed, black diesel smoke snatched at the sky. "Hey!" I shouted, but the big polished treads just kept grinding along. Sweat coursed over my body—streams, rivulets, mighty deltas—the sun raked my face and thrust a clawing hand down my throat. Beside me, Vogelsang danced in place, pogo-ing up and down like a Masai tribesman. Though his face was concealed, I took his body language to indicate that he was feeling as disturbed, confused and impotent as I was. A few minutes later Aorta limped up to join us, and after watching the bulldozer churn back and forth a moment longer, we turned as if by accord and strolled over to where Marlon stood in the shade of a twisted oak.

"Hello," Vogelsang said, peeling back his surgical mask. Marlon's immediate reaction was to bend awkwardly for the big plastic thermos and cradle it in his arms, as if he was afraid we'd come to snatch it away. He didn't say a word, merely blinked at us out of pale demented eyes. His head was cropped as closely as Aorta's, and it seemed disproportionately small against the bulk of him, the head of an ostrich or a sleepy brontosaur. "You know how far up the road your father's planning to go?" Vogelsang asked.

Marlon looked wildly from Vogelsang's face to mine, as if we'd asked him to betray his family to the Gestapo or drop his pants and recite poetry, before his eyes finally settled on Aorta. A change suddenly came over his face. He gave her a long, lingering, stupefied look, a look compounded of wonder, greed and unbridled anarchic lust, and then he flushed red and turned away.

"Marlon," I snapped, striving for that tone of inquisitorial menace and condescension mastered by schoolmarms, drill sergeants and professional torturers, "you're on private property now, you know—our property—and we want to know just what you think you're doing here." Meanwhile, I noticed with mounting panic that Sapers was moving his bulldozer back up the road in the direction from which we'd just come—toward the hill and our burgeoning secret.

Marlon looked down at his feet (they were encased in black sneakers the size of griddles), and then lifted the thermos to his mouth and took a huge slobbering swallow that left his chin streaked with dark liquid and his shirtfront damp. He bobbed his head and his mouth began to work, some terrible trauma pushing itself up from his inner depths to convulse his frame with seismic shudders. "Drinking Coke," he said finally with a sob. Then he turned his back on us and his great fleshy shoulders began to heave.

All at once there was a hoot of surprise from Sapers and we jerked round to watch him ram the bulldozer into neutral and leap down from the thing in a geyser of water. Even from where we were standing I could see the ruptured plastic pipe, snapped like a twig and flung over the cutting edge of the blade in a sorry inverted *V*. Water spurted thirty feet into the air—a magic fountain, a gusher, a lid-flipped hydrant on 142nd Street—and suddenly we were running again. Out of breath, crazed, our cards laid out on the table for anyone to read.

As we drew closer I could see that Sapers was clearly bewildered, the Willits Feed cap clutched in one grimy hand while the other scratched at the back of his head. "Lloyd!" Vogelsang shouted, stripping back goggles and hood, and Sapers turned to us with the blank uncomprehending stare of a flood or quake victim. "Lloyd, it's me, Vogelsang." Sapers had, of course, been aware of us all along, but had chosen to go about the business at hand rather than bother with social amenities. He had nothing to say to us in any case. Now, though, as I saw the look of enlightenment fan across his features, I realized that he couldn't have recognized Vogelsang in his jumpsuit. He'd probably mistaken him for an escapee from the burn ward or a commando versed in chemical warfare—just another manifestation of the hostile weirdness we'd brought to his sleepy corner of the woods.

We stood beside him now, Vogelsang grinning, Aorta scowling, the water slashing up into the burnt sky and plummeting down to explode in the dust. I felt like a circus animal—tiger, bear, lion—driven by the whip and making my final approach to the burning hoop. "What in God's hell is that?" Sapers said finally. He was referring to the plastic pipe, which we'd buried beneath the disused roadway some two weeks earlier. I shrugged. Aorta put her hands on her hips and gave him a why-don't-you-go-fuck-yourself stare. "Beats me," Vogelsang said. "Christ, Lloyd, you know I hardly just bought the place—there's all sorts of surprises here."

"But, but . . ." For the first time since I'd had the misfortune of meeting him, Sapers seemed at a loss for words. "But," he stammered, waving his hand to take in the entire scene, "I been grading this road for twenty years and there's never been no pipes in here before."

Vogelsang laughed, a maniacal, wound-up, child-molester's laugh. "Christ," he said, repeating himself, as if the invocation of a higher authority could somehow get him off the hook, "I just don't know how to explain it, Lloyd. It's as much a mystery to me as it is to you." Vogelsang patted frantically at his pockets, searching for the breath neutralizer, which he finally located and used with obvious relief. "I guess we'll just have to contact the DWP and see what they've been doing up here."

Sapers looked skeptical—he knew as well as I did that the water department had no business out in the hind end of the wilderness, that Vogelsang's implication was as preposterous and unfounded as if he'd attributed the pipe to Soviet intervention or UFOs. From skepticism, he shifted to suspicion. I could see the change in his face, could see that he was about to say something more, something tougher, something that would poke holes in the entire fabric of lies we'd thrown up to mask our real purpose, when suddenly the gush of water fizzled out. One moment it was spouting like Old Faithful, and the next it was the trickle of a child at a urinal.

"I'll be damned," Sapers said.

Vogelsang put on a look of consternation and wonder, a look as phony as mine. The water had given out for a simple and intelligible reason: the pump had shut down. As programmed. We'd gauged the amount of gasoline required to run the pump until all our reservoirs were filled—at that point, the pump ran out of gas and shut itself down. *Chuff-chuff, bang*. Simple as that.

We were standing around scratching our heads when suddenly a shadow fell across my back, and I swung round to confront a dejected Marlon, the thermos wedged beneath one fleshy arm, his eyes red with weeping. Behind us, the earthmover idled with a subdued chuffing roar, its surfaces glistening with water. Vogelsang had stepped forward to make a show of casually tossing the pipe aside, as if it meant nothing in the world to him—as if, like the rocks and trees and insects, it were just another manifestation of the marvelous in an endlessly puzzling universe—and was assuring Sapers that he'd look into the matter and straighten things out with the DWP or "whoever it was that was responsible." Marlon began to whimper.

"What's with you?" Sapers snarled.

The boy pointed a thick accusing finger at me. "He . . . he yelled at me, pop."

Sapers gave me a quick withering glance, a glance of contempt, hatred and disgust, then shot his eyes at his son. "Aaah, shut yer face, Fathead." Then he looked at me again, a wicked little grin tugging at the corners of his mouth. "So," he roared, "how's the writin' goin', Shakespeare?"

The third problem was neither mechanical nor human. It was instead a manifestation of the wilderness itself, of nature red in tooth and claw, of the teeming, irrational life that surrounds and subsumes us and that our roads and edifices and satellites struggle so hard to deny. It became evident about two weeks after the bulldozer incident. Vogelsang had long since repaired to the cool, umbrageous, sumac-free corridors of his Bolinas lodge, the sun had mounted a degree or two higher in the blistering sky, and the vital, life-sustaining flow of the irrigation system had settled into a pattern of smooth reliability we'd begun to take for granted. Then, one torrid morning (we watered in the morning and evening, for obvious reasons and in accordance with Dowst's superfluous instructions), as I picked up the hose to drench our Jonestown growing area in cool translucent aqua pura, I was stunned to find that none was forthcoming. Perplexed, I flailed the hose along its coiled length, stretched it, peered into the nozzle like a clown in a slapstick routine. Nothing. Next, I followed the hose to the nearest cluster of 55-gallon drums, only to find them empty, and finally made my lung-wrenching way up the precipitous incline to the main reservoir above the Khyber Pass. There I discovered that all six 330-gallon horse-troughs were dry, and concluded that the pump must have malfunctioned. But after stumbling back down the spine of the mountain, through thorn and briar and banks of stinging nettle, I found that the pump had in fact dutifully consumed its gas, pumped its water and shut itself down. So where was the water?

My cohorts were hunched blearily over breakfast when I stepped through the door and informed them that there was a major break somewhere along the pipeline. They yawned, scratched, farted, their eyes like hunted things. A fork rang out as it made contact with knife or plate, two pairs of lips sucked at the rims of coffee mugs. Since the heat had set in, we'd taken to staying up late into the night, drinking, shooting the bull, playing poker, Monopoly, and pitch, and resting through the ferocious dizzying heat of the afternoon. We alternated morning watering assignments, Dowst pulling his weight like the rest of us—when he was there. On this particular morning, as on most mornings, he was not there. No: he was in Sausalito, in his breezy, ocean-cooled apartment, no doubt knocking himself out to come up with the additional seeds we so desperately needed.

Gesh looked up from a greasy plate of scrambled eggs and chorizo and asked if I'd checked the pump. I nodded. Phil was bent over a sketch pad. The fires of artistic expression had been lately rekindled in him by the proximity of so much antique junk—an entire yardful of bedsprings, machine parts and dismantled automobiles—and he was working out the blueprint for a major new sculpture that promised to be "a monument to our heroic agricultural efforts." Without glancing up he asked if I'd checked the upper reservoir. "Uh-huh," I said, pouring myself a cup of coffee that looked and tasted like molasses laced with stomach acid.

There was a ruminative silence, during which a lizard darted out of the breadbox and lashed across the wall, and then Gesh set down his fork and drained his juice glass in a single decisive gulp. "Sounds like there's a break in the line," he announced.

We found it almost immediately. The main line from the pump

had been breached just below the Jonestown area, punctured in half a dozen places as if savaged with a sharp instrument or blasted at close quarters with a .22. "Kids," Phil said. "Fourteen-year-old punks." The pipe, which we'd simply laid out on the surface of the ground, certainly looked as if it had been intentionally vandalized. It was a tense moment. If adolescent vandals were roaming the woods, not only could they wreak havoc on our operation and make off with half the crop, they could expose us to the authorities as well—or perhaps they already had. I watched as the realization filtered through my companions' faces, fear and loathing and murderous intent flickering in their eyes. "Maybe it was Sapers," I said, knowing it wasn't. "Or Marlon?"

It was Gesh, the Angeleno, the city kid, who came up with the conjecture that proved conclusive. "Animals," he said. "Something big." We looked closer. Sure enough, there were the telltale signs: coiled heaps of dung flecked with berries, clumps of stinking reddish hair, tracks the size of Ping-Pong paddles. In the first rush of paranoia we'd somehow managed to overlook them, but now we saw clearly that the agency of destruction was animal rather than human. I guessed that the vandal must have been a bear, but if so, the creature's motives remained obscure. What was the attraction in a twenty-foot length of mottled plastic pipe? Gesh had an answer for this, too: the bear was thirsty. And lazy. Instead of clambering down the hill to the stream, he could drink his fill—and have a shower in the bargain—simply by puncturing any link of our aqueduct he happened across.

The existence of the presumptive bear was confirmed three days later when Phil, buzzing along the lower road on the 125-cc Kawasaki, rounded a corner to discover an obstruction in his path. The obstruction, on closer examination, turned out to be a lumpy, broad-beamed, auburn-colored thing squatting over a fresh mound of berry-flecked excrement: viz., the bear. With a blare of horror the bear lurched up, feinted to the right and then scrambled off down the roadway, Phil in pursuit. The animal's great shaggy hindquarters pumped at the dirt, Phil gripped the accelerator like a fighter ace zeroing in for the kill, leaves rushed by in a blur. One hundred yards, two hundred yards, three. And then, as if he'd been schooled in diversionary tactics, the bear suddenly skewed off into a scrub-choked ravine, while Phil, caught up in the heat of the chase, rammed a downed tree, tore the front wheel from the bike and did a triple-gainer into the stiff brown brush. The Kawasaki was wrecked, and Phil suffered a strained shoulder in addition to contusions both major and minor, but at least we'd firmly and finally established the identity of our antagonist.

An uneventful week slipped by, the heat like the flat of a sword, dull and stultifying, and then the bear struck again. This time he chewed through a pipe on the lower slope, and the enormous pressure of the gravity-feed shattered the plastic and sent a jet of water rocketing forty feet in the air. By the time we arrived on the scene, the dripping ecstatic creature had lumbered off, taking a section of deer fencing and eight healthy cannabis plants with him. "This has got to stop," Gesh growled, kicking angrily at the ravaged pipe. I watched his face through its dangerous permutations, watched as he flung sticks and stones at the mute leaves that surrounded us, bearlike himself in his bulk and his rage. Finally he turned to Phil and me to announce in a dead flat tone that the bear had to go: it was him or us.

Gesh put out poisoned baits that afternoon—marrow bones and kidneys soaked in strychnine—while Phil and I replaced the length of damaged pipe. The bloody heaps of flesh didn't look particularly appetizing, covered as they were with flies both quick and dead, but I assumed it wouldn't make much difference to a scavenging garbagophagist with a taste for plastic pipe and Campbell's Chunky Soup cans. I was wrong. As far as we could tell the bear never touched any of the baits, though one afternoon I did find a dead turkey vulture sprawled in the bushes like a discarded parasol.

As if in compensation for denying himself the baits, the bear took to rummaging through our garbage each night, disemboweling the green plastic bags with the alligator fasteners, gnawing cans and spreading a slick coat of mashed vegetable matter, grease and undifferentiated slime over the porch. Gesh saw this as a provocation. He spent the better part of an afternoon rigging up a battery-powered light system that would illuminate the bewildered scavenger's shaggy nighttime form just long enough to spell his doom. Pissed off, grim, wrapped in an old poncho and chain-smoking joints, Gesh sat up with the shotgun, waiting for the bear to signal his appearance with the fatal clank of can or bottle. When dawn spread her rosy fingers over the eastern sky, garbage was spread over the floorboards of the porch as usual, and Gesh was staring numbly down the barrel of his gun. "Never heard a thing," he said, his voice trailing off.

Then, in a succession of lightning raids, the bear consumed three quarts of motor oil, dragged a section of barbed-wire fence half a mile into the woods, punctured two more lengths of PVC pipe and knocked out the back window of the cabin to get at a case of apricot preserves (which he ate, shards of glass and all, without apparent harm). This time he'd gone too far: it was obvious that he had to be dealt with, and dealt with severely. We began to carry weapons when we made our rounds.

It was a clear, baking, Sonoran-desert sort of morning when I ambled through Julie Andrews's Meadow (now brown as the pampas) on my way to our most remote and least propitious growing area. The plants in the meadow were rigid, verdant and strong, two and a half or three feet high already, and I stopped a minute to admire them. I had a hoe slung over my shoulder, and the .357 magnum pistol tucked in my belt. The hoe was for weeding the sorry marijuana patch we'd dubbed "Duke's Heel," in ironic acknowledgment of George Deukmejian, the fanatical attorney general of the state of California, who'd been known to direct paratroop assaults on isolated marijuana farms and bring in a TV crew to record them; the pistol was for the bear. If I spotted him, I would shoot him. Or at least attempt to.

As I gave the springy serrate leaves a final proprietary pat and headed off across the meadow, I thought how incongruous it all was, how primitive, how much an atavism to go gunning for bear in an age when we couldn't even recognize true dirt. From childhood I'd been taught to revere wildlife, to raise my voice against the multinational corporations, corrupt shepherds, reactionary presidents and robber barons who would strip, rape and pollute the land. I'd sat through ecology classes in high school, turned out for Save the Whale rallies and Tree People boosters and fired off letters to congressmen protesting offshore-drilling amendments. I deplored the slaughter of the bison and passenger pigeon alike, recoiled from the venality of those who draped themselves in ocelot or wore boots fashioned from the belly of the gavial. Who wouldn't? But then it was easy to take a moral stance while munching an avocado-and-sprout sandwich in a carpeted apartment in New York or San Francisco. Now I was on the other side of the fence, now I was confronting nature at the root rather than lying back and reading about it. And at root, nature was dirty, anarchic, undisciplined, an enemy to progress and the American dream. Incongruous though it may have seemed, and though I was subscriber to the principles of the Sierra Club and a member of the Coyote Protective Society, I ambled across that field fingering the pistol and ready—no, seething—to kill.

Duke's Heel consisted of forty stunted plants concealed beneath the canopy of two rugged old serpentine oaks. We'd planted here without much hope, breaking a crust of hardpan to dig the holes for the late-sprouters and withered backup plants Dowst had managed to tease into existence. I was planning to hack out the weeds, water and fertilize the plants, and check the deer fencing. But when I descended the back slope of the meadow, I saw immediately that something was wrong. For one thing, the fence was down, and as I drew closer I saw that an entire section of chicken wire had been accordioned, balled up as if under the pressure of some immense crushing weight. For another—and this was a shock—the ground was barren. Where before there had been the sweet succulent green of the struggling plants, now there was only dirt, yellow-brown and naked. I threw the hoe aside, drew the gun from my belt and ran headlong down the hill.

After the glare of the sun on the open field, the shade beneath the trees was disorienting, and I drew up short, breathing hard, my eyes raking the shadows. A bear, I thought, and the thought was numbing: I'm going to shoot a bear. No rabbit, no squirrel, no soft-eyed defenseless doe: a bear. Tooth, sinew and muscle, four hundred pounds of raging hirsute flesh, claws the size of fingers, jaws that could deracinate limbs and pulverize bone. Standing there in the penumbra of the tree, blinking back panic and squinting till my eyes began to tear, I suddenly recalled a story I'd read as a boy in *True* or *Outdoor Life* or some such place: a grizzly had attacked an Aleut guide and raked his face off—

eyes, nose, lips, teeth—and the Indian had crawled twenty miles with his hamburger features and panicked an entire village. Then he died.

My hand quaked as I held the gun out before me. It was quiet, the only sound a distant hum of insects and the *chock-chock-chock* of some hidden bird. Aside from a scattering of leaves, there was no trace of the plantlings we'd put in the ground here—every last one had been uprooted. I looked closer and recognized the now familiar paddlelike tracks in the dirt. And then, with a start, I realized that I was not alone in the clearing beneath the trees.

For some seconds I'd been filtering out a steady and distinctive background noise—a low wheezing ripple and snort of air, an asthmatic sound, like the hiss of a vacuum cleaner with the slightest obstruction in the wand. Now the sound began to register, and I traced it to a tangle of branch and weed at the far perimeter of the growing area, no more than thirty feet away. In that moment I experienced a revelation that slammed at my knees and swabbed my throat dry: the bear was in that tangle. Not only was he in there, but he was asleep, and what I'd been hearing was the steady sibilant rise and fall of his snores. But why, I asked myself, would this canny night-raider leave himself wide open to the hurts of the world, laid out like a wino at the very scene of the crime—and in broad daylight?

The answer came like a fanfare: he was stoned, that's why. Obliterated, wasted, kayoed, down for the count, his great bruin's belly swollen with the remains of forty pot plants. I listened to his breathing, deep and restful, insuck and outflap: yes, the bear was in there all right, sleeping off a monumental high, snoring as contentedly as if he'd just toddled off to his den for a long winter's nap.

This was it, I thought, this was my chance. I could empty the magazine and fling myself into the highest branches of the tree before he knew what hit him. I scrutinized the welter of leaves with the intensity of a hit man, probing for a target. There, that was the cracked black sole of his foot, wasn't it? Yes! And there, buried in the vegetation, the immense mottled hulk of him, like a heap of moldy carpet someone had scraped from the floor of a flooded basement. I steadied the pistol with my left hand, as Vogelsang had demonstrated, and took aim.

A big bloated second ticked by, the bear snoring, my finger clutching the trigger as if it were my pass to the realms of glory. I remembered the scoutmaster, the bull's-eye target perforated with .22 holes, Vogelsang and the shotgun. But this was not the shotgun, this was the pistol, and its use required skill and concentration. What if I missed? Or merely wounded him? And if I killed him, then what? Would I bury him? Skin him and eat him? Leave him for the maggots? I lowered the gun. You'd have to be heartless, a degenerate blood-crazed butcher, to shoot a sleeping bear. There he lay in all his splendor, denizen of slope and glade, hibernator, bee-keeper, omnivore, symbol of the wild and born free: who was I to take his life? Perhaps I could simply fire in the air and scare him off. But that left open the possibility that instead I'd scare him into springing up and removing my face. I thought of slinking away, going for Gesh and Phil and the shotgun, sharing the danger and the terrible responsibility both. But no. There was no time for that. The bear was raiding our crops, destroying everything we'd worked and planned for, threatening the very success of the project itself. I raised the gun. *Kill!* a voice shrieked in my ear. *Kill!*

At that moment, my options were suddenly reduced to zero. For the bear, perhaps sensing on some deep instinctual level that he was half a step from eternity, awoke, and poked his huge grizzled snout from the bushes. He was lying on his side, raising his head wearily, like a commuter roused by the first buzz of the alarm clock. For an instant we regarded each other in bewilderment. His great chocolate eyes were striated with red veins, marijuana leaves hung from his drooping jaw, and his odor—the feculent, rancid, working stench of him—enveloped me. I was stunned. Terrified. Entranced.

The bear broke the spell. He rolled to his feet like an old sow shaking up from the dust, a sapling snapped under the weight of him and I fired. *BOOM!* The report of the gun was loud as a howitzer blast. *BOOM! BOOM! BOOM!* I fired again and again, backing away simultaneously, all my circuits open wide.

I missed.

When the smoke cleared, the bear was standing there precisely as he had been an instant earlier, but now his eyes were seized with intimations of mortality. He gave me one quick dumbfounded look, as if to say "You're really serious about all this, aren't you?," and then he was gone.

He took the back fence with him, and cleared a path through the scrub that would have accommodated Clyde Beatty's elephants. For a long while I could hear him crashing through the brush, and I listened till the sound was absorbed in the hum of the insects and the bored, quotidian *chock-chock-chock* of the hidden bird.

Chapter 2

Even before I could think to set down the sack of German beer, cold cuts and cannolis tucked under my arm, I'd hit every light-switch in the place, flicked on the air conditioner, tuned the TV to some cretinous game show and dropped the stylus on *Carmina Burana* at killing volume. This was living. I felt like Stanley emerged from the jungle, Zeus hurling thunderbolts; I felt liberated, triumphant, omnipotent. Machines hummed and clicked at my command, breezes blew and trumpets rang out. I was home.

Gesh followed me up the stairs like a page, his arms laden with wine, kaiser rolls, grapes, olives, anchovies, taco chips, Dijon mustard and artichoke hearts. It was two p.m., Friday, the start of the Fourth of July weekend, and we were a hundred and fifty miles from the heat, dust and disrepair of the summer camp. I was overjoyed. Save for a trip to Friedman Brothers' Farm Supply in Santa Rosa, this was the first time I'd left Willits in four months. Four months: I could hardly believe it. The world had gone on, governments rising and falling, economic indicators in a tailspin, people scheming, dying, erecting shopping centers and committing acts of heroism and depravity, and all the while I'd been sitting on my ass in the hinterlands, contracting poison oak and facing down rednecks and bears. But now, now at long last, sacrifice would have its reward: Gesh and I were on a three-day furlough, horny and wild and crotch-sore as drovers descending on Abilene.

Phil, who had experienced some measure of relief in Tahoe the previous weekend, had reluctantly agreed to stay behind and tend the plants. "I can handle it," he said, and then, playing on our fears, "so long as Sapers stays where he belongs and the bear doesn't come poking around again." We scarcely heard him. After sixteen weeks of abstinence—sixteen weeks during which we leered at sheep, slavered over farm girls in the two-hundred-pound class and built elaborate fantasies around the whores of Rio—we were strung just as tightly as the horniest zit-faced adolescent. Bears, cops, commandos, insolvency, failure, ignominy and incarceration: none of it mattered. Our eyes were glazed with romance, we were already lifting cocktails in lush gleaming bars full of secretaries, cosmeticians, poetesses and lutanists, the field of our perception narrowed to a single sharp focus. For the present, we had one concern and one concern only: women.

Gesh made the sandwiches while I showered and shaved. Then, while he was anointing himself, I made a few phone calls, hoping to connect with one of the girls I'd dated sporadically over the past year or so. I was disappointed. Amy and Marcia, I learned, had married, and I offered them my feeble congratulations. Giselle was in France, Corinne had joined the army, and Annie was dead. When Annie's phone didn't answer, I called her sister, who erupted in sobs at the mention of her name. It was a shock. Annie, declaimer of poetry, danseuse, cat-lover, Annie of the quick smile and athletic legs, had been laid low, cut down by a Coup de Ville as she crossed Market Street on her Moped. All I'd wanted was the fleeting comfort of pressing my flesh to hers—all I'd wanted was love—and instead I'd been given a whiff of the grave. *O Sorrow, cruel fellowship,/O Priestess in the vaults of Death . . .*

"Bummer," Gesh said, flailing his hair with a plastic brush.

I didn't mean to be insensitive, but I couldn't have agreed more: it was an inauspicious beginning, and the shock of it dampened my mood as automatically as would the news of an earthquake in Cincinnati or the outbreak of the Third World War. Gesh sat in the corner, a beer between his legs, subdued, watching me. What could I say? It was too bad, a shame and a pity and all that. Still, we were off the farm, and that alone was enough to ignite us again. Before long we were dribbling beer down our chins and bellowing along with Orff. We ate the sandwiches, drank the beer, graduated from Orff to the Stranglers, the Rude Boys and finally the Armageddon Sisters, and then flung ourselves out the door.

Our first stop was the Mexican laundry, where we deposited eight swollen sacks of towels, T-shirts and undershorts in varying stages of fermentation and stained with paint, grease, sweat, tomato paste, Rose's Lime Juice and the essence of bear. Next we drove up to Ashbury Heights to visit one of Gesh's acquaintances, a recreational pharmacologist who occupied the dingy servants' quarters of a twenty-room Edwardian mansion he shared with a lawyer and his wife, a lesbian couple, three Iranian students and an out-of-work carpenter. We passed through an iron gate, ascended marble steps. Gesh knocked.

There was a cacophony of canine yelps and snarls, a scrambling of paw and toenail against the inner door and then the irascible tones of a distant voice: "Coming. Coming." A moment later, a short angry character with a buzzhead haircut simultaneously swung back the door and kicked savagely at a pair of trembling Gordon setters. "Yeah?" he said, pinning us with a malevolent look.

"Rudy in?" Gesh said.

Without a word, Buzzhead simply turned and walked off into the shadows, leaving the door wide open and the skittish dogs shivering at the doorframe. I followed Gesh, pulling the door shut behind me, the wet noses of the dogs poking at my hands as we passed through a crepuscular entrance hall jagged with furniture—highboys, lowboys, armoires, sideboards. The entrance hall gave onto a drawing room heaped with boxes of clothes and books and smelling of cat litter. "This way," Gesh said, and we followed a paneled corridor past another disused room, descended a flight of stairs and pushed through a curtain into a small apartment.

There was an odor of onions, tobacco, rubbing alcohol. In the corner, stretched out on a bare mattress and spotlighted in the glow of a tensor lamp, a man with plaited hair held a paperback book to his face. Aside from the mattress, which lay on the floor, and a number of milk crates ranged against the wall and stuffed with books, shoes, clothing and newspapers, the only furniture in the room was a safe the size of a refrigerator. "Hey," the man said as we entered the room, and then he sprang up from the bed like a predator, snarling, "Get out, get out, you fucking beasts!"

He was referring to the dogs.

"Goddammit," he muttered, and there was real vehemence in his tone. "Stinking hairy bastards." Then he grabbed Gesh's hand and his face erupted in a grin. "Gesh!" he boomed. "How the fuck are you?"

Gesh said he had no complaints, and then nodded at me. "Rudy," he said, "Felix." I opted for the soul shake, but Rudy came straight on and twisted my hand around as if it were a salami on a string. Then he turned abruptly, padded to the safe and began spinning the tumblers. "So," he shouted over his shoulder, "you hear anything from Ziggy?"

Gesh responded to this—no, he hadn't heard from Ziggy but someone had told him he was waiting tables in Lahaina—while I studied Rudy. Aside from one or two of the pus-eyed reprobates clutching bottles in doorways off Mission Street, Rudy was the oddest, unhealthiest, most unsavory-looking character I'd laid eyes on in years. He was barefoot, wearing a torn pair of Jockey shorts and a ribbed turtleneck sweater with a NUKE THE WHALES button appended to the shoulder; his bare legs were hairless, the skin more yellow than white. His hair was plaited in tight cornrows that alternated with furrows of pink scalp as if his head were the blueprint for a maze, he was chinless and skinny as a concentration camp survivor, his nose was shoved up into his face and his eyes were too big for their sockets, stretching the lids like beer bellies poking out from beneath shrunken T-shirts.

When the safe swung open, I saw pharmaceutical scales, bags of mannitol and cocaine, plastic tear-sheets of Mandrax stacked like corrugated cardboard, a big food-storage Baggie full of twenties wound tight as pencils and secured with rubber bands. Rudy extracted a miniature medicine vial from the safe, and then fished around in one of the milk baskets for a bag of pot and a package of cigarette papers. For the next half hour we sat cross-legged on the floor beneath posters of John Lennon, Margaret Thatcher and the Pope, and deposited various substances in our oral and nasal cavities while we shammed the roles of host and guest. The conversation consisted of ejaculations like "Um, yeah, that's good," and a continuing exchange between Rudy and Gesh that invariably began with one or the other of them saying "What do you hear from X lately?" After a while they seemed to run out of mutual acquaintances and a paralyzing silence fell over the room. This was the signal for Gesh and me to rise and lay out half our weekend's allowance—painstakingly hoarded against our eight-dollars-per-diem salary—for two grams of coke and fifteen Quaaludes. Then we wished Rudy well and went out to tear the town apart.

It was six o'clock. We drove to North Beach, parked, and ambled down the street in a blaze of neon. I was feeling good, the pavement clicking beneath my heels, windows struck with light, people on the street, music in the air. After the months of exile, after the countless deadening hours that weighed on us like some wasting disease, this was exhilarating, a rush, and even the clash of traffic and the stink of exhaust gladdened my heart. I'd been around the world with Magellan, eaten my own shoes and seen the worst, and now I was home again. When Gesh said, "Let's have a cocktail," I was already dancing in the street.

The first place we stepped into featured thundering rock and roll and naked women grunting in a mud pit. We had two stingers and one quack apiece, and perked ourselves up in the men's room with a line of coke. I stood with my back to the bar, propped on my elbows, and watched the artificial mud cling to the nipples and moisten the crevices of the wrestling women. My teeth were on edge, and I found myself leaning into Gesh and shouting nonstop over the music as the coke worked on the verbal centers of my brain. This was good, I thought, this was what I wanted: excitement, cheap and loud. I felt expansive, generous, witty and invulnerable.

Twenty minutes later, as the effect of the coke waned and the methaqualone began to pour sand in my joints, I waxed philosophical. What was this need, I mused, for chemical oblivion? The world was full of drunks, junkies, kat-chewers and ether-sniffers. Kids stuck their heads in buckets of paint thinner, bears bloated on fermented berries, cats rolled in catnip. And here I was, stoned and getting stoneder, on holiday from my new vocation—itself an indictment—and watching a pair of big-titted women slog around in a tub of artificial mud. Understanding hit me like a truck: I was a degenerate. I was no part-time scholar and contractor on the rebound from the recession, I was a dope fiend and a dope dealer, saboteur of lives and minds, a gutless profit-monger and mammon-worshipper. Jerpbak had been right to single me out and pin me to the wall: I was dangerous, subversive. Suddenly I felt depressed, filled to the neck with sadness like a carafe with bad wine.

I sipped glumly at my drink and watched as one woman straddled the other, pinning an arm behind her back and mounting her rodeo-style. Then Gesh emerged from the men's room, pushed his way through the crowd at the bar, and slipped me the vial of cocaine. I took it, retired to a stall in the men's and did two quick toots. Within moments, I felt better. Immeasurably better. I was no archfiend, no blighter of lives or robber baron: I was just a regular guy, out on the town, feeling good, an entrepreneur providing a service for society. That's all. No harm. I ground my teeth and fluffed my hair in the mirror, the exhilaration returning. I was handsome, healthy, soon-to-be-rich, and I was sowing some oats. Big deal. When I shoved in beside Gesh at the bar, a murmur of appreciation rose from the patrons, and I turned to see that the mounted woman was forcing her antagonist's face into the mire while simultaneously slapping her flank like a jockey coming off the wire.

The next place had a pool table and smelled of hot grease. Two black dudes in purple pants and a silver-haired character in a suit sat at the bar. A frazzled blonde was shooting pool, the TV was tuned to a sitcom and a web of falsetto voices crooned from the jukebox over a thumping disco beat. Gesh went to the men's room. I ordered beers and pressed two quarters to the rail of the pool table. The blonde never even glanced up.

When she finished, I racked for eight ball and she broke with a shattering crash that sent a pair of low balls leaping for the pockets. I never even got to shoot. Gesh was next. She ran six and then missed. Gesh came back with a run of five before blowing an easy setup in the corner pocket. She missed. He missed. Then she sank the two remaining balls and made a neat cross-table cut on the eight to win it. "Nice shot," Gesh said. "Can I buy you a drink?"

"Tanqueray martini," she said. "Straight up."

Gesh introduced himself.

"Chinowa," she said, extending her hand.

"And this is Felix."

She turned to me, her mouth a pout of concentration, eyes like ceramics. "Rack 'em up."

We played her for the next hour or so, alternating games, and she never relinquished the table. She never seemed to lose control, no matter how much she drank, the cuestick flicking cleanly through the nest of her fingers as if it were tapped into her nervous system. Gesh and I, on the other hand, grew progressively weaker as the alcohol, in combination with the methaqualone, began to affect our coordination. She didn't seem to mind. In fact, she seemed to enjoy humiliating us, neatly cracking down ball after ball, executing tricky bank shots and wicked side-pocket cuts, while we lurched around the table, spilling beer and fumbling for the chalk.

We hung on. I don't know why—for her sake, I guess. I had begun to develop a deep and abiding appreciation of the way her calves flexed as she leaned over the table, the percussive clack of her heels dancing a cha-cha in my head. My third beer went down like water. I swallowed another Quaalude—for poise—and began to construct a scenario for the evening. Chinowa, who with her strong fingers and sure stick was obviously a bundle of seething erotic appetites, would phone her tall lusty roommate, the four of us would hit a few clubs and then retire to my apartment for foreplay and afterplay. Gesh leaned over a giveaway shot on the eight ball, his eyes dulled, tongue pinned in the corner of his mouth, and I knew he was envisioning a similar scenario. He would beat her with a flick of his wrist, beat her finally and authoritatively, and we could all relax and get out of this dump. As the Fates would have it, however, he miscued, the white ball skewing off impotently to kiss the far cushion and then perversely dribble back to the center of the table. Chinowa's laugh was sharp and disdainful. She bent over the eight ball and slammed it into the pocket as if she were hitting a punching bag.

We were reacting to this, tugging at our beards and fumbling for the necks of our beer bottles, when a short lilting whistle—the tinkle of a door chime, one note up and one down—penetrated the miasma of castrato "baby-baby" emanating from the jukebox. Slowly, like turtles cooking in the sun, we rotated our heads in the direction of the bar. Mr. Silverhair had pushed himself up from the barstool and stood smoothing his locks for a moment, and then, without a backward glance, strode purposefully out the door. Our heads swiveled back to Chinowa, who at the first fluttering note had straightened up as if she'd been slapped, dropping the cuestick to the floor with a clatter. Now she snatched her purse from a stool at the bar and hurried out the door, the *clack-clack-clack* of her heels echoing like gunshots in the sudden dramatic silence between songs.

"She wasn't worth a shit anyway," Gesh said, cramming the nether end of a three-pound super-chicken burrito into his mouth. We were outside, on the street, holding take-out burritos the size of skeins of yarn. "Yeah," I said, wiping guacamole from my face and fighting to talk, chew and maintain my balance all at the same time, "and besides, it's too early to get pinned down for the night yet." It was nine o'clock. Gesh examined his watch carefully, as if it could not only tell him the time but plot the progress of every available female in town to boot. "Yeah," he said finally. "Yeah, we got to get to these clubs, man, and start dancing."

It was a noble sentiment, nobly expressed. Unfortunately, as he formed the syllables of the final word, a word that connotes motion and grace, he lost his balance and staggered back against the window of a Chinese herbalist's shop. The shop was dark, the window resilient. The burrito, however, was not so resilient. It dropped from his hand and split open like a rotten banana. On his shoes. The shoes, and the cuffs of both pant legs, were smeared with a mélange of salsa, chicken, green chilis, sour cream, beans, onions, guacamole and rice. Gesh merely stared down at his feet, as he'd stared a moment earlier at his watch, a look of dim incomprehension creasing his features. He could have been the village idiot, puzzling over his intertwined shoelaces. A motorcycle snarled down the street, someone shouted from a second-story window. Finally Gesh waved his hand in a vague gesture of dismissal and said "Fuck it," his voice thick with retardation.

The events of the remainder of that evening—and especially their sequence—were never quite clear to me. But I can say with assurance that we drifted in and out of a number of clubs that featured heavy metal, new wave disco, punk, blues, bluegrass, reggae and bossa nova, and that we lurched across various congested dance floors with various women and made lewd, drunken proposals to all of them. Our breath was foul, our legs unsteady. We slammed into doorposts, stepped on people's feet, were twice refused service. At one point, I recall, Gesh took umbrage at the appearance of a massive, iron-pumping, head-cracking bouncer at a tidy little club in which everyone was neatly dressed and behaving himself. "Fucker looks like a neutered cat," Gesh growled, jabbing his finger in the direction of a young giant who lounged watchfully in the corner, his arms folded against a chest so muscle-inflated he might have been wearing a lifejacket.

Suddenly I was sober. "Are you crazy?" I said. "That guy's arms alone are bigger than my entire body."

Gesh's eyes were glazed, his face hard. In the candlelight, the scar that split his eyebrow had a dull sheen to it, like the white of a hard-boiled egg. For answer, he merely shrugged. I knew Gesh well enough to appreciate his volatility—I had only to think of his confrontations with Vogelsang, his impatience with Dowst, the rage that consumed him when the pump broke down or the Jeep failed to start—and I could see that something had set him off, could see that he was looking for trouble. "Come on," I said, "this place isn't for us. Come on, let's get out of here."

Gesh's gaze was fixed on the bouncer. For his part, the bouncer merely stood there, his eyes sweeping the room contemptuously. In front, elevated above a mass of straight-backed chairs and glossy cocktail tables, a folksinger perched on a stool and did early-sixties stuff about harmony and the brotherhood of man. "Cabbagehead," Gesh muttered, still glaring at the bouncer. "Sink licker." I tried to restrain him, but he brushed me aside. I watched as he made his way to the bar, ordered a triple crème de menthe—it came in a big water glass—cakewalked past the bouncer like a harmless high-spirited fraternity guy out on a date, then spun round and neatly upended the glass on the bouncer's head.

"Sorry," Gesh said with a sick grin.

For one stunned second the bouncer held himself in check—Is this guy serious? Should I be angry?—before hurling himself forward like a steel wrecker's ball. I remember thinking, as the viscous green slop congealed the bouncer's hair and startled his shirt, that Gesh had erred irretrievably, that we'd shortly be confronted by the police, and that I'd once again find myself digging deep for bail money. But Gesh surprised me. Stoned, drunk, and perverse as he was, he'd planned his move well—"Just counting coup," he later explained—and at the moment of truth, with exquisite timing, jammed a glossy cocktail table into the behemoth's knees. Reeking of mint, the big man took a fall, spewing drinks and crushing glass, wood and Lucite beneath him. The diversion gave Gesh—and me—time to dodge out the door, duck round the corner and stumble the length of a three-block alley like handicapped sprinters trying out for the Special Olympics. We finally pulled up behind an overflowing dumpster to catch our breath and erupt in nervous, triumphant, moronic giggles. This was silly, juvenile, undignified and ultimately unfulfilling, the sort of thing you did when you were sixteen. It was all that, but somehow it was hilarious, too.

In mid-laugh, as if it were a natural extension of the joke, Gesh suddenly doubled over to evacuate the contents of his stomach. I listened to his wet heaving gasps—the dying throes of a hero with a sword twisted in his gut—and began to feel queasy myself. "The smug son of a bitch," he choked, and then gagged again. When he was finished, he straightened up, wiped his mouth with the back of his sleeve and said, "What next?"

It was one-fifteen. We'd gone through the cocaine and all but six of the Quaaludes. The night had turned cold, and a dank insidious fog had begun to feather its way through the streets, smoothing angles, blurring distinctions. We headed away from Broadway, looking for a place I knew—or thought I knew—where we could have a nightcap.

I was feeling enervated, as if I'd been walking forever, part of a commando raid in Bataan that didn't quite come off, a misguided explorer hoofing it back to civilization. The night had been a disappointment, there was no doubt about it. We'd left the apartment in high spirits, needful, aching with desire, and we'd struck out. Bombed. Wound up empty-handed and addle-brained, with a bad taste in our mouths. The amazing thing is that we'd expected anything different—this was the way it always was and always would be, world without consummation, amen.

In a way, it was like fishing. Once a year, having forgotten how insufferable it is, I would go fishing. A day would come when I would awaken to think of hooks, lines, sinkers, the mysteries of the deep, and then of broiled halibut or rock cod in black bean sauce. Like Ishmael too long ashore, I would hurry down to the marina, snuffing the salt air. Then I'd fork over thirty-five bucks to the charter-boat captain, stand in a knot of drunken sportsmen and vomit over the rail for six hours. Fish? By the end of the day I couldn't imagine that that pounding pitching hell of an ocean was anything but the lifeless desert it seemed.

I was operating on this level of unhope when we pushed through the door of the bar I'd been looking for, only to find that this was a different place altogether. Strangers, clots of them, stared up at us—strangers who didn't give a shit if I lived or died or ever again experienced love in all my fruitless wandering years on earth. Candles glowed on rough-hewn tables, smoke rose like mustard gas from a hundred cigarettes, the jukebox rattled with slash-'em/tear-'em rock and roll. I saw long noses, drawn canine faces, earrings, nose rings, blue hair, orange hair. No one was smiling.

"Uh, listen," I said, taking Gesh by the arm, "I don't think this is the right place."

Gesh didn't look overconcerned. He merely shrugged, and was about to advance on the bar when a muscular voice cut through the jukebox frenzy to shout out our names: "Gesh! Felix! How the fuck you doing?"

It was Rudy. Chinless, noseless, skin the color of ripe grapefruit. He was standing at the bar with a guy so short and deformed he could have been a chimpanzee dressed up for the occasion. "Hey!" Rudy shouted, ushering us forward, "I'd like you to meet my friend Raul."

Raul was about four and a half feet tall, and there was something seriously wrong with his shoulders and torso. His shoulders were massive—big as a linebacker's—and swelled out in a lump at the base of his head. He had no neck, and his chest and abdomen were foreshortened, so that he looked as if he'd been compressed vertically. I shook his hand and nodded at the crazed glint in his black eyes.

"And this," Rudy was saying, "is Jones." I now saw that Raul was flanked by a guy about thirty, a cool character with short hair combed straight up and back and wearing a tie the width of a tape measure. He nodded, and then took my hand perfunctorily. "My friends call me Bud," he said.

"Hey, what you drinking?" Rudy shouted, and then asked where all the women were. "What," he said, "did you strike out? Yeah?" He handed me an Irish coffee. "Don't worry about it, man—me and Raul and Jonesie are on our way to this place where there's some real action—right, Raul?—and you guys are welcome to come along if you want."

Jones? Where had I heard that name before? Farmer Jones, Casey Jones, BoJo Jones. *I beat on the brat*, screamed the jukebox, *I beat on the brat,/With a baseball bat*. "Why not?" I said.

Outside, the fog had thickened. Cars vanished, parking meters were invisible at a range of ten feet, the light from storefronts was so diffuse it could have been spread with a butter knife. The five of us scraped out the door and shuffled down an alley, then crossed a street I didn't recognize. Someone lit a joint and handed it to me. We walked on, our voices pitched low. Nobody said much.

If I was disoriented earlier, I was totally lost now—at first I thought we were headed in the direction of Chinatown, but with the fog and the various turnings I was no longer sure. "A block more," Rudy said as we swung into a street as softly lit as a watercolor. I saw red neon off to my left, a sign winking on and off, but the fog was so dense I couldn't make out the lettering. Then Jones's voice, disembodied, was speaking somewhere behind me: "This is my street, man—see you tomorrow, Rude."

"Hey Jonesie"—Raul's voice—"what's the matter? No lead in your pencil?"

"Tired, man. Hey, good to meet you," Jones said, just a shadow now. "Ciao."

We walked on. I glanced up and saw that the streetlights were truncated, dissolved in cloud, earth and sky become one. "You know, that Jones is a real pussy," Raul said, and Rudy sniggered. I realized at that moment that I liked Rudy about as much as I liked snakes or trunk murderers, and that I liked his hunchbacked friend even less. And Jones—Jones was one of ten thousand people you meet casually and will never lay eyes on again, but still there was something about him that unsettled me. It was the name, I guess. Or the cool, faintly ironic look of appraisal he'd given me as we were introduced.

Suddenly I felt very weary of the whole business. Everything—Rudy and Raul, the dream of the summer camp, the fog, the hour, the city, my own lust-ridden, drugged and exhausted body—was shit. I wanted to go home to bed, but I didn't. I kept walking, listening to the mesmeric scrape of our footsteps on the wet pavement. Halfway down the block, as if to let me know he was still there and functioning, however minimally, Gesh pressed something into my hand. It was the stub of the joint we'd been smoking, cold and long dead. I flung it away. A moment later we reached the end of the block and crowded into the doorway of what looked to be a deserted storefront. Raul knocked.

"Yeah?" came a voice from within.

"It's me, Raul. I brought some friends."

There was the sound of a bolt sliding back. Fog closed in on us like the breath of a beast. "What is this place, anyway?" Gesh said.

The door opened on a dimly lit interior: bare linoleum floor, bare white fluorescent tubes, two graffiti-scrawled folding chairs leaning forlornly against the back wall. We shuffled in, hands in pockets, shoulders hunched. I had no idea what to expect—neither Rudy nor Raul would say anything other than "It's a trip," and "You're really going to dig this"—and found myself suppressing an urge to whistle as Raul closed the door behind us.

Inside, to the left of the door and invisible from the street, stood a makeshift desk—a slab of plywood set across the seats of four folding chairs. A man in suspenders and a dirty Tom & Jerry T-shirt was easing himself down behind the desk as we entered. He said nothing, merely glanced up at us without interest. A calendar hung crookedly on the wall behind him, open for some obscure and aggravating reason to November. The man's face was inflamed with some genetic skin disorder, corrugated with angry red lumps as if he'd blundered into a beehive, and strands of lank hair descended from his balding crown to his shoulders. A cigar box, a copy of *The Wall Street Journal* and a nightstick lay on the desk before him as if they'd been designed to complement one another. I'd expected a party, an after-hours club, a sleazy apartment with a couple of girls. But this? What was this?

The man—host, proprietor, whatever he was—looked bored. He pushed the hair out of his face and gestured at the blank wall that ran half the length of the room—plasterboard, painted white and already gray with grime, a cheap addition. I was puzzled. Storage room? Office? Then I noticed the holes. Holes punched at random in the flat smooth plasterboard face. There must have been ten or twelve of them, none higher than waist-level and all about two and a half inches in diameter.

"Ten bucks a pop," the man said.

Enlightenment came more quickly to Gesh than me. "You mean . . . you mean we stick our . . . and somebody . . . ?" It was as if he'd asked the waiter at Ma Maison what the silverware was for. The man behind the desk simply stared at him. "Shit," Gesh laughed, "and we don't even know who's back there, right? Be it man or beast."

We all swiveled our heads, even the proprietor, to contemplate the silent inanimate face of the wall.

"Who gives a shit?" Raul said, his eyes pools of oil. "What you going to do, go home and jerk off?"

I was stunned. This was crude, this was obscene, the ultimate in depravity, moral turpitude and plain bad taste. Talk about the zipless fuck, this was real anonymity, cold and soulless as an execution. I was repelled. But as I watched Raul, Rudy and Gesh count out their money, I began to see the perverse allure of it too. *Dear Mom, don't try to find me or anything but I'm writing to tell you I'm all right and I've got a steady job and plenty to eat.* I stepped up to the desk and gave Tom-&-Jerry a ten-dollar bill.

"Pick your hole," he said, handing me a ticket stub.

"What's this?" I said.

"This place is hetero, right?" Gesh's voice was slow. He was already standing before the wall, fumbling with his zipper.

No one answered him.

"The ticket goes in the hole, pal," Tom-&-Jerry said. And then his face changed expression for the first time, the hint of a grin lifting his lip a millimeter or two. "Like at the movies."

I moved to the far end of the wall, feeling foolish, feeling ashamed and naked, feeling stoned. The hole was neatly cut, edges smoothed, but it was encircled by a corona of dirt and some sad joker had scrawled *Abandon hope, all ye who enter here* just above it. What is lust? I thought, dropping the ticket into the aperture. What is flesh? What is mind? I unfastened my zipper, found that I had an erection, and penetrated the wall. Gesh was laughing, Rudy concentrating. Beside me, pressed to the wall like a penitent, Raul moaned softly, his features bloated with rapture. I could hear the hum of the fluorescent lights, sadness crushed me like a fist and someone—something—took hold of me with a grip as moist and gentle as love.

Chapter 3

Grim, silent, dehydrated and disappointed, hemmed in by eight bags of clean laundry, miscellaneous groceries and three coolers of ice, we passed under the great arching portals of the Golden Gate Bridge, skirted Sausalito and plunged into the blistering hellish heat of Route 101 North. We had six dollars left—for gas—the ravaged exhaust system screamed like a kamikaze coming on for the kill, and a cordon of semis—STAY BACK; DON'T TREAD ON ME; PETROCHEM LTD.—spewed diesel fumes in our faces. Gesh lit a cigarette. I flicked on the radio and got fire and brimstone, static, and Roy Rogers singing "Happy Trails." We were on our way back to bondage.

The previous day—the Fourth—we'd awakened sometime after noon to a barrage of cherry bombs and the *tat-a-tat-tat* of firecrackers. Startled from concupiscent dreams, I thought at first that war had broken out, made the groping but inescapable connection between the hiss of Roman candles and the birth of the Republic, and then snatched desperately for the glass of water standing on the night table. If I could just manage to reach that glass, there was a chance I might survive; if not, I was doomed. Sun tore through the curtains like an avenging sword, the sky was sick with smog and the stink of sulfur hung on the air. Straining, my fingers trembling with alcoholic dyscrasia, monkeys shrieking and war drums thumping in my head, I managed to make contact with and knock over the glass, and I lay there gasping like some sea creature carried in with the tide and left to the merciless sun and the sharp probing beaks of the gulls. My eyes failed at that point and I dozed (dreams of staggering across the Atacama Desert, ears and nostrils full of sand, tongue stuck to the roof of my mouth), until I was jolted awake again by the next concussive report. There was nothing for it but to get up and drink a quart of orange juice and six cups of coffee.

Gesh was sitting at the kitchen table, calmly spooning up poached egg with ketchup and green chili sauce, when I stumbled into the room. I tilted my head under the faucet and drank till I could feel it coming up, then tossed the coffee pot on the stove and found a can of orange-juice concentrate in the freezer. Gesh cracked a beer and smoothed out the sports page. "So what's on for today?" he said without glancing up.

As the block of orange juice sucked back from the can and dropped into the pitcher with a fecal plop, the ramifications of Gesh's query hit me, and I realized with relief that he was no more inclined than I to dwell on the previous night's debacle—spilled milk, water under the bridge and all that—but was looking instead, with courage and optimism, to the future. "There's a cookout," I said, and explained that I was planning to visit some friends, consume charred meat and watermelon, and lie creatively about my whereabouts over the course of the past four months. After that, there were the fireworks at Fisherman's Wharf, and then I was going to check out Aorta's band, the Nostrils, at a club on Haight Street.

Gesh scraped an English muffin and said he thought he'd pass on the cookout. He'd been thinking about getting cleaned up and going downtown around six for dinner and the fireworks.

When I got back at six-thirty, Gesh was just heading out the door. He was wearing a Hawaiian shirt that featured yellow parrots and blue palm trees, his hair was slicked down with water and he reeked of aftershave. "Great," he said, too loudly. "I thought you weren't going to show up. Listen"—he was drunk, excited, wound up about something—"can you give me a ride downtown?"

"Where to?"

He drew a crumpled bar napkin from his pocket, read off an

address and then hustled me down the steps and into the car. "Listen," he said, "I'm going to have to can the fireworks—if that's all right."

I shrugged, watching him. "Sure."

It seemed that he'd wandered into a bar full of women that afternoon—"Incredible, Felix: all of them foxes and they must have outnumbered the guys three to one"—and had made a date with one of them for the evening. Her name was Yvette, she was tall and high-busted and wore a slit skirt. Gesh tapped his comb to the beat of the radio and rhapsodized about her all the way downtown. "See you later," he said as I dropped him off, and he sauntered up the sidewalk like the romantic lead in a Broadway musical. Suddenly I felt depressed.

The fireworks went up and came down. *Pop-pop. Bang.* I watched them glumly, had a couple of greasy eggrolls and then drove over to the club where the Nostrils were playing. Three dollars at the door, a handstamp that showed two pig's nostrils like a pair of bifocals, more earrings and pink hair. I picked a table near the stage, chain-drank tequila and tonic because I felt conspicuous—*who is this joker sitting by himself, anyway?*—and settled down to wait for the show to start.

An hour later the Nostrils stepped out on the darkened stage, tuned their instruments and blasted into a pulse-pounding version of "God Bless America" as the lights came up. Almost immediately people began slam dancing under the stage, and a couple of harried-looking waitresses in change aprons began to clear the tables out of the way. I got up, stood at the bar, and because service was slow, ordered two drinks at once.

The Nostrils were an all-girl band. The lead singer, who looked like Bela Lugosi in drag, played guitar and fronted the group, while Aorta, standing beside a co-backup vocalist so emaciated she could have stepped out of one of the photographs of Dachau, ululated weird falsetto chants over the buzzsaw guitar riffs. At the rear of the stage, huddled over their instruments like praying mantises, the bass player and drummer hammered away at tribal rhythms. The music went on, without change, for an hour. One song segued into another, and all were alike—or perhaps they were simply doing an extended version of a single song. I couldn't tell. Then, in mid-beat, the music died so abruptly I thought the plug had been pulled, the lights faded and the dancers stopped slamming one another long enough to bellow incoherent threats through the sudden silence.

"Felix," Aorta said, threading her way through the crowd. "Glad you could make it. Got the weekend off, huh? How'd you like us?"

I shook her hand, forever cold, and wondered how to respond to this effusive rush of communication. For Aorta, this was practically filibustering. "Gesh and I came down for the weekend," I said.

"He here?" craning her neck to scan the crowd.

"No." I took a sip of my drink, and then lied: "The music was hot."

This was polite, and a neat conversational ploy as well, but Aorta didn't have a chance to respond. A girl had appeared beside her, and through the sweat, runny mascara and streaked pancake makeup, I saw that she was the Lugosi impersonator. "Vena, this is Felix—he's a friend of Vogelsang's."

Vena shot me a quick cool glance and then turned to Aorta. "You see who's in the crowd tonight?"

Aorta, never one to let her emotions show, imperceptibly widened her eyes as Vena named a name that meant nothing to me. "Who's that?" I said, and both women turned to look at me as if I'd just emerged from seventeen years in a Siberian gulag. From the gist of what passed between them, I gathered finally that he was a record producer.

"Let's tear his head off," Vena said, lighting a cigarette. "I think we ought to open with 'Burn Ward' and then hit him with 'Pink and Dead.' "

"The music was hot the first set," I said. "Anybody want a drink?" Elbows jostled me, voices shrieked with laughter, the ubiquitous jukebox started up with a roar. Vena was leaning into Aorta and shouting something in her ear. I tapped Aorta's arm, and she looked up a moment to give me a glance as empty as the spaces between the star—*Drink?* I pantomimed. *Do you want a drink?*—and then she turned back to Vena. What could I say? I backed up to the bar and ordered another tequila. I don't know what I'd expected from Aorta—sympathy, excitement, conversation, sex—but it was clear I wasn't going to get it.

Feeling sorry for myself, feeling as alone and friendless as a dieter at the feast of life, I went home to bed.

Now, buffeted by the chattering exhaust, billowing fumes and dust devils, I snuck a look at Gesh and saw that he hadn't exactly been exhilarated and revivified by the holiday either. He was staring out the window of the car, moodily sucking at his cigarette, stolid and silent as a rock. "Some bust of a weekend," I said, without taking my eyes from the road.

Gesh merely grunted, but there was an unfathomable depth of bitterness in that grunt, and though he hadn't said anything about his date with Yvette, I understood that it, too, had been a bust. He morosely tossed his cigarette out the window and into a clump of grass beneath a FIRE HAZARD sign, and then turned to me. "You don't know the half of it," he said.

"Yvette?"

Gesh flicked off the radio. "I wasn't going to tell you this—it's embarrassing—but the more I think about it, it's so pathetic it's funny." He paused to reach behind him and fumble through the cooler for a splinter of ice. "You know, right from the beginning I thought there was something strange about her—it was too good to be true, right? Paradise. A bar full of beautiful women and all of them hot. At first I thought she might be a hooker or something, the way she came on to me in the afternoon, but she wasn't. We did some kissing and groping at a booth in back and she didn't say anything so I asked her if she wanted to go somewhere else. 'I've got an appointment,' she says. 'But I'm free tonight.'

"Okay. So I'm all pumped up and I go over to her apartment thinking I've got it made and she meets me at the door in a pair of jeans and a tube top. She looks fantastic, but there's something about her that just doesn't sit right. She's big. Her shoulders are too wide. Then it hits me. But no, I think, that's crazy, and I look at her again and she's beautiful, stunning, like she just stepped off the cover of some women's magazine.

"We have a drink. She starts coming on like a nymphomaniac but I'm holding back because of that funny feeling I had. I'm on top of her, I'm trying to get her top down and her hands are all over me. 'Listen,' I say, 'I don't know how to put this, I mean

I hope you won't be offended or anything, and this is probably insane, but could you tell me something—it's really important to me.'

"She looks up at me, cold green eyes, eyes like the water under the Bay Bridge when you go fishing. 'What?' she says in this tiny little voice.

" 'Christ, I don't know: this is crazy. But tell me, do you . . . I mean, you wouldn't happen to have a penis by any chance?'

"Suddenly her eyes look like they're sinking into her head, her pupils shriveling up, and she looks like she's about to cry. And then she holds her hand up in front of my face, two fingers an inch apart. 'Yes,' she whispers, and I jerk back as if my shirt's on fire, 'but it's only a little one.' "

It must have been around seven when we hit the outskirts of Willits. The sun was dropping in the west and igniting the yellow grass of the hills, trees began to leap up along the road, and we passed a succession of neat little houses, as alike as pennies. Gesh was asleep, his head propped up on one arm and playing to and fro like a toy on a spring. I was thinking of the summer camp, of the plants flourishing in the stark sun, of the candy man who was going to buy the whole crop—cash up front—and of what I could do with a hundred and sixty-six thousand dollars, when I noticed that the car in front of me, a VW Bug of uncertain vintage, was behaving erratically. The car had slowed to a crawl and seemed to be listing to the right, as if the road had given way beneath it. As I drew closer and swung out to pass, I saw that the car was mottled with primer paint, bumper-blasted and rusted, and that the right front tire was flat to the rim.

I was already accelerating, humping up alongside to roar past and reduce the crippled Bug to a dot in the rearview mirror, when I turned to glance at the driver. What I saw was arresting: eyes you could fall into, a nimbus of black ringlets, the long, sculpted fingers and the open palm waving frantically for help. There was a desperation in that face, a needfulness that made my heart turn over. What she saw in return could hardly have inspired confidence—i.e., the battered Toyota, Gesh's big lolling shaggy head, my intrusive eyes and sweat-plastered hair—but she waved all the harder. My foot fell back from the accelerator.

Having been raised in New York, I was accustomed to turning my back on all such appeals for aid from strangers. I routinely gave the stiff arm to panhandlers, slammed the door in the faces of Bible salesmen, Avon ladies and Girl Scouts, ground the receiver into its cradle at the hint of a solicitation and strenuously avoided all scenes of human misery and extremity. Ignore him, my mother would say of a man twisted like a burned root, the stubs of three crudely sharpened pencils clenched in his trembling fist. Don't get involved, she'd hiss as a couple slugged it out over a carton of smashed eggs in the supermarket parking lot. But this was different. This was no half-crazed wino, wife-beater or terminal syphilitic—this was a flower, a beauty, a girl with a face that belonged to Amigoni's Venus. She pulled over to the shoulder, her damaged wheel rim clanking like a cowbell, and I swung up just ahead of her.

She was agile, urgent, pouring from the car in a spill of flesh. Nike sneakers, satiny blue jogger's shorts, a halter that left her shoulders and navel bare. Gesh had momentarily jolted awake as I rumbled up onto the shoulder, but now he drifted off again, snores ratchetting mechanically through his dried-up nostrils. I stepped out of the car.

"Oh, listen, thanks a lot," she gasped, snatching for breath like a miler. "I'm really glad somebody stopped—have you got a jack?"

She was standing directly in front of me now, too close in her urgency, shoulders shrugged and palms spread in entreaty. Her mouth was wide, nose cut like an *L*, skin dark. Italian, I thought. Or Greek.

"Because I don't know what happened to mine. I must've loaned it to somebody or something. Anyway, I've got a spare, and if you could just let me borrow your jack for a minute . . ."

I realized I'd been staring at her like a deaf-mute under sedation, and wrenched my face into a broad grin. "Sure, of course, no problem," I barked, swinging round to work open the trunk.

"I hit something about three miles back," she explained, peering into the trunk full of fast-food wrappers, rags, laundry, tools, cans of spray paint, torn tennis sneakers, and lurid paperbacks. "I figured I could limp into town, but then the rim started to go on me and all of a sudden the car was shaking like a roller coaster or something. Well, that was it. I started to get afraid for my pieces . . ."

I glanced up inquisitively, jack in hand.

"My pottery. I'm a potter. In Willits?" She took the jack from me as casually as if I were handing her a canapé at a cocktail party. "I'm right on Oak Street—it's just a little place, Petra's Pots. Between the real-estate office and the barbershop."

A mobile home the size of a DC-7 rumbled by as she bent to maneuver the jack under the frame of the VW and give the jack handle two quick twists. I stood above her, watching the coils of hair play across her bare shoulders, and then peered through the window of her car and saw that the back seat was stacked with flats of ceramic mugs and matching cream-and-sugar sets. Larger pieces—they could have been bongs or samovars for all I knew—were wrapped in newspaper and wedged into the floor space on the passenger's side. "Need any help?" I asked.

She was squatting beside the wheel now, fitting the cruciform wrench to the first of the wheel lugs, and she paused to glance up at me with a wide white smile: "No, thanks," she said, "I'm not the helpless type." Then she turned back to her work, and I watched her arms harden as she fought the lug. It wouldn't give. She strained until her shoulders began to tremble, then rose to her feet for better purchase.

"You're supposed to spit on your hands," I said, and she laughed.

Then she attacked the recalcitrant lug once more, throwing her entire body into it, teeth gritted, eyes clenched, halter bursting. Nothing. I watched her smugly, greedily—it was my right and privilege to study this beautiful woman, this stranger, because my stopping to help had forced us into an intimacy of purpose, and I knew it would be only a matter of moments before she would turn to me for the muscle she lacked. "Wow," she said finally, "that's a bitch," and she stood to wipe her hands on her shorts.

"Mind if I give it a try?" I said, arms folded across my chest.

"It must be frozen on," she said. "You know, rusted," but she was smiling softly, capitulating, and we both recognized that she was yielding ground, casting off the mantle of the woman warrior, if only for a moment.

As I bent to the wheel, I asked her if she was from Buffalo or Rochester, having detected a trace of vowel strangulation in her accent. "I was just curious," I added. "I've got a lot of friends from up around there."

"Chicago," she said, flattening the *a*. "My name's Petra, but I guess I already told you that."

I smiled up at her, gripping the prongs of the lugwrench like Samson fastening on the jawbone of an ass, introduced myself in a gasp and gave the wrench a mighty jerk. Nothing happened. "Tight," I grunted, flexing the muscles in my back.

"You from around here?"she said.

I jerked at the lug. It was immovable. With exaggerated care, as though the tool must be defective, I slipped the wrench from the lug and studied it.

"I mean," she prompted, "you look familiar to me."

"Oh," I said, judiciously fitting the wrench to another lug and preparing to slip every disc, rupture every muscle, and herniate myself into the bargain with one murderous herculean thrust, "not really. We live in Palo Alto, actually. But we just"—I broke off to jerk savagely at the wrench—"but we just like come up on weekends to go, to go"—I was running sweat, furious, distracted, and I nearly shouted the final word—"fishing."

"Looks like it's really on there, huh?"

"No, no," I said, bracing myself for another try, "don't worry. It's just"—again I heaved till I thought I could feel something give in my groin—"stuck, that's all."

It was at that moment, as if it had been choreographed by the Fates, as if all the hands of all the clocks that had measured time throughout history had been synchronized to mock that instant on that road on that day—it was then, when my guard was down and my passions piqued—that the CHP cruiser, revolving light aglow, glided silently up onto the shoulder behind us. I froze. Became a sculpture in living flesh: *Man Changing Flat*. Petra glanced up at the opaque window of the police car and put her hands to her hips.

The door of the car swung open and a glistening boot appeared. Then, six-two, one-eighty-five, as lean and tough as a strip of jerky and with every hair of his mustache clipped to regulation length, Officer Jerpbak emerged from the cruiser. He was carrying his summons book in one hand, and his mirror shades flashed malevolently. "What's the problem here?"

"Nothing we can't fix ourselves," Petra said. Her voice had turned acid.

A pickup rattled by on the road, cloely tailed by a convertible that lurched into the outside lane with a blast of the throttle and then vanished in the distance. I straightened up—slowly, cautiously—still gripping the lugwrench and wondering what to do. Should I avert my face, throw my voice, drop the wrench and stroll casually back to the Toyota, start it up and drive off? The wrench weighed twelve tons, my heart was in my ears. Here he was, at long last, Jerpbak. Jerpbak the enforcer, Jerpbak the hound. In the flesh. "It's just a flat tire, Officer," I said, my voice hollow, withered, gone flat and out of key.

"Well," said Jerpbak, ignoring me, "Miss Pandazopolos." He sauntered up to the VW, put a foot on the bumper and thumbed through his summons book. "And her junk-wagon."

"Oh, come on—get off my case, Jerpbak." She flattened the final vowel until it trailed off in a bleat.

If to this point Jerpbak had seemed faintly amused, in the way of a nine-year-old with a bare wire and a pan of frogs, he turned abruptly serious. "In the car, lady," he snapped. "I'm conducting a spot inspection of this vehicle right here and now."

Petra fixed him with a stare of such intense, incendiary hatred I thought he'd burst into flame, and I realized with a thrill that she and I—that this fantastic, wide-mouthed, long-legged, dark-skinned, furious woman and I—had a bond in common. She opened her mouth as if to protest, but Jerpbak, impenetrable behind his shades, was already scribbling in his summons book, and she stalked round the car and slammed into the driver's seat instead.

At this point, Jerpbak turned to me. "And who are you?"

"Me?"

"Yeah, you."

"I'm nobody. I mean I, uh, just stopped to help when I, uh—?"

"You a local?"

"Me? No, no. Just passing through, never been here before in my life. I live in San Jose. With my mother."

"Funny," Jerpbak said, scratching meditatively in the dirt with the toe of his boot, "you look familiar." And then he hit me with the question that gave me nightmares: "Ever been to Tahoe?"

"Where?"

"You hard of hearing? Tahoe. Lake Tahoe."

Shit, I thought, and I felt something give way, a piece of elastic frayed to the breaking point. "Yeah," I said. "I've been there." And then: "Look, what's this all about, anyway? You charging me with being a good Samaritan or what?"

There was a long silence. Jerpbak's glasses were like the eyes of a predacious insect, huge, soulless, unfathomable. Drums thundered in my head, my chest was exploding, a truck shot by with a climactic whoosh. "I don't like you," Jerpbak said finally. "I don't like your shirt or your shoes or your haircut or the tone of your voice. In fact, I like you so little that if you're not in that piece-of-shit Toyota and out of here in thirty seconds flat, I *am* going to run your ass in. Don't tempt me." Then he turned his back: I was dismissed.

Jerpbak was hovering over Petra's window now. She stared straight ahead, rigid as a catatonic. "License and registration," Jerpbak said. She didn't move. He repeated himself.

Petra's voice was soft. "Don't do this," she said.

"License and registration."

"All right," she said. "I forgot my license. It's at home somewhere."

I watched the back of Jerpbak's head, studied the square of his shoulders. "I'm afraid I'll have to take you in then," he said. Take her in? I was stunned. The man's psychotic, I thought. A bullyboy. A brownshirt.

"Shit!" Petra shouted, flinging herself from the car. "You know goddamn well I have a license—you've harassed me enough over it, haven't you? How many tickets have you given me in the last three months? Huh? What do you mean I don't have a license?" She was six inches from him, veins standing out in her neck, eyes throwing punches.

Jerpbak never flinched. He just stood there, erect as a ramrod, idly fingering the buffed leather of his holster and the hard plastic grip of his revolver. His voice was almost weary. "Up against the car," he said.

She hesitated; he grabbed for her arm. Just that: he grabbed for her arm, and then spun her around. I don't know what came over me—some misguided chivalric impulse, I suppose, or perhaps it was even more basic than that, something archetypal, primordial. *Kill, fuck, eat*, the id tells us, and sometimes we listen. In this instance it was all tied up with sex, of course. Would I have interfered if Petra had looked like Edith Sitwell or Nancy Reagan? I stepped forward. I think I said something penetrating like "Hey, no need to get rough," and I may have reached out with the hazy notion of restraining Jerpbak's arm—or no, I merely brushed him, that's all. Accidentally.

Brushing, restraining—I could have clubbed him with the lug-wrench and it wouldn't have been any different. One hundred and twenty seconds later I found myself handcuffed to Petra and seated in the rear of the cruiser, my wrist aching, knees cramped, heart hammering, and facing a probable string of charges ranging from interfering with a peace officer in the line of duty to assault, mayhem and attempted murder. The police radio chattered tonelessly, inanely, sun screamed through the windows. I watched as Jerpbak sauntered up to the Toyota and shook Gesh awake. I was as wrought up as a pit bull with blood in his nostrils.

Petra's free hand reached out to pat my shackled one. "I'm sorry," she said. Her eyes were wide and wet, stricken like the eyes of tear-gas victims. "It's just that . . . this guy is crazy. He thinks that I . . . he, he persecutes me." She leaned into me, and I could feel her body percolating with hurt and anger until the first sob rose in her throat. A moment later she broke down, sobs churning like waves on a beach, the very frame of the car heaving with the force of her emotion. I'd been thinking wildly of escape, of smashing Jerpbak and running for it, and then more somberly of lawyers and jail cells, the collapse of the summer camp and of how now, finally and irrevocably, I'd let my partners down—thinking of my own circumscribed and miserable self. Now, without thought or hesitation, as instinctively as I would reach out a hand to someone who'd fallen or hold open the door for a child with an armful of groceries, I drew up my free hand to take her shoulder and press her to me. What else could I have done?

Chapter 4

I was advised of my rights, photographed, fingerprinted, relieved of my personal property and consigned to the local jail, where I was escorted to a communal cell occupied by two happy-hour drunks, an acne-ravaged shoplifter, a vagrant Indian, and a middle-aged man who had assaulted his seventy-five-year-old mother in a dispute over a can of sugar-free Dr Pepper. I was charged with interfering with the duties of a peace officer and assault and battery. Bail was set at $2,000.

The cell was big, fitted out with Murphy cots, tile floor (easy to hose down, like a cage at the zoo), and two crappers. The Indian—I thought at first he might have been one of the pool players from Shirelle's—was leaning against the bars, dragging on a cigarette, as I stumbled into the cell. A toothpick jutted from his mouth, and his eyes were like cups of blood. The others sat or lay on their cots in silence, gripped by the peculiar lassitude that sets in when the cell door clanks shut and you find yourself locked away and powerless. After a moment the Indian nodded at me and said, "What they get you for?"

I was feeling stupid, ashamed, guilty. I'd acted impulsively, foolishly, replaying my first encounter with Jerpbak to the letter, déjà vu. I wanted to hang myself, throttle Jerpbak, make love to Petra, Chinowa, poor dead Annie, I wanted to sit around the table at the summer camp and drink gin rickeys with Phil and Gesh and even Dowst; I did not want to hunker down behind the broomhandle-thick bars of the Willits jail and open up my heart to a vagrant Indian. "Murder," I said.

The Indian's lower lip protruded until it entirely obscured the upper, and he nodded his head slowly and solemnly. No one else said a word to me until Phil came to bail me out six hours later.

Six hours. For six hours I lay on my cot and listened to the tortured ratchetting snores of the drunks and the *mea culpa*s of the mother-beater ("Mama," he moaned at regular intervals, "Mama, forgive me"); for six hours I reflected on my crime and its consequences for the summer camp, and tried to focus the image of Petra, already dissolving in my memory like a teaspoon of sugar in a water tank. There were the distant echoes of footsteps, blown noses, cleared throats. A single yellow bulb burned in the hallway. "What they get you for?" the Indian asked the shoplifter.

In the car on the way in, and while we sat shackled wrist to wrist in the anteroom of the Willits Police Department, Petra had given me an insight into Jerpbak that made my blood boil. Not that I wasn't already coddling with fear, excitement and rage, my nervous system like a leaky gas jet over which someone was fumbling with a pack of matches, but this was a real provocation, this was heinous: Jerpbak had sexually harassed her. I was outraged and disgusted. He was no ascetic, no true believer—he was venal, an extortionist, an amatorial strong-arm man. He was a sinner like the rest of us.

It seemed that Petra had first run afoul of him shortly after he'd been transferred to the eastern Mendocino region. He'd stopped her for a routine check, stopped her because he was bored, because she was a pretty girl and he was a lean, tough, sinewy, head-cracking, doper-busting, macho highway patrolman. I pictured him—the jackbooted swagger, the short-sleeved shirt with the chevron on the shoulder, the iron triceps and rigid spine—as he ambled up to the car. Petra was ready for him. She held out her license and registration like offerings, like tribute, and concentrated on the nervous chatter of her car's engine. "What's this?" he said, stooping to lean in the window and slip back his sunglasses like a knight lifting his visor. "My license and registration," Petra said, glancing up at him. His hair was fine, parted at the side and cut close in what used to be called a regular haircut; equally fine hairs flattened along his forearm as a truck whooshed by on the highway. "I don't want to see those," he said, holding her eyes. "I just want to chat a minute, that's all."

He chatted. Came on strong, made a stab at wit (Petra didn't elaborate, but I could guess what passed for wit in Jerpbak's circle—adolescent double entendre gleaned from sitcoms and game shows). Petra didn't respond. "Can I go now?" she asked finally.

Jerpbak again held her eyes, Jerpbak the hound, the married man, the former star halfback, and lowered his voice to a seductive whisper: "Only if you'll let me take you to dinner some night this week."

Three days later he appeared in her shop. "Hi," he said, dressed in civvies that looked like a uniform—white pants, polo shirt, the inevitable shades. "Remember me?" She again rebuffed him, and he stormed out of the shop like a wounded buffalo; thereafter, Petra was prominent on his shitlist. In due course he discovered that in addition to making mugs, saucers, plates, cream and sugar dispensers, flower pots, bowls and pickle trays, she also made stoneware bongs for a head shop in San Francisco. This gave him a foothold, an angle, a justification for putting pressure on her. She was now, in his view, a blot on the community, an undesirable engaged in an activity if not actually illegal, then certainly reprehensible and corrupting.

Shortly thereafter he stopped her as she was driving off to an arts and crafts fair, her Volkswagen laden with bulky frangible pieces, and conducted a search of the car while writing out a sheaf of violations. He asked her if she wasn't aware that narcotics implements such as she produced were commonly used by minors. He asked her if she had no sense of morals or community responsibility. Finally, after she'd been delayed over half an hour and was exasperated to the point of tears, he offered to tear up the tickets if she'd agree to go out with him just once. She refused. "All right," he said, sunglasses snapped down to shield his face as if he were preparing for battle, "but you're going to regret it."

From across the cell, the shoplifter's voice twitched with the modulations of the hormonal imbalance. "Shoplifting," he said.

"Me," the Indian said, "I'm in here for nothing. Breathing, that's all. I'm in here because I don't own a Lincoln Continental."

There were footsteps in the hallway, I heard the clank of a metal door and then a voice calling out my name. I jumped up. The big medieval key rattled in the lock. "Nasmyth," the voice repeated. "Come with me."

Phil was waiting for me in the anteroom. He clutched a bulging business envelope in one hand and he was grinning sheepishly, as if he were the one who should be apologizing. The office was small and cramped; the night-shift cop sat at his desk shuffling papers and looking worn and weary. Phil embraced me in the traditional back-slapping way, then counted out twenty crisp one-hundred-dollar bills for the man at the desk, folded the receipt away in his wallet, and led me out the door. "You all right?" he said.

I mumbled a reply, hangdog, mortified, not knowing what to say. Gone were the visions, fled the dreams. I felt I'd let everyone down, felt that I alone had stuck the pin in our balloon and destroyed what nosy neighbors, hostile townsfolk, anarchic bears and inclement weather couldn't. How could we go on now? I'd attracted the notice and aroused the enmity of Jerpbak. The summer camp was dead.

We climbed into the Toyota in silence. Phil drove. He insisted on it, in fact, treating me like an invalid, as if the six hours I'd spent behind bars had so sapped me I was unable to depress the pedals or manipulate the shift lever. He left the police station headed in the wrong direction, made several stops—for cigarettes, for gas, for an It's It—pulled in and out of driveways, looped back on himself, and finally emerged from an obscure dirt road just opposite Shirelle's Bum Steer. For a long while we merely sat there, the engine idling raggedly, as he studied the blacktop and peered into the rearview mirror with the intensity of a U-boat captain lining up a target on his periscope. Then, without warning, he hit the accelerator and the Toyota leapt out onto the roadway like a drag racer. Phil glanced at me in the rushing darkness. "Evasive action," he explained.

It was the first thing either of us had said since we'd left the police station. We'd been lost in our own thoughts, measuring out the sentence of doom, trying to accommodate ourselves to disappointment and failure. "So how's Vogelsang taking it?" I said.

I studied Phil's profile in the glow of the dashboard. It was unrevealing. He was all nose, chin and Adam's apple, like a caricature. I thought at first he might be suppressing a grin, but I couldn't be sure—he might have been frowning, too. Just then the tires squealed, we lurched around a corner and slowed as we hit the pitted surface of the road up to the summer camp. Phil shrugged. "He's up there now, waiting for you. Everybody's in a panic."

"Look," I began, and the weight of what I was about to say nearly choked me, "maybe I ought to quit the project. I mean, get out of everybody's way. You guys don't really need me now that the heavy stuff's over with."

The car shivered on its worn springs, bushes scraped at the side panels with the rasp of knives on a whetstone. "You don't have to do that," Phil said, his voice soft. He glanced at me, then turned back to the road. "We'll work something out."

It was two a.m. We rumbled into the field in front of the house and jerked to a halt beside Vogelsang's Saab. It was a moonless night, stars high and cold like pinpricks in the fabric of the universe. There was the usual chorus of nocturnal insects, the uncertain hump of Dowst's van and the shadowy displacement of space that indicated the pickup and Jeep. I glanced up and saw that all the windows of the cabin were aglow.

I'd been gone a little over sixty hours. Gesh and I had clambered into the car on Friday like escapees from the chain gang, like troupers boarding the bus for home after a tour of Piscagoula, Little Rock and Des Moines. Now it was Monday morning, and I was back. For months I'd been desperate to leave the place, ticking off the days like a prisoner in solitary, looking up from shovel or come-along and seeing cement, brick and asphalt, lying in my sweaty sheets and dreaming of cold beers, hot showers, checkered tablecloths and discerning waiters; but now, as Phil and I mounted the steps of the porch, I felt I'd come home. It was odd. In a moment we would push through the door to dirt, heat, chaos, to the feeble glow of Coleman lanterns and the scuff of lizards on the wall—and it would be all right. Suddenly I was crushed with regret. I was going to have to face them all—Vogelsang, Dowst, Aorta, Gesh, Phil, my co-workers and comrades—and tell them I was going to quit. Walk out with nothing. Sacrifice myself for the good of all. I didn't know what I'd do if they took me up on it.

The door swung open and four faces turned to look up at me as if I were a specimen in the zoo. There was a stink of rancid garbage, insects batted at the Coleman lanterns, shadows clung to the corners. My business partners were seated at the kitchen table, ranged round the Monopoly board, beleaguered by coffee cups, an empty rum bottle, brightly colored cards, the spurious lucre of the game's treasury. They looked anxious. And tired. I couldn't help noticing that Vogelsang held the deeds to half a dozen properties, had accumulated a mountain of cash and erected hotels on Boardwalk and Park Place. Gesh picked up a *Go Directly to Jail, Do Not Pass Go* card as we stepped in the door.

"Felix," somebody said, and then they were all on their feet, nosing around me like hounds worrying the carcass of a rabbit. All except Vogelsang, that is. He sat there stoically, his features inscrutable, thumbing through his play money like Joe Stalin examining photographs of disloyal party chiefs. Though it was the middle of the night, and he had no intention of stepping out the door or coming into contact with any form of vegetative life, let alone poison oak, he was nonetheless wearing his NASA jumpsuit. I tried not to look at him.

For the first few minutes everyone was solicitous. Gesh poured me a shot of vodka, the only thing we had in the house, Dowst brewed some lukewarm tea, Aorta regarded me with interest, and Vogelsang asked some indirect questions pertaining to the nature of my confinement and how much the law knew about me. I alternately sipped warm vodka and cold tea, my stomach curdling with the bitter culture of guilt and dereliction, while Gesh tried to make sense of things.

Like the others, he was puzzled. What had I done? What was it all about? One minute he'd been snoring against the window frame, and the next he was staring into the whipcrack face of a highway patrolman. The patrolman said nothing, merely pointed to where I sat in the back seat of the cruiser, returned to his car and thundered up the highway. Gesh stared after us, incredulous, then drove to a phone booth and called Vogelsang. Vogelsang asked what had happened, and Gesh was only able to say that I'd been handcuffed to some woman and hauled off by the police. Gesh looked at me for confirmation, elucidation, enlightenment. I looked down at the floor.

Gesh's voice faltered, then picked up again. Luckily, Vogelsang kept some cash on hand for just such an emergency, and promised to get on the horn to his lawyer and then drive up to Willits with the bail money. Fine. Terrific. Gesh had hung up, feeling relieved, but then found himself at a loss. He didn't dare go near the police station, for fear he'd be implicated in whatever it was I'd done, and he couldn't very well sit by the phone booth for the rest of the night. All at once it occurred to him that he should hustle up to the summer camp and alert Phil, in the event that legions of troopers were even then surrounding the place. They weren't, and he'd had no recourse but to sit tight and soothe his frazzled nerves with alcohol. This he'd apparently succeeded in doing, as he was half drunk at the moment, the words clinging to his lips as if they'd been written out on strips of paper and pasted to the roof of his mouth. When he finished, everyone turned to me. I'd never known a more miserable moment.

"It was really stupid," I said finally, and the room fell silent. The sound of the moths beating against the lamp screen transferred itself to my head, a frenzied thumping patter of drums. Beyond the windows, something—some creature of the night—let out a short sharp yip of pain or bloodlust. Hesitantly, like a man on the couch trying to reconstruct a dream, I told them what had happened, sparing no detail, and concluded by reasserting that the whole thing had been a foolish mistake, which I heartily regretted. No one said a word. "I feel like I've let everybody down," I said after a moment. "I mean, Jerpbak's got a vendetta against me now. I don't see how I can go on."

Dowst was watching me like a shark moving in on a gutted mackerel. Vogelsang was so alert I thought he was about to snap to attention and salute. Phil and Gesh averted their eyes.

"What I'm saying is, for the sake of the project I think it would be better if I quit."

"No," Gesh said. "You can't do that."

Phil screwed up his lazy eye and gave me a look of loyalty and camaraderie, a look that said teak tables and marble-topped oyster bars be damned. "I don't see why you can't stay on," he said. "It's not as though you got busted for a drug offense or anything, and Vogelsang already said his lawyer can postpone the trial till after the harvest. . . ."

"How much would you want?" Dowst said. "I mean, how would we split?" And then, in a rush: "Because you'd be breaking your contract."

"That's up to us, isn't it?" Gesh shot back. "Me, Phil and Felix are together, remember?"

"Just asking, that's all." Dowst tugged at the flange of his long Yankee nose. "But I think he's right—he ought to quit. For the sake of us all."

Gesh had been sitting on the kitchen counter, legs dangling. Now he leapt to his feet. "Yeah, and maybe you ought to quit, too. You don't do jack-shit up here anyway. Maybe you ought to just hump off to Sausalito and write a couple of articles on the chokeberry or something, huh?"

"Wait a minute," Vogelsang said, pushing himself up from the table, "there's no reason to get excited. I think there's a rational solution to all this. You've got to remember"—pacing now—"we've got a thousand plants in the ground and we need Felix to help water and harvest them. We're a long way from home yet."

A thousand plants? What was that all about? Was he saying we had only half what we'd projected? I did some quick figuring, couldn't help myself: one-third of $250,000 equals $83,333.33. Shit. All this for a lousy eighty-three thousand dollars? It wasn't worth it. But then another part of me just as quickly grasped at it as if it were untold millions, as if I were a fever-wracked explorer clutching the map to the elephant burial ground in my trembling insatiable hands.

"I don't see how—" Dowst began, but Vogelsang cut him off.

"How about this," Vogelsang said, spinning round to face us like Clarence Darrow delivering his peroration. "Felix stays. But for the next four and a half months," and he ticked them off on his fingers, "July, August, September, October and the beginning of November, neither he nor the Toyota ever leaves the property."

They were looking at me appraisingly now, the jury bringing in a guilty verdict. "No time off for good behavior?" I said, trying to make a joke of it.

"It's up to you, Felix," Vogelsang said. "I don't see any other way. It's going to be tough—you won't even be able to go into town for groceries or anything. But that's it. We can't take the risk." He was fumbling in his shirt pocket for something, the vial of breath neutralizer, no doubt, found himself frustrated, and then glanced back up at me. "You agree?"

I sat there in my chair like a prisoner in the dock, my face expressionless, a surge of joy and relief rising like a shout in my chest. I'd expected the worst—doom and exile—and I'd merely been sentenced to life at hard labor. Four and a half months of the farm. No Petra, no Chinowa, no fresh bagels or Sunday paper, no music, no films, no leisurely cups of capuccino at coffeehouses in North Beach. Nothing but tedium, dust, lizards and heat. And a chance to make it work.

"Well?" Vogelsang said.

Did I have a choice? I nodded my head. "Agreed."

Chapter 5

Let me tell you about attrition. About dwindling expectations, human error, Mother Nature on the counteroffensive. Let me tell you about days without end, about the oppression of mid-afternoon, about booze and dope, horseshoes, cards, paperbacks read and reread till their covers fall to pieces, let me tell you about boredom and the loss of faith.

First off, Vogelsang was right. There *were* only a thousand plants in the ground. Or to be more precise, nine hundred fifty-seven. I know: I counted them. It was the first thing I thought of when I woke the day following my sojourn in the town jail. Early on, we'd planted better than one thousand seedlings, and then Dowst had managed to sprout and plant some six or seven hundred more—at least. Or so he'd said. We were aware that we'd fallen short of our original estimate, but we had no idea by how much. Five percent? Ten? Fifteen? It wasn't our concern. We were the workers, the muscle, the yeomen, and Dowst and Vogelsang were the managers. The number of plants in the ground and the condition of those plants was their business; ours was to dig holes, string and mend fences, repair the irrigation system, and see that each plant got its two and a half gallons of H_2O per day. And so we'd never counted the plants. Never felt a need to. There were so many, after all, forests of them, their odor rank and sweet and overpowering, that we simply let ourselves get caught up in the fantasy of it, the wish that fulfills itself: of course we had two thousand plants.

But Vogelsang never made mistakes, and now I wasn't so sure.

I lay there a moment atop my sweaty sleeping bag, a soiled sheet twisted at my ankles, and then staggered into the kitchen for a glass of water. It was one-thirty in the afternoon and the house was already so hot you could have baked bread on the counter. Phil was stretched out on the sofa behind a tattered copy of an E. Rice Burroughs novel, perfectly inert, a tall vodka collins in his hand. I peered through the yellowed window and saw that both van and Saab were gone. "Vogelsang and Dowst leave already?" I said.

Phil snorted. "What do you think—they'd stick around here a second more than they had to?" From above, in the insupportable heat of the loft, Gesh's snores drifted down, dry as husks.

I drank from the tap, wiped my mouth with the back of my hand. "Last night," I began, rummaging through the refuse on the counter for a knife, peanut butter and bread, "Vogelsang said we've only got a thousand plants in the ground—that's crazy, isn't it?"

Phil shrugged. I was watching his face and he was watching mine. "I don't know, seems like there's a million when you're watering."

"Yeah," I said, "I know what you mean," but fifteen minutes later I was out there in the feverish hammering heat of midday, notebook in hand, counting.

Bushes had gone brown, the grass was stiff and yellow. I trod carefully, terrified of the rattlesnakes that infested the place. (I had a deep-seated fear of snakes, of their furtiveness, their muscular phallic potency, the quickness of their thrust, and the terrible rending wound they left in the poisoned flesh. I always carried a snakebite kit with me—but of course I knew the rattler would never be so cooperative as to puncture my foot or hand, but instead would fasten onto my ear or eye or scrotum, thus negating the value of the kit—and during the cold weather, when there was no more than a chance in a million of encountering a snake of any kind, I'd worn leather gaiters. As soon as the heat had set in, and the snakes emerged, the gaiters had become too uncomfortable and I'd abandoned them.) I made a mark for every plant on the property, four across and a slash for five, and found that fewer than a thousand had survived the root rot, blight, and over- and under-watering that had afflicted them. Not to mention the hundreds—thousands?—that never emerged from the tough withered husks of their seedpods or succumbed to the depredations of various creatures, from the insects in the greenhouse to the bear. Nine fifty-seven. That was the figure I came up with, and that was the figure I presented to my co-workers after dinner that evening.

The evening watering was done, and we were standing out front of the house in the long shadows, pitching horseshoes for a dollar a game. "Vogelsang was right," I told them, "we've got less than a thousand plants." It was awful to contemplate: in one fell swoop our profits had been cut in half.

"Bummer," Gesh said, and pitched a ringer to win the game. "That's what, thirty-six dollars you owe me now, Felix."

But this was just the beginning of our troubles, the first clear indication that we would have to revise our expectations downward. There were more to come. A week later, we began to notice that some of our healthiest plants—chest-high already and greener than a bucket of greenback dollars—were wilting. On closer inspection we saw that a narrow band had been cut or gnawed in the stem of each plant. We were bewildered. Had deer leapt eight feet in the air to vault our fences, bend their necks low to the ground, and nibble at the hard fibrous stems of the plants rather than graze the succulent leaves? Obviously not. Something smaller was responsible, some rabbity little bounding thing with an effective range about ankle-high and the ability to crawl under a deer fence. "Rabbits?" Phil guessed. "Gophers?"

It was then, with fear, loathing, regret and trepidation, that I remembered the dark scurrying forms I'd encountered that first day in the storage shed; a second later I made the connection with the rat traps we'd found scattered about Jones's main growing area. "Rats," I said.

We phoned Dowst. Rats, he informed us, live in the city. In garbage. A week later we'd lost upward of fifty plants, and we phoned him again. He looked preoccupied as he stepped out of the van, and I noticed that his skin had lost its color, as if he'd been spending a lot of time indoors, hunched over his notes on the virgin's bower or the beard lichen. We walked down to Jonestown with him, squatted like farmers socializing outside the courthouse, and showed him the ring of toothmarks that had bled a vigorous plant dry in a week's time. I watched as he ran a finger round the moist indentation and then brought it to his mouth to taste the fluid seeping from the wound. He was silent a moment, then looked up at us and announced that rabbits were decimating our crop. "They're thirsty," he explained, "and here you've got a standing fountain, seventy percent water." He rose to his feet and brushed at his trousers. "The only thing to do is peg down the fences so they can't get in underneath."

We pegged. Crawled on our hands and knees through the rattlesnake-, scorpion- and tarantula-infested brush, the sweat dripping from our noses, and hammered stakes into the ground, stretching our chicken wire so tight even a beetle couldn't have crawled under it. It took us a week. Dowst stayed on to supervise, to potter around the growing areas exuding expertise, and even, on occasion, to lend a hand. When we got the whole thing finished—all the fences in all the growing areas nailed down tight—I observed that we were still losing plants to the mystery gnawers, and suggested that the big bundles of twigs and downed branches we regularly came across in the woods and had as a matter of course enclosed within the confines of our now impervious fences were in fact rats' nests and that rats, not rabbits, were the culprits. Dowst demurred. But two days later, as the plants continued to wither and the toothy girdles to proliferate, he authorized Phil to drive into Santa Rosa and purchase two hundred rat traps at Friedman Brothers' Farm Supply.

By now it was early August, nearly a month since my fateful scrape with the law. We had something like eight hundred and forty six-foot plants—bushes, trees—burgeoning around us. The boredom was crushing. We alternated early watering chores—two days on, one day off—so that each of us could sleep late two days a week. I almost preferred getting up early. At least you felt alive in the cool of the morning, traversing fields damp with dew, ducking through silent groves of oak and madrone, catching a glimpse of deer, fox, bobcat. We'd get back to the cabin at nine-thirty or ten, the temperature already past ninety, stuff something in our mouths and fall face forward on our worn mattresses. It would be one or two by the time we woke to the deadening heat, our nostrils parched, throats dry as dunes, and joined the late sleeper in the continuous round of drinking, pot smoking, cards, and horseshoes that would put us away, dead drunk and disoriented, in the wee hours of the morning.

Each day was the same, without variation. Occasionally the pump would break down and Gesh would take it to a repairman in town and attempt to be casual about what he was doing with twenty-five-hundred gallons of water a day, or Dowst would pay a visit with magazines, newspapers, vodka and ice. But that was about it for excitement. The cards wore thin, the walls developed blisters from the intensity of our stares, we began to know the household lizards by name. "Gollee," Phil would say, slipping into an Atchafalaya drawl as we sat silently over our fiftieth game of pitch, "I haven't had this much fun since the hogs ate my baby sister."

If we saw Dowst once or twice a week, we rarely saw Vogelsang. As the plants blossomed into hard evidence, he made himself increasingly scarce, more than ever the silent partner. "Look, I've got too much to lose," he told us one night after he'd been summoned to repair the kick start on the surviving Kawasaki. "I just can't take the risk of being seen up here or identified in any way with this operation. I've got business interests, property in three states, a number of other deals in the works . . ." and he waved his hand to show the futility of trying even to intimate the scope of his interests. We watched that exasperated hand in silence, thinking our own thoughts about how much he had to lose, and by extension, how little we had. To lose.

For my part, the euphoria of being allowed to stay on was quickly exhausted, and I'd come to feel as oppressed as my coworkers by the drudgery and the unvarying routine. During the long slow hours of the interminable sweltering afternoons, propped up in a chair with a tall vodka and tonic and some moronic sci-fi paperback Phil had picked up at a used-book store in Ukiah ("The *classics*, Phil," I'd tell him, "get me something fat by Dostoevski or Dickens or somebody"), I began to feel I was aestivating, my clock wound down, brain numbed. It was then, more than ever, that I would find myself thinking of Petra.

One evening, while we stood round the horseshoe pit, winning, losing and exchanging chits, Dowst's van slid through the trees along the road and swung into the field, jouncing toward us across the brittle yellow expanse of the yard like a USO wagon come to some remote outpost. We were shirtless, bearded, dirty, our jeans sun-bleached and boots cracked with age and abuse. Behind us the sun flared in the sky, fat and red as a tangerine, and a host of turkey vultures, naked heads, glossy wings, converged on the carcass of some luckless creature struck down behind the shed. Puddles of crushed glass glinted at our feet, the sagging out-buildings eased toward the ground like derelicts bedding down for the night, and the cabin, pale as driftwood, radiated heat in scalloped waves until you had to look twice to be sure it wasn't on fire. For an instant I saw the scene from Dowst's eyes—from the eyes of an outsider, an emissary from the world of hot tubs and Cuisinarts—and realized that we must have looked like mad prospectors, like desert rats, like the sad sun-crazed remnants of Pizarro's band on the last leg of the road to Eldorado.

Dowst backed out of the van, crablike, his arms laden, and disappeared into the house. A moment later he emerged, newspaper in hand, and crossed the yard to join us. He was wearing white shorts and an alligator-emblazoned shirt, tennis shoes and pink-tinted shades. "Hi," he said, gangling and affable, as relaxed as a man who's just played two sets of tennis before brunch, and then held out the newspaper as if it were a new steel racket or a Frisbee. "I thought you guys might want to see this."

See what? VOGELSANG ELECTED MAYOR; POT SOARS ON COMMODITIES MARKET; JERPBAK TRANSFERRED TO JERUSALEM. We saw the front page of the *Chronicle*, blocks of print, a murky photograph. Puzzled, we crowded round him, scanning the headlines, passing quickly over the stories of corruption in government, poverty in the Third World and carnage in the Seychelles, until the following story leapt out from the page to seize us like the iron grip of a strangler:

WAR DECLARED ON POT GROWERS

The Drug Enforcement Administration and the State Department of Justice have formulated plans for a federally funded assault on growers of high-grade sinsemilla marijuana along the Northern California coast, the *Chronicle* learned today. A federal law-enforcement grant of $400,000 has been rushed through to enable the newly formed "Sinsemilla Strike Force" to begin operations before the fall harvest season. The strike force will coordinate federal agents and local police departments in "sniffing out illicit growing operations," as one source put it, in Mendocino, Del Norte, and Humboldt counties. Aerial surveillance, including the use of infra-red photography, will, it is hoped, pinpoint the locations of so many of the large-scale farms, while a program of special cash rewards for turning in growers is expected to help in exposing others.

"People are tired of this sort of thing," a source close to the strike force said, "and they resent the outsiders that come into their community for illegal and often highly lucrative purposes. We're confident that the reward system will make it easier for local residents to help us identify and apprehend the criminals in their midst."

Operations could begin as early as next month, the source disclosed.

Dowst was grinning sheepishly, a slight flush to his cheeks, as if he'd just told an off-color joke at a lawn party. "Not such great news, huh?"

For some reason, the story didn't affect me as it would have a few months earlier. I was alarmed, certainly, all the vital functions thrown into high gear as I read on, but I wasn't panicked. In fact, relatively speaking, I was calm. Perhaps my run-in with Jerpbak and the little scene I'd gone through with Savoy—*everybody knows what you guys are doing up there*—had made me fatalistic. Perhaps I expected a bust. Perhaps I wanted it.

Gesh was not quite so calm. He snatched the paper from Dowst's hands, balled it up and attempted to punt it into the trees. Then he turned on him, his face splayed with anger. "What next?" he shouted, as if Dowst were to blame. "Christ!" he roared, and spun round to face the empty hills.

Phil was pale. He tried to laugh it off, improvising a half-hearted joke about infra-red pot and reading glasses for the eye in the sky, until his words trailed off in a little self-conscious bleat of laughter.

Then, in what had almost become a reflex gesture for him, Gesh wheeled around to jab a thick admonitory finger in Dowst's face. "Between the rats and the bears and you and Vogelsang and now the fucking federal government, there's going to be precious little of this pot to split up, you know that?"

Dowst knew it. And so did we.

But that wasn't the worst of it. The following day, after he'd made a tour of the plantation and monitored the growth of each leaf, stem and twig, Dowst announced that he'd begun sexing the plants and that within a month all the males should have emerged. "Around the end of September, after the photoperiod begins to decline; that's when we'll get them all."

Phil and I were playing checkers; Gesh was dozing on the couch, a newspaper spread over his face. It was mid-afternoon, and the heat was like a wasting disease. "Huh?" I said.

"You know," Dowst was rattling through the cans of soup in the cupboard under the sink, "for sinsemilla pot. We've got to weed out the male plants."

That was something we'd known all along, in the way we knew that chickens laid eggs whether there was a rooster or not, or that Pluto was the ninth planet in the solar system—it was part of our general store of knowledge. But we hadn't really stopped to think about it, to consider its ramifications or work it into our formulae for translating plants into dollars. Any fool knew that in order to get sinsemilla pot you had to identify and eliminate the male plants so that the energy of the unfertilized females would go toward production of the huge, resinous, THC-packed colas that made seedless pot the most potent, desirable and highly priced smoke on the market. Any fool. But to this point we'd conveniently managed to overlook it.

I watched Phil's face as the realization of what Dowst was saying seeped into his nervous system and gave vent to various autonomous twitches of mortification and regret. "You mean . . . we've got to . . . to . . . *throw out some of the plants?*"

Dowst had found a can of Bon Ton lobster bisque and was applying the opener to it. "Usually about fifty percent. It could be higher or lower. Depending."

Phil looked like a man being strapped into the electric chair while his wife French-kisses the D.A. in the hallway. "On what?"

The lobster bisque was the color of diarrhea. Dowst sloshed it into his spotless Swiss aluminum camp pot and stirred it with a spoon he'd carefully disinfected over the front burner. "Luck," he said finally, and he pronounced the word as if it had meaning, pronounced it like the well-washed Yankee optimist he was, a man who could trace his roots back to the redoubtable Dowsts on the *Mayflower*. Besides, he had his van, a condo in Sausalito and a monthly stipend from his trust fund. He didn't need luck.

I thought of Mendel's pea plants, x and y chromosomes, thought of all those hale and hearty many-branching glorious male plants that would be hacked down and burned—fifty percent of the crop in a single swoop and the second such swoop in a month's time. Numbers invaded my head like an alien force, a little problem in elementary arithmetic: *Take 840 pot plants and divide by 2. Divide again, allowing for one-half pound of marketable pot per plant, to solve for the total number of pounds obtained. Multiply this figure by $1600, the going rate per pound. Now divide by 3 to arrive at the dollar value of each share—the financier's, the expert's and the yeomen's—and finally divide by 3 again to find the miserable pittance that you yourself will receive after nine months of backbreaking labor, police terror and exile from civilization.*

Dowst was whistling. Phil gnawed at the edge of a black plastic checker, expressionless, his eyes vacant. My half million had been reduced to $37,000. Barring seizure, blight, insect depredation and unforeseeable natural disasters, that is. It was a shock. If Jerpbak, ravenous rodents and the "Sinsemilla Strike Force" had driven a stake through my heart, Dowst had just climbed atop the coffin to nail down the lid.

I awoke the following morning to the tortured rasping of the pickup's starter and the hacking cough of combustion that eventually succeeded it. Bleary, disoriented—what time was it, anyway? Five-thirty? Six?—I rolled out of bed and trundled up the hallway and into the front room, where I stood in my underwear and peered groggily out the window. The pickup sat motionless in the high weeds, a coil of shadowy exhaust winding from the tailpipe as I watched with a vague, unformed curiosity, emerging from dreams as from a lake. Then a dull tooth of light glinted from the pickup's windshield as the vehicle heaved forward and rocked across the tarnished field, tailgate clanking, stiff grass giving way, birds bitching in the trees: there was the valediction of the brake lights, and it was gone. I stood there a moment longer, perplexed, scratching at my privates, until a voice spoke at me from the gloom of the far corner. "Gesh and Phil," the voice said.

Dowst, I saw now, was sitting at the kitchen table over a bowl of granola, shaking vitamin tablets into his palm from a forest of plastic vials. A soft, aqueous light suffused the room, pressing like a swollen balloon against the familiar objects of the place, softening corners, spreading shadows.

"What time is it?" I said.

"Five."

Five. I let that register, still scratching, then allowed my awakening mind to seize on the next question. "Where are they going?"

Dowst sighed. His eyes, pale in the best of light, were rinsed of color in the incipient gray of the morning. "Tahoe," he said.

"Tahoe?"

"For three days. R and R, they said. Both of them said they couldn't sleep."

Little wonder, I thought, after the cheering news of the past few weeks (slash, hack, another integer bites the dust). It was my turn to sigh. I poured myself a cup of coffee and sat down across from Dowst.

So they were gone. Disheartened, disillusioned, shorn of hope, spirit and animation, heads bowed, tails between their legs, the oyster bar reduced to a burger counter, the yacht to a dinghy. For one disjointed instant I wondered if I'd ever see them again, wondered if they'd decided to bag it, write the whole thing off and go back to the lost world of prawns, Mai Tais and teriyaki. But then, as I considered it, certitude came over me in a rush, and I knew—categorically and beyond the shadow of a doubt—that they would be back. Of course they would. A hundred and sixty thousand, eighty thousand, forty, twenty—what difference did it make? It was all they had. They needed this thing as badly as I did—if it failed, after all the hope and sweat and toil we'd invested in it, then the society itself was bankrupt, the pioneers a fraud, true grit, enterprise and daring as vestigial as adenoids or appendixes. We believed in Ragged Dick, P. T. Barnum, Diamond Jim Brady, in Andrew Carnegie, D. B. Cooper, Jackie Robinson. In the classless society, upward mobility, the law of the jungle. We'd seen all the movies, read all the books. We never doubted that we would make it, that one day we would be the fat cats in the mansion on the hill. Never. Not for a moment. After all, what else was there?

Dowst and I did the morning watering; then I went back to bed. When I woke about noon, bathed in sweat, Dowst was perched on the edge of the couch, his duffel bag packed, leafing through an issue of *Fremontia*. "Listen," he said, "I wonder if you could handle the watering by yourself tonight. I'm supposed to meet this friend of mine in the botany department at Berkeley—we're going to have drinks and dinner in Santa Rosa. It's really important. I could wind up with a two-year appointment there if things work out."

I was being deserted for the second time that day. I was hot, disappointed, lonely, restless and beset with vague fears. I shrugged.

"Because I'd really appreciate it," Dowst said, getting to his feet. "I mean, uh, I'll probably be back late tonight—no, I'll definitely be back tonight—so I can help you with the morning watering. And for the next couple of days, too—until those guys get back."

I nodded wearily, and he was gone. I listened to the smooth rumble of the van's engine until the sound was swallowed up in the rattle of insects and the harsh glottal complaint of a crow perched outside the door. The house blistered around me. I heard a shingle crack, watched a lizard emerge from a rent in the wall and disappear behind the couch. It was then that it seized me. An idea, a point of perspective, an exhilarating, lubricious, uninhibited foretaste of forbidden fruit. I was alone. I could do anything I wanted—anything—and no one would be the wiser.

But no. I'd given my word. Jerpbak lay in wait for me out there, the Sinsemilla Strike Force was poised to strike. Besides, I couldn't leave the place unguarded—what if Sapers came nosing around? Or if some hiker or cowboy blundered across our sweet fields of money trees? No, I couldn't leave the place, I couldn't.

Thirty seconds later I was in the bedroom, poking through the mound of clothes in the corner and sniffing socks and T-shirts to discover the least offensive. It's been over a month, I was thinking as I dug the dirt from beneath my nails with the blade of a pocketknife. From somewhere below, the crow let out a long rasping laugh and then flapped past the window like a knot of rags. My twice-brushed teeth gleamed at me in the mirror, my eyes were feverish. I eased down on the edge of the bed and pulled on a pair of white jeans, lamentably stained in the crotch with a blot of red wine but otherwise presentable, and then spit-polished my Dingo boots. Over a month. She wouldn't even remember me. I held the keys in my hand. Would she?

Chapter 6

The shop bell made a prim, little-girl-peeing sort of sound, the sun blasted the back of my head, a smell of sweet herbs and the music of the spheres enveloped me, and I shut the door on a cool, leafy potter's paradise. Outside, the streets were like furnaces, dust, glare, hot tires on hot pavement; here was the peace of a pine forest, soft-lit from the skylights above, suffused with the sweet scent of the sachets that clung to the beams like cocoons, viridescent with plants spilling from hanging pots, reaching for the ceiling from ceramic floor planters, sending tendrils out to embrace the weathered barn siding that silvered the walls. I stood there a moment, my back to the door, catching my breath like a man emerging from the sauna to plunge into a cold bath. Gentle breezes wafted, hidden speakers filled the room with a chorus of voices that rose and fell in passionate certitude—Bach, wasn't it? Yes, J. S. Bach sending a glorious full-throated missive to a merciful and present God.

I looked around me and saw the colors of the earth. Muted browns, sienna, umber, the palest of yellows. I saw Boston fern, philodendron, wandering Jew, myrtle and jade. I saw pottery—vases, planters, tureens, amphorae, urns, earthenware cups, glasses, pitchers, plates, finger bowls. There were ceramic bells and windchimes, massive cookpots, diminutive snuffboxes. And all arranged with taste and discrimination, set out on shelves, sideboards, a huge walnut table with place settings for eight and a delicate faience vase of cut flowers as a centerpiece. I felt as if

I'd stepped into a bower, a bedroom, a church. I pushed my hair back, wiped my sweating palms on the thighs of my pants and waited.

Nothing happened.

I listened to *kyrie eleisons*, examined this pot or that, discovered a fat orange cat and stroked its ears. Then I noticed a smaller bell, the familiar businesslike tinny sort of thing I've always associated with elementary school classrooms and hotel lobbies. I depressed the plunger—*bing-bing*, *bing-bing*—and was rewarded, a moment later, by the appearance of Petra.

She emerged from a door at the rear of the shop, dressed in a smock that flowed from her like a gown. She was barefoot, and a thin silver chain cut a *V* at her throat. I watched her official smile give way to a look of misplaced recognition. "Hi," I said.

"Oh," she murmured, stalling for time like a game-show contestant who's just been shown, for the purpose of identification, the monumental color slide of a bearded president. "Hi."

We smiled at one another.

"Fred?" she said.

"Felix," I corrected.

"Felix," she said.

I told her I'd dropped in to see how she was doing. She said she was doing fine and asked me how the fishing was. Her teeth were white, flawless, like something out of a toothpaste ad. "Fishing?" I repeated, puzzled, caught off guard, thinking of teeth and lips and the ache of enforced celibacy, until I remembered the lame story I'd concocted over the jack handle on that eventful evening a month back. "Lunkers," I blurted, "we've been catching lunkers. Yellowtails, guppies and monkey-faced eels."

To my relief, she laughed, and then turned to lift a ceramic teapot from a hot plate and offer me a cup of herb tea (rose hips or some such crap, which I detest and normally refuse, but managed somehow to accept gracefully). And then, stirring our tea, something magical happened—in a single leap we were able to extricate ourselves from the slough of trivia and small talk, and focus on the subject that bound us in intimacy: Jerpbak. Jerpbak, our mutual tormentor and bitterest enemy, our jailer, the agent that had brought us together, wed us, bound us flesh to flesh. I watched her eyes over the teacup and saw the back seat of Jerpbak's cruiser. "Is he still bothering you?" I said.

She shook her head. We were sitting at the big walnut table holding ceramic cups, while cars rushed by the window and Bach marched steadily forward, taking little figures and swelling them to great ones. "Uh-uh," she said. "Not since . . . well, not since I saw you last. I mean, when we met." She coughed into her fist and colored a bit.

I waved my hand as if to say *It's no big deal, I'm glad I stopped, I'd do it again anytime, swim out to Alcatraz and do thirty years in the federal pen for a glance from you, babe*, and told her—with all the flourishes—of my scrape with Jerpbak at the Eldorado County jail.

"God, that guy is nuts," she said. "He's not responsible for his actions. If they don't do something with him he's going to hurt somebody one of these days." She took a short angry sip of her tea. "Do you think he recognized you?"

"Who cares?" I said, hot and reckless, the tough guy, and then tried to shrug the whole thing off by telling her I'd got hold of a lawyer (which was true) who had assured me I would get off on all counts (not true), as I really hadn't done anything, when you came right down to it (also true).

"You were acting like a rational human being, that's all," she said, fixing me with the kind of look Joan of Arc must have taken into battle with her. "I'll testify to that."

We sat there a moment in silence, brooding over the wrongs done us, and then she observed that the whole thing was ironic in a way.

"Ironic?"

"Yes, well," she said, lowering her eyes, "I was the cause of the whole mess, and I actually got off easier than you. A lot easier. Compared to what you went through, I was lucky." The resisting arrest charge, it seemed, had merely been a threat, and Jerpbak had not followed through on it. She'd been booked and then released on the promise of returning in the morning with her license, and given forty-eight hours to correct the defects Jerpbak had ferreted out in the antique hulk of her VW Bug—from improperly displayed license plates to inoperable signal lights and eviscerated muffler—in lieu of paying the fines. It had cost her a hundred and twenty dollars in repair bills, she said, but at least she was free of it. And then her voice dropped to a whisper and she gave me the sort of look only martyrs nailed to the cross have a right to hope for: "I'm really sorry you had to get involved. If there's anything I can do . . ."

There was plenty she could do, I thought, in terms of local anesthesia and release of tension, and to avoid leering at her—she was feeling sorry for me, feeling sorry and grateful, and I didn't want to blow it by leaping at her like a sex maniac—I looked at my watch. It was one-thirty. Lunchtime. While I debated asking her to lunch (no doubt she'd already nibbled an alfalfa-sprout-and-feta-cheese sandwich while hunched over the potter's wheel), I bought a vase I couldn't afford, thinking I'd use it to enliven the décor at the summer camp or else ship it to my ninety-year-old maiden aunt in Buffalo.

"You sure you want this?" Petra asked me.

I nodded vigorously, mumbling something banal about the quality of the craftsmanship and the intricacy of the design.

"Do you know what it is?"

"A vase," I said.

She laughed—a short, toothy, ingenuous laugh—and then informed me that it was a funerary urn. "For ashes."

"Okay," I said, "you got me. I was going to put flowers in it." I held up a qualifying finger. "Dead flowers."

I was the soul of wit. We laughed together. She poured me a second cup of the wretched acidic tea (it tasted like a petroleum derivative) and asked if I'd like to see her workshop. "We'll call it an educational tour," she said, rising from the table.

I followed her into a brilliantly lit back room—cement floor, lath-and-plaster walls, high banks of gymnasium windows. It was hotter back here and the place smelled strongly of the clay that dominated it, coating everything in a fine thin layer, like volcanic ash or the residue of a dust storm. Petra took me round the room in a slow sweeping arc, pointing out the plastic bags of clay, the potter's wheel, her kiln the size of a gingerbread house, the buckets of glazes and the greenware in the drier. I smelled the ferment of the earth, fingered the clay and marveled at its moistness and plasticity; I saw her in her smock and her bare feet and felt I knew her. When I thought I'd seen everything and was trying to wrest the flow of the conversation from ceramics and push it in the direction of lunch, she gave me an odd look—eyes half-lidded, lips curled in a serene inscrutable smile—and asked if I'd like to see her real work.

"Real work?" I echoed. The room was as still and dry as an ancient riverbed; pots uncountable and in every phase of production littered the floor, the makeshift shelves, the drying racks and firing trays. I was puzzled.

She crooked her finger and I followed her—she in jogger's shorts, her long naked legs leaping from the cutaway smock, me in my least offensive T-shirt and most imbecilic smile—to a doorway at the far end of the room. I'd seen the door earlier and taken it for a closet, but now she flipped a light switch and led me into still another room. Perhaps the blandness of the workroom and my growing preoccupation with lunch had lulled me, but this was a surprise: suddenly I found myself amidst a host of strange figures, colors that pulsed, glazes that dazzled. If the shop was a potter's paradise, then this was the treasury of the gods. Or no: this was the dwarf kingdom. Bearded, mustachioed, long-eared and thick-browed, fifty faces leered at mine, their expressions crazed, demented, vacant. Human figures, two-thirds scale, stood, sat and crouched round the room, their heads pointed, eyes veiled, lips curled with private smiles or fat with the defective's pout. It was like being on a subway in Manhattan. I laughed.

Petra seemed relieved. She was grinning. "You like them?"

I was making various marveling noises—tongue clucks, throaty exclamations of wonder, giggles that rose in crescendo to choke off at the top. I stroked the slick, brightly glazed dunce cap of a man perched on the edge of a park bench and reading a newspaper. "Todd Browning," I said. "Fellini."

She nodded. "And Viola Frey. And Robert Arneson."

"And you," I said.

"And me."

A trio in buskins and leotards—men? women?—groped for a ball suspended from a string; a child with the drooping features of Leonid Brezhnev played at jacks. "These are great," I said, unraveling my arm to indicate the full range of them. "They're hilarious and weird, they're grotesque. Has anybody seen them?"

Petra was leaning against an enormously fat woman in a bridal gown decorated with dancing fishes. "A few people," she said, and I felt a surge of exhilaration (she was showing them to me, I was one of the chosen) and a corresponding jolt of jealousy (to whom else had she shown them?). Pots and creamers and orange-juice pitchers were okay, she said after a moment, and she enjoyed doing them—but she was an artist, too, and these pieces were an expression of that side of her. She was collecting them for a show in San Francisco.

I asked her if she knew anything about metal sculpture, and then if she'd ever heard of Phil Cherniske. "He does—he did—these big preposterous things in metal," I said. "He used to be known as Phil Yonkers?"

She looked as if she hadn't heard me, looked distracted, but she said, "No, I don't think so." And then: "Have you had lunch yet?"

"No," the word a hurtling shell, my lips the barrel of an artillery gun, "no, I haven't."

"Because I was going to close early—now, in fact—and go to a barbecue at this little country bar just outside of town. You know, steak and ribs and whatnot. They're celebrating national heifer week or something and a friend of mine who runs a health-food store made up some of the salads. I mean, I'm not that much into red meat, but I thought it might be fun."

"Sure," I said, marveling at how easy it was. "Sure, sounds like fun."

She was smiling like all the angels in heaven. "Great," she said. "Let me just take off this smock and get my purse," and she started out of the room, only to swing round at the doorway and lean into the post for a moment. "Maybe you know the place? It's on the Covelo road?"

One of the ceramic pinheads reached out and punched me in the solar plexus but I held on, praying, gasping for breath, feeling the great hot tongs of fate fishing around for me as if I were a lobster in a pot.

"It's called Shirelle's."

Chapter 7

The parking lot at Shirelle's—that barren wasteland, that tundra—was as packed with vehicles as a used-car lot. There were pickups, RVs, Mustangs, Bobcats and Impalas, choppers, dirtbikes and Mopeds, Trans Ams and Sevilles, woodies, dune buggies, vans—and the monolithic cherry-red cab of a Peterbilt truck, a machine among toys, rising like an island from the sea of steel and chrome. Beyond the cars I could make out cowboy hats and tiny sun-flamed faces and the metronomic dip and rise of the head of a grazing horse. I recognized the scene. Bingo under the trees, the church picnic, county fair. Children ran squalling through a blue-black haze of barbecue smoke, dogs yelped, Frisbees hung in the air. Over it all came the inevitable twanging thump of amplified country music—*Duckett, duckett, duck-etttt/Duck, duck, duck-etttt*—and the hoots and yahoos of inebriated giants in big-brimmed straw hats. I swung into the lot with a crunch of gravel and found a parking spot between two glistening, high-riding pickups. "Well," I said, turning to Petra, "this is it, huh?"

She was leaning forward in her seat, legs long and naked and brown, scanning the lot with the intensity of a child at the fair. "There's Sarah's car," she said, "and that's Teddy's motorcycle." She shot a look past me. "And good, good. Alice is here, too." Her hand was on my arm, light as a breath of air, heavy as a shackle. "I think you're really going to like them."

Odd, I thought, emerging from the car, that I'd barely noticed all this on my way into town an hour and a half ago. (I'd been aware of an unusual level of activity—cars swinging in and out of the lot, music blaring—but had been afraid to look too closely for fear I'd find myself staring into Savoy's face, or Shirelle's or Sapers's or George Pete Turner's.) Odder still that we'd taken my car—the interdicted Toyota—but I'd felt, for reasons that have to do with the masculine ego and the need to assert it, that I should be in command. Despite the fact that Petra had offered to drive and that the very sight of the Toyota was a provocation to every law enforcement officer within a thirty-mile radius.

I slammed my door. Petra slammed hers. I stood there a moment in the hellish sun, the smell of burning meat in my nostrils, and felt as naked and exposed as a sinner at the gates of Dis. Twice before I'd trod this very ground, and twice before I'd found myself in deep trouble. The place was a sink of enmity, a nest of yahooism, as fraught with danger as the Willits police station. (Quick clips of the leering faces of Sapers, Marlon, Shirelle, Savoy and Jerpbak passed in review through the contracting lens of my consciousness.) Good God. I'd gone back on my word, left the farm wide open to discovery and paraded my car about the streets, and now here I was, strolling blithely into the lion's den as if I had nothing to fear. What am I doing? I thought, suddenly seized with panic. Couldn't I control my urges, get a grip on myself, act like an adult? Of course I could, yes, of course. It wasn't too late. I'd tell Petra that I didn't feel well, that I hated fairs, country music, sunshine, that my parents had been missionaries roasted by cannibals and that the smell of the barbecue pit turned my stomach. But then she took my hand to lead me forward, and something rose up in me that had neither regard for danger nor respect for fear, and I felt nothing but bliss.

Admission, FOR ALL THE MEAT, BEER AND SALLID YOU CAN HOLD, was six dollars, and we stood in front of a card table manned by a rapier-nosed, watery-eyed old fellow in a plaid shirt while Petra dug through her purse and I examined the contents of my pockets. I had about fourteen or fifteen dollars to last me the rest of my life, but for the same reason I'd insisted on driving, I attempted to pay for both of us. I came up with two fives and two singles that were so worn they looked like leaf mulch, and laid them on the table, but Petra wouldn't hear of it. "No way," she said, scooping up the bills and forcing them into my front pocket. "I invited you, remember?"

The old man looked confused. He stared up at us out of pale, swollen eyes, then produced a handkerchief and blew his nose carefully, tenderly, as if he were aware that each blow might be his last. "Two?" he said, his voice distant and cracked, and then held out a trembling pink hand to take the twenty Petra offered him. As he fumbled for change in the cigar box at his elbow and then carefully tore two pale orange stubs from a wheel of all-purpose tickets, I couldn't help thinking, with shame and mortification and an odd sensation of arousal, of the makeshift desk at the suck palace and the ten sordid despairing minutes I'd given up there. I took the ticket guiltily—ADMIT ONE—and followed Petra, my guide and support, into the roped-off area that enclosed the sickly tree, the gaping dark entrance to the bar and the smoking pit.

For the first few minutes I kept my head down, tense and wary, concentrating on bits of broken glass in the dirt, on the sharp, minatory toes of cowboy boots, on bare ankles, painted toenails and snub-nosed sneakers. Petra led me to the beer booth, where I studied the footprints in the beer-muddied earth and the way the froth dissolved at the bartender's feet. "What'll it be, honey?" the bartender asked, twanging the verb until it fell somewhere between *bee* and *bay*.

"Two beers," I said, addressing his belt buckle.

Petra laughed. "Don't mind me," she said. "My voice is changing."

I stole a glance at the guffawing bartender, expecting Lloyd Sapers or George Pete Turner, and was relieved to find myself staring into the grinning, wild-eyed, gold-toothed, sun-blasted face of a drunken stranger in a Stetson hat. "Good beer, boy," he said, handing me two plastic cups filled to the rim. "Drink up. We got a bottomless keg here."

I nodded, wrenched my face into a simulated grin and gave the crowd a quick scan (the backs and profiles of strangers, naked shoulders, sunburned beer bellies, bola ties and blue jeans), and then ducked my head again, expecting the blade to fall at any moment. Then Petra said, "There's Sarah," and nudged me in the direction of a maze of tables heaped with food.

Sarah was tall, broad-shouldered and bosomy, dressed in Danskin top and jeans, her hair teased straight out from her head until it looked like one of those furry hats worn by the guards at Buckingham Palace. She sat at a long table behind a sign advertising her health-food store—THE SEEDS OF LIFE—and served falafel, tahini, tofu salad and carrot juice as alternatives to the ceremonial slabs of bloody beef that made National Heifer Week the event that it was. She wasn't doing much business. I took her hand as Petra introduced us, then watched as she scribbled "Out to Lunch" over the store logo and laid a sheet of plastic wrap over the tofu salad. "Everybody's over here," she said, and we followed her past the smoking barbecue pit (out of the corner of my eye I saw billowing smoke, vague menacing figures, the glow of hot coals) to a blanket spread out in the shade of the building.

The three occupants of the blanket—Teddy (a little guy in racing leathers whom I took to be Sarah's beau), Alice (a health-food nut, thin as a refugee), and a big, box-headed character with a wire-thin Little Richard mustache—smiled benevolently at us as we eased down amidst a clutter of paper plates and plastic cups, denuded ribs, puddled grease and pinto beans. I sat between Petra and Sarah, and sucked the foam from my beer. Flies hovered, the big P.A. speakers crackled, smoke spun off into the sky.

Petra introduced me—everyone seemed to be familiar with our connection, and this pleased me—and then Little Richard said that he'd just got back from three weeks in Hawaii, tuning pianos. This led to two distinct but rapidly converging threads of conversation: the Islands and the trade of piano tuning. Sarah said she was tone deaf. Teddy said that he once swam with humpback whales off Maui. Alice looked up from a plate of shredded carrots and said that she preferred Debussy's Etudes to anything Chopin ever did—especially when she was in Hawaii. Did the tropical air make tuning more difficult? Petra wondered. Richard tied up the loose ends neatly with an anecdote about sun bathing in Kaanapali with his tuning forks, and then turned to me and said, "So what do you do, fella?"

These were dangerous conversational waters, and I could see the shoals and reefs prickling about me. Earlier, in the car, Petra had asked the same question and I'd begged off by saying, "You know—a little of this and a little of that." "Sounds like a pretty evasive answer," she'd retorted, and I'd dropped the corners of my mouth and said, "You're right. Actually I run guns to Libya." Now I opted for the straightforward approach. I looked Richard in the eye and told him I inspected airplane fuselages for stress fractures.

"Oh," he said, and then the conversation rushed on past me, expanding to touch on methods of tofu preparation, the heat, the shameless behavior of a number of people I didn't know, and the political situation in Central America. I leaned back on the blanket, scanning the crowd for trouble, smiling amenably at Petra's friends and whispering nonstop witticisms in her ear. And oh, yes: drinking beer. It seemed that every time I took a swallow or two someone would hand me a fresh cup. This had a two-fold effect—of relaxing my guard (so what if I ran across Sapers or one of the other yokels—they had nothing on me) and suppressing my appetite. When Petra got us a plate of potato salad and chili beans, I did a couple of finger exercises with my plastic fork and then drained another beer.

After a while the conversation went dead, the C&W band lurched into some rural funk, and Sarah and Teddy got up to dance. Little Richard was passed out at the edge of the blanket, the sun filtering through the leaves to illuminate each separate astonishing whisker of his mustache, and Alice excused herself to go tend Sarah's health-food stand. I thought of asking Petra to dance, but since I hate dancing, I decided against it. Instead I told her that I hadn't meant to be flippant or to hide anything when she'd asked me what I did for a living, and sketched in what I'd been doing for the past year or so—that is, refurbishing Victorians in a slow market and reading banal, subliterate freshman papers as a part-timer at Cabrillo Community College. I didn't mention the summer camp.

She looked disappointed. Or skeptical. "So you live in San Francisco?"

I nodded. "But I'm up here for the summer with a couple of friends—just to get away, you know?"

"I know. Fishing, right?"

We smiled at each other. "Yeah, well, we do actually go fishing sometimes. But mainly the idea is just to rough it, you know, get out of the city, listen to the crickets, hike in the mountains."

"I know what you mean," she said, her voice so soft I could barely hear her, and then she dropped her head to trace a pattern in the blanket. I felt then that she saw right through me, knew as well as Vogelsang what I was doing in Willits. Lies beget other lies, I thought—now's the time to come clean, to start the relationship off right. But I didn't come clean. I couldn't. I was about to say more, to get myself in deeper, when she lifted her glass and said "Cheers."

For the next hour or so, while the sun made a molten puddle of the parking lot and the band hammered away at their guitars as if the instruments had somehow offended them, we talked, getting to know each other, comparing notes. I learned about Petra's childhood in Evanston, summers spent sailing on the Great Lakes, her talent for design and the first misshapen piece she'd ever fired (a noseless bust of Janis Joplin). Her father was an architect, her mother was dead. Auto accident. She had a sister named Helen. She liked green chartreuse, Husky dogs and old-time Chicago Blues. She was twenty-nine. When she was in the tenth grade, attending a private school, she'd met a guy two years her senior, an athlete, high achiever and verbal whiz. They dated. He was class president, she was secretary of the Art Club. He went to the University of Iowa, she went to the University of Iowa. They dated strenuously, lived together, got married. He went to law school, she worked (in a Kentucky-style-chicken franchise where they went through thirty gallons of lard a day). When he graduated and got a job with a firm in San Francisco, they moved to a skylit apartment on Dolores Street and she began doing ceramics in earnest. One night he told her he was bored. Bored? she said. I don't want to talk about it, he said. Two days later he was gone. She called the law firm. He hadn't been in for over a week. Later she heard that he was in Amsterdam, living on a barge, then someone saw him at a jazz club in Oslo. With a Danish girl. After that, she stopped asking.

I made sympathetic noises. How could anyone—be he deaf, dumb, blind, castrated—walk out on her? I was thinking, and then realized that someone, somewhere, could be thinking the same thing about Ronnie. Square pegs, round holes.

We drank beer. Petra stretched her legs, applied tanning oil to thighs and forearms, offered me potato salad as if it were caviar. It was hot, it was dry, there was too much dust, too much noise and there were too many people, but I hardly noticed—I gave my full attention to Petra, mooning over her like some ridiculous lovelorn swain out of Shakespeare or Lyly, ready to jump up and swoon at the drop of a hat. We drank more beer. Teddy and Sarah fumbled back to the blanket, panting and running sweat, stolidly drained their warm beers and staggered back to the dance floor. Then Petra handed me her empty cup and rose to her feet. "I've got to go to the ladies'. Would you get me another beer?"

"Sure," I said, reckless, foolish, drink-besotted, hurtling mindlessly toward some fateful collision. I sprang up from the blanket. We were standing inches apart. I put my arm around her shoulder and we kissed for the first time, dogs yapping and chords thumping at the periphery of my consciousness, my whole being consumed with pure urgent animal lust. "Be back in a minute," she said, her voice soft as a touch, and I stood there, empty cup in hand, watching helplessly as she receded into the crowd.

I looked around me. The heifer bacchanal was in full swing, heads, shoulders, torsos and hips flailing in time to the music, feet shuffling and legs kicking, incisors tearing, molars champing, throats gulping—beef, beef, beef—as the smoke rose to the sky and abandoned shrieks cut through the steady pounding din of the drums. To the left of the dancers was the barbecue pit, which I would have to negotiate on my way to the beer booth, and beyond that the appalling dark entrance of the bar.

I began to maneuver my way through the crowd, thinking of Petra's blue shorts and the couch at the summer camp, when someone set off a string of firecrackers and fifty hats sailed into the air accompanied by a chorus of yips and yahoos. Ducking hats and elbows, clutching the plastic cups in one hand and extending the other to forestall interference, I snaked through the mass of carnivorous bodies at the barbecue pit and was just closing in on my destination when a two-hundred-pound blonde in pigtails and a fringed Dale Evans outfit stepped in front of me and asked if I wanted to dance.

"Dance?" I repeated, stupefied. But before I could go into my hard-of-hearing-with-a-touch-of-brain-damage routine, she jerked my arm like a puppy's leash, spun me around and propelled me toward the dance floor. This was no time for argument: I danced. She pressed me to her—breasts like armaments, big grinding hips—then made the mistake of releasing my hand as she fell into momentary rapture over the musical miracle of her own rhythmically heaving body, and I dodged behind a barefoot lumberjack with beard, belly and ratchetting beads, and clawed my way to the beer booth.

The bartender had his back to me, bending to crack a fresh keg. "Two beers," I said. "When you get a chance." I stole a look over my shoulder to see if my dancing partner had missed me, but there was no sign of her. I was safe. I would give the dance floor a wide berth on the way back, hand Petra her beer and then suggest that we go to my place—or rather her place. Yes, that's what I'd do. We'd been here long enough, I'd taken foolish risks, and now it was time for my reward.

Absently, I studied the work-hardened hands of the bartender as he positioned the spigot over the cork, screwed the collar tight and rammed the plunger home. Somewhere behind me a raft of firecrackers snapped and stuttered. And then, in the half-conscious way we register minor changes in our environment, I saw that this bartender, with his sun-ravaged neck, graying hair and outsized ears, was not the good-natured cowboy of two and a half hours ago, but someone else altogether, someone who from this angle almost looked . . . familiar.

Before I could make the connection, Lloyd Sapers spun around, spigot in hand, and said, "Two beers coming up." The beer was already hissing into the first cup, yellow as bile, when he glanced up and found himself staring into my stricken face. There was a moment of shocked recognition during which his eyes fell back into his head and his lower jaw dropped open to reveal teeth worn to nubs and a lump of shit-colored tobacco, and then his face lit with a sort of malicious joy. "Well, Christ-ass, if it isn't Ernest Hemingway. Gettin' a bit dry up there on the mountain, hey?"

My first impulse was to laugh in his face in an explosion of nerves, like the killer at the denouement of a Sherlock Holmes movie (*Ha! You've caught me! Ha-Ha! Yes, yes: I did it! I killed her! Choked her with my own hands, I did. Ha! Ha-Ha, Ha-Ha! Ha!*). Fortunately, I was able to stifle that impulse. What I did manage to do, after struggling to get a grip on myself, was force my face into the jocular it-wasn't-me expression of a good ole boy caught in a minor but quintessentially manly transgression. "You know how it is," I said, grinning sheepishly, "the road to hell is paved with good intentions."

"Don't I know it," he roared and nearly choked on his own laughter. I watched as the level of beer rose in the second cup, already shifting my weight to turn and make my escape, when he leaned forward and said, "You didn't bring that big fella with you, did you? The one that shoved me around?"

I shook my head.

"Good," he said, dropping his voice from the usual roar. His straw hat was askew and he smelled as if he'd been dipped in used Kitty Litter. "I don't like him," he said confidentially, capping off the beer with a crown of foam. "The man just ain't neighborly."

I hooked two fingers over the lips of the plastic cups, preparatory to lifting them from the table and making my exit, but Sapers wouldn't release them. Held fast, I could only mumble something to the effect that Gesh was sometimes hard to get along with.

"Ha!" Sapers bellowed. "Now that's an understatement." And then he snatched the beers from my grasp and swished them in the dust. "You got a couple of chewed-up cups there, friend—what'd you do, pick 'em up off the ground?"

"No, I—"

"Here," he said, producing clean cups and clicking them down on the table, "I'll fix you up with some fresh ones," and I watched as he prolonged my agony by pumping up the keg and meticulously tipping each cup to accept a slow steady stream of headless beer. I was sweating. I closed my eyes a moment and watched a dance of red and green paremecia on the underside of my eyelids. "Here you go," Sapers said, and pushed the two full beers toward me.

Could it be this easy? I reached for the beers, about to thank him and go, when he ducked his head slyly, spat out a stream of saliva and tobacco juice and said, "So I hear you boys been doin' a little gardenin' up there. . . ."

I stood stock-still, my hands arrested, like a man at a picnic who glances up from his sandwich to find a two-inch hornet circumnavigating his head. Sapers was regarding me steadily, his eyes keen and intent. I remembered that first morning in the cabin, the way he'd dropped the mask of the yokel for just an instant and the foreboding I'd felt. He was clever, he was dangerous, he bore us ill will. And I was half drunk. As nonchalantly as I could, I lifted one of the beers to my lips, took a swallow and said, "Whatever gave you that idea?"

"Marlon," he said, blinking innocently, the hick again. "He says you got all these drums of water and hoses and—"

I cut him off. "Marlon?" Illumination came in a rush: the big lumbering half-wit had been spying on us, slipping through the woods like a cousin to the bear, fingering our hoses and sniffing our plants. "You mean he's . . .?" I couldn't quite frame the words.

Sapers looked apologetic. "Oh, listen, I hope you and your friends'll understand—the boy's a bit, you know," he said, tapping a gnarled finger to the side of his head. "He don't mean no harm."

"But our place is private property—we've got signs up all over the place." My voice was a squeal of outrage. "Vogelsang would hit the ceiling if he heard about this."

Sapers spat again, then picked up my beer and took a long swallow. "Aw, come on," he said, "it's no big deal, is it? What have you got to hide?"

"Nothing," I said, too quickly. "But it's the principle. You see, Vogelsang's afraid somebody'll get hurt on the property and sue him—he's got a real hang-up about it. And Gesh, you know how Gesh is." I shrugged. "Me, I could care less. I mean, shit, we've got nothing to hide."

Sapers was watching me like a predator, no hint of amusement in his face. "So what have you got in the ground over there anyways—sweet corn?"

What was he doing—playing games? Making me squirm? I didn't know what to think—maybe I was having a paranoid episode and he knew nothing at all—but at least I had the presence of mind to play along. "What else?" I said, as if in epicurean contemplation of that succulent, many-kerneled farinaceous vegetable. "Nothing but cattle corn in the supermarket, right?"

Sapers was impassive, his face locked like a vault.

"Of course, we're growing other stuff, too—for the exercise, you know? Beets, celery, cucumbers, succotash—you name it."

Stroking his chin thoughtfully, Sapers shifted the wad of tobacco from his left cheek to his right. "The only reason I ask is because I been havin' the devil of a time with the coons this year—for every ear they eat they spoil five. They hittin' you pretty hard, too?"

"No," I said. "I mean yes. Or we didn't know it was coons. Something's been getting into the garden, anyway—Phil thought it was bears." I chortled at the absurdity of it, but the joke fell flat. Something made me glance to my right at that instant, and I saw to my alarm that I was flanked by the immensity of Marlon and the wiry whiskery spring-coiled figure of George Pete Turner.

Marlon was wearing a dirty white T-shirt maculated with barbecue sauce, in the tenuous grip of which the great naked ball of his belly hung like a wad of soggy newsprint. He clutched a two-quart plastic bottle of Safeway cola in one hand and held a red helium balloon—HEIFER HIJINKS, WILLITS, CA—in the other. When he saw that my attention was focused on him, his eyes rushed round the thick lenses of his wire-framed glasses and he giggled.

George Pete Turner glared at me out of red-flecked eyes, then took a hit from a pint bottle of Old Grand-Dad. The last time I'd seen him he'd punched me in the side of the head. I looked from him to Sapers and then back again. "They let just about any scum in here, don't they?" George Pete observed, staring down at my shoes.

"Well," I said, an easy little chuckle breaking up the mellifluous double *l*s (who was I to take offense, the whole thing just a harmless little joke, a wisecrack, wit, persiflage, that's all). I followed this with "Heh-heh" as a sort of bridge, raised my hand in a quick farewell and ducked away, abandoning the beers.

It was at this point, nearly panicked now, running scared, that I found myself making eye contact with the big blonde in the Dale Evans outfit. Though I immediately glanced away, I could see out of the corner of my eye that she was making her way toward me through the crowd. I had nowhere to turn. Sapers behind me, the she-woman in front of me, the pit to my left and the dark portals of Shirelle's to my right. If in such situations the hearts of heroes expand to enable them to flail their enemies into submission, tuck heroines under their arms and swing to safety via conveniently placed gymnasium ropes, then I benefited at that moment from a similarly expanding organ—that is, my bladder. All at once my body spoke to me with an urgency that was not to be denied. I took a deep breath and plunged toward the shadowy entrance of the bar and the rushing release of the men's room that lay beyond it.

I was met by the roar of electric fans, a clamor of chaotic voices, and darkness. After the steady, harsh, omnipresent glare of the summer sun, the darkness here seemed absolute, impenetrable, the darkness of mushroom cellars, crypts, spelunkers' dreams. I edged out of the doorway in the direction of the bar, feeling my way through the pillars of flesh and barking drunken voices until my eyes began to adjust. The place, I saw, was packed. People pressed up against the bar, stood in tight howling groups with cocktails clenched in their hands, sat six or eight to a table tearing at ribs and hoisting pitchers of margaritas. For some reason—temperature control? atmosphere?—the curtains were drawn and candles glimmered from the tables. I stood there a moment, tentative, my shoulders drawn in, a canny old quarterback scouting the defensive line. Then my bladder goaded me and I started across the room.

Unfortunately, a great bleary white-haired hulk of a man in denim jacket and string tie chose that moment to lurch back and deliver the punch line of a joke with a lusty guffaw and an emphatic stamp of his rattlesnake-hide boot. The emphatic stamp caught me across the bridge of my right foot as the jokester's audience exploded in laughter. "Excuse me," I murmured, backing off, when I felt a pressure on my arm and swung round to stare bewildered into Savoy's foxy triangular little face. "Hi," she said. "Long time no see."

Something caught in my throat.

"Felix, right?" she said, treating me to a blinding, full-face smile. I felt like a prisoner of painted savages running the gauntlet over a trench of hot coals—reeling from one blow, I pitched face forward into the stinging slap of the next. I watched numbly as she fished a pack of cigarettes from a tiny sequined purse, shook one free and lit it.

"I was just going to the men's room," I said.

Savoy breathed smoke in my face. "So how do you like the party?" she said, ignoring me. The smile was fixed on her lips, as empty and artificial as the smile of a president's wife or a dime-store mannequin, but effective all the same. I didn't want to be within six miles of her, the pressure on my bladder was like a knife in the groin, I was in trouble, out of luck and I'd begun to feel queasy, and yet still that smile spoke to me of erotic delights unfolding like the petals of a flower. "You've got to admit," she said, pulling the cigarette from her mouth to nudge me and emit a chummy little giggle, "the place is shit-for-sure livelier than usual."

I had to admit it. But my stomach plunged like an elevator out of control and the ocean of beer I'd consumed was, according to the first law of gastrophysics, seeking an outlet. I belched.

This was hilarious. She clapped her hands and laughed aloud, as if I'd just delivered an epigram worthy of Oscar Wilde. "Far out," she gasped, still laughing. "I know what you mean." Then she gave me that beaming, wide-eyed, candid look and took my hand. "Listen," she said, "I'm over here at the bar. Why don't you come and join me for a minute so I can buy you a drink and introduce you to a few friends?"

Introduce me? This was the girl who had turned to me with the same smile, the same seductive eyes and insouciant breasts and announced, as if she were giving me an injection, that she had us cold. *Everybody in town knows what you guys are doing up there*. I pulled away. "No, no," I said, "I've got to go, really," knowing that she was poison, that she was out to trip me up, that her eyes were trepans and her smile a snare.

"Oh, come on," she said, tugging my hand as insistently as the big blonde had. "One little drink."

The flesh is weak, but the mind is weaker. I followed her.

We made our way through the crowd—men in wide-brimmed felt hats, women in print dresses clutching patent-leather purses—to the only unoccupied bar stool in the place. Two women—one middle-aged, the other about thirty—flanked the empty stool like sentinels. They smiled in unison as Savoy led me up to them.

What was going on here? I wondered vaguely, my brain numbed with love for Petra, lust for Savoy, heat, guilt, alcohol and the successive shocks of standing face to face with the handful of people in the world I most wanted to avoid. Why was Savoy, whom I barely knew, taking the trouble of introducing me to anyone? What was in it for her, for me? Was she just a friendly, ingenuous, lovely expansive teenager, or was she a conniving, hardened slut who wanted to lead me to destruction and make me betray my friends? For that matter, what was I doing here? Why wasn't I in the men's room, at Petra's apartment, crouching under the bed at the summer camp?

"This is Felix," Savoy was saying, "the guy I was telling you about?" *Telling them about?* The phrase sank talons in my flesh. I saw drinks on the bar—a glass of something clear—the hard foraging eyes of the older woman, the soft inquisitive gaze of the younger. Both women nodded, and I had the queer, light-headed sensation that the room was moving.

Savoy was watching me. The two women were watching me. I felt like a lion or an elephant at the moment of plunging through the concealed bamboo to the pit below. "This," Savoy said, indicating the older woman, "is Mrs. Jerpbak, and this," nodding toward the younger, "is her daughter-in-law, Jeannie."

At first the names didn't register. I rarely picked up names on a first introduction, even at the best of times. Mrs. Humpback, Mrs. Runamok: what difference did it make? But then, as the elder woman leaned toward me and mouthed "So what do you do, Felix?" the plugged channels of my brain opened up and the full horror of what was happening came home to me: I was standing amicably in a public place and trading polite chitchat with the wife and mother of my deadliest enemy. Joe McCarthy would as soon have sat down to tea with Ethel Rosenberg and Mao Tse-tung. Even worse, Savoy was obviously intimate with them—no doubt they were old family friends who watched TV and shampooed their dogs together, attended church socials arm-in-arm, observed one another's birthdays and shared a bottomless revulsion for dope growers, pickpockets and other specimens of urban depravity. *This is the guy I was telling you about*, Savoy had said. It was all up. We'd been fingered. Ten years, intoned the judge.

If I'd been able to pull myself together in the face of Sapers and George Pete Turner, now I broke down. Totally. Absolutely. Without hope or redemption. I leered down at this woman in the pink pants suit and cement hair (who reminded me disconcertingly of my own mother) and shrieked like a madman: "Ha-Ha! I did it! Yes, yes: I killed her!"

The elder Mrs. Jerpbak's face shrank until it resembled something you might stumble across in a root cellar. She jerked back in her seat like a whiplash victim and clutched at the neck of her blouse. "Ha, ha, ha!" I crowed, turning on the younger Mrs. Jerpbak with the exultation of the Superman, beyond civility, beyond law, beyond reason. "Killed her with my own hands, I did. And by God, I enjoyed it!"

People began to turn their heads. Savoy dug her fingers into my arm and hissed in my face like some scaly thing prodded with a stick: "We were just talking about the rewards for turning in dope farmers, did you know that? Huh? Did you hear about that?" Her face was twisted and ugly, furious, vituperative, the face of an extortionist.

I didn't feel well. I snatched the glass of clear liquid from the bar and downed it at a gulp. It was gin. I gave Savoy a sharp savage look—oh, the bitch, the bitch—folded my face up like a deck of cards (the floor heaving and swaying, faces melding in a blur as if glimpsed through the windows of a hurtling train), and then turned and vomited in the elder Mrs. Jerpbak's lap.

Petra was sitting with Teddy and Sarah when I returned, beerless, my bladder full and stomach empty, reeking of my own intestinal secrets and flailing through the crowd in a galloping, braying, headlong panic. "Felix," Petra said, "where have you been?"

I could barely speak, locked in the paranoiac's delirium, envisioning Jerpbak calling out the National Guard to avenge the assault on his mother, looking at Petra and seeing a horde of keypunchers and savings-and-loan men in fatigues, jaws grim with a spoiled weekend, their shiny new high-laced boots trampling through the scrub outside the cabin. Hounds bayed, helicopters hovered. *We know you're in there, shithead*, Jerpbak bellowed through a megaphone, and then his voice faltered and broke: *Ma*, he bleated, *Maaaaa!*

"Felix?"

"Listen," I said, panting, jerking my neck wildly as beefy faces lurched in and out of my field of vision, "listen, I've got to take off, I mean something's come up, it's, uh, well it's my mother. Her, she—"

Petra was on her feet. "Are you all right?"

I could think of one thing only: slamming up the road to the summer camp as fast as the Toyota would take me and burying my head in the sleeping bag. "Can you, do you think you could get a ride back to town?"

Teddy and Sarah were standing now, too, their faces pinched with distrust: I was nobody, a stranger, an untouchable. I could have been a Hare Krishna begging change in the airport lobby. Petra's jaw hardened. "Is this a joke?"

"No, listen, I'm sorry," I said, already backing away.

"Felix." There was impatience in her tone, exasperation. But there was something else, too: the hint of a plea.

"I'll call," I blurted—gutshot, terrified, stung by bestial urges and the frenzy of the doomed—as I turned to run for the car.

"Don't bother," Petra said.

I was running. No time to look back. I ran with all the force of the panic rising in my chest, ran in shock, ran as if the entire Jerpbak clan, Savoy, Sapers and George Pete Turner were chasing me with a pot of tar, ran till my lungs were heaving like a drowning man's and the burning red door of the Toyota jerked back on its hinges and I plunged the key like a sword into the hot slot of the ignition.

I drove without thinking, fast and hard. Seventy-five, eighty, bad tires keening round the curves, my stomach churning. I hit the dirt road to the summer camp at fifty, slammed over scree, fallen limbs, the rock-hard hump that rose between the ruts like bread in a pan, and careened to a halt in a tangle of poison oak and stinging nettle. I shoved out of the car, fell to my knees and puked till I could feel my digestive tract strung out on a wire from throat to sphincter. My eyes watered, my head ached. I watched indifferently as a glossy black beetle crawled between my fingers and a party of ants discovered the sour eruption in their midst, then rose shakily, relieved the pressure on my bladder and forced myself back into the car. After grinding back and forth a dozen times, I managed to jerk the Toyota from the bushes and out onto the hardpan surface of the road.

It was then that I noticed the other car. An old MG, slung low, the grill like meshed teeth. It was parked on the Covelo road, almost directly across from the entrance to our driveway. I put the car in neutral and backed to the edge of the blacktop for a closer look. The car was in prime condition, newly painted, not a nick on it. There was no one in sight. Where was the driver? Had the car broken down, run out of gas? Or was this some backpacking Sierra Club freak ignoring our posted signs? I sat there a moment, studying the inert vehicle in the rearview mirror, then started up the road for the cabin.

Everything was as I'd left it—the tumbledown shack with its cloudy windows and peeling tarpaper, the gutted outbuildings, mounds of garbage. The Jeep sagged forward on its bad spring, the open hood testimony to my frustrated efforts to start it. It was six-thirty. The sun hung over the cabin as if stalled, a hushed expectant stillness in the air. Dowst wasn't back yet.

I felt a hundred years old. My clothes were sweat-soaked, my mouth tasted of bile. I'd left the plantation for six hours and the wrath of the gods had fallen on my head. There was no doubt about it, I thought, trudging across the moribund field to the house, Savoy meant to blackmail us. And I'd have to tell them. Tell Phil and Gesh, my partners and fellow sufferers, my buddies. Tell Dowst. Tell Vogelsang. Tell them I'd gone back on my word, tell them I'd fucked up. I stepped up on the porch, scattering lizards, and the tiniest hope flared in my scored brain: Vogelsang. Maybe he could sound her out, buy her off, kidnap her and ship her to Bolivia in a crate of machine parts. Anything was possible. After all, he was used to working miracles—and he never lost. Never. Not to anyone.

The door pushed open with its usual whine of protest—bed, I was thinking, an hour's sleep, that's all I'll need and then I can sort things out—when I caught a whiff of cigarette smoke and turned to see a figure seated on the couch. It wasn't Dowst, it wasn't Vogelsang, it wasn't Phil or Gesh or Aorta. I stood there frozen in the doorway, stupefied, blinking at the gloom. I saw ankle boots, skinny tie, short hair brushed straight up and back.

"Hello, Felix," Jones said.

Chapter 8

I heard the minutest sounds: the drip of the bathroom faucet, the rattle of a fly trapped against the windowpane. *Tap-tap, tap.* The fly threw the husk of its body against the glass—blindly, uselessly—until the rasp of those cellophane wings became unbearable. For an instant, as if in a dream, the objects of the room lost definition (shadows and shapes, shapes and shadows) and then materialized again. I saw a bag of garbage spilled beneath the stove, cobwebs, dirt, a deck of worn cards on the kitchen table, I saw Jones. The moment was timeless, eternal. *Tap-tap, tap.* Jones made no move to rise from the couch. Finally, the seconds swelling like blisters, he attempted a smile, the sort of smile one ten-year-old gives another before shoving him over the back of a crouching conspirator. "Don't you remember me?" he said.

My first thought was to close the door, trap him so he couldn't escape. But then what? Strangle him with his tie? Get him in a headlock and wait for reinforcements? Jones. The wonder of it, the perfidy, the wicked baffling collusion of chance and circumstance: he'd known all along. I slammed the door with a savagery that shook the house.

"No need to get upset, brother," Jones said, dragging on his cigarette. "I just came to talk business, that's all."

I measured the room in six long strides and stood over him, hands clenched at my sides. "Get the fuck out of here," I said.

My voice was strained, distant, as harsh and punchy as a drumroll echoing across an open field.

Jones didn't flinch. He just looked up at me, cool as an assassin, arms folded and jaw set. *I don't give a shit*, his eyes said. *About you, the social contract, hard work, sweat, toil, aspiration. . . . I want*, they said.

I wanted, too. I wanted tranquillity, soothing pleasures in every part, an end to fear, madness and the frantic driven wide-eyed rush of the pursued, I wanted my friends to make money and the summer camp to succeed. And though I hadn't struck anyone in anger since I was thirteen and a kid named Sammy Wolfson told me to get my dirty ass out of his mother's begonias, I wanted to strike Jones. Right then. Swiftly, savagely, with power and immediacy and all the hammering force of righteousness. I wanted to blast him, flatten him, cripple him, concentrate all my rage and bile in one annihilating, bone-crushing blow and lay him to waste. I'd had it. I looked at Jones and knew I could kill.

If he could read my thoughts, Jones gave no indication of it. He crossed his legs as casually as if he were lunching at the finks' club, and then flicked the ash from his cigarette. On the floor. "All's I want is ten thou."

"Get out!" I roared. I was trembling.

Jones uncoiled himself and cautiously rose from the couch. We were standing two feet apart. "You want to fight?" he said. "I'll fight you, motherfucker."

This was it, the project gone to pot, the wolf at the door, violence and criminality. "Get out," I repeated, senselessly, and my voice dropped with resignation: there were no more words.

"Hit me, man," Jones said, backing off a pace. "Go on. But I'll walk straight into the Willits police station and collect a thousand bucks for turning you guys in. You like that?"

I didn't like anything. I didn't care. I cocked my fist.

Just then, *salvator mundi*, there was the sound of a car in the field outside, and Dowst's van eased into view beyond the window. We watched silently as the van jerked to a halt in a maelstrom of dust and Dowst emerged in shorts and sandals, looking as if he were on his way to a croquet party. Jones exhaled a cloud of smoke and eased himself down on the arm of the couch. "The other partner, huh?" he sneered. "Let's let him in on this, too."

Dowst came through the door with a sack of Santa Rosa plums, two bags of ice and a big-toothed companionable grin. When he spotted Jones slouching there against the arm of the couch like a delinquent outside the principal's office, he stopped dead a moment, as if afraid he'd entered the wrong house, then continued on in and set his burden down on the kitchen counter. His face had flared briefly—with surprise, passion, outrage—and then fallen in on itself like a white dwarf. Now he stood there at the counter, his mouth puckered in a lower-case *o*, struggling for some reason to replicate the call of a familiar woodland bird.

"Jones," I said.

"Jones?"

"The famous dope farmer," I said. Jones grinned. "He's here to blackmail us."

"All's I want is ten thou," Jones said, replaying a tape.

I watched comprehension filter into Dowst's face, and then I watched him get angry (it began with his ears, which flushed the color of spiracha chilis, as if they'd been tweaked, and then seeped into his face, settling in a tight intransigent line across his lips). "We're busy here," he said. "We've got no time for leeches. As Dowst waxed, I waned. I found that my own anger had dissipated, choked on itself like the mythical beast that swallows its own tail. All I felt now was despair.

Jones ground out his cigarette on the arm of the couch and then adjusted the knot of his tie. "You're busy," he mocked. "Well, so am I. So's the sheriff. He's busy looking for assholes like you."

"We know about you," Dowst said. He was puffed up with self-righteousness now, the Yalie remonstrating over a trick question on a botany quiz. "You were busted last summer."

Jones shrugged. "Then they'll know my information is reliable, right?" He pushed himself up from the chair arm and moved past me toward the door. "Look," he said, pausing at the doorway and glancing from me to Dowst, "I'm not asking, I'm telling you. Ten thousand bucks. Cash. You don't give it to me, I'll have a talk with the sheriff."

The color had gone out of Dowst's face as the gravity of the situation hit home: we were powerless. We could bait, bluster and threaten all day, we could coddle and cajole, appeal to Jones's better nature and then pin him down and work over his ribs and groin till he couldn't stand, but he had us. Short of murder, there was nothing we could do to stop him. Dowst looked sorrowful, penitent, deeply hurt and appalled; he looked as if he'd been punched in the wallet. "But we haven't got that kind of money," he said. "It's all wrapped up in the plants."

"Monday. Noon."

"You know that," I said. He was giving us two days. "You of all people . . ."

Jones turned to me with a look of malice that made me want to wring my hands, tear out my hair and out-howl the damned in the lake of fire. "Ask Vogelsang," he said, and the name sounded natural on his lips, the thought sensible and apposite, until I realized that this was Jones speaking, a stranger, someone who couldn't possibly have known who was behind us . . . *unless*—picture mountains toppling into the sea, great slabs of granite shearing off and hammering the pitching waters, and you'll have an idea of how this insight was to hit me—*unless Vogelsang had been lying to us all along*, *unless Jones* had *been his man*. Dowst must have had the same thought. Slap. Crash. Thud. His mouth gaped and his hands fluttered at his sides as if he'd gone into neuromuscular collapse.

The door was open. Jones was framed in the glare from the dead yellow field and the dead yellow hills beyond. His expression was gloating, triumphant—he could have been a grand master maneuvering his bitterest rival into checkmate. I watched in a daze as he lifted his index finger in hip valediction. "Ciao," he said, and the door pulled shut.

I was sunk uneasily in the easy chair, simultaneously studying Vogelsang's back, tapping my foot to a manic nine/eight beat and devouring corn chips with a compulsion that verged on frenzy. Something was about to happen, something final and irrevocable, but I didn't know what. Vogelsang's back (the dapple of brown and green in the jumpsuit, the undershirt of muscle rippling and contracting as he gestured with his hands and upper body, the hard black excrescence of the .44 at his side) was the center in a storm of uncertainty, a cipher, something to hold on to. I studied it as the setting sun smeared the windows with blood.

Vogelsang was talking, talking nonstop, and we were in the midst of a crisis. The crisis. The crisis of crises. At long last, after all the scarifying feints and shuffles, after all the alarms in the night, our troubles had erupted and the hour of our sorrow was at hand. *Be ye ashamed, O ye husbandmen; howl, O ye vinedressers, for the wheat and for the barley; because the harvest of the field is perished.* Oh, yes.

All the principals were gathered, Dowst in his kerchief and I in my cap, Gesh, Phil, Aorta. Dowst was sitting across from Vogelsang at the kitchen table, an expression of censure and distaste ironed into his stern Yankee features. Aorta hunched beside Vogelsang in an imitation-leopardskin jacket, examining her nails with a bowed head, and—this got my heart pounding—looking scared. Propped up against the stove, his face a mask of rage—curled lip, Tatar cheekbones, bristling beard—Gesh could have been an advance man for Genghis Khan. His eyes were lidded with exhaustion and the torpor of methaqualone abuse, and the sleeves of his shirt had been cut away to reveal the cables in his arms. Phil was gone, a mere ghost of himself, stretched out on the couch behind me like a narcoleptic. He and Gesh had rolled into Tahoe at about the time I'd stepped into Petra's shop, and they'd worked diligently at obliterating all thought of the summer camp until Dowst's hysterical summons reached them at three-thirty the following morning. Then they climbed back into the pickup and watched the broken yellow line eat up the road.

My hand went to the bag of chips, then to my mouth, then back to the bag: hand, bag, mouth, hand, bag, mouth. Phil's snores were like stones dropped on a polished surface. Vogelsang's voice rattled on. Immanent, inescapable, like beat of blood and thump of heart, the little creatures of house and wood saturated the auditory spectrum with clicks, rattles, hisses and grunts. Twenty-four hours had passed since I'd walked into the house and found Jones on the couch.

"All I know about Jones is what Strozier told me. He must have been guerrilla farming up here—Strozier didn't even know it himself till he came up from the city one day and saw the garbage the idiot left behind." *Psssst, psssst.* Vogelsang freshened his breath. "If Jones named me he probably looked up the deed to the property and took an educated guess."

My hand paused at the bag's aperture, my foot stopped drumming. I'd created half this crisis—Savoy was all my own doing—and I didn't have a right even to open my mouth at this point. But I surprised myself. "Vogelsang," I said. "You're lying."

At first, the secret of Savoy had clung to me like a mussel to a rock, tenacious, immovable, held fast despite the crash of the waves and the suck of the tide. Reeling from the confrontation with Jones and the gallery of horrors to which I'd been subjected at Shirelle's, I was too deep in shock even to think about my weakness, treachery and guilt, let alone confess them. For a while I even toyed with the idea of keeping the whole thing to myself. Forever. If we were busted, the fink-of-choice was Jones. Savoy? Never heard of her. I sank low in that moment, as low as I've ever sunk, but my better self won out. There was a moral imperative here: I was a sentry and the barbarians were creeping up on us, dirks clenched between their teeth and blood in their eyes, and it was up to me to sound the alarm. I'd already left the gate open. Could I stand by and see my mates butchered in their bunks?

Still, confession hadn't come easy. Just after Jones had made his exit, Dowst and I had dodged frantically round the room for half an hour or so, ritually weeping, wailing and gnashing our teeth, before it occurred to Dowst that he should *(a)* remove himself as quickly as possible from the scene of the crime, and *(b)* use the phoning of the absent partners as a pretext for that removal. He was gone for hours. The night revolved round my guilt. The house was dark, and I lay in my bed like a sacrificial victim on the block, the jetliners at thirty thousand feet screaming in my ears, each rustle of leaf or sigh of branch the dread footfall of the high priest. And then, at the stroke of some dark, forlorn hour, there came the closing rumble of a vehicle making its way up the hill. Dowst? Jerpbak? G. P. Turner and a mob of vigilantes? I didn't wait to find out. My legs exploded beneath me and I was out the door in a bound, across the field and into the woods by the time Dowst's headlights illuminated the trees at the far end of the front lot. It was four a.m. I hadn't slept an instant. I huddled there in the crushed leaves, spiderwebs and squirrel shit, crying out for absolution, ready to crawl on my hands and knees up the thousand steps of the temple, ready to bare my soul and take my pricks and kicks.

I told Dowst. (I don't remember how I broached the subject. Lamely, I'm sure. "Uh, Boyd, uh, guess what? You want to hear something funny?") Then, when they arrived at noon—burned out, hung over, and terminally wired—I told Phil and Gesh. Finally, when Vogelsang pulled in at five in the afternoon, I choked back my swollen tongue, hung my head and told him, too. He listened stoically, lines ironed into his cheeks. "I'm disappointed in you," he said when I'd finished. His tone of voice was a marvel—distant, superior, lugubrious and sarcastic to the point of flagellation—a tone precisely calculated to induce writhings of guilt in its auditor. "First the thing with the CHP, and now this. You're out of control, Felix." He was the crestfallen coach and I the star player caught with a bag of Dexamyls in his locker. "I thought you were the rock of this project, someone I could trust. That's why Boyd and I came to you first." Dowst was irate. He insisted that I forfeit my share and get off the property posthaste. Gesh raged, Phil clucked his tongue. I was stupid, they said, a fool. Pussy-crazed. I'd let them down. I was a first-class schmuck, an airhead, an oaf and a poltroon. They said all of this and more, my co-sufferers and fellow peons (every time I glanced at Gesh he came up with a new insult), but they stood by me.

We'd waited for Vogelsang through the endless afternoon, waited as a beleaguered and vastly outnumbered army waits for reinforcements, for the order to withdraw, for the old campaigner who can turn defeat into victory. He'd marched in with a stiff back, strung as tightly as any of us, jumping at the slightest sound, but trying his best to maintain. My confession had given him a chance to take the offensive, but when we'd exhausted that ground and turned back to Jones, he'd begun filibustering. He was selling and we weren't buying. Confusion, panic and the withering fire of recrimination assailed us, we beat our breasts, shrieked in one another's faces. Accusations flew, tempers flared. We cursed one another, raged and receded, plotted wildly, imagined untold horrors and parceled out blame.

The biggest parcel was mine. I was blameworthy in everyone's eyes, my own included. I was incontinent, unreliable, about as trustworthy as a shaggy-legged satyr at a Girl Scout jamboree. Dowst was culpable, as far as Phil, Gesh and I were concerned, for having failed to come up with sufficient seedlings and to plan for a host of contingencies—from root rot to rodents to the birth of Jerpbak—but he was absolved from blame in the current crisis. Vogelsang was unanimously guilty—of duplicity and underhandedness, of failing to shield us from harsh eventuality, of having walked into my living room on that rainy winter's night. There were two innocents among us. Oh, they could have dug more holes or killed more rats, but at this point they were nothing more than aggrieved victims.

Now, the sun dipping behind the ridge and bringing us that much closer to the hour Jones had named, one of those aggrieved innocents spoke up. "Felix says you're lying, Herb," Gesh growled, his voice the ominous rumble of some cave-dwelling thing, some bear or wolverine roused from hibernation.

The filibuster had stopped cold. Vogelsang looked tense, shifty, he looked like a perjurer tripped up on the witness stand, he looked like a liar. "I'm not," he said. "Trust me." And then he was off again, as if afraid to stop talking, reassuring us, marshalling arguments against our quitting, admitting that things had come to a dangerous pass through my irresponsibility and other factors beyond his control, but reminding us that nothing had happened yet and insisting that he would do his fixer's best to right the cart. Or something like that. I remember only that he used the orator's stratagem of exaggerating the adversary's guilt and opposing it to his own innocence, and that he finished by assuring us that he would ferret out Jones and Savoy and see what he could do. "Don't worry," he said. "I'll take care of them."

Take care of them? I thought. What was he going to do—

buy them off? Cut out their tongues? Run them down in his Saab? Take care of them. He'd promised to take care of us, too.

"Jones," Gesh repeated. The name was a summons, a challenge, a kick in the face. He was leaning forward now, his fists clenched, his eyes swollen till they looked like cueballs. "You're lying, Herb. You're shit-faced with it."

"Christ, stop bickering," Dowst snapped, leaping up from the table. "The police could be at the door any minute. I say we harvest what we can and get out now."

I could see it coming, see it in the way Gesh shifted his weight forward and swung away from the stove, and though I hurled myself out of the armchair, I was half an instant too late. There was a thud as Dowst hit the wall, a muted cry from Aorta and then the wet brutal slap, as of a canoe paddle brought down on the surface of a still lake, as Gesh caught Vogelsang across the cheekbone with six months of rage and frustration. It was a lurching, graceless blow, and Gesh staggered forward under his own momentum, fist, arm, shoulder and chest describing a single arc that brought him and Vogelsang to the floor in a deluge of flesh. The table leapt, the chair splintered. Coffee mugs skipped across the linoleum. Vogelsang was on his back, hugging Gesh in a lover's embrace, cords standing out in his neck, jaw clamped, eyes feral and frightening. Gesh fought for purchase. "Motherfucker," he spat, over and over, as if it were a battle cry.

They were scraping across the floor, hugging each other, the shuffle of hands and feet like a chorus of sweeping brooms. Gesh was breathing hard, grunting, cursing; Vogelsang grappled in silence. By now Dowst had recovered from his initial shock and was leaning over the combatants like a referee. "Knock it off!" he shouted, as if it could have the slightest effect. "Come on, break it up!" Feet churned over the floor, the end table went down. Aorta had backed up against the far wall, Phil looked up groggily from the couch. I didn't know what to do. I stood there, trembling, caught up in the killing violence, watching Gesh hammer at Vogelsang and wanting both to wade in and separate them and to let it go on. Vogelsang was down. The untouchable, the serene, chief god of his own pantheon and victor of every contest he'd ever entered. He was down, and something moved in me with every blow.

It's hard to say exactly how it happened. Gesh was on his knees, swinging mechanically, Vogelsang struggling to ward off the blows and Dowst leaning forward clumsily to snatch at Gesh's collar like a teacher in the schoolyard. Then suddenly Vogelsang was free and scrambling to his feet while Dowst hit the wall again and Gesh rose from the floor like a wounded bear. "Gesh!" I shouted, and I understood in that instant that I was cheering him on, goading him, backing him, calling out his name in partisanship and affirmation as the ranks of hometown fans call out the single name of the champion stepping up to bat. For them. For us. Gesh moved forward, huge, the street fighter, the brawler, blood on his knuckles.

I glanced at Vogelsang. His face showed nothing. His right eye was swollen and there was a thread of blood at the corner of his mouth. The .44, swift death, steel in an arena of flesh, clung to his hip. He ignored it. Instead, he cocked his open hands in the kung fu pyramid and stepped forward.

"No!" I shouted.

"Vogelsang!" Dowst called.

It was so quick. So quick I barely saw it. Gesh swung, Vogelsang parried the blow and caught him twice in the throat with the flat of his hand and then struck him in the groin with an exploding foot. As Gesh pitched forward, Vogelsang's knee went to the small of his back and I could hear the chiropractor's crack as he jerked Gesh's head back in the Montagnard death grip. And then, before I could realize what was happening, Phil was up off the couch with the misaligned .22 in his hand and I was flinging up my elbow to deflect his aim—too far, this had gone too far—when we all stopped dead at the sound of Aorta's voice.

She hadn't screamed—no, it was far more chilling than that. "Oh, my God," she said, and it cut like a knife to the core of everything we were—stark, animal, squeal of bushpig, howl of monkey—and we understood somehow that the words had no reference to the silly morality play we were enacting. We looked up—all of us, even Vogelsang, even Gesh. Looked up and saw that there was a face in the kitchen window, framed against the darkening sky. Round and huge, moonlike, a face, watching us.

PART 4

Harvest

Chapter 1

The fire put things in perspective. It came like a judgment, singeing, cleansing, burning with a pure, fatal, almost mystic candescence, eating away at the old growth of our baited lives to make way for the new. Immediate, deadly, it put us back in touch with ourselves. If we'd sat around the stove on a rainy spring night and traded tales of cheating death, now we fought for our lives. We burned. Inhaled smoke, rubbed our eyes raw. We dropped into the inferno and emerged again. Singed. Cleansed. Alive.

It was a stifling, bone-dry night in early October, a month from harvest (with hope, fear and a nod to the demons, we'd chosen my birthday, circled in black on the apocalyptic calendar, for the day we would reap what we'd sown). Gesh was gone, damping his inner fires in the anodynic embrace of Tahoe Nelda, and Phil and I were sitting up late—well past midnight—drinking big glasses of vodka and tonic, smoking pot and playing pitch. The fuel in the ancient Coleman lantern was burning low. I shuffled the cards. All the world was as hushed as if it were about to plunge into eternity.

Phil took the bid, and I could tell he had a killer hand by the way he let his eye wander casually over the room (he was contemplating the appointments, struck with the smart conjunction of couch, armchair and splintered end table, cards the furthest thing from his mind). He threw the queen of spades (the son of a bitch, I knew he had the king and jack back there, too), just as the lamp began to flicker. "Damn," he said, raking in my deuce and slapping down the king. The light was fading fast. I studied his king for a long palpitating moment, as though debating the loss of another point card, and then with a grin laid down the ace. Of spades. "I'll get it," Phil said, jumping up to refill the lantern. "Make me another drink, will you?"

I got up and shuffled to the cooler in darkness as Phil fumbled for the flashlight, snatched the lantern from the table and hurried out the door. Ice. I pawed around, dropped some cubes in a pair of fresh glasses and felt the house rock gently as Phil thumped across the porch. CAUTION: DO NOT REFILL WHEN HOT, warned the inscription on the base of the lantern. I poured from bottles. *Glug-glug-glug*. Outside were the stars, the trees, the endless blanched hills. I settled in the darkness, drink in hand, and listened to the slow weary moan of the storage shed door as it pulled back on its hinges.

In August, I never thought I'd see September on the farm, let alone October. Any shred of hope I may have nurtured after the earlier disappointments—the reemergence of Jerpbak, my confinement to the property, the ongoing decimation of the crop—was dashed by the leapfrogging catastrophes of that nightmarish two-day period at the end of the month. In the space of just over thirty hours I'd managed to rearouse the viper's pit of the Bum Steer, alienate Petra, sully Jerpbak's mother, feel the pinch of Jones, witness the eruption of physical conflict between my partners and experience the onset of cardiac arrest in the terrible moment in which Aorta had gasped and I looked up to see that leering face in the window. Was ever man so beset by demons? I was ready to hang it up, flay myself through the streets, run to the authorities and turn myself in: I saw that face in the window and knew we'd reached the end. But here it was October, and we were alive and well and unincarcerated, and looking forward to reaping not thorns but dollars.

We'd been spared. For the moment, at any rate. The great jaws had come near, gaping so that all we could see was the darkness within, and then they'd rushed on by to gobble up some other luckless creature while we bobbed helplessly in the wake. August had left us with two choices: run or stay. If we ran, we would take next to nothing with us, the plants having barely begun to bud. If we stayed, we faced loss, disorder, sorrow and ruination. We stayed. Through inertia more than anything else. We were stuck in gear, crushed by indecision and apathy, unable to throw down our shovels and hoses no matter what the cost. Like the mule that goes on pulling its cart after the muleskinner drops dead of sunstroke, we went on. Out of necessity. Out of boredom, fatigue, confusion. Out of habit.

It was in this state that we awaited Jones. We waited through that long Tuesday, Phil, Gesh and I (Dowst and Vogelsang had vanished, of course), waited grimly, heroically, waited like prisoners on death row. Jones wanted ten thousand. Between us we had sixteen dollars and forty-two cents. Noon came and went. No Jones. We were puzzled, anxious. Had he gone to the police after all? Had he forgotten the whole thing? Had he died and gone to hoods' heaven? Night fell. We sat in darkness so we could see him approaching. We emptied half a gallon of vodka. Gesh smoked two packs of cigarettes. Jones didn't show. By the third or fourth day the tension began to ease, and we forgot him for minutes at a time as we went about our chores and fought the tedium with the usual round of drinks, bombers, cheap paperbacks, tortured naps, horseshoes, Monopoly and cards.

A week after the appointed date, we were jolted from our postprandial torpor by the throaty roar of a foreign car negotiating the hill. I looked into my co-workers' eyes and saw fear, despair and resignation. We shuffled outside and stood in a grim knot on the porch. We weren't running. I chewed my lip and watched the trees for the first heartless red flash of Jones's MG. Phil began to whistle tunelessly. As the sound of the engine grew closer, I began to whistle, too. *Oh, Susannah*, I whistled, *don't you cry for me*, but then Vogelsang's Saab rounded the corner and lurched into the field, and I felt as if I'd been resurrected from the dead.

Unfortunately, the appearance of Vogelsang's Saab did not necessarily indicate the appearance of Vogelsang (though we didn't realize it at the time, he'd already paid his final visit to the summer camp). Aorta was alone. We watched as she slid out of the car and made her sinuous way toward us, a flat white envelope clutched in her hand. "Hi," she said, her face as expressionless as the late Mao Tse-tung's. I saw that she'd dyed her hair anew: a two-inch azure stripe now ran from her brow to the nape of her neck, giving her the look of some bush creature, some weirdly striped antelope or prowling cat. "Vogelsang said to give this to you."

"Where is he?" Gesh demanded. "What's he doing about all this shit that's coming down?"

"Jones never showed," I said.

She glanced up at me, then focused on the crumpled Pennzoil can at my feet. "We know," she murmured. "Read the letter." And then, as if she were messenger to a colony of lepers, she turned to hurry off before we could contaminate her.

I tore open the envelope, which bore my name across the front in the blocky misaligned characters kidnappers clip from magazines in gangster movies. The letter inside was pasted up in the same way:

> Felix:
>
> I have contacted J., having found his address in the court record for his arrest. He will not bother us further. I was able to bargain him down to $5,000, which I paid him in cash. The money, of course, is a debit against out net earnings, and will have to be deducted from our respective shares.
>
> The other problem, the problem of S., has I think been resolved, and far less painfully (see enclosure).
>
> The Fates are smiling on us, yes?
>
> Yours,
>
> V.

Phil and Gesh read over my shoulder.

"Five thousand bucks," Phil said. "Ouch."

"I'd kill him for five hundred," Gesh muttered, and I wasn't sure if he was referring to Jones or Vogelsang.

"What enclosure?" I said.

The car door slammed. *Vroom*, the engine turned over with a low sucking moan. *Vroom-vroom*. I glanced up, noting absently that Vogelsang had removed the license plates, than bent for the crumpled envelope. Inside, equally crumpled, was a newspaper clipping. LOCAL GIRL MISSING, I read. *Savoy Skaggs, 17, a June graduate of Willits High School and a resident at 1990 Covelo Road . . .* No, it couldn't be, I thought, the moment poetry, sweet as revenge, victory, the beatific light that shines on the darkest hour. . . . *no leads . . . investigating the possibility* . . . Of course, of course. She's run off to consort with Eugene, suave and irresistible offshoot of G. P. Turner, the gentleman pugilist. I pictured her hitchhiking to Wiesbaden, thumb out, skirt hiked, sick to death of being a conniving country bitch and bar slut, hastening to marry off her little mangoes before they rotted. Love conquers all.

My comrades were frowning over the letter. The Saab had begun to creep forward. "Hey, look at this!" I shouted, nearly whooping with the joy of it and waving the newsprint like a flag at a parade. But then I stopped cold: *investigating the possibility of foul play.* Foul play?

Suddenly I was running. "Stop!" I shouted. "Wait up!" Aorta was still in first gear, taking it easy over hummock and hump, but picking up speed. Something snatched at my foot. I went on, shouting, waving my arms. I caught her as she was swinging onto the road.

There was a whine of brake discs, the car humped forward and then back, dust rose. Aorta looked alarmed. "What? What's the matter?"

I thrust my face in the window, dripping sweat. "Vogelsang." I gasped, lungs heaving, air too thick to swallow. "He didn't have anything to do with this? He didn't . . . ?"

Aorta's face was white, ghoulish, the eyes sunk deep in her head. Zombies, I thought. Murderers. Kidnappers. "What do you mean?" she demanded.

Exhaust bit at my throat, dust settled on my forearm. I noticed the license plates on the seat beside her. "Savoy, Vogelsang wouldn't have, have done anything, would he?"

She made a heroic attempt at working incredulity into her face, slash eyebrows lifting a degree, eyes fighting for the ironic glance. "Don't be silly," she said, her voice tinny as a party horn. She goosed the gas pedal. "Of course not," she said, eyes forward, and then she popped the clutch and shot off down the road. I stood there, inhaling dust that tasted like ashes and wondering just how much all this would redound to my future happiness and well-being.

Then there was the face in the window.

It was a large face, pale and childish, tapering at the brow and expanding like a prize eggplant in the region of the jowl. Above, there was a bristle of close-cropped hair and a long-billed cap; below, a congeries of chins. When I recovered from my initial shock, I realized that the face belonged not to a sheriff's deputy, spare extortionist or special investigator from the DEA, but to our own witless, puerile and very likely subhuman neighbor, Marlon Sapers. Who else?

"Oh, my God," Aorta had said, and we'd frozen in our worst moment, the moment of our dissolution and grief. Vogelsang had Gesh in a lethal chokehold, I was wrestling the .22 from Phil, Dowst was shouting, Aorta gasping, garbage climbed the walls as if it were alive and chaos roared in our ears. Phil was the first to react. He swung the rifle around like a skeetshooter and took out the upper left panel of the window as neatly as if he were potting a clay pigeon. *Pow!* The face disappeared from the window, Vogelsang sprang up as if he'd been scalded, Gesh struggled unsteadily to his feet, Dowst hit the floor. Looking pleased with himself, looking as if he'd just solved the better portion of the world's problems in a single flamboyant stroke, Phil lowered the gun. It was then that I made the association between those fleshy befuddled features and Sapers's son and heir, and I called out his name in shocked reproof. "Marlon!" I cried. "You come back here!"

The next thing I remember, Vogelsang and I were crashing through the scrub behind the house, pursuing Marlon. What we intended to do with him once we caught him was a question that begged further consideration. We didn't stop to consider.

To his distress, Marlon was not built for flight. Clumsy, lumbering, reeling from the shock of discovery and rattled by the deadly crack of the gun, he lurched blindly through the brush, heading first in one direction, then another. We caught up with him between the storage shed and the propane tank. Perceiving our closeness, he turned at bay, a frantic, crazed, trapped-beast sort of look in the eyes that loomed huge behind the thick lenses of his glasses. "Go away!" he screamed, his body shuddering under the force of conflicting impulses and aberrant emotions. "Leave me alone!" I pulled up short, half a dozen feet from him, but Vogelsang, caught up in the chase and the bloodlust of his clash with Gesh, dove for his legs like a tackler.

If he could have paused to think things out or had he been a fraction less keyed up, I'm sure Vogelsang would have acted differently. As it was, he saw almost immediately that he'd made a mistake. A grave mistake. Marlon let out a shattering, high-pitched, psychotic shriek—the shriek alone enough to commit him to Mattewan—and flung Vogelsang from him as if he were made of sawdust and paper. Then he turned to me. Vogelsang lay in the bushes, stunned, birds flew cursing into the trees, the sky darkened. Marlon was in a rage. He stamped his feet and shrieked again, pounding his fists up and down like pistons. I backed up a step. "Marlon," I said, trying for a reasonable, soothing tone. "No one wants to hurt you."

"*You* do," he choked. "You don't like me." There were beads of sweat on his face, he was turning color—his usual chalky pallor giving way to the angry swollen red of a sore about to burst—and his eyes jerked around the perimeter of the glasses like fish trapped in a sinking pond. Here was the psychopath, the disturbed adolescent who'd nearly crushed his grandmother after she'd scolded him, the inhabitee of the padded cell at Napa State. "I know you," he blubbered, his voice so constricted it sounded like the hiss of a deflating balloon. "You, you hollered at me!"

The great reddening hulk of him was awash in inflammatory chemicals, burning secretions from bad glands. His teeth chattered, his neck foundered on its chins like a ship going down. I backed up another few steps, poised to run, when suddenly he let out a terrible scourging shriek, bent low, tore up a bush the size of a bale of hay and heaved it at me. Branches scraped my chest, roots, dirt, I felt something wet at the corner of my mouth. When I looked up, Marlon was spinning round as if in a game of blindman's buff, dust beating about his frantically churning legs, a high choking whinny of rage and terror stuttering through his clenched teeth. Suddenly he lurched off, erratic as a drunk, all thought of fleeing subsumed in the peremptory urge to nullify his immediate environment, to beat the visible world to dust. Before him stood the propane tank, big as a submarine. He never hesitated. Just lowered his shoulder and galloped into it, pounding it repeatedly until it fell from its cinder-block stand with a single deep booming reverberation.

I didn't know what to do. We'd set him off, and he was unstoppable. Vogelsang didn't look as if he had any ready solutions either. While Marlon was distracted by the propane tank, he'd dodged out of the way, holding his side. Now he stood at a discreet distance, looking dazed and helpless, as Marlon turned his attention to the storage shed. Huge, savage, amok, Marlon reared back and hit the side of the building with the force of an artillery shell, and I heard something give, the brittle snap of stud or beam. Then he began pummeling the weathered panels with his fists and forearms until he'd managed to punch a hole in the wall. Then again and again, tearing at the hole, his fists bleeding, face warped with hatred and anguish, the ancient flimsy structure rocking on its foundation. He was awesome, brutal, mindless, King Kong hammering dinosaurs into submission. "Marlon!" I shouted over the clamor. "How about a Coke?"

No response.

"A Mars bar?"

Nails screamed, boards wheezed. A plank tore loose and flew into the field.

It had begun to look as if he would reduce the entire lodge to splinters when there came a sharp imperious roar from the ravine at my back. "Marlon!" the voice boomed, deep as the rumble of ruptured earth, hard as a wall of granite. "You stop that now!" I turned my head. There, blasting up out of the thicket like Grendel's mother was the biggest woman I had ever laid eyes upon—not your typical fat woman or bearded lady, but a monument to flesh, twice the size of the shot putter for the Soviet women's team. Or for the men's team, for that matter. Trudy Sapers. I didn't need an introduciton.

Neither did Marlon. As enraged as he'd been an instant earlier, as frenzied and disturbed and out of control, he now shifted gears, suddenly caught up in a new paroxysm of blind, destructive, mother-mortifying fury. His jowls shuddered convulsively, he stamped and raged in full tantrum, put the great log of his sneakered foot through the wall. But his mother knew him too well. On she came, six-two at least, five hundred pounds or more, moving across the field with a purposive grace, with a mammoth, unimpeachable dignity, undaunted in an ankle-length dress the size of an open parachute. She took hold of him by the upper arm and firmly but gently, almost tenderly, threw him to the ground and sat on him.

There was nothing to say. In the face of such a fit and so monumental an act of melioration and tenderness, Marlon's voyeurism seemed hardly worth mentioning. I stood there awestruck through a long aphasic moment as Marlon's breathing gradually became easier and Sapers himself emerged from the bushes behind me. He could have been emerging on a battlefield. Vogelsang was still cradling his ribs and I was licking blood from the corner of my mouth, there were three jagged rents in the face of the storage shed, and the propane tank lay on its side in the bushes like a beached whale.

"Heh-heh," Sapers said, and he spat nervously. "Heh-heh. My apologies about all this, boys. No harm done, I hope. Heh-heh." He spat again, the stream of tobacco juice like some part of his anatomy, a coiled brown tongue lashing in and out as if to test the air before each breath. "Ohhhh, don't you worry a bit, I'll pay for the damages, a course."

Vogelsang stood off in the brush, looking dazed. His eyes were shrunken with pain. I saw him wince and snatch at his side when he lifted his hand in a gesture meant to reassure Sapers.

Phil, Gesh, Dowst and Aorta were peering down from the shattered kitchen window, mouths agape, as stunned and bewildered as tourists witnessing bizarre rites in the heart of a savage and little-known region. I was feeling bewildered, too, as if my life had somehow become confused with a Fellini movie.

"So," Sapers roared, startling me, "I don't know if you've had a chance to meet my wife?"

And thus the menace had withdrawn, retracting its claws as suddenly as it had shown them: Jones, Savoy, the face in the window. Days passed, weeks. We went about our business like blind men, like drudges, the sky didn't fall, the earth didn't tremble and the cells at the county jail remained as recondite as the tunnels beneath the Potala. We licked our wounds, drew a deep collective breath and went on weeding and watering, cooking meals, consuming vodka and hauling manure. I began to feel easier (relatively speaking, of course—think of the plummeting skydiver, his parachute tangled behind him, who sees that he will not after all be impaled on the nasty black pointed spires of the wrought-iron fence but hammered to pulp on the sidewalk instead), yet one problem still nagged at me: Petra. I wanted her, wanted her with an ache that tore at my dreams and soured my morning coffee, wanted her as a native of the searing plain wants the distant white-tipped mountains. And yet I was powerless to do anything about it. I couldn't leave the property to phone her, not after what had happened, and I wouldn't be free to see her until November. The thought was torture. Would she be there in November? Would she want to see me? I could confess to her then, of course, the plants harvested and sold and the operation wrapped up, but how would she react?

It took me a week to hit on the idea of writing her. Phil lifted the phone book from the local Circle K and I found her address—same as the store—and wrote her a fifteen-page epistle in longhand. The first three pages consisted of an elaborate (but witty and self-justifying) apology for my behavior at the heifer festival, and this was followed by an eight-page dissertation on my background, motives, beliefs and desires, and thoughts on subjects ranging from ceramic sculpture to Wordsworth's "Lucy" poems (from which I quoted liberally). The concluding pages marked a return to the exculpatory mode and hinted at the dark, dangerous, enigmatic and stimulating circumstances in which I now found myself, promised full disclosure in due time and concluded with a desperate plea for patience and understanding. I signed it "Love, Felix," and gave Dowst's Sausalito address.

Two weeks passed and there was no answer. I wrote again. Twenty-five pages' worth, a letter so thick I had to have Phil mail it in a nine-by-twelve manila envelope. If the first missive was poised between pathos and wit, this was a howl of anguish, written out of despair and loneliness and the sting of rejection. It was demanding, insinuating, the sort of thing that convinces the addressee to move to Toledo and neglect to leave a forwarding address. I dissected my dreams, compared myself to Manfred, young Werther and James Dean, writhed on the page like an insect pinned to a mounting board and generally made an ass of myself. I even confessed that I loved her (a mistake under any circumstances), and insisted that I would change my name and emigrate if she didn't return my feelings. The day Phil mailed the second letter, Dowst showed up with a reply to the first.

"Dear Felix," she'd written in a bold cursive on the back of a prestamped postal service card, "I have neither the time nor patience to play games or carry on a correspondence with an underground man. If you want to see me, see me. But please, no more tortured letters." She signed it, "Best, Petra."

She never wrote again.

Neither did I.

Yes, and then there was the fire.

The night was hushed, moonless and black, the night of desert and outback and the wild places of the world beyond the ken of linemen and meter readers. I sat in darkness, thinking nothing, thinking one more drink, another couple of hands, a cold shower, bed. Phil was in the shed refilling the lantern. He was drunk. I was drunk. We'd been playing pitch, talking in low voices against the oppression of the night and the place, killing our various hurts with alcohol, when the lantern fizzled out. DO NOT REFILL WHEN HOT. Though I couldn't see it, the kitchen door stood open. I listened to the sounds I'd heard a hundred times, flesh, metal, wood: the groan of the hinges as the storage shed door swung open, the rattle of the gas can, Phil's murmuring heartfelt curses as he blundered into this object or that and burned his fingers on the spigot at the base of the lantern.

But then—sudden, chilling, anomalous—a new sound intruded on the familiar sequence, a sound like the low sucking whoosh of a stubborn gas jet, and before I could react the night exploded with light, a single coruscating flash that illuminated the doorway as if it were noon. My first thought was that lightning had struck the shed, but instead of the rumble of thunder I heard Phil's shout and the deadly incendiary clank of the gas can hitting the floor. This is it, I thought, flinging myself from the chair as Phil cried out again and a second can of fluid went up with a sickening rush of air. My feet pounded across the rotten planks of the porch, the shed glowing like a jack-o'-lantern before me, and I understood that this was the nightmare that had brooded over us all along, this was the trial—not police, not helicopters, dogs, poachers or informers, not rats, locusts or bears, but the quick licking flames of the refining fire.

When I reached the shed, I saw the spitting lamp, the overturned fuel cans, cold blue flames spilling across the floor in liquid fingers. And I saw Phil, in shock, his torso flaring like a struck match. He'd staggered back against the wall, frantically swiping at his crackling T-shirt and the corona of flame that clung to his head, the flesh of his right arm coated in burning fluid and hissing like a torch as he swept it through the air. More: I saw the flames at the walls, the burning newspapers, collapsed furniture, garbage, the big ten-gallon cans of gasoline lined up like executioners in the far corner.

Drowning in fire, Phil clutched at me. He was dancing—we were dancing—whirling and shouting, frenetic, Laurel and Hardy dropped in the giant's frying pan. My nostrils dilated round the chemical stink of incinerated hair, my flesh touched his and I burned. For a single terrible runaway instant I was caught up in his panic, frozen, unable to act—WOULD-BE RESCUER DROWNS IN FOUR FEET OF WATER—until I got hold of myself and shoved him from me. His face heaved, he shouted out my name. But I was already on him again, slapping the crown of his head, tearing at his shirt until it dropped from him in luminous strips, and then driving him through the door and out into the merciful night. Tangled like wrestlers, we pitched over the edge of the porch and I pinned him to the ground, buried him beneath me, rubbing, massaging, beating at the flames until they gave in.

We looked at each other, the moment crystallizing round the pained gaping incomprehension of his face, the feel of the blistered flesh of his arm, the dust cool as balm. Phil's mouth was working, fishlike, trying to close on a bubble of shock, his pompadour was gone and the wicked hungry glare of the fire glistened in his eyes. There was no time for assessments, repairs or solicitude: the jaws were making another pass. "Quick!" I hissed. "The hose, the hose!" And then I was back in the shed, flinging things at the flames—a box of newspapers, a pillow, a pair of gutted mattresses—anything to give us a second's purchase. Flames sprang up, I slapped them down. The overturned lamp spat like a torch, I kicked it across the room. I felt nothing—neither the heat on my face nor the burns on my hands and arms—nothing but the imperative of the moment: we had to quench the fire, kill it before it killed us and took the house, the woods and the mountain with it.

Even then, even in those first few frenzied seconds, I knew that our lives were at stake, that the fire, once loosed on the parched fields, would burn to Ukiah. We'd gone five months without water. Alder, manzanita, pine, hollow grass and withered scrub—it was all kindling, stacked and waiting. This was no grassfire we had here, no mere acre-scorcher or garage fire, this was the germ of the conflagration, the blaze that leaps into the air and rushes through the trees like apocalypse, the fire that outruns you, chokes you, incinerates you. I fought it. No thought of quitting, running, ducking out: this was the end of the line.

I stood just inside the doorway, flailing at the flames with an old overcoat. Across the room—through a gauntlet of heaped refuse and sudden startling splashes of fire—stood the jerrycans of gasoline. Four of them. The fire flowed toward them like the tide rising on a beach and I saw that they would be enveloped in a matter of minutes, and thought of teenaged Phil in the dump truck, too stupid to realize he was about to die. I was stupid, too. Beating back the flames with the smoldering overcoat, breathing fire, my eyes tearing with the smoke and ears slapped and stung by the roar, I pictured that moment of crushing combustion: my flesh—fat and lean—sizzling like bacon, roiling clouds of fire, the house going up as if napalmed. They'd never even find my bones.

At this juncture, Phil appeared in the doorway. He was shirtless, his sneakers were steaming and his head looked like a scorched onion. In one hand he held an intermittently spurting garden hose, in the other a dripping mop. Though his eyes gave away his terror—the sockets could barely contain them, the wild ducking eyes of horses trapped in a burning barn—he trained the hose on the heart of the blaze and began swabbing the heaps of burning refuse like a frenetic scrubwoman. Encouraged, I edged forward and lifted the nearest mattress, itself aflame now, and slammed it down again, momentarily damping the fire so that I could tear through the room to the cans of gasoline.

I tore. Through Stygian gloom and Tartarean fire, through a smoldering clutter that would have given a fire marshall nightmares, kicking aside paint cans and leaping mounds of fuming rags and discarded clothes. When I reached the far side of the room I couldn't see Phil or the open doorway. The jerrycans were hot to the touch. I crouched over them, bending low to snatch a quick breath beneath the loops of smoke raveling down from the ceiling, thinking *What next?* Was I really going to sprint through that inferno with a pair of ten-gallon cans of gasoline tucked under my arm? Twice, no less? I saw smoke, flames like teeth. I couldn't seem to catch my breath. Insidious, the image of a Buddhist monk, his charred frame the center in a whirling jacket of fire, came to me. So this is heroism, I thought, feeling like the buck private who flings himself on the hand grenade to save his buddies in the foxhole, the platoon, the general and his chiefs of staff, and by extension the whole of the United States and the American way of life. I.e., foolish.

Protean, the flames licked at the walls, roared beneath the elevated floorboards, tendrils and creepers of some spontaneous, irreversible growth. I was coughing, my lungs turned inside out like a pair of rubber gloves. The jerrycans weren't getting any cooler. As from a great distance I heard Phil shouting my name, but I'd begun to feel dizzy, sleepy somehow. Smoke inhalation, I thought numbly, and inhaled more smoke, pinching my eyes shut against the acid haze. In another moment I'd be too groggy to stand, let alone heft eighty-pound cans of gasoline.

It was then—the pyre awaiting me, my throat constricting, inertia pinning me to the spot—that I became aware of an almost imperceptible shift in the atmosphere, a flow of cooler air, the soft incongruous touch of a breeze on the back of my neck. I jerked round to discover the rents Marlon had torn in the back wall—jagged, night-black, rents the size of jerrycans. The fire talked to me, harsh and sibilant, but I didn't listen. One, two, three, four, the cans were gone, tumbled in the grass, and I was ducking across the room like a deserter in no-man's-land. Phil gave me a wild desperate look as I flung myself past him and out into the open, where I fell to my knees and coughed till I thought I was about to give birth.

Twenty minutes later we were still at it. Stripped to the waist like stokers, soot-blackened and viscid with sweat, we plied shovels, hauled buckets of dirt, stamped out a grassfire on one side of the shed while flinging burning rubbish out of the door on the other. It was impossible, maddening, a losing proposition: one minute we'd think we finally had things under control, and the next flames would be spitting in our faces. We might have escaped the holocaust—the single scorching gasoline-fed blast that would have decided the issue once and for all—but the steady incremental force of the fire was beginning to take its toll. Phil was hurting, his chest and shoulders scoriated with whiplash burns, his right forearm slick with pus. He looked tired, scared, worn, looked as if he were about to throw down his shovel and bolt for the car. I didn't feel much better. Though we'd worked like automatons, oblivious to heat, thirst, pain, worked without remit and in perfect accord, grunting instructions to each other, rushing from one threat to the next in feverish concentration—though we plumbed the depths of our physical and spiritual resources, reached down deep inside ourselves for that something extra and got it—we were barely running even. And we weren't getting any stronger.

If we'd had water pressure it might have been different. But the hose, drawing on the spring-fed tank that supplied the house, could deliver no more than a trickle. (The water table was low, the tank small—a class of thirsty kindergartners could have come in off the playground and drained the entire thing without blinking. In better times—that is, when our lives weren't imminently threatened by an advancing inferno—this was merely an annoyance; now it was critical.) Within minutes Phil's mop had gone up like a pitch-pine torch, and we began to recognize the futility of attempting to fight a three-alarm blaze with teacups of water. We turned to the mattresses as a stopgap. Flung at the core of the conflagration, they would smother the flames for a minute or two while we frantically scattered burning debris and parried fiery thrusts with our shovels. Of course, this procedure had its drawbacks. Unlike more conventional fire-fighting agents—

water, sand, CO_2 foam—bed ticking and cotton batting are themselves flammable, and periodically the mattresses had to be dragged out into the grass and beaten. Soon the grass was ablaze, and we were fighting fires on two fronts.

At some point we'd decided to abandon the mattresses in favor of dirt, and I found myself standing in a knee-deep trench just off the edge of the porch, shoveling like some crazed and fever-racked desperado atop a chest of doubloons. My hands were raw, the fire in the shed spoke with a steady implacable hiss, the mattresses leaked flames into the grass before me. I shoveled. Two scoops on the porch, one in the red-flaming grass. Phil stood above me on the porch, a cutout, flat against the glare, pitching the dirt through the open doorway. This was the shovel brigade. Dig, heave, dig: there was no other rhythm in the world.

I was in the act of lifting my six- or seven-hundredth shovel-load when I was arrested by a new sound from the shed—a fruity, nut-cracking sound, fibers yielding, tree limbs snapping in a gale—and turned to see that a section of the floor had caved in, spewing sparks and glowing cinders into the scrub behind the house. Unleashed, flames shot up through the gap, beating like wings, swelling and shape-shifting till they reached the ceiling. Phil staggered back from the doorway and dropped his shovel just as a can of something volatile 2paint thinner?—went up with a percussive wallop. I stopped, too. For the first time since Phil had cried out and I'd started up out of the darkened kitchen, I hesitated. It was overwhelming, hopeless. The shed was engulfed in flame from beneath, the brushfire at my feet was spreading faster than I could cover it, and now the scrub out back was going up, too. I stood there transfixed, my hand clenched round the haft of the useless shovel, the familiar chalky taste of surrender creeping up my throat.

That was when Gesh appeared.

At the stroke of that moment—the paint thinner flaring in triumph, the hole in the floor feeding oxygen to the flames like an outsized bellows, Phil stunned and tired and hurt, my will wavering and the quitter's taint rising in me like an infection—that was when Gesh emerged from the darkness like all the king's horses and all the king's men. He came out of the night in white chinos and sandals, his hair slicked down, beard trimmed and aloha shirt pressed, trailing a scent of aftershave. He was running. Head down, shoulders hunched forward, the big man held in reserve for the crucial confrontation, for single combat, the goal-line stand. No time for questions, strategies, appraisals: he slammed through the grassfire, took the porch in a bound, snatched up Phil's shovel and plunged into the burning shed.

The effect was almost immediate: flames that had leapt to the ceiling were suddenly hobbled, the brilliant dilating light diminished as if Gesh's bulk alone could displace the flames, as if he were a true believer cast into the burning fiery furnace, a Joe Magarac able to cool molten steel with a touch of his hand. I heard the scrape of his shovel, the snarl of the flames, and then I watched as a steady swirling arc of fire disengaged itself from the conflagration and struck the surface of the porch in an ignifluous rush: a smoldering rug materialized, the charred headboard of a forgotten bed, smoke-spewing cans, scraps of lumber, blazing boxes of rags and newspapers. Shovel flailing, shirt aflap, Gesh stood rooted in the heart of the inferno, a shadow closing over the jagged sheet of flame, choking it, defusing it, stealing its fire. Revitalized, Phil danced round each heap of combustion as it shot through the doorway, poking and stamping like a bushman with an effigy. I came alive too. Suddenly the shovel was light in my hands, a toy, a stick, and I was dumping dirt on the brushfire like a backhoe in high gear.

This was teamwork. With Gesh hacking away in the shed like a hook and ladder company on the eve of a three-week vacation and Phil dredging up some final deep-buried reserve of grit and energy, I was inspired, a shoveling genius. Though the flames snaked through the grass and rose up to hiss in my face, though bushes exploded in a rush of streaming sparks and the ground went hot beneath my feet, I drove myself like a long-distance runner coming into the home stretch, my will undeniable, inexorable, victory in sight. The shovel rose and fell with a mechanical insistence until the last pocket of fire closed on a fist of darkness. Then I turned back to the shed.

Inside, the heat was dizzying, the smoke a noose round the throat. The atmosphere seemed denser now, blacker, and I remember wondering vaguely if this was a good sign or bad. As I inched my way in I thought I could make out Gesh's form through the haze, but the fumes stabbed at my eyes and tore at my lungs until I found myself backing out the door like a crab. How could he stand it? He'd been in there five minutes, ten minutes, he'd been in there long enough to suffocate and collapse. I suddenly pictured him gasping for breath, going lightheaded, losing his bearings and tumbling into the flames like a man of straw, and then I was back in the shed, shouting his name as Phil had shouted mine over the simmering jerrycans. "Gesh!" I called, the vacuum of my throat torn by the smoke that rushed to fill it. At first I saw nothing, heard only the steady flap of the flames. I called out again. Then, out of a confusion of vacillating shapes, Gesh suddenly appeared, naked to the waist, wielding his shovel like a trident. I plunged forward. Took hold of his arm. Shouted in his face with all the frantic urgency of the rescuer lowered into the fuming pit. "This way!" I shouted. "Hurry!"

The aloha shirt trailed from him in spangled tatters, his face was rigid with fury, his eyes like open sores. "Get out!" he roared, snatching his arm away and turning to fling a bucket of earth at the fiery column rising through the gap in the staved-in floor. I glanced round. He'd managed to clear the floor, prop up the ceiling with a fallen beam and hammer out a section of the wall I'd last seen burning like a Yule log. I tried to pitch in, but quarters were close and he inadvertently slammed into me as he bent, cursing, for a second bucket of earth. Amazed, I watched as he hurtled round the room like a man trapped in a runaway locomotive, damping the main blaze in a chiaroscuro of furious movement, scattering debris, levitating buckets of dirt. The heat was cooking my skin, the smoke curing my lungs. I got out.

If Gesh was getting a grip on the fire in the shed, the blaze out back was the most concentrated threat now. Not only was it feeding the conflagration under the shed, but it was leapfrogging toward the drought-withered trees of the ravine and creeping along the base of the house as well. I turned to it like an outflanked cavalry officer, galloping round the corner of the shed with my spade held out before me like a lance; unfortunately I bowled into Phil, who was hunched feebly over his own digging implement and coughing into his fist like a tubercular orphan.

"You all right?" I screamed, staggering past him, everything a shout, the whole world a roar. And then I was bellowing instructions at him and we were shoveling yet again, steel biting earth, earth flying. Together we were able to clear a corridor to the base of the shed, and we began pitching dirt at the flames blossoming beneath the floorboards as Gesh fought them from above. Smoke ran for the sky, the shovel tore at my blistered hands. Flames coughed, sputtered, flared up again with an insidious cackle. We moved dirt, truckloads of it, and eventually we began to prevail; the fire under the shed cringed, shrank, backed off to devour itself in frustration. There was a single astonishing moment when the light suddenly died and I looked up at the shed in stupefaction: it was no longer burning. Gutted, charred, smoking, a sagging depthless web of lines lit only by the sickly glow of the fire at my back, the shed was no longer burning.

The rest was anticlimax. There was Gesh hurtling along the edge of the ravine with a splitting axe, clearing brush, taking down thorn and manzanita as if he were picking flowers, forcing the fire away from the trees and back toward the ground it had already blackened. There was Phil protecting the back wall of the house as if it were Buckingham Palace or the Louvre, Gesh and I cutting swaths through the single fire, dividing it once, twice, and then dividing it again, the heat attenuating, the light fading. We watched, shovels flicking like tongues, as the isolated fires burned themselves out, watched as the coals glowed hot on the charred ground and then faded into the enveloping night. Half an hour after Gesh had emerged from nowhere to snatch up Phil's shovel and fight his way into the shed, the threat was over.

The night had suddenly grown dark again. In the garish glow of the embers, Phil's face looked like some Polish Christ's, gaunt and long-nosed, suffused with suffering. Gesh's hair stood straight out from his head, his face was blackened, the yellow strips of the aloha shirt trailed from him as if he were peeling. I was trying to catch my breath, experience relief, savor the first few moments of life without frenzy, when Gesh turned to me, the lines of his face underscored with soot and locked in the grid of rage he wore into battle. "Well, what are you waiting for?" he growled. "Can't you see Phil's got to be taken to the hospital?"

I glanced at Phil. His right arm had crusted over and the welts on his chest and shoulders were raw; a slashing wet wound cut back into his hairline. He was a mess. "Can you . . . ?" I began, turning to Gesh. I meant to ask if he was sure he could handle things in the event the fire started up again, but I was jittery still and unable to find the words. As I faltered, the brush began to flare in a pocket out by the propane tank.

"I can drive myself," Phil said, so softly I could barely hear him. He looked like the survivor of a DC-10 crash, his clothes reduced to rags, body scorched, hair gone.

"Bullshit," Gesh said. "You take him, Felix."

I felt sapped, felt as if I'd just come off a two-week shift in the coal mine—felt as if I'd been trapped in a coal mine, for that matter, buried under tons of hot rock, breathing noxious fumes and drinking beakers of acid. My shoulders and arms ached, I was bleeding in half a dozen places, my hands stung as if I'd dipped them in a deep fryer and then rubbed them with alcohol. I felt like shit, but I also felt transcendent, exhilarated, able to leap tall buildings at a single bound. I'd stayed with it, fought the odds like a square-jawed hero, and won. "Sure," I said.

Gesh had already begun to move off toward the presumptuous little blaze licking at the propane tank, but he paused to look me in the eye. "Go," he said, and it sounded like a benediction.

Chapter 2

Trees cowered along the road, signposts and mileage markers backed off like startled animals, the pavement itself seemed to plunge away from the clutch of the headlights as if dropping into oblivion. It was four a.m. by the dashboard clock, and I was coming into Willits at eighty, Jerpbak and his jackbooted legions be damned: I was the one on urgent business this time. Full of grace, the lark ascending, survivor, victor, hardass, I took the curves like a teenager with identity problems and sucked the straightaways into the future with a blast of exhaust. A road sign—it sprang up like a puppet in a Punch and Judy show and then vanished instantaneously—announced the city limits. SPEED LIMIT 35. I slowed to sixty. Through the town center, past the nightglow of the Willits Diner, the neon lure of motels and quick-stop restaurants, stoplights falling away like leaves in a windstorm, *noli me tangere*.

Phil slouched in the death seat, eyes lidded. His neck had sunk into his chest and his head pitched and rolled with the road's abrasions, his face impossibly heavy, a thing of stone. He hadn't uttered a word since we'd left the farm. Was he asleep? In shock? Withdrawn in the web of his pain like a crippled animal, like a dog licking its mangled paw in the dark void beneath the house? I glanced over at him. He'd propped himself against the window, raw back arching away from contact with the seat, his near shoulder stippled with blisters, pitted, cratered, rough as toadskin. "You okay?" I whispered, watching the road.

He began to cough into his fist. I stepped on the gas. "Another minute, Phil," I murmured, lurching round the only other vehicle on the road—a creeping heedless bread truck—with a desperate jerk of the wheel. Phil didn't even lift his head.

The hospital was like a medieval leprosarium, poorly lighted, neglected, falling into ruin. Cheap additions fanned out from the main building like the wings of a crippled bird, the sloping drive was afflicted with potholes, slabs of pale green stucco peeled from the walls like sloughed skin. I thundered past the lions couchant and Ionic columns of the main entrance (long since boarded up) and did a sloppy power slide into the AMBULANCE ONLY/NO PARKING/TOW AWAY zone in front of the emergency entrance. Phil clawed his way out of the car as if emerging from a tomb and tottered toward the doorway on stiff legs, his fists clenched at his sides. I swung open the door for him and we found ourselves in a scuffed hallway cluttered with plastic plants, cheap furniture and collapsible wheelchairs.

"Yes?" The night nurse sat stiffly at a pine desk outside the emergency room, alert as a three-headed dog. She was blond, forty, a victim of dry skin and a lifetime of suppressing emotion. Beyond her I saw a dull wash of light, a clutter of chairs, the janitor, feet up, white socks, masticating a bologna sandwich and devouring a Louis L'Amour Western.

"We've had an accident," I said.

"Name?"

"Mine or his?"

Bent over a printed form, her pen poised to record information, the nurse's cap cleaving her head like a scythe, she expelled a long withering depthless sigh of exasperation. "The name of the individual to be admitted," she said without looking up.

Phil croaked out his name.

"Sex? Age? Height? Weight? Medical insurance? Allergies?" The questions came like body blows in a prizefight, cumulative, unending, wearying. Phil stood there in the sepia light, burned raw, the collar of his incinerated T-shirt still clinging to his neck, charred underwear poking through the holes in his pants. We were both in blackface.

"Look," I said, cutting her off in mid-phrase—was she really asking about his bank account?—"the man is in pain, can't you see that?"

"Savings?"

Phil looked as if he were about to go down for the count. "Crocker," he gasped.

"Major credit card? Next of kin? Religion?"

"Listen," I said. She ignored me.

"Sign here." As she pushed the form toward Phil, she focused her colorless eyes on him for the first time, and I saw with a jolt that there was nothing there. Neither curiosity nor concern, sympathy or interest. She might have been home in bed, dancing in a casino, married to the Aga Khan. But she was here. In Willits. At four-ten in the morning. She'd witnessed resuscitation and expiration, stroke, hemorrhage and loss of hope, seen the human form twisted and degraded, hacked, torn, bathed in blood, pus, mucus, urine, she'd seen blue babies and blanched corpses. We were nothing. Scabs, vermin, dirt. The contact lenses clung to her eyes like blinders.

Phil signed.

As Phil stooped painfully to drag pen across paper, the doctor appeared as if on cue. He came flashing through the emergency-room door in a pristine scrub shirt, young, perfect, his head a mass of imbricate hair, mustache impeccable, teeth aligned, skin clear. "Well," he crooned, jocular as an anchorman delivering the news of three hundred thousand fatalities in a Hunan earthquake, "so we've had a little mishap?" He was winking, nodding, grinning, as if we were sixth graders caught in some minor peccancy—playing with matches or peeping into the girls' locker room. "Sensitive, is it? Yes, yes," he purred, taking Phil by the elbow and steering him toward the back room in a flurry of one-liners and sympathetic tongue-clucks. As they passed through the doorway I heard the doctor's voice rise in screaming falsetto as he broke into a mock Negro dialect: "And then she says, 'Lordy, lordy, this dude done got burned!' " There was a single wild bray of laughter, and then the door swung to with a click.

I took a seat in the waiting room. The janitor had finished his sandwich and was tenderly examining the ball of his right foot, from which he'd removed the sock. A bucket of filthy water stood beside him, the mop handle protruding from it like a reed in a swamp. I leaned my head back against the wall and closed my eyes. I was feeling weary, numb, the stirrings of a nameless dread pounding in my organs like jungle drums, a subtle chemical abstersion flushing my veins of the adrenaline that had kept me going over the past two hours. Freud, coming down off his cocaine, knew the feeling. So did Sherlock Holmes and the speed freaks on Haight Street. I'd felt exultant, energized, potent, rushing with stamina and inspiration, and now all I felt was empty. It was over, the crisis past. I'd consumed enough vodka before the fire erupted to be drunk now, but I didn't feel drunk at all. I felt tired. Frightened. Depressed. I opened my eyes once and saw that the janitor hadn't moved—he was fixed in the cloudy frame of my vision, feet forever white, rubbing, rubbing.

When I woke, the janitor was sloshing dirty water across the floor and the beaming physician was standing over me. "Your friend," he said, "Phil?"

I nodded, rubbing my eyes. "Yeah?"

"He's been burned pretty severely—right shoulder, right forearm, chest, back, hands—and he's lost a lot of fluid." He was rocking back and forth on his heels, grinning like a talk-show host.

"Is he going to be all right?"

Oh, he was beaming now, this doctor. There was no cancer in his body, he'd never bled, bruised or burned, his heart was like a piston. This was the question he'd been waiting for, this the reason he'd poked at preserved cadavers in a chilly basement in Guadalajara and interned at Cleveland General—for this moment and the infinitude of others like it. *He* was in no danger. He jogged ten miles a day, forswore tobacco, alcohol, caffeine, cholesterol, food additives and TV. But Phil? "We'll have to keep him overnight. At least."

The doctor wasn't moving. He was winking again now, nodding and tossing his eyebrows like a stray Marx brother. "What about you?" he said, looking down at my hands.

"Me?" It hadn't occurred to me that I might need treatment, too. I lifted my hands and examined them as if I'd never seen them before.

"You've got a second-degree burn there." He smiled. "Blistering, extravasated fluid, risk of infection." He looked pleased with himself.

Ten minutes later I was bent over the nurse's desk, a pain killer dissolving in the pit of my stomach, my hands imprisoned in gauze. The sixty questions had passed the nurse's lips, the responses had been duly recorded and the form shoved at me for confirmation. I was fumbling with the pen, struggling awkwardly with my gauze mittens and attempting a clonic, looping two-handed signature, when the outside door flew back with the sort of histrionic boom that announces Mephistopheles in Gounod's *Faust*. Windows rattled up and down the corridor, a dull metallic echo resounded from deep in the hospital's bowels. I looked up. Bullet head, frozen spine, boots like truncheons: Officer Jerpbak stepped through the doorway.

He was not alone. Cradled in his right arm, dead weight, was a Halloween ghoul, a bloodslick puppet, an extra from a sleazy flick about knife-wielding maniacs. Heels dragged, blood flowed. Signal 30, I thought, disintegrating sports cars, overturned logging trucks, head wounds, multiple contusions. I backed off as Jerpbak, one arm thrown out for balance, staggered down the hallway under his burden. I'd never seen so much blood. It maculated the floor, darkened the front of Jerpbak's uniform, blotted the features of the limp, spike-haired kid locked under his arm. Jerpbak's face was drained, the hard line of his mouth unsteady: he looked up at me and saw nothing.

The nurse's pen was poised, her head bent to yet another form. "Name?" she said, barely glancing up. Jerpbak stood before the desk, dazed, bewildered, his mouth working in agitation—there was a wild, urgent look in his eye, the look of the harried shopper bursting into the kitchen with four splitting sacks of groceries and no place to set them down. He'd lurched to a confused halt, bracing his legs to support the kid's weight, right arm girdling the kid's chest, left cradling his head: bloody Mary, bloody Jesus. The kid was unconscious. His leather jacket shone wet with blood, blood like oil, black and slickly glistening; his face looked as if it had been slathered with finger paint, as if a twenty-five-cent bamboo back scratcher had been dipped in a pot of gouty red enamel and raked over his eyelids, nose, cheekbones, mouth. He couldn't have been more than eighteen. I saw the lids roll back like defective shades, I saw the dull lifeless sheen of his eyes.

"Goddammit!" Jerpbak leaned forward to slam the desk with the flat of his hand. "Are you alive or what?" He was addressing the nurse. Roaring at her. Barking out the question, his voice a primal yelp that cut through the nurse's apathy like the physical threat it was: she'd seen it all, yes, and now she was seeing this. She sprang from her chair as if she'd been stung, took the room in five amazing strides and plunged through the emergency-room door like a diver. At the same time, Jerpbak lost his grip on the inert kid and staggered forward with him, inadvertently slamming the kid's body across the desk like a slab of boneless meat—if he hadn't caught himself at the last second he would have fallen atop him. I heard the sound of an electric motor starting up somewhere down the corridor, the lights dimmed, then came back up. Jerpbak leaned over the prostrate kid like a beast over his bloody prey, breathing hard. Then he pushed himself up from the table as if he were doing a calisthenic, caught my eyes—his were punctured with shock—and reeled into the waiting room shouting incoherently.

I saw the white flash of the janitor's hair as he looked up from his mop, and then the young doctor pushed through the swinging doors and into the waiting room, his face rushing with hilarity as he rehearsed his stock of cops-and-robbers jokes. He looked first at Jerpbak, the grin turning quizzical, and then beyond him to where the kid's limp form was flung across the desk.

His face went cold. Forget the charm-school manners, the easy quips, pain with a smile: this was no joke. He was on the kid in an instant, a man with a thousand hands—checking for heartbeat, clearing nose and mouth, stanching the flow of blood—all the while shouting instructions over his shoulder. I watched as nurses, orderlies, aides—a hidden white-clad army—slammed through the door with a jangling gurney, descending on the kid like a snowstorm.

Jerpbak, his uniform dark with the kid's blood, stood at the doctor's back, tugging abstractedly at his own stiff shirtcuffs. "He fell," Jerpbak said, as if it mattered, "fell and hit his head."

The doctor gave him a quick sharp glance and then he was gone, the gurney squealing across the wet floor, voices parrying, the flurrying hands concentrated now on the kid's face and head.

The whole episode, beginning to end, had taken no more than sixty seconds. Jerpbak stood with his back to me, watching as the gurney was swallowed up in the embrace of the swinging doors. The night nurse had vanished; the janitor shook his head slowly and went back to swabbing the floor, erasing the gurney's tracks with a sleepy dreamlike motion. The form I'd signed lay on the desk still, a single smear of blood cutting it in two. I lowered my head, put one foot in front of the other and walked down the hallway and out into the night.

Amber light, red. Jerpbak's patrol car stood at the curb, engine running, rack lights flashing. At first glance the car seemed empty, and I was shuffling toward the Toyota, thinking only to get out of there before Jerpbak turned his mind to other matters, when I was arrested by the pale glimmer of a face floating in the obscurity of the back-seat window. I saw the glint of an earring, the turned-up collar of a sad leather jacket like the one the kid had been wearing, a pair of pinned mournful eyes. I came closer. Behind the stark wire mesh of that back-seat prison I knew only too well, a second kid sat, the desolation of his face punctuated by the sickle-shaped bruise under his right eye. I stared at him. His tongue flicked out to lick a split lip, the radio crackled, the engine stuttered and then caught again. He was a tough guy, this kid, sixteen years old. He looked as if he'd been crying.

When I stuck my head in the open driver's window, I saw that the kid was handcuffed to the mesh. He said nothing. I said nothing. I reached in, twisted the ignition key and killed the engine. Then, the keys rattling in my hand like swords, like the fierce, sharp, stabbing edge of righteousness, I cocked my arm and pitched the wheeling clatter of them into the flat black envelope of the night.

The Toyota drove itself. Down the ruptured drive and out onto the dark highway, the nasal blast of the exhaust setting shaded windows atremble, each shove of the gearshift rending the car's guts anew: I didn't want to go back to the farm. Not yet. I didn't want to look into Gesh's drained and soot-blackened face, didn't want to contemplate the razed shed, charred stubble, the big greedy bite the passing jaws had taken out of our lives. It was just past five. My conscious mind had shut down, but something deeper, some root calibrator of need, led me into the macadam parking lot outside the Circle K and on up to the dimly glowing phone booth that stood before it like a shrine: I suddenly knew what I was going to do.

I fished through my wallet for the number, relayed the information to the operator in a voice so low she had to ask me to repeat myself, and listened to the suspenseful rhythms of long-distance connection—*tap-a-tap-clicketa-click-click-click*—as I cupped the receiver in my bandaged hands. It would be eight o'clock in New York.

When at long last the line engaged—with a final, definitive and climactic click—my voice leapt into the void on the other end: "Hello?" I demanded. "Hello?"

I got a recording: the number had been changed. I traced a pattern in the grime of the window as the operator dialed the new number and together we waited for the mice to stop running up and down the line. There was a distant ringing. Three thousand miles away Dwight lifted the receiver.

"Hello, Dwight?" I blurted, barely able to contain myself through the operator's preliminaries, "it's me, Felix." The words came in spate, I couldn't get them out quickly enough: I was afraid he'd left for work already, was he okay, we'd had an accident. Yes, Phil. In the hospital. Burns. I was all right, yes, just a bit shaken up.

He mumbled something about a weird coincidence. I asked him to read me something, anything, pick a day. How about this date in '65, I said. I'm upset, I said. Help me. Read me something. Be late for work.

There was something wrong. His voice was strange, and for an instant I thought I'd somehow got the wrong number. "Dwight?" I said.

"It's a weird coincidence." He was repeating himself. "I mean that you guys . . ."

I couldn't hear him. He was speaking so softly I couldn't make out what he was saying. "Dwight," I shouted, "I can't hear you. What's the matter?"

"The fire," he said.

"I know," I said. "But we're all right. We made it. I'm picking up Phil tomorrow."

"No," he said.

"Read me something."

"I can't. I'm talking about my fire, in the apartment. My old apartment."

It was then that I began to understand, then that I slipped out of myself for a moment, then that I shut up and listened. Dwight's building had gone up while he was at work. Two weeks ago. He'd lost everything, every record he'd ever kept, every note, every figure, every last fragment of the past. It was as if he'd never lived. "I can't believe it," I said.

"Believe it." His voice was choked. bewildered. "I've been trying to remember," he said. "For two weeks I haven't been in to work—all I'm doing is trying to reconstruct it all, trying to get *something* down on paper anyway."

I looked out at the night through the streaked grid of the booth's window—*Al & Jolene*, *Suck This*, *Go Wolverines*—and saw the nodding head of the all-night clerk in the frantically lit quick-stop store. Open all night. Got everything you want. Milk, razor blades, whiskey, Kaopectate. It was a clean, well-lighted place.

"Remember Mrs. Gold? Third grade? It was me, Bobbie Bartro and Linda Lurlee in the far row up against the map of the Fertile Crescent, remember? And you sat where—two rows over, right? Behind Wayne Moore. But what I can't remember is where Phil sat . . . or the name of the girl with the braids and buck teeth—Nancy something—that moved away in the fifth grade."

His voice was a plaint, a drone, remembrance of things past and funeral oration wrapped in one: I didn't want to hear it. "Dwight," I said. "Dwight."

"I'm getting senile. Really, I mean it. Like that game in Little League when we were twelve—we were the Condors, remember? We were playing the Crows, or was it the Orioles? Anyway, Murray Praeger got knocked unconscious in a rundown with somebody, remember? I can get that much. But it's incredible,

I'm really losing my grip: I can't remember whether we won or lost—"

"Dwight," I said. And then I hung up.

I felt as if someone had taken a vegetable peeler to my nerves. Hands wrapped in gauze, face smudged, clothes in a bum's disarray, I stood there in the phone booth like a postulant, staring at the inert receiver as if I expected it to come alive, as if I somehow expected Dwight to call back and tell me he'd only been joking. After a while a pickup truck wheeled into the lot and two men in long-billed caps and coveralls emerged and ambled into the store, where the somnolent clerk served them coffee in paper cups. It wasn't getting any earlier.

I fell into the Toyota like a dead man, animated the engine, flicked on the lights. Exhaust rose through the floorboards, the truncated tailpipe rattled furiously against the rear bumper. Three pale faces stared out at me from the blazing sanctuary of the quick-stop store as I backed around, slammed the car into gear and shot out onto the highway with a squalling blast. Suddenly I felt crazy, fey, psychopathic. Come and get me, Jerpbak, I thought, popping the clutch and fishtailing up the road. I got it up to seventy by the time I reached the town limits, then swung around and roared through the sleepy hamlet again. I was baiting the Fates, measuring the gape of the jaws. Nothing happened.

I found after a while that I'd somehow turned off the main drag, negotiated a tricky series of cross streets and emerged on the broad, tree-lined corridor of Oak Street. Now I was creeping, the exhaust a muted rumble. My hands were on the wheel, my foot on the accelerator, but the car rolled forward under its own volition, no arguing with destiny. Houses drifted past, white shutters, picket fences, shade trees, then a block of storefronts. I glanced at myself in the rearview mirror. Red-veined and sorrowful, the eyes fell back into my skull like open sores. I swiped at a black smear on my nose, tried to pat my hair in place. The headlights were tentacles pulling me along.

The shop was dark. I found the stairway out back. White railing, ghostly. Potted plants, leaves black and smooth to the touch, lovesick cat off in the bushes, smell of rosemary or basil.

I stumbled on the first step, floundering in the darkness like a dog-paddler gone off the deep end; something crashed to the ground with a sick thump. I kept going. I didn't think, didn't want to think.

A moment later I stood on the second-floor landing, breathing hard and peering off into the abyss below. More plants. I turned to the door, knuckles poised, not thinking, not thinking, and made sudden cranial contact with what must have been a bowling ball suspended at eye level. It hit me once, hard, just above the bridge of the nose, then swung off into space to come back and crack me again, this time on the crown of my bowed head. All at once I felt desperate. I'd meant to knock deferentially—it was past five in the morning, after all—or at least wittily, but I found myself hammering at the door like the Gestapo. *Boom*, *boom*, *boom*.

From inside I could hear confused movement: shuffling feet, probing hands. A light went on, a voice called out. *Boom*, *boom*, *boom*, I hammered. Then the porch light, mustard yellow. A hanging planter materialized, reeling past my left ear; a ceramic dwarf looked up at me quizzically. "Okay, okay," came the voice from within, "enough already." I stopped pounding. There was the sound of lock and key, a bolt sliding back.

I spread my bandaged hands, lifted my shoulders in a deprecatory shrug: I was ready to capitulate.

Chapter 3

Petra stood in the doorway, her face soft with sleep, a dragon-splashed kimono pinched round her throat. There was a look of utter stupefaction in her eyes, a look of bewilderment and incomprehension, as if she'd been wakened from a sound sleep and asked to name the fifty volumes of the Harvard Classics or the capitals of all the countries of the South China Sea, beginning with Borneo. A square-headed cat brushed up against her bare ankles and then froze, blinking up at me mistrustfully.

I'd twisted my face into a strained grin and fixed it there until I must have looked like a funeral-home director in a novelty shop. Since I couldn't think of anything to say, I grinned wider.

"Felix?" she said. It was a question.

I nodded.

This exchange was succeeded by an ever-lengthening moment of silence, during which I struggled to think of some witty opener, the mot that would break the ice and precipitate a mutual flood of verbal good will, while Petra's look went from puzzlement to a glare of irate recognition. She was studying my sorry hair, soiled face, scorched clothes and mummy-wrapped hands, recalling no doubt that the last time she'd laid eyes on me my behavior had been eccentric to the point of offense, and that our only communication since had been my mad, interminable, demanding, love-struck letters, the tone of which made *Notes from Underground* seem the tranquil recollections of a lucid mind. Behind her I could see buffed linoleum, a ceramic pig devouring ceramic corn, more plants. "I'm sorry," I began, staring down at my feet and losing my train of thought: a ragged hole the size of a silver dollar had eaten through the canvas of my right sneaker, dissolving the sweatsock beneath and exposing the serried rank of my upper toe joints. Stiff, naked, red, the toes looked as if they should be cracked and dipped in drawn butter.

The cat nuzzled Petra's ankles. Out of the corner of my eye I saw that the oscillating planter had begun to lose momentum, winding down like a hypnotist's watch. In the space of time I'd been standing on her doorstep groping for words, a legion of tired old men had breathed their last, interest had accrued, vows been exchanged, and the worldwide army of hollow-eyed widows had brewed enough tea to fill all the petroleum storage tanks in Houston. Finally Petra stepped back and held the door open. "My God," she said, "what was it—a car crash?"

I told her everything.

We sat at the kitchen table amid a welter of corn plants, rubber plants, dracaena, coleus and African violets, sipping Postum and watching the night sky fall away to tatters in the east, while I told her about the model hole, about the bear, about the half million that had gone through more permutations than the federal arts budget. I told her about Gesh, Phil, Vogelsang, Sapers, Marlon, about the rain, the heat, the rattlesnakes, airplanes, poison oak. I told her about the fire.

The sky was pale, the trees beyond the windows brightening as if a filter had been lifted, when I closed out my apologia with the harrowing tale of the hospital and Jerpbak's latest victims. "I threw his keys in the woods," I said, my voice lifting with the memory of it.

Petra got up from the table and put the kettle on again. "More Postum?"

Postum. It tasted like boiled cinders. "Sure," I said.

I'd been talking for over an hour. I'd begun hesitantly, guiltily, alluding obliquely to my conduct at the heifer festival and then staring down at the spectacle of my clasped hands. "I've been keeping something from you," I said. If she'd looked angry, tired, sympathetic and apprehensive by degrees as she'd opened the door, let me in and offered me a seat, now she gave me a look of concentrated attention: the enigma was about to be unraveled.

Yes, I'd insulted her friends, deserted her on our first and only date, plagued her with rambling letters and appeared on her doorstep at five in the morning—but there were extenuating circumstances. I was a nice guy—trustworthy, loyal, sane and sympathetic—really, I was. "We're not up here for our health," I said.

Her laugh surprised me. She reached out to pat my bandaged hand. "I can see that," she said.

I acknowledged her point with a tight, rueful smile, then lowered my head again. "We're growing pot."

Petra had looked at me curiously, as if in that moment I'd emerged from darkness to light, as if I'd molted, sloughed off a strange skin and metamorphosed into the familiar. "So that's it," she said, smiling a wide, beautiful, close-lipped smile. "I should have guessed. And I thought you were schizophrenic or something. Or married." She was watching me over the rim of her cup, her eyes flaring with amusement. "Remember Teddy? And Sarah?" I nodded. I wanted to get it over with, give her all the sorry details, I wanted to justify myself, I wanted absolution. "They've got a patch too. So does Alice." She gestured at the dark windowpane. "I've even got five plants myself, buried out there in a clump of pampas grass. Everybody grows around here—it's no big thing."

This was my moment of confession, yes, my moment of humiliation, my scourging—but she'd gone too far. Did she think I was some piker, some weekend dirtbagger, some Teddy? "I'm talking two thousand plants."

She shrugged. "Alice knows a guy up in Humboldt with twice that. He's got his own twin-engine plane. He even contributed to the sheriff's reelection fund last year."

What could I say? We were losers, schmucks, first-class boneheads. We weren't paying off politicians or reconnoitering the skies—we were too busy dodging our own shadows and setting fire to storage sheds. Chastened, I dropped any pretense of coming on like the macho dope king and gave her the story straight. I described rampant paranoia, xenophobia, self-enforced isolation. I told her of sleepless nights, panic at the first sputter of an internal-combustion engine, suspicion that ate like acid at the fabric of quotidian existence. I told her how Vogelsang appeared and disappeared like a wood sprite, how Phil slept with his sneakers on, how Dowst would insist that we change the hundred-dollar bills he gave us for supplies *before* we bought groceries, on the theory that only dope farmers would flash a hundred-dollar bill in the checkout line. She was laughing. So was I. It was a comedy, this tale I was telling her, slapstick. We were ridiculous, we were cranks, sots, quixotic dreamers—Ponce de León, Percival Lowell and Donald Duck all rolled in one. When I'd told her everything—the whole sad laughable tale—she'd said "Poor Felix," and patted my hand again. Then she'd asked if I wanted more Postum.

Now, as I watched her at the stove, the first splash of sun ripening the window and firing the kimono with color, I felt at peace for the first time in months. Annealed by the fire, shriven by confession, I rolled the cup in my clumsy hands and felt like Saint Anthony emerging from the tomb. I'd revealed my festering secret and nothing had happened. Petra hadn't run howling from the room or telephoned the police, the DEA hadn't burst in and demanded my surrender, the stars were still in their firmament and the seas lapped the shores. No big thing, she'd said. She was right. For the moment at least I'd been able to put things in perspective, separate myself from the grip of events, see the absurdity of what we'd come to. If the best stories—or the funniest, at any rate—derive from suffering recollected in tranquility then this was hilarious. In telling it, I'd defused it, neutralized the misery through retrospection, made light of the woe. My trip to Belize? Oh, yes, I lost eight layers of skin to sunburn while snorkeling off the barrier reef, turned yellow from jaundice, got mugged outside the courthouse and couldn't get a grip on my bowels for a month. Ha-ha-ha.

Petra's kimono was slit to mid-thigh. Her skin was dark, even, smooth as the slap of a masseuse's palm. I felt deeply appreciative of that revelation of skin, that sweet tapering triangle of flesh, and was fully lost in its contemplation when she turned to me and asked if I was hungry. I wasn't. She was standing there in the nimbus of light, looking at me as if I were the UNICEF poster child. "You know what," she said finally, two cups of fresh noxious Postum steaming in her hand, "you're a real mess."

I liked the tone of this observation, liked her concern. After all, I hadn't come to her doorstep looking for indifference, abuse or rejection, but for sympathy. Sympathy, and perhaps even a little tenderness. I lifted my eyebrows and shrugged.

Her voice dropped. "You may as well spend the night," she said. "Or the morning, I mean."

If I'd been feeling the effects of my cathartic night, feeling leaden and listless, suddenly I was alert as a bloodhound at dinnertime. My first impulse was to decline the invitation ("You don't have to do that; oh, no, no, I couldn't"), but I suppressed it. "I'd like that," I said. I looked her in the eye as she set the ceramic mug down before me—the mug was implausibly ringed by what seemed to be the raised figures of dancing nymphs and satyrs—and added, "That would be great. Really. You wouldn't believe how depressing the farm is. Especially now."

I was playing for sympathy, trying to gauge her mood. Was she asking me to spend the night in the way a Sister of Mercy might ask an invalid in out of the cold, or was she asking me to share her bed, clutch her, embrace her, make love to her like a genius? Out of uncertainty, out of nervousness, I began to rattle on about conditions at the summer camp—the stink of burned garbage and raw excrement, the dance of the rats and spiders, the humorless air, slashing sun, filthy mattresses and reluctant water taps—when she cut me off. "You'll want a shower," she said.

"Yes, yes," I agreed, nodding vigorously, "a shower."

I was standing suddenly, watching her closely, fumbling toward the first move, a touch, a kiss, never certain, suspended in the moment like an insect caught in a web. She stood three feet from me. Morning light, ceramic pig, a stove that shone like the flank of a Viking rocket. She sipped her Postum, watching me in turn, her lips pursed to blow the steam from her cup. Now, I thought, hesitating.

"The shower's through here," she said, setting down her mug and drifting through the kitchen in a liquid rush of dragons and lotus flowers. The living room was on the left, her bedroom on the right. She stood at the door of the penumbral bedroom—bed, dresser, patchwork quilt—ushering me forward. Dimly visible in the far corner, a clutch of ceramic figures gazed at me with stricken, sorrowful eyes that seemed to speak of lost chances and the bankruptcy of hope. I followed her through the room, past the broad variegated plain of the big double bed and the eyes of the gloomy figures. Then the bathroom door swung open, a splash of underwater light caught in the thick, beaded, sun-struck windows. "Here's a towel," she said, shoving terrycloth at my bandaged hands, and then I was in the bathroom, door closing, click, and she was gone.

My pants were a trial. Fingers like blocks of cement, fumbling with the catch, the zipper. Scorched, frayed, reeking of smoke and dried sweat, the pants finally dropped to the floor. Then the rest: sneakers fit for the wastebasket, T-shirt a rag, socks and Jockey shorts smelling as if they'd been used to mop up the locker room after the big game. The tiles felt cool under my feet, the windows glowed. I was nude, in Petra's bathroom. Though the shower awaited, I couldn't resist poking through her medicine cabinet—take two in the morning, two in the evening and feed the rest to the ducks—and peeking into her dirty-clothes hamper. I studied her undergarments, her makeup, her artifacts and totems. I used her toothbrush. Counted her birth-control pills, took a swig of Listerine and swirled it round my mouth, found a plastic vial of what looked to be Valium, shook out two and swallowed them. Then I slid back the opaque door of the shower stall, stepped inside and took the first hissing rush of water like a bride in the ritual bath.

One minute passed. Two. Water swirling round my feet, my head bowed to the spray, hands held high to keep the bandages dry. When the stall door slid back, I turned like a supplicant before the oracle. Petra was smiling. The kimono dropped from her and that naked interesting leg engulfed her, pulled her forward. The water beat at me, at us, purifying, cleansing, doing the work of absolution. "I thought you might need help," she murmured, holding me. "What with your hands and all."

Phil was waiting for us amid the plastic ferns in the hallway-cum-lobby of the Frank R. Howard Memorial Hospital. At first I didn't recognize him. He had his back to us, and he was slumped in a burnt-orange imitation-leather easy chair, thumbing through a twelve-year-old copy of *Reader's Digest*. An old man, so wasted his flesh looked painted on, dozed in a wheelchair beside him, while a thick, stolid, broad-faced woman who might have been Nina Khrushchev's cousin from San Jose sat directly across from him, stolidly peeling a banana. I stepped through the main door, Petra at my side, and took in the scuffed linoleum, battered gurneys, the pine desk, which now bore a placard reading "Receptionist," the little group ranged round the cheap furniture and plastic plants. Nina's cousin gave us a brief bovine glance and then turned back to her banana. I saw the nodding old man, I saw the back of Phil's head (which was not Phil's head at all, but the shorn and gauze-wrapped cranium of some stranger, some poor unfortunate from whose afflictions one instinctively and charitably averts one's eyes). "Maybe he's still in his room or something," I said, steering Petra toward the receptionist's desk.

Gone was the sour night-nurse. In her stead, a motherly type beamed up at us, dispensing smiles like individually wrapped candies. "May I help you?"

Beyond her, the emergency room stood empty, no trace of the kid's bloody passage. "Phil Cherniske," I said, with an odd sense of déjà vu that took me back to the Eldorado County jail. I'd phoned the hospital from Petra's apartment half an hour earlier, and Phil had told me he was all right—a little sore, that was all—and that he'd meet me in the lobby at two. It was ten after. "He's due to be discharged?"

She gave me a peculiar look, a web of creases suddenly emerging to snatch the smile from her lips. "But he's right over there," she said, indicating the trio among the ferns.

Petra and I turned our heads in unison, the old man in the wheelchair woke with a start and shouted something incoherent, Nina's cousin tucked the nether end of the banana in the pocket of her cheek and Phil looked up from his magazine. "Phil," I blurted, my voice echoing down the corridor, "over here."

He stood. Pale as a fish, dressed in his soot-blackened jeans, greasy workboots and a pale green hospital gown that fell away in back to reveal bandages upon bandages, he looked like an invalid, a refugee, one of the homeless. They'd shaved the crown of his head, and he wore a listing slab of sticking-plaster and gauze on the left side as if it were a jaunty white beret. I crossed the hallway and gave him the Beau Geste hug, gingerly patting his bandaged shoulders with my bandaged hands. "Christ," I said, stepping back, "you look terrible."

Phil's stubborn eyes had come into alignment, and he was surveying me head to foot with a tight sardonic smile. I was wearing the punctuated sneakers, my beat pants and a Boy Scout shirt of Petra's that was so small it looked like a bib. And my bandages, of course. "You don't exactly look like the Barclay man yourself, you know."

"You are all right, though, aren't you?" I said. His right arm was taped and bound, his chest, back, shoulders; where a tongue of flesh protruded from beneath the gauze, it was rough and raw, as if someone had taken a cheese grater to it.

Phil shrugged. "I've got to change the bandages once a day and rub this shit that looks like green toothpaste . . ." He broke off in mid-sentence. A look of bewilderment had come over his face, and he was gazing beyond me at Petra as if she were a cross between La Belle Dame Sans Merci and the Dragon Lady.

I turned and slipped my arm round her waist. "Phil," I said, "this is Petra. Petra, Phil."

Phil shook her hand numbly.

"Who the hell are you?" bawled the old man in the wheelchair, glaring at the wide-faced chewing woman. She'd been sitting there, motionless, staring off into space and absently turning the banana peel over in her hands as if she were molding clay. "You," the old man raged. "Fat face. What the shit, piss and fuck do you think you're doing in my bathroom?"

The woman looked alarmed, terrified, as if she'd been denounced in a purge and was facing a howling mob. She rose to her feet, gathering up a handbag the size of a pig's head and looking wildly around her, as we moved off down the hallway, away from the commotion. Phil was giving me an are-you-crazy-or-what look, the look of a conspirator betrayed, a look of disbelief and mortal offense. I ignored him.

We passed through the double doors and out into the sunshine. I was holding Petra's hand, couldn't seem to stop touching her in fact. I'd never in my life felt better. "I told her everything, Phil," I said.

He stopped short. Petra attempted an awkward grin; I put on

my sober, prisoner-in-the-dock expression. We stood there in the driveway for a long moment, the three of us, facing one another like footballers in a huddle. I watched as Phil absorbed the news, watched as his lips and eyes tried out one expression after another, sorting through responses like ties on a rack—he looked like a stand-up comic trying to play Lear, Cordelia and the Fool simultaneously. Finally he just dropped his shoulders and gave us a bald-headed, green-gowned, wild-eyed, gap-toothed smile. "At least you didn't tell the Eyewitness News Team . . . or did you?"

The café Petra chose for breakfast/lunch was, of course, the very one in which I'd had my first paranoid episode, the one in which I'd conjured the specter of Jerpbak and gone into ataxic shock while Phil blithely related the adventures of Bors Borka, intergalactic hero. That was back in April. I hadn't been near the place since. Now, as I swung the Toyota into the parking lot and nosed up to the cinder-block foundation between the inevitable pickups and dusty Ford sedans, I felt the slightest tremor run through my digestive tract. Phil was rattling on about hospital food, oblivious as usual. "They gave me lime Jell-O for breakfast, with a little shit-smear of that fake whipped cream—you know, that stuff they make out of leftover fiberglass? For lunch it was grape Jell-O with fruit cocktail in it. I mean that was it. No bread, no milk, no meat, eggs, nothing. Jell-O." He scratched the bristle of his head. "Maybe it's some kind of new miracle food or something."

"Haven't you heard?" Petra said. "It prevents cancer."

We were laughing as we ascended the front steps, grinning like fools as we stepped through the door. The place was crowded. Puffs of starched hair, cowboy hats, cigarette smoke, a rumbling clatter of cheap silverware and busy voices and the faint, countrified pulse of the jukebox. Petra was leading us past a row of congested booths to a table by the far window, when a hand reached out to grab my wrist.

I stopped. Looked down. Lloyd Sapers was grinning up at me, a plate of runny eggs and grits at his elbow. Beside him, the massive spill of goggle-eyed Marlon, an avalanche of flesh in a T-shirt the size of a bedspread. Sitting across from him, and eyeing me wrathfully, was George Pete Turner. "Howdedo, howdedo," Sapers was saying, the chin bobbing up and down on his neck like a rubber ball attached to a paddle. "Looks like you boys mighta had a little accident, huh?"

Phil and Petra had stopped, too, and were looking back at me questioningly. How many times had I been through this, I wondered, watching the mock-innocent expression hang on Sapers's face like a kite in the wind, how many times had I played the whipping boy to this crew of in-bred, shit-shoveling, tobacco-chewing rednecks? Things had changed. I'd been through the fire and my life was something new. I jerked my hand away. "What's it to you?" I said.

"Just asking, that's all," Sapers roared as if addressing the entire restaurant. A sly smirk creased the stubble of his cheeks and he licked his lips. "Just being neighborly."

"You want to be neighborly," I said, leaning forward and resting my bandaged fists on the edge of the table, "why don't you come up with some cash to cover your son's rampage a month and a half ago? Like you promised."

He was glib, Sapers, chameleonlike, but I had him. His face folded like a lawn chair and he began to fidget in his seat. Marlon, who'd been lustily attacking a double Super Chili Beef Burger in a sea of French fries, reddened and stared down at his plate.

"Come on, Felix," Phil said. He was standing behind me, the hospital gown tucked into his jeans, impatience hardening his face: he didn't like Sapers any more than I did.

Sapers was on the defensive now, mumbling something about an operation for Trudy and a stud bull with the bloody scours. I cut him off. "You owe me," I said.

Through all this, George Pete Turner had been glowering up at me with his wicked slanted vigilante's eyes, no doubt privately implicating me in the disappearance of his daughter-in-law-to-be and a thousand other crimes, not the least of which was my insistence on continuing to draw breath and occupy space. Now I turned to him, straightened up and folded my arms across my chest. I felt like Shane unleashed, like Kid Lightning, hands wrapped, warming up for the main event. "And you, friend," I said, "don't *I* owe *you* something?"

The question seemed to take him by surprise. He glanced at Phil and then Petra, as if for clarification.

I was a firefighter, a hero, a lover. I looked him in the eye, two feet away, and prodded him: "Like a good shot to the side of the head, maybe?"

"Hey-hey," Sapers said, roaring again. "We're all friends here, aren't we?"

George Pete was rangy, tough, hard as a knot. He was wearing a plaid shirt, a hand-tooled belt and a string tie. His eyes were the color of water vapor. He didn't say a word.

"Come on, stand up," I said. "I'll take you on right here and now, bandages and all." I don't know what had come over me, but I was suddenly hot with outrage, self-righteous as a preacher, vengeful as a man wronged. I was ready to fight to the death, bite the heads off chickens, anything.

A nerve twitched under George Pete's right eye. Plates rattled and voices hummed around us. Marlon swished the ice in his glass, Sapers was silent. George Pete suddenly became interested in the design of his napkin. "Fine," I said, and an era had ended. I turned my back on them contemptuously, the matador walking away from a spiritless bull, and led Petra and Phil to a table in the corner.

Something had changed. Some subtle alteration had taken place in the balance of things—I'd cut a new notch in the chain of being, and I could feel all the myriad creatures of the earth, from slippery amoebae and humping earthworms to the hordes of China, shoving over to make room like passengers on a crowded bus. As if in confirmation of this new state of things, the ancient waitress responded instantly to my merest gesture, though the place was packed. She poured us hot coffee, freshly brewed. The food came so quickly I suspected the cook of clairvoyance. It was hot, properly seasoned, tasty. The rolls were airy, the butter firm and pale. Phil and Petra discovered the common ground of sculpture and became fast friends almost instantly. When I looked up, Sapers and his party had vanished.

"No," Phil was saying, "I haven't done anything in years."

"But you wouldn't catch him dead without his blowtorch," I said.

Petra smiled. She was wearing white—a peasant blouse, embroidered gentians twining the sleeves. I watched her lift the sandwich to her mouth, pat her lips with the napkin, and then watched her smile widen like the wake of a sailboat cutting across a flashing depthless sea. When the two highway patrolmen lumbered through the door, keys clanking, gunbelts creaking, and heaved into the booth behind us, I barely glanced up.

Chapter 4

Unseasonable, freakish, the rains began in earnest the last week of October. I woke one morning to the sound of rain on the sheet Styrofoam of the roof—it was like the rattling of a snare drum—and to the slow steady drip of the runoff making its way through the seams and spattering the kitchen floor. At first I was elated. Like one of Noah's unwitting contemporaries on the first blessed day of rain, I thought only of the crops standing tall in the fields, of the even, invigorating, pluvial wash laving leaves, buds, stems, percolating down to the thirsting roots. Lulled by the sweet percussion, I turned over and fell back into my dreams: there would be no need to start up the pump, I thought, not today.

Three days later it was still raining.

Now I woke to the hiss of it as to a pronouncement of doom, thinking of the generations of plowmen gone down, from the Mesopotamians to Virgil's *agricolae* to the pioneers of the Midwest and their mechanized descendants—tilling, seeding, fertilizing and watering, waiting, praying, sacrificing to the gods—only to wake one morning to the rattle of hail or the cutting rasp of the locusts' wings. My bed was damp, my clothes damper still. A single day's rain was cause for celebration, a boon—just the thing to coax the buds into a final pre-harvest frenzy—but this was a disaster. Sodden, the heavy colas would pull the branches down till they snapped, the plants would die premature deaths, the buds would develop mold and wind up tasting like coffin scrapings. Where was the season of mellow fruitfulness, plumping kernels and deluded bees?

I was making breakfast—fried-egg sandwiches with green salsa and melted jack cheese—when Gesh rumbled down the stairs from the attic like a tree dweller dropping to earth. He was wearing a hooded black sweatshirt and a pair of grease-stiffened corduroys, and he was cursing. The curses were elaborate, heartfelt, rhythmic and persuasive, and they were directed at the weather, at Vogelsang, at the Powers That Be and life in a disappointing and ultimately tragic universe. For five minutes or more he stood at the yellowed front window, hooded like a monk at prayer, cursing into the windowpane. The glass clouded over: it was cold. Once again. And of course we hadn't laid in even a stick of wood, thinking only of the maturing sun, the crop—attenuated though it was—coming to golden fruition, money in the bank, release, the life of the city. Why stockpile wood against a winter we'd never see?

When Gesh finally joined me at the table, he announced (yet again, litany of disaffection) that he was fed up with the whole thing. I watched as he slathered ketchup on his eggs and thumped the bottom of the salsa bottle. "I mean it," he said, as if I'd questioned him. "Just get in the truck, drive to Tahoe and forget the whole fucking mess."

I sympathized with him. Who wouldn't? I had the same feelings myself. But I was determined to see those plants harvested if I had to do it in a boat. Alone. With both hands manacled behind my back and Jerpbak circling overhead in a helicopter. It was no longer a question of money (the crop had been so decimated we'd be lucky to wind up with a fraction of even our most despairing estimate), reason (if I'd been reasonable I would have been sitting in front of the stove in Petra's kitchen) or pride—no, it went deeper than that. Call it stubbornness, call it stupidity. I was beyond caring. Grim as the shipwrecked fanatic who survives six weeks on the open sea only to be offered rescue within sight of shore, I was determined to stick it out to the end. "Maybe we ought to go out there and check on the plants," I said. "Or give Dowst a call."

"Fuck Dowst," Gesh said. Predictably.

A muted subaqueous glow drained the room of light until it

began to feel like a dungeon. Behind me there was the steady syncopation of the water dripping from the ceiling into pots, pans and buckets. The kitchen smelled like a mushroom cellar.

I was thinking that phoning Dowst wouldn't be such a bad idea—especially as it would give me an excuse to drop in on Petra as long as I was in town—when Phil emerged from the shadowy depths of his room as if from the Black Hole of Calcutta. His eyes were watery and flecked with red, his bandages dirty. A joint glowed in his hand and a haze of marijuana smoke seemed to seep from his ears and cling like a phantom to the shorn crown of his head (he'd been sedating himself diligently since the fire—to ease the smart of his burns, he insisted—but changing the bandages far less faithfully). "Morning," he said, shuffling across the room to the stove, where he fired up all four burners and held his hands out flat as if he were roasting weiners. We watched him pour himself a cup of coffee, cradle it in his hands, blow on it and take a tentative sip, watched with open-mouthed concentration, as if we'd never before seen so subtle and astonishing a feat. "What about it," he said finally, swinging around to face us. "The weather stinks, Vogelsang's a liar and I'm the mummy's ghost. Let's get stoned."

Stoned, straight, drunk, sober: it didn't make a shred of difference. "Why not?" I said.

We mopped up our eggs and then huddled over the stove, glumly sharing a joint, gearing ourselves up for yet another critical decision. (We were smoking our own product now, heady stuff—shake leaves from fourteen-foot female plants with colas the size of nightsticks. The leaves were so saturated with resin they stuck to your fingers like flypaper.) We drank coffee, smoked a bit more, stood around staring off into space. Then, as if at a given signal, we shrugged into our rain gear and trundled out into the downpour to make the rounds and assess the damage.

Outside, water had begun to collect beneath the gutted storage shed and in a wide scimitar-shaped depression in the front yard. The Jeep, which hadn't run in a month, sloped forward in a reddish pool that already threatened to engulf the front bumper. There was no wind, no slant to the rain, no indication that the storm was moving on. Clouds clung to the earth as if strangling it, the main drive had reverted to its primitive state—i.e., it was a riverbed—and a network of parched gullies that were nothing more than scars in the dust suddenly churned with angry, braided streams. It was March all over again.

We trudged down the road to the Jonestown growing area—the only one that ultimately produced anything—and fought our way through the dripping undergrowth to the rat-trap-strewn enclosure we'd thrown up in the vain hope of protecting our crop from the quick-toothed vandals of the wood. Our plants—what was left of them—had been doing well, flowering for better than a month now, putting out buds on top of buds. This was the climactic growth we'd been waiting for, fey, penultimate, triggered by the autumnal equinox and the declining days that succeeded it. Dowst had been busy throughout September, identifying and eliminating the male plants, foiling nature. I'd watched as he cut down one healthy plant after another—each the culmination of months of coolie labor, of digging, hauling, fertilizing, watering—and tossed them aside to decompose. It hurt. But it was necessary. Frustrated, aching, desperate for completion, the females spread themselves ever more luxuriously, the flowers swelling, growing sweeter, more resinous and potent; budding more and still more, our harvest battened on the vine.

Now we stood confused amid the apparent ruins of it. Raindrops tapped at our backs like insinuating fingers, water puddled the ground, streamed from our hats and shoulders. The trees drooped like old men with back problems, the fierce jungle smell of ripe pot stunned the air, raw and chlorophyllific; the carcass of a rat lay twisted and dumb-staring in a trap at my feet. None of us had been out of the house since the rains had begun, and we weren't quite prepared for the transformation they'd wrought. Whereas three days earlier we'd been tending plants twelve and fourteen feet tall with branches arching toward the sun like candelabra, now we were confronted with broken limbs, splayed growth, the declining curve. Fully half the plants had ruptured under the water-heavy burden of the flower bracts, and all were bent like sunflowers after a frost. In the lower corner of the plot I found a six-inch cola—prime buds—immersed in a soup of reddish mud. It was as if someone had gone through the field with a saber, swiping randomly at stem, branch, leaf and bud.

My thoughts were gradual. Still stoned, I looked round me

in a slow pan—everything seemed to be moving, divided into beads of color, as if I were looking through a microscope. Somehow my heartbeat seemed to have lodged in my brain.

"What now?" Phil was standing at my side, Mr. Potatohead, carrot nose and cherry tomato eyes. The rain thrashed the trees like a monsoon in Burma.

"I don't know," I said.

So much water was streaming from my hat I had to turn my head and look sideways to see him. We might as well have been hooked to the conveyor track in a car wash. "This could go on forever," he said.

I couldn't think of anything to say. Anything positive, that is.

"So what do we do?" he said. "Wait and hope it clears up, try to harvest now, or what?"

It was a resonant question, pithy, full of meat and consequence, the question I'd been asking myself for the past several minutes. "We call the expert," I said.

Half an hour later, after schussing down the driveway in the Toyota, fighting erratic windshield wipers and skirting Shirelle's Bum Steer, Phil, Gesh and I crowded into a phone booth at a Shell station just outside Willits and phoned Dowst. I did the talking.

"Hello, Boyd?"

A pause. I could picture him hunching over his typewriter in a glen plaid shirt, sipping hot chicken-noodle soup and typing out his notes on the wild onion or the water wattle. "Christ, I thought you guys would never call," he said. "What's going on up there?"

"It's raining."

Another pause, as if we were speaking different languages and he had to wait for the translator to finish before he could respond. "Well, yes, of course. What I mean is did you get the stuff in yet?"

"You mean the plants?"

We hadn't seen Dowst in a month, since he'd finished culling the crop. Just before he left, he'd strolled up to the horseshoe pit and announced in sacerdotal tones that all the remaining plants were females and that we had nothing to worry about, and then he'd taken me aside. He was wearing a sober don't-jump-on-me-it's-out-of-my-hands expression, partly defensive, partly apologetic—he could have been a surgeon breaking the news that he'd made a slight miscalculation and removed my liver rather than my gall bladder. "Felix," he said, "you know we're going to harvest a lot less than we expected. A lot less." Yankee farmer, Yankee farmer, I thought, looking into those eyes rinsed of color through the generations of toil in the bleak rocky fields of New England. Lizards scurried in the dust, the clank of horseshoes beat at the moment like a blacksmith's hammer. "I know," I said. Then he shook my hand in a way that disturbed me, a way that seemed both empathetic and final. It was a scene from *Kamikaze Hell* or *Zero Hour Over Bataan*: he was bailing out. "I got that job, you know—did I tell you? At Berkeley. I start in the spring."

What could I say? We'd worked side by side, pitched horseshoes and played cards together, and yet I felt nothing, nothing but bitterness. My smile was fractured, inane, a grimace really. "Great," I said.

"See you," he said, turning to head for his van. A woodpecker drummed at dead wood off in the forest; overhead, in the reaches of space, lightwaves bent like coat hangers as they responded to the gravitational tug of distant suns. "You'll be back soon?" I called, thinking of the harvest. Perhaps he didn't hear me. I remember the way the sunlight glanced off the side panel of his van as he rolled across the lot.

Now it was raining. Gesh's shoulders crowded the booth's open doorway; water spilled from the upturned collar of his khaki overcoat. Phil pressed himself flat against the glass beside me. On the other end of the line, Dowst raised his voice. "Don't you guys realize that a rain like this is going to sap the plants? You'll get withered stigmas and the gland heads'll wash away, which means you're going to get one hell of a less potent harvest—you leave it out there much longer, you're not going to get shit."

I found Dowst's usage disturbing: the genitive form of the personal pronoun had shifted from "ours" to "yours." We were asking for help, advice, for the expert judgment he'd contracted to deliver, and we were getting a brush-off. Dowst wasn't in trouble; we were. He'd cut us adrift, lost interest. He'd written the whole thing off as a failure and had no intention of showing his face again—except to pick up his share of the proceeds. Anger rose in me like some hurtling, uncontainable force—a spear thrust, a rocket blast. "What the hell do you mean?" I said, my voice choked tight. "You're in on this, too. You're the so-called expert here, aren't you?"

At this juncture, Gesh snatched the phone from me and shouted into the receiver. "Get your ass up here, scumbag!" he roared, the phone like a throttled doll in his huge, white-knuckled fist.

I wrestled the receiver away from him. "Boyd?" I said, but Gesh, his face like hammered tin, tore it out of my hands and screamed "I'll kill you!" into the inert black bulb.

"Boyd?" I repeated when I'd regained control of the receiver. "Are you there?"

His voice was distant, cold. "Get the plants in."

I appreciated the injunction, but just how were we supposed to go about it? It had been apparent for some time that Dowst, Gesh, Phil and I would be on our own when it came to harvest. No one mentioned Mr. Big any more—clearly the deal was off. He only dealt with major operators, the guys who grew pot like Reynolds grew tobacco. We were nothing. Not only would we have to harvest and slow-dry the plants, we'd have to manicure the buds and peddle them ourselves. But Dowst's expertise was essential to all this: without him we were helpless. "Wonderful," I said, "super," a heavy load of sarcasm flattening my tone, "but how?"

"That's up to you. Rent a truck or something."

"But what then? I mean where are we going to dry it and all?" The plan had called for giving the crop another two weeks or so to come to the very cornucopian apex of potent, fecund, resin-dripping fruition, after which we would hack the plants down and string them across the lower branches of oaks, madrones, etc., to desiccate in the dry seasonal winds. Meteorologically speaking, the plan was all washed up.

There was a pause. Phil tilted his rainhat back, exposing a swath of filthy gauze; the set of his mouth, a certain redness about the lower nostrils and a roving rabbity gaze betrayed his anxiety. Gesh stared straight into the receiver, as if his eyes could hear. "What's wrong with your place?" Dowst said.

"My place?" The suggestion was outrageous, preposterous—he might as well have named the Oval Office or the lobby of the Chase Manhattan Bank. Hundreds of pounds of marijuana strung up like dirty wash in my apartment? In the middle of the city? How would we get it in—or out?

Dowst's voice pricked at me like a hatpin. "Look, I don't know," he said. "All I know is that it's supposed to rain for the rest of the week and you'd better get that shit in and dry it someplace." The line crackled as if with the dislocations of the storm. "Harvest," he said. "Now." And then he hung up.

Phil and Gesh were looking at me as if I were a runner bringing news of foreign wars. "Well," Gesh said, "what did he say?"

Rain spanked the glass walls of the phone booth; a dank wind rose up out of nowhere to assault my nostrils. Suddenly it didn't matter. Inspiration came, joy, uplift. All at once I knew what we were going to do, and how. But even more important was the electricity of the understanding that came with it: we were free. The project was finished, harvest upon us. All we had to do was cut the plants, pack up and turn our backs on the place. Forever. No more Jerpbak, Sapers and the rest, no more lizards and rats, heat, dust, rain, cold, no more alarms in the night or bathing in a tub fit for crocodiles, no more Dowst, Jones, Vogelsang: it was over.

"Well?"

I was grinning. The rain fell steadily, dropping like the curtain on the final act of a wearying and protracted drama. "We harvest," I said. "Now."

Ever since the fire, I'd felt that the three of us had drawn apart in some subtle, indefinable way. We were still close—as close as any band of guerrillas under attack, as close as survivors, comrades, buddies, blood brothers—but the fire, as I've said, altered our perspective. As it became increasingly evident that the whole ill-fated project was a bust and that we'd sweated and agonized and given up nine months of our lives for nothing, we began perhaps to feel a bit shamefaced, embarrassed for ourselves, as though we were rubes taken in by a good but transparent pitch, as though we should have known better. The profits would be negligible, Mr. Big was an interdicted subject, the hazards mounted as the crops ripened, but it was understood among us that we would stick it out. We no longer bothered to perform calculations on the mental ledger sheet—solving for *x* was too unsettling. We were going to persevere, grimly, stolidly, Tess cutting sheaves at Flintcombe-Ash, Job staggering under the burden of calamity, and we didn't want to know the score.

And so, once united behind the myth of success—the yachts, the restaurants, the equal shares of half a million dollars—we now by necessity drew into ourselves to avoid confronting its rotten wasted core. Gesh brooded. He took long plodding walks through the fields, his fierce Slavic gaze fixed on the ground, hair in a tangle, great bruising hands wadded behind him like tissue paper. Restless, he made a twenty-four-hour run to Tahoe for pharmaceutical meliorants; exhausted, he slept twelve hours a day. He seemed distracted, cankers of rage eating at him like some alien growth, disappointment, self-reproach and the ravages of heartburn sunk into his eyes. Increasingly taciturn, cryptic even, he became the evil genius of the place, a bristling presence to whom the least gesture of day-to-day life was a wellspring of bitterness. Throw a ringer to beat him at horseshoes, draw the winning card from the deck, and he looked as if you'd run a sword through him.

If Gesh was tangled up in himself, rootbound with frustration, Phil was the sensitive plant. For the first few days after his return from the hospital, he drifted from one room to another like a ghost, scratching idly at his crotch or the desolation of his crown, smiling little, saying less. He picked at his guitar for hours at a time (mournful single-string meanderings that sounded like lamentations for the dead), he stopped eating, chain-smoked pot; his bandages glowed in the dark. I came in from irrigating the plants or stood at the stove stirring a kettle of tuna, noodles, and cream of celery soup while Gesh glared at a tattered skin magazine and Phil gazed out the window as if he were witness to rare visions or rehearsing for the rapture. Acid emotions, short-circuited brainwaves: I felt pinched between them. "Phil, are you okay?" I asked after a day or two. No response. I repeated myself. "Me?" he said finally, as if he were one of hundreds present. "Oh, yeah, sure, no problem."

Finally, just as I'd begun to suspect that the flames had somehow scoured the inside of his head as well as the outer tegument, Phil roused himself to action. It was early morning, four or five days after he'd got back from the hospital, the weather sere and hot, snakes stirring, rats nibbling, rain an impossible proposition. Gesh and I were on our way back from ministering to a thirsty if depleted crop, stepping gingerly, our ears attuned to the least rustle of leaf or twig (I held the shotgun out before me like an assegai, wary of snakes and poachers alike), when Gesh grabbed my arm and dropped his voice to a tense whisper: "What was that?"

"What?" I said, my chin the end-stop beneath the flaring exclamation point of my mouth, nose and brow.

"That noise."

We were cutting cross-country to save time, up to our knees in dense, reptile-nurturing brush, no more than fifty yards from the cabin. "I don't hear anything," I whispered, hearing it. It was a hiss: faint, sibilant, saurian, nasty. I released the shotgun's safety catch. Cautiously, slowly, with more reluctance than curiosity, we made our way to the edge of the field that lay before the house.

What we saw was Phil. He was bent over something, his back to us, intent as a cannibal at breakfast. As I drew closer it became apparent that the hissing was not an expression of ophidian rage but rather the constant fulminating rush of burning gas: Phil was fooling around with his acetylene torch, playing with fire, shaping something. We came up behind him. Sparks flew. Rumpled, twisted, dull as dried blood, the dismal, rusted shapes of discarded machine parts lay in a jagged heap beside him like the debris of foreign wars. Phil was in the process of joining the spin basket of an abandoned washing machine to the amputated fender of a deceased Packard I'd tripped over at least sixty times since March. I asked him what he was doing.

Behind him loomed the charred skeleton of the shed; the blackened grass fanned out around him like a stain. I watched as he steadied the spin basket with one hand and carefully drew the torch along the base of it with the other. He finished the connection before he turned to look over his shoulder at us.

"It's a bird feeder, right?" Gesh said.

Phil was wearing goggles. The dirty bandages clung to him like a second skin. He could have been a downed fighter ace, injured but game, hunched hopefully over the husk of his gutted jet. For a long moment he simply regarded us as if he'd never laid eyes on us before, the blue flame spitting from his fingertips as if in some magic act. After a while, he turned back to his work.

By nightfall a chin-high pyramid of conjoined junk rose from the ground where the greenhouse had once stood. I'd watched Phil from the shadowy interior of the cabin as morning became afternoon and the roving sun beat at his long nose and naked brow, watched as he dragged bedsprings across the stubble, caressed fenders scalloped like giant ashtrays, probed the slick bulging bellies of his objets trouvés with the burning finger of his torch. He sifted through the ash and debris of the storage shed until he came up with the decapitated head of a pitchfork with its scorched and twisted tines, crabwalked across the back field like a man with bowel problems as he struggled with the gearbox of the weed-whipped Hudson that straddled the cleft of the ravine like a beached ship. He hammered, burned, melted, bent, wedged, clattered and thumped. There was noise, there was heat, creation blossomed amid the rubble, ineffable design confronted physics. When it was fully dark, Phil staggered into the kitchen to take nourishment.

"Is it done?" I asked. My tone was buoyant, warm, shot full of enthusiasm. Phil had been a zombie since the fire, not yet dead but not alive either, and to see him snap out of it was a relief. "Whatever it is," I added. "What is it, anyway?"

Phil was bent over the gas burner, lighting a joint. I suppose the cannabinoids contributed in some mystical way to the purity of his vision—I was standing knee-deep in a bog and he was scaling creative Annapurnas. "No," he said, exhaling fragrant smoke, "it's not done yet." Dried sweat chewed at his bandages with yellow teeth, his wild eye spun in its socket like a lacquered lemon in a slot machine. "It's a, it's—" He broke off to take another hit. "It's a tribute to us, I mean to the whole thing we're doing up here."

Gesh was slumped in the easy chair, his huge bare feet splayed out across the floor. "You mean like a memorial to the dead, right?"

"Come on, give us a break," I said.

"What about the eye in the sky?" Gesh drew himself up and leaned forward. "You don't think they'll spot that pile of junk from anywhere in the range of five hundred to thirty thousand feet? You might as well put up a neon sign: 'Pot, a hundred and twenty dollars a lid.' "

Phil wasn't listening. He was spooning papaya-coconut chutney on a slice of white bread and staring off at the flat black windows as if his gaze could drive back the night and illuminate the yard. The creative fit was on him.

It took him a week. After the second day he had to use a ladder. I went outside one morning to see how he was doing and found him perched ten feet off the ground, nesting in the crotch of his metallic aerie like some gangling unfeathered big-winged chick, the blue flame licking here and there, parts accruing. "How's it going?" I shouted. Aloft, grinning, begoggled, he held up two fingers in the victory sign.

Gesh bitched. Lizards began to frequent the structure's lower verges, twitching in the dazzling light, doing short-armed push-ups and yelping from soft trembling throats. Birds shat on it, rats toured its tortuous walkways like prospective tenants looking over an apartment complex. The sum of its parts, Phil's monument grew in unexpected directions, mad, random, sensible only to the inner vision that spawned it. Twice the artist made frantic trips to town to replenish his supply of brazing rods or refill one or the other of his tanks. Aside from those two brief hiatuses, he worked from dawn till dusk, skipping meals, ignoring his chores, his comrades, the plants blooming like medallions in the fields. Frayed, the bandages whipped round him in ectoplasmic flux, his pants and T-shirts were spattered and singed, skin began to peel in transparent sheets from his sunburned nose. On the sixth day he worked late into the night, the glow of the torch dimly visible beyond the darkened windows of the cabin. On the seventh day he rested. He rose about noon and summoned Gesh and me outside. Tottering on the porch, his eyes glowing feverishly, he gestured toward the mound of welded junk with a flourish and said "*Voilà.*"

Gesh gave me a sidelong glance. I tried to maintain my equanimity.

"What do you think?" Phil said.

Think? The thing was monstrous, anarchic, a mockery of proportion and grace of line. It looked like a heap of crushed and rusted French horns and tubas, it looked like a dismantled tank in the Sinai, it looked like the Watts Towers compressed by an Olympian fist. I walked round it, Phil at my side. Twenty feet high, wide around as my bedroom floor, it was monumental, toothy, jagged, unsteady, a maze of gears, bolts, hammered planes and swooping arcs. "Nice," I said.

Gesh's hands were sunk deep in his pockets. He was grinning, fighting down a laugh, his face animated for the first time in days.

Phil took my arm and backed off a pace or two, maneuvering for a better perspective. "I was thinking of calling it *Agrarian Rhapsody*," he said, "but now I'm not so sure. What do you think of *Burned*?"

If my co-workers had motivational problems during those declining weeks at the summer camp, I had my bouts of self-doubt and despondency, too. I felt useless, I felt as if I'd been sold a bill of goods, deceived, I felt like Willie Loman at the end of the road. But just when my spirit had shrunk to a hard black knot, the fire delivered me up to Petra and I felt my priorities shift like tectonic plates after a seismic storm. I'd been standing on one side of the rift, and then as the gulf widened I'd leapt to the other. Gesh ate himself up, Phil sought solace in art, I was in love.

The others didn't like it, not a bit. By introducing Petra to our inner circle, I'd compromised the project, weakened our position irretrievably. First I'd screwed up with Savoy, and now I'd willfully violated our vow of secrecy and my promise to remain on the property as long as Jerpbak roved the streets and the plants grew straight and tall. Phil looked the other way, Gesh muttered and swore, Vogelsang—had he known—would have mounted the pedestal of righteousness and denounced me for a turncoat and a fool, but nearly every afternoon during that three-week period between the fire and the rains, I cranked up the Toyota and drove into Willits. I couldn't help myself. Didn't want to. The summer camp was moribund; this was newborn.

I would saunter into her shop at four each afternoon—horny as a tomcat, aching, throbbing, my eyes and fingertips, my tongue, lips, and nostrils swollen with lust—and feign indifference as she chatted with a customer or watch transfixed as she sat at her wheel, shaping clay beneath the pyramid of her long tapering fingers. The shop closed at five. I would have been up since seven, tending the plants for the first hour or two, then killing time with walks, cards, trashy paperbacks, the ritual of meals, the one-o'clock siesta, all the while palpitating for the hour of my liberation like a dog awaiting the scrape of his master's heel on the doorstep. If there were no customers, I'd walk straight in, soothed by the music of the bell, the shadows, the cool plants and glistening triumphant pots, the music of Boccherini, Pachelbel, Palestrina, find her in her smock before the glowing oven or bent over the wheel, and stick my tongue in her ear. Sometimes she was busy, and I would wait; other times we would wrestle on the floor, naked in the clay, and let the angels sing.

I liked it best when there were customers in the shop. Then I could browse, anonymous, a customer among customers, pondering this object or that, my fingers tracing the persuasive, gently swelling convexity of a vase or cupping a smooth glazed bowl as if it were an object of erotic devotion. This was the season of the late-blooming tourist, the golden ones, retirees in Winnebagos and Sceni-Cruisers, smiling their wan beneficent smiles, dropping Mastercard slips and traveler's checks like manna. I heard madrigals and watched her lips, I hummed along with motets and saw the pregnant look she gave me over the stooped white heads of couples who'd been married fifty years. The anticipation was delicious. I watched her, ogled her, coveted her in the way a child covets the foil-wrapped gifts beneath the Christmas tree—the breasts pushing at her smock, the long impossible fall of her legs, the even white teeth, and the flawless tender expanse of her lips as she beamed at some sunny old character's blandishments. Five o'clock would come and I'd help her close up the shop, draw the shades, count out the receipts with trembling fingers, touching her, and then I'd take her upstairs and ravish her. Or rather, during that first week when my hands were still bandaged, she ravished me. Upstairs, on her bed, under the greedy voyeuristic gaze of her dwarves and elves and pinheads, she undressed me, button by button. Then she took off her smock.

We would drink a bottle of wine, eat a lazy dinner—tofu salad or veggie delight from Sarah's place or three-pound garbage burritos from the Mexican restaurant two doors down—go back to bed, smoke, drink, talk. We talked about our respective childhoods, childhood in general, about the relative virtues of growing up in Chicago and New York, about sculpture, movies, books, the tide of illiteracy rising steadily to undermine the country's intellectual foundations. We talked politics, art, religion, talked blues and plainsong, considered the variety of life on the planet and the argument from design, wondered about life after death and dismissed reincarnation. I confessed that like most children of the Wonder-bread era I hadn't believed in God past the age of awareness, but that lately I'd begun to feel the tug of the irrational. She told me she'd wanted to be an artist since her discovery of fingerpaints in kindergarten; I told her I'd always been fascinated with dirigibles. Lighter than air, I said, as if the phrase were magical.

"Felix, listen," she said. Her hand was on my arm. She gave me a look, lips drawn tight, eyes extruded, that reminded me of Michelangelo's *Pietà*. "When he left me like that—my husband, I mean—it was the worst thing that ever happened to me. I felt like I had a disease or something—I felt like I *was* a disease."

"You know, I quit on my wife," I said.

She just looked at me.

"It was a career thing. Or no, it was me, I was immature, hung up on role playing, you know?" I told her about Ronnie, how when we met she'd seemed so helpless, so utterly adrift—unable to eat in a restaurant by herself, incapable of locking a car door or paying the phone bill before they disconnected her—and how good it had made me feel to think that she needed me, that I was her champion, her foundation and support. I told her how all that had changed, how she'd grown up and abandoned the little-girl-in-search-of-a-daddy role like a dress that no longer fit her, how she'd suddenly taken an interest in local politics,

Afghan hounds and assertiveness training, how she'd asked me for a quid pro quo—to support her through her M.B.A. program as she'd supported me through my abortive Ph.D.—and how I'd quit on her. When I finished, I glanced at Petra like a guilty child, like a thug, a criminal, a male supremacist and backward boor, and flashed her a tentative smile. She was holding an empty teacup. "You know something?" she said. I shrugged. "The way you smile—with your whole face, with your eyes—it's like a certificate of trust."

One night, I don't remember how—who but an insomniac can retrace the web of association of even his own thoughts, let alone recall the progress of a free-ranging dialogue—we got on the subject of babies. It was not a subject to which I readily warmed. Raised as an only child in a neighborhood where it was thought impolite to have more than two children, I'd never had to deal with either sibling rivalry or sibling bonding, had never been supplanted at my mother's breast by a little gene-shuffler, had never cooed into half-formed faces or wiped up infantile secretions. I knew more of dogs, cats or even goldfish than I knew of children, and my experience of the last-mentioned had been exclusively negative. Children—babies—were loathsome to me, all open orifices and dribbling body fluids, they were the noose around the throat, an end to youth, an eternal responsibility, anathema. But on this night, this otherwise triumphant, golden, redolent night, babies was the subject.

"I'm twenty-nine now," Petra said, running a reflective finger around the edge of her wineglass.

"Yes," I said.

"I'll be thirty in two months."

I nodded, wondering what this had to do with anything. I felt a twinge of panic. Was she making an oblique comment on our relationship? Was she too old for me? Was I too young for her? Had she been doomed by some genetic infirmity to collapse on the brink of her fourth decade?

"You know," she said after a moment, "I could never be serious about anybody—a man, I mean—who didn't want children." We were in bed. Her legs were wrapped around me. At the mention of this highly charged term with its suggestion of sex, love, tenderness, and affliction, of generations gone down and generations to come, with its messy implications and terrible responsibilities, my poor organ rose briefly with the inflammatory thought of the act involved, and then immediately collapsed under the weight of the rest.

"The child is father of the man," I said, apropos of nothing. "Speaking of Wordsworth, do you know what Whitman had to say about childhood?"

She was resolute, unswervable. "I'm no religious nut," she said. "Or one of these virginal types out of a Victorian novel who can't relate to good clean healthy athletic sex—it's nothing like that." She sat up, arranged herself against the headboard in the lotus position and then reached out to the night table to refill our wineglasses. I watched her breasts move.

"It's just that when you look at it, no matter how much our generation has tried to postpone the issue of adulthood and all the responsibilities that go with it, you've got to grow up sometime and realize that having a family is just a part of life, maybe the biggest part." She shoved her hair back, took a sip of wine and went on to talk about the life force, mayflies, the great chain of being and the nesting habits of birds. She was philosophical, and she was nude. Somehow, everything she said made perfect sense. "It's nature," she said. "I mean, all these nerve endings, the physical thing, you know . . ." She dropped her eyes. I took her breast in my hand like a sacred object. I knew. "It's all there to ensure the survival of the species."

I was sitting up now, too, sitting close, my hands on her. "You sound like Charles Darwin."

"No, I mean you go through life in stages and at each stage everything changes. You're a kid with a doll or bicycle and every day lasts six years, then you're a teenager counting pubic hairs and waiting for the phone to ring."

"You too, huh?"

She smiled, nodded, took a quick sip of Bardolino. I hunkered closer.

"Then you're twenty, twenty-five, and you want to have a good time—why get tied down? Hedonism, right? The Me Generation?"

My hands were on her, and now hers were on me. There was something moving in me, and it wasn't philosophy.

"I'm all for it," she said. "But I want something else, too. I want to feel complete—you know what I mean?"

At this point I could only murmur. I was rising up on my haunches like a satyr, falling into her as into a warm bath.

And then all of a sudden she was gone. Pushing herself up from the bed, swinging her legs out, padding across the floor to the gnome that sat on her dresser. "I loved being a kid," she said, running a thoughtful finger across the gnome's fallen forehead. "Loved it. My mother was a big woman and she would take me shopping or walking along the lakeshore and I would feel like I was in the grip of some god and that nothing could go wrong, that everything would last forever, like in a painting—like in Seurat's *La Grande Jatte* . . . you know it?"

I shook my head.

Then she was crossing the room to the bookcase, everything in motion, and bending like one of Degas's nudes to pluck up a book of reproductions of the French Impressionists. She handed me the book, open to Seurat's idyll. I saw a day of milky sunshine, kids, dogs, sunbonnets, a warmth and radiance that never ends, no quitting allowed. Or even contemplated. Petra was watching me. "Come here," I said, setting the book aside. She came, and then we sank back into the bed and I gave myself over to impulse and the tug of the life force.

The following day I strolled into the shop at the usual hour and found her bargaining with an old road warrior over a four-hundred dollar stoneware table setting.

"Four hundred," she said.

The old man was heavyset, pouchy and grizzled, in a new white T-shirt. His face was broad and sorrowful, collapsing on itself like a decaying jack-o'-lantern. "Three hundred," he said.

"Four hundred."

"Three-fifty."

"Four hundred."

"Three seventy-five."

Light, airy, elegant, Debussy's *Children's Corner Suite* fluttered effortlessly through the speakers as I walked in, wondering at the coincidence: was she trying to tell me something? Petra flashed me a smile, I winked in surreptitious acknowledgment, then turned to examine a soup tureen as if I'd never before encountered so exquisite an object, as if I could barely restrain myself from having it wrapped immediately and whirling round to bid on the old man's crockery.

"Three-eighty," he said, "and that's my final price."

But Petra wasn't there to answer. She'd swept across the room, locking her arm in mine and effectively blowing my cover as the disinterested and anonymous pottery-lover. "Felix," she gasped, grinning till all her fine teeth showed, strangely animated, ebullient, ticking away like a kettle coming on to full boil, "have you heard? Have you seen the paper?"

I hadn't seen the paper. I lived like an ignorant pig farmer in a sagging shack three miles from the nearest hardtop road. "Heard what?"

"Jerpbak. They got him."

"Who?" I cried, believing, disbelieving, already lit with a rush of anticipatory joy, already panting. I wanted to hear the worst, the vilest details, I wanted to hear that he'd murdered his wife, vanished without a trace, been run down by a carload of ganja-crazed Rastafarians. "What are you talking about?"

"Wait, wait, wait," she said, skipping back to the counter for the newspaper. Befuddled, the old Winnebago pilot stood at the cash register, a two-pound ceramic plate in one hand, a sheaf of traveler's checks in the other.

The story was on page six, tucked away amid a clutter of birth announcements and photographs of bilious-looking Rotarians and adolescent calf-fatteners. It was simple, terse, to the point. Jerpbak had been suspended from active duty pending investigation of assault charges brought against him by the parents of two juveniles he'd taken into custody earlier in the month. Charles Fadel, Jr., 16, son of the prominent Bay Area attorney, had been admitted to the Frank R. Howard Memorial Hospital in Willits suffering from facial contusions, concussion, and fractured ribs; his companion, Michael Puff, 17, of Mill Valley, had sustained minor cuts and bruises that did not require emergency care. According to the official police report, Officer Jerpbak encountered the pair at 3:45 a.m. on the sixth of October as they were hitchhiking along Route 101 just south of Willits. They allegedly refused the reasonable request of a police officer in declining to identify themselves and subsequently resisted arrest, at which time the officer was constrained to subdue them. In filing charges, the parents of the juveniles contended that the arresting officer had violated the youths' civil rights and had used unwarranted and excessive force in detaining them. (Oh, yes. I could picture the dark road, Jerpbak wound up like a jack-in-the-box; I closed my eyes and saw the bloody kid splayed out on the nurse's desk.) CHP officials declined comment.

I read through the story with mounting exhilaration, then stopped to read it again, savoring the details. I clenched my fist, gritted my teeth: they were going to stick it to him, they were going to hang his ass. I felt as deeply justified, as elated and self-righteous as I had when I first heard the news of Nixon's resignation. Jerpbak had got his comeuppance. There was justice in the world after all, justice ascendant.

Petra and I embraced. We danced round the shop, arm in arm, homesteaders watching the Comanches retreat under the guns of the cavalry. "We've got to celebrate," I said.

Forgotten, the old man slouched behind his belly, watching us out of cloudy, lugubrious eyes. We were dancing in each other's arms; he had a bad back, bad feet and an abraded memory. "All right," he said, setting down the plate and scrawling his signature across the face of the topmost check, "I'll give you four hundred."

We went to the classiest restaurant in town, a place called Visions of Johanna that crouched like a tortoise behind the Blue Bird Motel. The cuisine was haute Mexican: carnitas, menudo, pollo en mole. We ate, we drank. The subject of niños, which had lain between us like the sword in Siegfried's bed, never came up. Petra paid. Vindicated, victorious, flushed with passion, tequila and a sense of universal well-being, we went home to make triumphant love.

That was four days ago. When the sun was shining and the fields were blooming, when God was in His heaven and all was right with the world. Now it was raining. Phil, Gesh and I slumped open-mouthed round the telephone outside the forlorn Shell station, trying to cope with the sudden, monumental, liberating effect of Dowst's injunction. "Harvest now," he'd said, and it was a cutting away of the bonds, a dropping of the shackles. We were grunts in the trenches and the general himself had sent us the word: we're going home, boys!

My mind was in ferment. I hadn't seen Petra since the night of the restaurant, and I didn't know when I'd see her next. We would be caught up in a seething rush of activity for the next several days, weeks even. We were harvesting. Packing up. Evacuating. And once we'd evacuated we'd have to find a place to dry, manicure, weigh and package the stuff, to say nothing of unloading it. "Listen," I said, "I've got to make a phone call. Could you guys wait in the car?"

The back of Gesh's trench coat was soaked through. He was breathing in an odd, fitful way, his mind in the wet fields, flashing like a scythe. "We're going to need a truck," he said. "Something enclosed."

Phil was nodding in agreement.

"Okay," I said, "great. Just let me make this phone call and we'll discuss it."

I watched as they dodged off through the downpour, hitting the puddles flatfooted and snatching at their collars. Then I dialed Petra's number and counted the clicks as the rain drummed at the tinny roof of the phone booth.

She was in the shop. Her voice was a pulse of enthusiasm, quick, high-pitched, barely contained. She was firing a new piece—a figure—her work was going well in the sudden absence of tourists. No, it wasn't a grotesque, not really. She was going in a new direction, she thought: this figure a swimmer on a block of jagged ceramic waves, limbs churning, head down, features not so much distorted as unformed, raw, in ovo—she couldn't seem to visualize the face. Weird, wasn't it?

"Strange," I said.

How did I like the rain?

"We're harvesting," I said.

Her voice dropped. "So soon? I thought—?"

"I just talked to Dowst. This much rain is going to kill us, it's going to weaken the crop and make the smoke a lot less potent. We have no choice."

A gust of wind rattled the booth, raindrops tore at the glass like grapeshot. I couldn't hear. "What?" I said.

"So you're leaving, then."
"Yes."
"Going back to the city."
"I'll call," I said.
"Sure," she said.

We rented a twenty-four-foot U-Haul truck and bought two hundred double-reinforced three-ply extra-large plastic trash bags and three sickles. It was getting dark by the time we introduced the truck's big churning wheels to the riverine bed of the driveway. Gesh was behind the wheel of the truck and I was in the deathseat; Phil preceded us in the Toyota. There were no surprises. The truck staggered like an afflicted beast groaning in every joint, Gesh fought the wheel like Hercules wrestling the Hydra, I braced myself against the dashboard with both hands and feet, branches slammed at the great humped enclosure that rose up behind the cab and the wheels bogged down in mud. Six times. We took down saplings and beetling limbs with bow saw and axe, we propped up the wheels with skull-sized stones and rotted logs, we shoved, sweated and bled. Expert at this sort of thing, we managed to clear the top of the hill in a mere two and a half hours. The rain slacked off just as we rolled up outside the cabin, the clouds parted and the pale rinsed stars shone through the gap like the sign of the covenant. "Hey," Gesh said, slamming the big hollow door of the truck and cocking his head back, "you know what? It looks like it might just clear up after all."

Phil and I gazed hopefully at the heavens. Just then the moon emerged, cut like a sickle, and the clouds fell away in strips. "Yeah," I said after a while, "I think you might be right."

He wasn't.

In the morning it was raining again. Hard. The earth sizzled, the sky was a cerement, the rain heaved down brutally, retributively, with crashing fall and stabbing winds out of the northwest. Inside, it wasn't much better. Brownish swill drooled from the ceiling, filling and overfilling the receptacles flung randomly across the kitchen floor, wind screamed through the planks, the sodden beams groaned beneath my feet like arthritic old tumblers at the base of a human pyramid. The house was sapped, enervated, falling to ruin. I couldn't have cared less. If, as in some vaudeville routine, the entire place collapsed the moment we slammed the door, so much the better.

Shivering in the early-morning cold, I eased down on the living room floor to pull on my socks and shoes. I wasn't sitting at the kitchen table or on the couch or easy chair for the simple reason that they no longer existed—at least in the form we'd known them. In a festive mood after winning the battle of the U-Haul, we'd dismantled the furniture, feeding the combustibles into the wood stove while toasting our imminent departure with the dregs of our liquor larder (two fingers of bourbon, three of Kahlua, a faint whiff of vodka and half a gallon of soured burgundy that tasted like industrial solvent). I laced my boots to the mocking chatter of the rain, and then, hosed and shod, I sloshed my way to the stove as Gesh rambled about overhead and the decelerating rhythm of Phil's snores indicated that he was about to emerge from the grip of his dreams.

The kitchen was a palette of life, blooming with rank growth, with festering sludge and the primordial agents of decay. A rich blood-red fungus that apparently throve on periodic incineration clogged the stove's jets, exotic saprophytes stippled the walls, the counters were maculated with splotches of blue-green mold from which black filaments arose like trees in a miniature forest. The smell was not encouraging. If the place had been barely habitable when we moved in, it looked now as if a troop of baboons had used it for primal therapy. I shrugged and struck a match, surveying the room for the penultimate time. Then I shoved aside the crusted kettle in which the remains of our last supper were slowly congealing, and put on the water for coffee.

We tackled the Khyber Pass first.

Up the precipitous slope, stumbling over mud-slick streams like Sherpa rejects, the rain driving at our faces. We wore improvised rain gear—plastic trash bags, hastily tailored to admit necks and arms—and we carried our sickles like weapons. Slash, hack, slash. Top-heavy, the plants gave way at the first swipe. We caught them in a dazzling rush of leaves, shook them out like big soggy beach umbrellas and unceremoniously stuffed them into trash bags. The bags skipped gracefully down the slope, and we followed them, staggering, careening, already as mucked over as alligator wrestlers. Then we proceeded to Julie Andrews's Meadow and Jonestown, and finally to the marginal areas that lay on the far wet verges of the property.

We were finished by three in the afternoon, every leaf, bud and twig bundled up and stowed away in the rear of the U-Haul. Stacked up there like sandbags atop a levee, the bulging bags of pot looked like a king's ransom, like paydirt and wealth abounding. We knew better. After drying, the bulk of the crop would be so much dross: it was only the buds that concerned us, and well we understood how few they were likely to be. Still, we felt elated. Despite the rain, and considering the sweat, toil and emotional trauma that had gone into raising it, the crop had been surprisingly simple to harvest. We were rapid reapers, the cat burglars of the open field, snatching the goods and filling our sacks. Cut, bag and load. That was it. We were done. The summer camp was history.

Gesh hustled his paper sack of dirty underwear and other worldly baggage out to the Toyota while Phil packed up his priceless mementoes, disintegrating sci-fi paperbacks, his guitar and torch. I bundled my clothes, stuffed them into the sleeping bag and collected the coffee pot and colander we'd liberated from my apartment in the city. The rest we left. The mile and a half of PVC pipe, the cattle troughs, the water pump, the motorbikes, the pickup and the nonfunctional Jeep. Not to mention the shotgun and the crooked .22, the ruptured sacks of garbage and Phil's heroic junk sculpture. It all belonged to Vogelsang. Let him come and get it.

My partners launched the U-Haul down the hill, twice foundering on dangerous shoals and once coming within a tire's breadth of pitching over the side of a precipice cut like the face of the Chrysler Building. We encountered our Charybdis in the guise of a swirling spectacular pothole that nearly wrenched off the left wheel, and then moments later our Scylla loomed up on the right in the form of a stray chunk of pillow basalt the size of a Volkswagen. The trees dug their talons into the flanks of the truck as if to hold it back, the front end shimmied like a school of anchovies in distress and the rear doors flew open twice, spilling bags of pot into the free-flowing roadway. Minor impediments all. We made the necessary repairs and adjustments and floated the big treasure-laden truck down the drive like a stately galleon. I saw my comrades out to the blacktop road, gave them the thumbs-up sign and started back up the hill for the Toyota.

It was getting dark by the time I reached the cabin. Hurrying, I emerged from the grip of the trees, strode across the field and past the waiting Toyota, up the steps of the porch and into the house for my final look around. The place was silent, penumbral, already haunted by our absence. Nothing had changed, but for the disappearance of the furniture, and yet the low, littered rooms had been transformed—whereas before they'd had the look of healthy seething squalor, now they stood derelict. After all that had gone on in these rooms, after all the confrontations, disappointments and anxieties, after all the bullshit sessions, card games and miserable meals—after all the living we'd done here—the place was dead. I felt like a historian pacing off the battlefield at Philippi. I felt like a grave robber.

I stood there in the center of the room for a long moment, watching the shadows swell and darken like living organisms, listening to the inexhaustible rain as it spanked the ground beneath the eaves. What was I waiting for? What was I doing? I shook my head like a drunk under the shower and then walked down the hallway to my room to see if I'd left anything. The door pushed open to the scrape of frantic feet and there was a blur of movement as the rat flew along the baseboard and vanished in the shadows; he'd been digging into the stained and stinking underbelly of my mattress as he might have dug into a corpse. Naked tail, a brush of whisker and the quick flashing eye: he'd been reinstated, restored to his rightful dominion. The mattress, the fetid soup cans and mouldering chicken bones, the 3-in-1 oil and the complete adventures of Bors Borka: these were his legacy.

Looping filaments of dirt festooned the walls, the floor sagged in the center as under the force of some invisible weight, a lustrous tan spider slid up and down the guys of its trembling web like a finger on the neck of a banjo. I hadn't forgotten anything. The wastebasket was full, scraps of glossy magazines (idealized photos of food and women, in that order) slashed at the walls, newspapers, torn flannel shirts and worn jeans lay heaped on the floor. I'd left them consciously, purposely, as I might have left them in a burning building or a foundering ship: why bother, after all? The whole run-down, gutted, roof-rent slum was nothing more than an oversized refuse bin, was the essence of trash itself.

I turned to go—as I'd turned nearly nine months earlier, fresh from the city and stunned by the desolation of the place—and found myself confronting the calendar on the back panel of the door. I'd seen it a thousand times, ignored it, mocked it, forgotten it, but there it was. Still. The woman in the cloche hat with her face averted, the rubric of the year, the page splayed out and defaced by an unknown hand in forgotten times. A bad joke, nothing more.

We'd harvested prematurely, nearly two weeks ahead of the designated date. Today was the thirty-first—Halloween—and we were gone. Or going. Whatever the orphic calendar portended for the thirty-second anniversary of my birth—joy or calamity or provocation—no longer mattered. I reached out, slipped the calendar from the rusty nail that secured it, folded it once and tucked it into my back pocket.

The rain seemed heavier as I maneuvered the Toyota down the drive, past the block of pillow basalt and the downed tree limbs, and out of the clutch of the angry grasping branches. Water fanned out over the windshield faster than the spastic wipers could drive it back, the headlights made phantoms of the steaming tree trunks, my breath clouded the windows. I was picking my way carefully, maintaining momentum to keep from bogging down, my thoughts on Phil and Gesh and our rendezvous later that night, when all at once I found myself hallucinating.

There, against the soft stagy backdrop of the trees, was an apparition, the ghost of harvest past, the clown prince of the scythe, in motley and whiteface. Huge, swelling to gargantuan proportions under the approaching headlights, the figure slogged to the far berm and stood frozen beside the road. As I eased by, the flaring point of highest illumination giving way in a flash to invisibility, I understood that this was no hallucination. No, this was flesh, flesh with a vengeance: beneath the frippery I recognized the big bones and broad vacant gaze of Marlon Sapers. Marlon Sapers, mannish boy, got up as superabundant clown, replete with bulbous nose and pancake jowls, in a drenched ruffled shirtfront and baggy suit with dancing polka dots and writhing stripes, Marlon Sapers, come to mock me. I stopped. Rolled down the window to the teeth of the blow and peered back into the rubicund glow of the taillights. I could barely make him out. "Marlon?" I called. Water rushed past the wheels with the thousand moans of the drowning, rain drilled the roof. There was no answer. But then, reedy, childlike, as tinny as a bad recording, his voice came to me over the crash of the storm—he seemed to be complaining, or no, he was offering something. "Suck your feet?" he asked.

For a moment I lost him. The car coughed and spat, mist seeped out of the earth. Then he took a step forward and his face emerged from the night, pink, garish, huge, floating in the wash of darkness like an orb in the infinite. His expression startled me. He seemed to be grinning—Cheshire Cat, Robin Goodfellow—grinning as if in contemplation of some killing, suprahuman jest.

The pillowcase appeared from nowhere, legerdemain. It was bulging, wet as skin, its neck gaping wide between his big buttery fists. "Trick or treat?" he said.

Chapter 5

I got into San Francisco about half past ten to find the mud-spattered U-Haul parked directly in front of my apartment—and poorly parked at that. One wheel was up on the curb, the cab obscured a sign that threatened TOW AWAY come seven the next morning, and Gesh had managed to straddle two and a half prime, precious, hotly sought-after and fiercely contested parking spaces. To cap it off, he'd settled beneath a high-intensity streetlamp that lit the rear of the truck like a stage. Our plan had been to meet at Vogelsang's—we would surprise him with the truckload of pot and coerce him into allowing us to string it up to dry in his cavernous rooms and endless hallways—but the plan had fallen flat. Typically. As I discovered on arriving at the Bolinas manse, Vogelsang had eluded us once again. The gates were locked, the house was dark, the lewd mannequins stood guard. I found a note from Phil and Gesh pinned to the main gate. It read, simply, *Fair Oaks.*

My co-conspirators were sunk into the furniture in the front room as I plodded up the stairs with my suitcase and Phil's guitar. They were drinking beer, testing the limits of the stereo system with an album called *White Noise Plays White Noise*, and watching a sitcom about a quadraplegic detective who ferrets out evildoers through astral projection. I was wet, weary, hypnotized to the point of catatonia by the incessant frantic swipe of the Toyota's windshield wipers. The suitcase plummeted from my grip, Phil's guitar dropped into the rocking chair. I cut the volume on the stereo and offered an observation. "You made it," I said.

Still bandaged, still depilated, his bad eye blazing with the awakening joy of the exile returned, Phil swung round to acknowledge the soundness of my observation. Gesh set his beer down. "Vogelsang wasn't there, the son of a bitch," he said.

Outside, in the close, shadowy depths of the U-Haul van, a hundred bags of sodden marijuana stood ready to mildew, rot, deliquesce into soup. "So I noticed," I said.

Another thing I noticed was the shopping bag at Phil's feet. The paper was crisp and unblemished and it bore the logo of the corner market. Inside, atop a six-pack of generic beer, were five spanking-white cellophane-wrapped coils of clothesline. Phil was watching me closely. In the background, White Noise's keyboard virtuoso was attempting an auditory re-creation of the siege of Britain. Gesh was watching me too. The bombs fell, the machine guns rattled. "What now?" Phil said.

We brought the pot in, a bag at a time, just after three. The streets were quiet, the glare of the streetlamp softened by a milky drizzle. Up the stairs and down, the landlord wondering at the thump of our footsteps, the sacks of contraband like body bags, like pelf, like the insidious pods in *Invasion of the Body Snatchers*. We worked quickly, silently, our shoulders slumped with guilt, our eyes raking the streets for the first stab of the patrol car's headlights. Phil stood in the back of the truck and tossed the bags forward, while Gesh and I hustled them up the stairs like ants scrambling under the burden of their misshapen egg cases. At one point a car stopped just down the street to discharge a passenger, engine rumbling, headlights slicing into the rear of the truck. We froze. A pair of voices echoed through the haze and bounded off the wet pavement, and a moment later a gangling teenager in a Gumby costume ambled up the street and into our midst. We gave him stares like swords. He looked down at his feet.

Upstairs, I regarded the spill of slick plastic bags as I might have regarded the debris of a natural disaster or the baggage of desert nomads. The living room was inundated, the kitchen piled high, the spare room glimmering with the dull sheen of plastic. Already Gesh had begun to string the rope across the living room, securing the ends with a quick booming convergence of hammer and nail. Phil twisted open the wet bags, shook the plants over the carpet in a tumult of rasping leaves, shuddering buds and precipitant moisture, inverted them with a flick of his wrist and hooked them over the clothesline like so many wet overcoats. I cracked a window, wondering what I'd let myself in for now. Then I set the thermostat at 95 degrees and started up a pair of ratchetting fans I dug out of a box in the basement. We worked furiously, noisily. Clumsy with exhaustion, we stumbled into one another: the hammer thumped, the bags rippled, our footsteps played a frantic tarantella across the ceiling of the apartment below. As Gesh's hammer rapped at the wall for perhaps the fiftieth time, my landlord, a middle-aged bachelor with a viscid Armenian accent, rapped at the outside door. This rapping, unidentified at first, put us in mind of agents of the law and gave us a final nasty shock, a coda to the demonic symphony of such shocks we'd endured over the course of the past nine months. But then the landlord's voice rose faintly from the well of the stairs—"Fee-lix!"—and I knew we'd been delivered once again.

I met him at the base of the stairs, regarding him warily from my end of the security chain. He was wearing a skullcap and a pair of dirty striped pajamas that looked as if they'd been lifted from an internment camp, he was barefoot and his sleepy eyes were riddled with incomprehension. "What is happening here?" he said, his mouth working beneath the blue bristle of his beard. "This, this . . ." and he held his hands like claws to the side of his head, "this thrumping and bang-ing."

I told him my mother had died and that my brothers and I were constructing the coffin ourselves, in deference to the traditions of the old country. Wired, beat, my apartment devastated and body sapped, I didn't have much trouble looking appropriately distraught. "Old country?" he said. "What is that?"

"Boston," I told him, sober as a motherless child.

He looked at me for a long moment, the whites of his eyes crosshatched with broken blood vessels, lids crusted and inflamed. Three-chord rock and roll and the *boom-boom-boom* of the hammer filtered down from above. Breath steamed from his big flared nostrils; he shuffled his bare feet on the wet pavement.

He looked puzzled, disoriented, looked as if he were about to say something but couldn't quite get it out. After a while he turned, muttering, and slammed into his apartment.

By dawn, my roomy Victorian had the look and feel of a curing shed in Raleigh, North Carolina, and smelled like the alley out back of a florist's shop doused with agent orange. The atmosphere was stifling, barely breathable, the rank wet seething odor of the pot pungent as spilled perfume. It was 107 degrees in the living room. Desert winds roared from the vents, an electric space heater glowed in the corner opposite the crackling fireplace, the fans screamed for oil and we sweated like jungle explorers. As the windows were turning gray we strung up the last of the plants, nearly twenty-four hours after we'd plunged into the fields with our flashing sickles. We were worn out, frayed to the bone. We sat at the kitchen table, sipping coffee from cardboard containers and staring off into space. I felt like Sisyphus taking a five-minute break, like Muhammad Ali at the end of the fourteenth round in Manila. Gesh's head slumped forward, Phil lapped absently at a frosted doughnut. Outside, it was still raining.

I got up and made my way through the vegetation to the living room. Bending to my record collection, I thought back to the night I'd played *The Rite of Spring* and Vogelsang had thumped up the stairs with his mad proposal. The room smelled like a silo, sweat dripped from my nose. I straightened up and put on a record—Strauss's *Death and Transfiguration*. It could have been my theme song.

The crop dried in five days. During that interval Gesh lay roasting like a pecan on the couch, the perpetual beer clutched in his perspiring hand, while Phil and I escaped the deadly whirling sirocco breezes of the apartment by planting ourselves in the front row of the unheated ninety-nine-cent movie house around the corner, where we regaled ourselves with popcorn that tasted like Styrofoam and a succession of kung fu/slasher/biker/car-chase flicks with Spanish subtitles. Now that I had leisure for it, I also spent a disproportionate amount of time worrying. I worried about the steady wind wafting from my front window to perfume the entire block with the essence of torrefying pot, I worried about the dark looks my landlord gave me when I ran into him on the front stoop, I worried about the disposition of the U-Haul truck, which we'd somehow neglected to move and which had subsequently been towed away and impounded by municipal drones while we rested from the labors of our harvest. And then of course my personal finances were a mess: rent and utility bills on the apartment had pretty well eaten up my meager savings during the course of my exile, and we were a long way from realizing any profit on the marijuana that littered the apartment from floor to ceiling (we still had to trim, bag and peddle it). Nor could I forget my pending court appearance, though Jerpbak's demotion could be expected to play in my favor.

I worried about Petra, too. I phoned her several times from the pay phone outside the Cinema Latina, my home phone having been disconnected in my absence, but was unable to reach her. Was she distracted by the roar of the kiln? Was she out digging clay in some remote streambed? Had she left town for good, found a new man, flown to Puerto Vallarta for two weeks in the sun? I didn't know. Couldn't guess. I just hung on to the receiver and listened to the flatulent busy signal as if to some arcane code.

Dried, that is deprived of the water weight that composed seventy percent of its bulk, the crop took on an increasingly withered and reduced look. Leaves shriveled, buds shrank. Plants that had been big as Christmas trees now seemed as light and insubstantial as paper kites. On the afternoon of the fifth day we gathered in the saunalike atmosphere of the front room to sample the product and determine its fitness for sale. Phil and I sat sweltering on the couch while Gesh broke a long squirrel's-tail cola from a brittle branch and pared away the leaves that protruded like tongues from between the flowers. Then he plucked two of the neat fingertip-sized buds from the stem and crumbled them over a creased cigarette paper with a slow circular rub of his palms. No one said a word, the moment as drenched in ritual as a high mass at the Vatican. We watched as he rolled the joint with sacerdotal solemnity, sealed it with a sidelong lick and held it up before our eyes as if he were blessing the host. Sere leaves rustled overhead, the fans hummed and the heat swabbed at the back of my throat as Gesh struck the ceremonial match and held the joint out to me as to a communicant at the rail. I took it to my lips and inhaled.

After the smoke had been around three times, I found myself concentrating on the big trimmed cola that lay before me on the coffee table like one of those toy evergreen trees you get with model-railroad kits. It was worth, roughly, a hundred and fifty dollars. We'd grown it from nothing, from a seed you could barely see, from a speck of lint. Entranced by the marvel of it, I lifted the cola from the table as a diamond buyer might have lifted a gem from the tray, slowly turning it over in my hands. It was stiff as a bottle brush, the rich dark green of it touched here and there with the gold and white of the tiny stigmas. I exhaled and wiped my brow. Gesh was smiling serenely. The smoke was smooth, slightly sweet and minty, and as good as or better than what we'd been sampling in the field over the course of the past six weeks. I felt a rush of pride, discovering in that instant the exultation of the creator, the nurturer, the husbandman with the prize pumpkin: we'd done it.

"What do you think?" Gesh asked.

I didn't need to consult Dowst for this one. I raised myself in the chair, astral specks and phantom amoebae floating unchecked through my field of vision. "It's ready," I said.

The final phase of the harvesting process—separating the wheat from the chaff, as it were—commenced immediately. We rose as one from our seats and threw open the windows, cut the thermostat, and unplugged the fans and space heater. Then we lifted down the skeletal plants, removed the flowering tops and arranged them on a folding aluminum banquet table I hastily set up in the middle of the front room, and fed the rest—leaves, branches and the horny fibrous stems that looked like the lower legs of storks or spoonbills—into the fireplace. (This gave rise to a steady spew of viscous black smoke that poured from the chimney for two days, casting an industrial pall over the neighborhood and twice prodding my landlord out of the garage with a garden hose.) After sampling another bud or two—purely for analytical purposes—we sent out for beer, turned up the music, sharpened our scissors and sat down to the tedious business of manicuring the tops.

Early next morning, Gesh called Rudy. I didn't like Rudy—didn't like the way he looked, didn't like his locker-room humor and half-witted street talk, and especially didn't like his connection with Jones. But Rudy, dealer in stimulants and sedatives, was going to do us a service. For five dollars an hour and all he could smoke, he was going to help us trim, weigh and bag our lovely top-grade sinsemilla, and then he was going to take our share on consignment at $1,400 a pound and peddle it to his clientele. We would take a beating to the tune of $200 a pound, but we figured it was well worth it to avoid the hassle of having to unload the stuff ourselves.

Rudy came sniffing up the stairs like a bloodhound. His eyes bulged as if under some abnormal internal pressure—as if there were something alive in there trying to get out—and the boneless dollop of flesh that passed for his nose was twitching in agitation. Under his right arm, cradled like an attenuated football, he carried an Ohaus triple-beam scale in a paper sack. "Hey man, how the fuck you doing?" he said, clapping Gesh's shoulder with a hand shriveled like a bird's claw. He greeted Phil with a "What's happening?" and nodded at me in passing.

"Holy Christ," he said, pushing his way into the living room, "what are you guys trying to do here with all this shit—get yourselves busted or what?" He hovered over the fire, warming his hands. Beside him, stacked up like cattle fodder, was the dross we'd yet to burn. "You know it smells like there's a truckload of pot on fire out there?"

I knew. My landlord, eager to inquire into certain disturbing phenomena (such as the irregular hours I was keeping, the prodigious belch of black smoke emanating from the chimney and the five-day period during which the oil burner never shut down), had cornered me half an hour earlier as I was coming up the front steps with a grease-stippled bag of fried wonton. He'd traded in the yarmulke for a faded Giants cap, from the nether margin of which a band of hair the color and texture of an Airedale's projected at a peculiar angle. "I am not sleeping last night," he said, delivering this information as if it were momentous, revolutionary, as if he were announcing the discovery of a new planet or the cure for cancer. I told him I was sorry to hear that. He peered at me questioningly out of his black perplexed eyes, and I had the feeling he was sizing me up, trying to reconcile his memory of me with the wild-eyed apparition standing before him. It was as if he weren't altogether sure I wasn't an imposter.

"So," he said suddenly, glancing up at the fuming blanket of smoke that flew up from the roof as from the depths of a refinery, "you are cold? With open window?" Just then I caught a whiff of it, a smell reminiscent of rock festivals in packed concert halls. "The fire, you mean?" He nodded. A few months ago I would have made an effort, I would have soothed him with a flurry of apologies, promises and plausible lies—but now I found that I just couldn't muster the energy. Instead, I ducked my head, gave him a grief-stricken look and told him we were burning my mother's mementoes in accordance with her last wishes. "You know," I added, "photo albums, diaries, old seventy-eights of the Andrews Sisters and whatnot." He cleared his throat respectfully and told me I had one month to get out.

For all his loudmouthing, though, Rudy didn't seem especially concerned. Smoke was smoke, and who was to say we weren't burning sandalwood or green mesquite—or creosote telephone poles, for that matter? He knew it as well as we did. Unless you walked up the block thinking pot, you'd never notice a thing. Of course, the whole fiasco had been ill-advised from the start. Bringing a hundred pounds of pot into the heart of the city in a U-Haul truck was beyond mere fatuity—it was irrational, irresponsible, the act of desperate men. But whereas we'd spent nearly nine months in a state of perpetual xenophobic panic in an area that contained fewer people in ten square miles than lived on this very block, we now tended to view things more dispassionately. Perhaps we felt safe in the very absurdity of what we were doing (weren't all the narcs out sniffing around in the woods, after all?). Or perhaps we just didn't give a shit. At any rate, I took Rudy's comment for what it was—a means of staking out the territory, setting the record straight: we were bunglers and fools, dangerous even to ourselves, callow freshmen in the school of pharmaceutical usage and abusage, and he was professor emeritus.

The first thing Rudy did was roll himself two joints. He tucked one in his shirt pocket for future reference and settled into the easy chair with the other. I watched him fuss over it like a cigar buyer in Havana—licking it, sniffing it, drawing deep and exhaling with a sigh—as he smoked the thing down to a stub. He sat there ensconced in the chair like a guru. After a while he said, "Good shit," and pulled himself from the grip of the chair to set up his scales. First he weighed out a pound of the trimmed tops; then, for comparison, a pound of the raw stuff. I was sitting at the aluminum table with Phil and Gesh, doggedly snipping away with my scissors, my mind on other things: viz., Petra, my lack of employment or capital and my coming eviction. The TV was on, as it had been continuously since we'd stepped through the door (some soap opera rife with hard-drinking, tormented middle-aged men in Lacoste shirts and a host of apparently sex-crazed teenage women), and the radio pulsed softly to the thump of a synthesized disco beat.

Rudy nosed through the entire crop—colas big and small—poking around like a rodent, a big swollen two-legged rat come down from the mountain to take another bite out of our profits. I asked him when he was going to sit down and start earning the five bucks an hour we were paying him to trim pot. He didn't answer, but a moment later he turned round and said, "You know, I'd say you guys got about thirty pounds or so here—plus maybe a couple pounds of shake."

Thirty pounds. Gesh looked at Phil. Phil looked at me. No one said a word, but the calculators clicked on in our heads. Our share would be ten pounds, split three ways. At $1,400 a pound—that is, minus Rudy's commission—we would come out with something like $4,600 apiece, or about $162,000 short of our original estimate. And oh yes, each of us would have to kick in $555 of that to cover the $5,000 Vogelsang had laid out for Jones, the extortionist. It was a shock. We'd known the figure would be low, but this was less by half than our most dismal estimate. After a moment or so, long enough for Rudy's words to sink in and for the figures to materialize deep in our brains and work their way forward, Phil's voice rose in a kind of plaint from the end of the table. "You sure?"

Later—it was nearly dark, the hills beyond the window cluttered with palely lit façades, houses like playing cards or dominoes—I was out in the kitchen opening a can of cream of tomato soup when Rudy sauntered in, looking for matches. He was stoned, big dilated pupils eclipsing the insipid yellow irises, his lower lip gone soft with fuddlement. "What's happening?" he said. I ignored him, concentrating on the way the soup sucked back from the can; I reached for the Worcestershire, black pepper. Rudy circled the room, vaguely patting at his pockets, poking into drawers. Finally he stopped in front of the stove. "Got a match?" he said.

I was irritated. Pissed off. The place was a mess, I was a failure and Rudy was a jerk. I dug a pack of matches from my pocket and flung them at him without turning my head.

The soup was the color of spoiled salmon, carrots gone tough in the ground. I stirred it without interest or appetite, watching the spoon as it broke the murky surface, vanished and reappeared. There was the rasp and flare of a match, the stink of sulfur, and then the supple, sweet odor of marijuana. "Hey, man," Rudy said at my elbow—I was stirring the soup, stirring—"no reason to feel bad about it. You guys at least got something out of it."

"What?" I snarled, turning on him like an attack dog. "What did we get out of it? Four thousand bucks?" I was frothing. "Big shit."

"Better than Jonesie."

Jonesie. The diminutive, no less. Ah, if I'd felt bitter to this point, chewing over my hurts and losses behind the snip of the scissors and the rattle of the spoon in the pot, now I was enraged, ready to strike out at anything that came into range. "Jonesie," I echoed, mimicking him. "The leech. The cocksucker. He did nothing, nothing at all, not a lick—and for your information he's going to wind up with more than any of us three."

Rudy's eyes dodged mine. "I can't do nothing about that, man—don't take it out on me." Then he went into a little routine about how he knew the dude and all, but that didn't mean he was his mother or anything, did I see what he was getting at? I saw. But there was something in his eyes he couldn't control, a shiftiness, as if he was holding something back. He proferred the joint. I refused it. Vehemently. "Besides, I didn't mean this year," he said, exposing his gamy brown teeth in a conciliatory smile. "I mean *last* year. Vogelsang really screwed the guy."

"Vogelsang?"

Rudy looked put out, angry and resentful suddenly, as if I'd spat down the front of his shirt or torn the stitches out of a knitting wound. For an instant I thought he was going to hit me. "Yeah," he hissed, "your pal, the big wheeler-dealer, the dope king. Vogelsang."

"Vogelsang?" I repeated, as, lost and directionless, I might have repeated the name of a distant subway stop in a foreign country. Something was up, toil and trouble, all my brooding suspicions congealing like the soup in the pot before me.

"It cost me *money*, man." Rudy, of the downsloping chin and punished nose, of the pigeon chest and hepatic skin, was outraged, the thought of it more than he could bear. Take my mother, my sister, my old hound dog, but don't you come near my blue vinyl checkbook.

I dropped the spoon in the pot, feeling weak, staring into his tumid glistening eyes as into matching crystal balls and groping toward illumination—or rather toward confirmation of what I'd known in my heart all along: Vogelsang had done us dirty.

Rudy shuffled his feet in agitation, bent to rub his knee; smoke tugged at both sides of his head like a hot towel wrapped round a toothache. "Son of a bitch talked me into putting up three grand. Two hundred pounds, he said, easy. We'd split even, me, him and Jones."

Vogelsang, Vogelsang, the syllables pounded in my blood with evil rhythm. I felt betrayed, I felt hot and vengeful. I saw myself slipping into his shadowy museum, lifting one of the Cambodian pig stickers down from the wall, and creeping up the hallway; I saw the door to the bedroom, the waterbed, Vogelsang.

Loose-lipped, spilling his grievances like spew, Rudy went on. "So when Jonesie goes and gets popped, Vogelsang insists—*insists*, even though it's no skin off his ass, I mean he's not even up there or anything—that the plants have to go. Bud says no, don't panic, it's no big thing, and Vogelsang went up there and did it himself. At night. With his flashlight and his fucking gun. He cut the whole crop down and burned it, and you know what I got out of it? Shit. Zero. I'm the one that got burned."

I felt reckless, stupid with fury, felt as I had when Jerpbak took hold of me in the Eldorado County Jail or when Jones stood sneering before me in the hot still cabin, the blackmailer's filthy demand on his lips. And why hadn't Rudy told us all this when his old friend Gesh and I visited him over that long and fruitless Fourth of July weekend? I knew, I knew now: to ask the question was to answer it. Because he was in collusion with Jones, that's why. Because he wanted his money back. From anybody. From us.

I could smell the soup burning behind me. Rudy stood there, bones in a sack, lips pouted and shoulders sunk under the weight of the world's injustice. Poor Rudy. He was drawing on the joint, about to say more, when I slapped it from his hand and shoved him against the wall. "Get out," I said, my voice like an ice pick. "Get your sneaking ass out of my house."

Shock and fear: Rudy was featureless, a smudged drawing, something to hate. I had him by the throat like a madman, his breath was sick in my face, his wrists clutched at mine as if we were playing king of the mountain or fighting for a football. "Hey," he said, "hey," terrified by the look on my face, writhing like something fished out of the mud, "leave me alone, man, I haven't done nothing." I held him there against a wall bristling with kitchen implements—graters and choppers, the cleaver, the butcher knife—held him like a goose or turkey to be throttled, twist of the neck, pluck him clean. "You've got two minutes," I said.

Then I was out in the hallway, my jacket torn from the hook, rattle of car keys, Phil's face, Gesh's, the long aluminum table heaped with our sad, diminished and tainted gains, my feet on the steps, the outer door, the porch, the car. The engine caught with a roar and I lurched out into the street. I didn't see traffic lights, flashing neon, the sweeping turrets of the Golden Gate Bridge. Through the glare of the oncoming headlights and the shadows lashing at the windshield, I saw one thing only: Vogelsang.

Chapter 6

The night was clear, the moon a gift in the sky, a sharp unforgiving stab of cold on the air. Though the main gate was locked—barricaded like the portals of Teste Noire's castle—I could see lights in the distance, and faintly, as in a midsummer night's dream, I could hear snatches of music. He was home. I contemplated the glowing spot of the buzzer, the dark grid of the squawk box. Should I ring and announce myself like a dinner guest—or bound over the wall like a renegade? I'd come to the end of the line. I wanted answers, apologies, amends, I wanted to see Vogelsang on his knees, stigmatized by his guilt and begging forgiveness in a spew of *mea culpas*, I wanted to see him humbled like a Harijan outside the temple—maybe I even wanted blood. I don't know, I wasn't rational. Or I was rational in the way of a Son of Sam or a George Metesky, stealth and calculation on the surface, violence burning beneath like a primordial itch. I turned away from the buzzer.

Gravel crunched as I maneuvered the Toyota alongside the gate, squeezing in parallel, inches to spare. I had no thought—no conscious thought, anyway—of closing off the gate as if I were laying siege to the place, but that was the effect. My idea had been to use the car as a ladder, but as I hoisted myself from the Toyota's roof to the top of the gate, I saw that I'd also managed to set up a blockade—as long as the car was there, no one was going anyplace. Blood sang in my ears; I heard the soft thump of drums from the direction of the house. Slowly, cautiously, with the grace that comes of necessity, I lowered myself down the inner side of the gate—it must have been ten feet high—and dropped into the darkness below.

All was quiet, save for the fitful melody drifting across the night from the dimly lit house. There were no crickets, no locusts, no katydids, the seething generation of insects that had chattered and gibed at me through the summer's crises dead now, trod under. I moved toward the light, stealthy as an assassin. Down the drive, past Vogelsang's faintly gleaming Saab and the pale backdrop of the eucalyptus grove—but what was that? The familiar outline of the Jeep, and beside it the Datsun pickup. Vogelsang had been busy.

Through another gate, circling round, and up the redwood steps to the back deck. No pets to worry about, no scurrying Siamese or lurching old hounds, no surprises or alarms. Breathing hard, I inched my way along the rear wall, a cloud of water vapor clinging to my face like a mask. The shades were drawn on the first window—kitchen or bedroom, I couldn't remember which—but dead ahead a long parallelogram of light cut across the deck where the ballroom would be. Carefully, carefully. I edged toward it, the music dying and starting up again, louder now, more distinct: tabalas and tambourines, some sort of weird goatherd's serenade pierced at intervals by an intermittent reedy piping that suggested a hobbled old fakir sporting a turban and dying of emphysema. *Chink-chink, doom; chink-chink, doom.*

I was forcing myself to move slowly, counting one, two, three seconds between steps, concentrating on images of bushwhackers, scalp-takers, naked sly Iroquois to whom the snap of a twig meant the difference between life and death, when all at once a cold stiff hand shot out to snatch at my arm. I jerked back reflexively, there was a sharp rasping as of a chair shoved back against a parquet floor, and next thing I knew I was frantically juggling one of Vogelsang's mannequins. The mannequin had been propped against the wall, minding its own business, and I'd blundered into it. Now, eyeless, faceless, it came at me, toppling like a cut tree, like a corpse dislodged from its niche in the catacombs, and I was already shrinking from the crash, the alarmed footsteps, the burst of the floodlights and the click of the shell in the chamber of that black blazing shotgun, when I lurched forward at the last second to catch it with the plunging manic swoop of a tango instructor at the graduation ball.

For a full minute I hunched there, motionless, the mannequin clutched to my thundering chest. I listened for footsteps, waited for the shout of discovery. Nothing. The music went on as before, the piping intertwined now with a flat nasal moan that rose and fell like smoke over a campfire. I didn't know exactly what I was doing on Vogelsang's back porch in the dead of night—or what I was going to do—but somehow surprise seemed the key. For once I wanted to catch him off guard, take him by storm, blitzkrieg his sensibilities and blast his composure—for once I wanted the upper hand. And so I froze there, barely breathing, the slow seconds digging into my scalp like tomahawks, until I knew I was safe. Soundlessly, with relief and gratitude and oh such care—picture the novice paramedic lowering a nonagenarian with back problems onto the stretcher—I set the mannequin down. Then, still hunched low, I crept forward.

Vogelsang was sitting at the long table in the center of the room, his back to me. A pair of antique brass pole-lamps flanked him, lighting the table like a ticket booth, and he seemed to be deliberating over the arrangement of a welter of pale, rigid and faintly yellowed objects spread out before him—if I hadn't known better I might have taken them for ivory backscratchers and chopsticks, for nose flutes and tortoiseshell combs dumped from the bag of a Hong Kong street peddler. Looking closer, I saw the cusp of a mandible, the swell of a partial ribcage, and at Vogelsang's elbow, the thin-boned dumb-staring skull. Or no, a pair of skulls, face up, worn the color of weak tea and tessellated like parchment. I watched him pick up a polished toe- or finger-joint and compare it with another, then lift a heavy magnifying glass from the table and peer through it as if he were grading gems.

Barefoot, dressed in a short oriental robe with a sash round the waist, Vogelsang could have been a samurai taking his ease in the geisha house. His movements were slow and circumspect, the lamps cast an aureole about him, the fireplace flared as with a ritual blaze. There were the remains of a snack—fish flakes and ginseng, no doubt—and a bottle of wine and three glasses on the table beside him. To the far left, in the darkened stereo/ TV nook, the fiery red light of the amplifier glowed, and the VU needles of the tapedeck dimly registered the percussive clank and moribund whine of the goatherd's serenade. I saw the guns and knives climbing the walls, the dancing bobcats, glittering display cases and all the rest; there was no one else in the room.

I stood, a fragment of the night, a Ch'en Ta Erh hovering over the go-between's bed, and tried the handle of the sliding glass door. The door was unlatched. One finger, the slightest pressure, and I'd cracked it an inch. The music sharpened suddenly, all edges, and I could feel the warmth of the room on my face. I hesitated, steeling myself, fishing for an opening line—what do you say to someone who's violated a trust, used and manipulated you, who plays dirty yet never loses, someone lounging in his pajamas in his own living room and fiddling with a heap of discolored bones while the walls bristle with guns and knives and swords? *Naaah, naa-aaah-naaah* sang the goatherd, *chink-chink, doom* went the drums. It was then—just as I'd screwed up the nerve to throw back the door and spring into the room like an avenging demon—that Aorta swung through the kitchen door with a coffee mug in her hand. But it wasn't the mug that caught my attention: no, not that. The first thing I noticed was that she was naked.

Thirteen years old, I'd peeped through the curtains at sad yeasty middle-aged Marge Conklin and watched her roll the sepia stockings from legs like suet, until I lost heart—something terrifying there, something claustrophobic and fatal—and sank into the bushes as if I'd been clubbed. I felt the same way now. Forbidden fruit, systems overload: I was electrified. Aorta crossed the room, her breasts gently swaying, the swath of hair caught like a juggler's prop between her legs, and stopped to lean over Vogelsang and his sepulchral booty. She showed me her backside, tight, solid, slightly parted legs, ass wagging, as she brushed Vogelsang's cheek with her lips and set the mug down on the table. I was riveted, turned on, hot as a moth doused with pheromones, but feeling guilty, too, ashamed: I'd come with high purpose, I'd come to vanquish deceit and wave the banner of decency, truth and honor, and here I was shuffling around outside the window with a hard-on like some pubescent Peeping Tom. I backed off and pressed myself to the wall.

When I looked again, Vogelsang was alone. Aorta had moved off into the shadows at the far end of the room: I strained to make her out. So long as she was in the room—and especially so long as she was prancing around in her skin as if she were about to rub herself down with coconut oil or powder her privates—I couldn't burst in and confront Vogelsang. Could I? But why not, I thought, feeling a rush of evil, remembering my hurts. I'd come to take him by storm, right? How better terrorize him than to spring through the door with a bloody shout just as he mounts her amid the phalanges and vertebrae? Yes, I thought, grinning like a deviate, and I began to pray that she'd stop fiddling around in the dark and come back to distract him from his bones.

It was too fond a hope.

I was crestfallen—as voyeur and sadist both—when a moment later she emerged from the shadows in a short robe identical to Vogelsang's and made for the kitchen again. But wait a minute. Was this Aorta? Stiletto nails and black lipstick, yes, the upthrusting breasts and liquid legs, but there was something different about her—was it her hair? It seemed longer, darker, and the broad badger stripe was gone. Or was it something else—her chin, her nose, the way she moved? I couldn't be sure. The kitchen door swung to, and she disappeared.

Now was my chance. I thought of Jones, Rudy, thought of nine months down the tubes and threw back the door with an apocalyptic rumble. Vogelsang glanced over his shoulder—casually, with the barest interest, as if he were dining at Vanessi's and the cocktail waitress had dropped a glass at the bar—and then all at once his face went numb and I saw the spasm of alarm, the panic that froze in his eyes till they shone like the glass buttons of his badgers and bobcats. I was huge, I was terrible. A wave of malicious joy swept over me. "Felix," he said, fumbling for my name as if he'd forgotten it.

I stepped into the room. Saying nothing.

Anyone else would have expressed shock, surprise, outrage, fear, anyone else would have demanded an explanation, reached for the shotgun or ducked under the table. But not Vogelsang. No: he was never surprised, never startled; like some serene alien being, some exemplar of cool, some god, he merely turned his back to me. I'd broken into his house in the middle of the night while his woman strutted around naked, I'd sprung from the shadows to strike terror in his heart and make him think, if even for an instant, that his reckoning had finally come, and he turned his back on me. I was stupefied, enraged, cheated even in this. Was he deliberately baiting me? I was about to bellow his name in stentorian wrath, scream it till the windows shook, when he turned slowly round with the bottle in his hand. He held it aloft, offering it. "Wine?" he asked.

I looked beyond him to the three glasses on the tray and in that moment felt the balance shift—if for a second the momentum had been with me, I'd lost it now. Three glasses. Why three? It was uncanny, unsettling: it was almost as if he'd been expecting me.

"It's been a while," he said, pushing the chair back and standing to face me.

My throat was constricted, as if I were standing before a packed courtroom and trying to swallow a lump of cold egg noodles while cross-examining a witness. "Why'd you lie to us?"

He was pouring wine into a long-stemmed glass. "Bordeaux," he said, "Haut Brion, 1972. Ever so slightly tart." He stepped toward me, then thought better of it, and set the glass back down on the table while he bent to refill his own. We were playing at host and guest—the ceremonial offering, the gracious smile and easy banter—and all the while billowing little bursts of rage were detonating in my head. Even at the best of times the wine was an affectation, like his stilted diction and his sangfroid. Something to have, to know about, to control. I'd never seen him drink more than half a glass in my life—why would he? Alcohol softens you, takes the edge away. The competitive edge.

"We're celebrating tonight, did you know?" He gestured toward the table. "Cocopa. A woman and child. We found them together, in a single grave, just across the border in Sonora."

This was archaeology night. Here we were, pals, a pair of old bone collectors sharing a bottle of good wine prior to the slide show. Well, I was having none of it. I stood there fuming, intransigent, waiting for an answer: I would not be put off. "You lied," I said.

He rolled the glass between his palms, deciding something. I watched the light catch his hair and the way his shadow loomed toward me as he rocked back and forth on his heels. "All right," he said finally, "I admit it. I lied to you."

If there was a moment at which things could have gotten physical, it had passed, and he knew it. I could have flung myself at him like a kamikaze, I suppose, and I'd been close to it in that gut-tightening instant when he'd turned his back to me as if I were nothing—a child, a cripple, a pup—but we both knew he could have taken me easily. I had only to think of the night he'd brought Gesh down, of the primal look that had come into his eyes and the terrifying mechanical response of his body, to understand how futile it would be. I'd come to recover my dignity. Lying prone beneath Vogelsang as he applied the Montagnard death grip was no way to start.

I stood there in the doorway, itching like a gunfighter called out back of the saloon. There was a cold draft on my neck, the night smelled of wet leaves and eucalyptus buttons, I heard the ring of silverware from the kitchen, the sad stiff bones glowed under the lights, the dancing bobcats grinned at me. "You're a worthless son of a bitch," I said. "You're a cheat and a liar."

Vogelsang accepted this with his bemused little schoolmaster's smile. Then, shaking his head as if I'd just misconstrued some basic theorem at the blackboard, he circled round me to the open door. "Mind if I shut this?" he said, sliding it closed. "Cold, you know?"

I'd backed off a step or two, and found myself wedged between a bust of Oscar Wilde and a potted palm; somewhere at the periphery of my consciousness the goatherd's serenade slipped into a sort of slow, clangorous threnody. Vogelsang strode back across the room, barefoot, his calves creased with muscle, looking as if he'd just taken two out of three falls for the championship. I felt the bitterness in me like a hot wire. "But how could you?" I demanded. "I mean, what's the point? You use somebody to make a few extra bucks for yourself like, like . . ." I was worked up, spilling over, bad brew. "What do you think you are, some fucking robber baron or something?"

Vogelsang settled into his chair, the inflammatory smirk still creasing his lips, and gestured for me to have a seat. He was in control now and he knew it. Unruffled, composed, calm as a pasha sated with figs and partridges whose sole worry was to relieve himself of a bit of gas before calling for his dancing girls, he fiddled with the sash of his robe, lifted the glass to examine his wine and then tipped it to his lips for a leisurely sip. I wanted to snatch a thick-knobbed femur from the table and drive it into his skull. I ignored the chair. I stood. Like a pillar.

"And what did you get out of it, anyway?" I said, digging in, trying to nettle him, my anger and frustration building in proportion to his calm. "Subtract for that bloodsucker Jones and your share's going to be worth less than fifteen thousand bucks—you went and screwed us and you're not even going to make your expenses back. You're hurting, too. You lost. For once in your life, you lost." My voice was stretched like wire, a whine, a taunt. I was a benchwarmer ragging the home-run hitter who's just struck out, a playground brat with a mouthful of orthodonture jeering from the stands. I was getting personal.

And that was it, the key I'd been looking for, the way in. Vogelsang's smirk suddenly fell in on itself. I could call him a cheat and a liar all night and it was Brer Rabbit in the briar patch—he throve on it; it fed his self-concept; he was the wheeler-dealer, the manipulator, the crafty, tough, amoral Übermensch who rises above the grasping herd to prevail—but to be accused of failure, called a dupe, a loser, was more than he could bear. I'd hit home. Bull's-eye. "Face it," I said, twisting the arrow, "you're a loser."

"No, Felix"—his tone had changed, the amusement dried up—"you're a loser. You and Cherniske and that other halfwit. And Dowst, too. I made out, don't you worry."

What was he talking about? He'd made nothing, he'd made a mistake. "Bullshit," I said.

Suddenly he was on his feet, catty, clonic, the old Vogelsang. He paced to the end of the table and swung round. "I bought that property in February, like I told you. But not this February. February two years ago. You know what I paid?"

I knew nothing. I was a loser.

"Ninety-two."

Chink-doom, went the goatherd, *doom-doom*.

"You know what I'm getting—what I *got*? Already?" The cords stood out in his neck like stitches in a sweater. "I signed over the title yesterday—the deal's been cooking for months. Months." He was twitching, jerking, dancing in place like an Indian whooping over the corpse of an enemy. "One-seventy. And do you know why? Because you improved the place for me."

I sat down. Hard.

"That's right. I had a deal with Sapers—and don't give me that look, I played straight with you: he knew nothing about the pot. If I fenced the property line he'd let me tap into his electricity. I told him my writer friends would do it for the exercise."

A cavern was opening up inside me, a pit, a chasm in which I could hear the faint reverberations of all the coppers, pennies, yen, groschen, forints and centavos of all the sad, grasping, multifarious generations as they plunged into the everlasting gloom.

"And I'll tell you something else. I'll do a little work on that Jeep and that pickup and I'll unload them for more than what I paid for them. The PVC pipe is stacked in the garage right now. The generator and pump, too." He'd moved closer now, his fingers dancing on the tabletop. The smaller skull was in his hand—alas, poor Yorick—and he was gesturing with it. "Don't be naive, Felix," he said in a voice that could have humbled the chairman of the board at ITT, "don't be stupid. I don't lose."

My own voice was a croak, a dying crippled thrust of rebuke. "Jones. He *was* your man. You got together to cheat us."

"Where did you get that idea?"

"Rudy."

He held the skull up before his face and gazed into the empty eye sockets; I thought he was going to crush it, but he set it down gently beside its mate and fussed over the arrangement for a moment before responding. "Rudy made a bad investment," he said. "Jones is a leech." And then: "Jones figured it out, that's all. He talked to Rudy, he saw you and Gesh when you were in town. I assume he made a little reconnaissance trip up to the property to check things out and then he decided to squeeze us."

Vogelsang's eyes went hard with the thought of it. "I guess he figured I owed him something."

I rose slowly from the chair, feeling the tug of gravity like a gouty old pensioner with an inner tube of fat round the middle, like an arthritic horse or elephant about to receive the coup de grace. The load was too heavy, the taint too deep. I was digging a garden, thinking turnips and corn and fat, dewy beefsteak tomatoes, turning over the earth and finding garbage, layer upon layer of it, reeking, alive with the seething white ferment of decay. "But we were friends, weren't we?"

He shrugged. "I offered you a deal. You could have said no."

"You didn't have to lie to me, use me like something you wipe your ass with."

"Oh, come on, Felix, drop the martyr act, will you? It's wearing thin. Just because I offer you a deal doesn't mean I have to lay out my whole financial history and give you the FDIC seal of approval, does it? You didn't ask me for a prospectus when I told you to buy zirconium, did you? I've made you money. And don't forget, you put up nothing on this project. None of you did. I'm the one who bought the land and put up the capital, I'm the one who gave you the chance to make it."

"We were doomed from the start." All the blood seemed to have left my head. I felt like a moth sucked dry in the spider's web. "You said two thousand plants, one thousand pounds. But you knew damned well we'd have to start with four thousand plants to wind up with two. I mean, you and Dowst come breezing into my living room and make it sound like you're laying half a million dollars in my lap or something, when all along—"

He was holding up his palm. "No, no. I wanted it to go—I really thought it would, I believed in it. Why else would I even bother to set it up? Boyd's the one. I relied on him and he let me down." Vogelsang was calmer now: the threat had passed. He'd let me know, low as I was, that he was that much higher—he'd taken a couple of shots below the belt maybe, but he'd gone the distance and he was still the champ. "That was my biggest mistake," he said after a pause, "—trusting Dowst."

I just looked at him, stupidly, obtusely, the slow learner in a class of whiz kids.

"He swore he could come up with the seeds. And that half a pound per plant was the *low* estimate anyway, figuring for unviable seeds and bad weather and all the rest, that even if we ran into problems we should get a pound or more out of most of them. Plus he looked the place over and assured me he could grow a forest up there, a jungle—no problem."

This was funny. Vogelsang was showing his teeth in appreciation, the bobcats were madly whirling, and the goatherd abruptly gave up his dirge for the merry *scritch-scratch-scritch* of the stalled stylus. But there was something else, too. A titter. From the shadows. I jerked my head round and saw, in the far corner of the room, the bare pale outline of a human figure hunched down on the couch. When she stood and moved toward the turntable to change the record, I saw with a shock that this was Aorta, naked still, rising from the dark corner like a naiad rising from her pool, and that her hair was bleached white and cropped close as ever. Buttocks, breasts, nipples, thighs, the tattoo on her left flank (a scorpion?)—each was like a jab in the arm, a skipped heartbeat. But what made me drop my lower lip and gape like a defective was that broad hacked bristling blue stripe that cut a swath through her hair.

I blinked at Vogelsang, dumbfounded. He was still smiling—or rather lifting his lip back from his teeth in the weird strained way of a Bible salesman or a friend of the opera. Was I going crazy? I glanced again at Aorta as she stood fussing with the record on the far side of the room, and then, with dawning comprehension, swiveled my head a hundred and eighty degrees to stare at the hard, cold, unrevealing slab of the kitchen door.

The door swung open at that moment, as if on cue, and she stepped into the room and came toward us, grinning hesitantly, showing off those fine even little baby's teeth and the pink ripple of gum. She balanced a tray in one hand and held an open beer in the other. The kimono had fallen open partially, and I could see the slant of one little tittie, and below, a glimpse of pale pubic fuzz. Makeup, haircut, height, weight, walk, she could almost have been Aorta's twin—but I knew her now, knew her instantaneously, knew her with a rush of amaze, envy, hatred and lust that came like the first jolt of electroshock. "Savoy," I whispered.

The tray held delicacies—smoked oysters, artichoke hearts, the black spittle of caviar—an antipasto. Or anticoito. I watched her eyes as she set the tray down among the bones, beside the half-empty bottle and the three glasses. She gave me a single sharp, brazen look, brazen and triumphal both, and then slipped her arm round Vogelsang's waist. "Hi," she said. She was smiling, though her lip trembled just perceptibly. "Long time no see."

If the state of shock is a deep sleep of the senses that protects us in our cores from the sharp edges of the world, then I was deeply thankful for it at that moment. I felt it come over me like a blanket, like a drug, felt my lips go numb, my eyes glaze. I wasn't thinking of perfidy, rottenness, greed: I was thinking nothing.

"It's not what you think, Felix," Vogelsang said. He looked embarrassed, caught with his hand in the jar; he grinned till the long pale roots of his teeth showed. "I never laid eyes on her till you sent me down there to talk to her. I swear it."

"My mother's an asshole," Savoy said, as if we'd been discussing mothers and assholes for the past fifteen minutes.

"I made a deal with her. An arrangement. She wanted out of little Appalachia and I told her she could come stay here with me and Aorta if she'd back off the project."

I was aware of a movement to my left. Aorta had come up and was standing at my elbow, stark naked. We made a foursome, I realized, a grouping, huddled round the scattered bones and the tray of goodies like actors in a necrophilic epic plotting out the next coupling. Music was playing, something I didn't recognize, percussive, nasty, like the hissing of adders. I glanced at Aorta. Her expression was noncommittal. I felt drunk. My face was on fire, my groin throbbing.

"Eugene's an asshole, too," Savoy said.

Vogelsang reached for his wineglass, breaking the tableau, Aorta scratched herself absently and reached for a cracker, Savoy threw back her head to take a swig of beer. Uneasy on my heels, my eyes riveted to Aorta's crotch, navel, nipples, I stuffed my hands in my pockets and backed off a step. It was then that I caught the scent of it. Rank, hot, urgent, it was the odor of sex, the musky perfume Vogelsang and Aorta had been wearing the night we'd lifted our glasses to the success of the summer camp. I snuffed it like a tomcat, like a caveman, and it had a rotten edge to it. The bones lay on the table, Aorta was watching me, the music hissed in my ears, and I hated them all. I hated cabals, plots, schemes, hated the hungry clawing fornicating faces of the world, I hated myself.

I turned and made for the door, for the smell of eucalyptus, the night, the wind, medicine for my hurts. My hand was on the latch. "Felix," Vogelsang said, and I paused to look back at him. "You can stay if you want."

I didn't want.

Across the redwood planks, legs pulling me along, legs and feet, past the fallen mannequin and down the steps the way I'd come. A wind had risen to shake the trees. I was around the corner of the house when I heard his voice coming at me—he must have been standing at the door. "The calendar," he shouted, "it was only a joke."

I don't know how long I sat in the car. Ten minutes? Twenty? An hour? The wind drove in off the ocean, steady as a hand, the moon lay across the hood of the car like a cheap bauble. I was thinking. Of chinless Rudy, of Jones, Vogelsang and Savoy, all the stingers and stingees of the world, all the beat deals, the scams and the hustles, and I realized how precious little it all mattered. Go for it, they said, get it while you can, early to bed and early to rise. Well, I'd gone for it and now I was out of work, out of money and out of luck, I had a trial coming up and no place to live, and I felt like an emotional invalid, like a balloon without the helium. I sat there, getting cold, and I thought of Phil and Gesh back in the apartment clipping away at the shreds of their yachts and restaurants with scissors that grew duller by the moment. *Money, give me money*. Then I thought of Petra. No, I saw Petra. Her hands, sunk in the raw clay, kneading it like bread, molding it, pulling the hard, lasting stuff from its shifting, shapeless core. Wet, yielding, fecund: I could smell the clay, I could feel it.

I slipped the key into the ignition and started the car with a roar that sounded like applause, like a hundred thousand hands clapping in the dark. Then I backed out from under the shadow of Vogelsang's gate, wound my way up the driveway and past the ghostly stripped trunks of the eucalyptus trees, and turned north, for Willits, a long rainy winter ahead of me, time to think things over, break some new ground, and maybe even—if things went well—to plant a little seed.